Titles by Jasmine Guillory

· · · · ·

The Wedding Date
The Proposal
The Wedding Party
Royal Holiday
Party of Two
While We Were Dating

While We Were Dating

Jasmine Guillory

Berkley
New York

BERKLEY
An imprint of Penguin Random House LLC
penguinrandomhouse.com

Copyright © 2021 by Jasmine Guillory
Penguin Random House supports copyright. Copyright fuels creativity,
encourages diverse voices, promotes free speech, and creates a vibrant culture.
Thank you for buying an authorized edition of this book and for complying
with copyright laws by not reproducing, scanning, or distributing any part
of it in any form without permission. You are supporting writers and allowing
Penguin Random House to continue to publish books for every reader.

BERKLEY and the BERKLEY & B colophon
are registered trademarks of Penguin Random House LLC.

Library of Congress Cataloging-in-Publication Data

Names: Guillory, Jasmine, author.
Title: While we were dating / Jasmine Guillory.
Description: New York: Berkley, [2021]
Identifiers: LCCN 2021003777 (print) | LCCN 2021003778 (ebook) |
ISBN 9780593100844 (hardcover) | ISBN 9780593100868 (ebook)
Classification: LCC PS3607.U48553 W48 2021 (print) |
LCC PS3607.U48553 (ebook) | DDC 813/.6—dc23
LC record available at https://lccn.loc.gov/2021003777
LC ebook record available at https://lccn.loc.gov/2021003778

Printed in the United States of America
1st Printing

Title page art: © Shutterstock/EL BANCO04
Book design by Ashley Tucker

To Jill Vizas
Thank you for always answering the phone
when I call, for thirty plus years and counting

One

BEN STEPHENS WAS RUNNING LATE TO WORK, CLUTCHING A cup of coffee, and about to get on the bus when his boss called.

Shit. He'd meant to get to work early this morning because of that pitch they had later for a huge client, but he'd woken up in the bed of last night's date and had to race back home, shower, change, and then get to work. He was honestly proud of himself for only running fifteen minutes late, and now this.

"I hope I caught you before you left home," Lisa said.

He looked from side to side. Was he being watched? Was this a trick question?

"Um, no, I'm on Muni, on the way to the office," he said. Which was true! He was one step onto Muni by the time he said it.

"Okay, well, go back home and get your car," she said. "I know we were supposed to drive down to that pitch together today, but I'm stuck at LAX, along with everyone else who was supposed to be there today; if it was any other client we'd postpone, but if we do it for this, they'll just give the ad campaign to someone else."

Ben was already off the bus and on the way back to his apartment.

"So do you want me to do it alone?" He felt a burst of adrenaline at the thought of it. He was great at client pitches, and he never got to lead them at this ad agency. But this was a much more top-down agency than the ones he'd been at before, and while he'd gotten to work on some fantastic campaigns, he had a lot less autonomy.

"We may not have a choice," Lisa said. "We're scheduled to be on another flight that leaves in an hour, so if traffic is with us, we may not be there too late, but you'll almost certainly have to at least start it on your own. Can you handle it? I just emailed Vanessa and told her to meet you there; she'll bring everything you need. You already have the PowerPoint."

He didn't just have the PowerPoint, he'd written almost the entire thing, but they both knew that.

"Sure, I can handle it, no problem. I know the vision for this ad campaign inside out." Which was absolutely true. He'd done the bulk of the work for it, but he'd always known he wouldn't play much of a role at the pitch today. He knew he would be there partly so they could look to him to fill in the blanks they didn't know, and mostly to show the "diversity" of their ad agency.

He could hear the relief in his boss's voice.

"I knew I could count on you, Ben. Even if promptness isn't your strong point, your ability to win over clients is. And I know how hard you worked on this. See you soon, I hope. Text me if you need anything, okay?"

He let himself back into his building and pretended he hadn't heard that crack about his promptness. Especially since it was true.

"Will do."

He changed into his lucky shoes, grabbed his car keys, and headed to his car. This ad campaign was top secret—it was to launch a splashy new phone, and they'd all had to sign the most draconian nondisclosure agreement he'd ever seen in order to even get to work on it. The client had already secured the talent—an actress who they were paying untold amounts of money to do this. His agency had done a bunch of work for them, but then, so had lots of other ad agencies—three of them were pitching today. Which was why he was now on 101 South alone, wishing that he could read through the PowerPoint as he drove.

He wasn't nervous about the actual presentation—his boss was right, he was great at that part. It was the pressure of having this huge pitch on his shoulders that made him want to study.

He called his brother as soon as he hit traffic.

"I need a pep talk," he said when Theo answered the phone.

"*You* do?" Theo asked. "This is Ben, right? My little brother? The one who always has a supreme amount of confidence in everything he does?"

Ben managed to shift into a slightly-faster-moving lane.

"Yes, yes, your brother, your only sibling. Now that we've gotten that over with—I have a . . . big work thing that I just realized I can't tell you the details of, but trust me, it's big. And I want to get it right."

He'd caught himself just in time before he told Theo everything. He took a very careful gulp of coffee. He definitely couldn't spill today.

"Okay," Theo said. "Do you know your shit? Really, do you know it, inside and out?"

He thought about how hard he'd worked on this.

"Yeah. I really know it."

"Then you're going to be fantastic, no matter what this is," Theo said. "You're going to kill it. You know that."

He did know that, actually. But it helped to hear Theo say it.

"I sure as hell am."

An hour later, he pulled into the elaborate tech company campus and gave his name to the security guard. He grabbed his bag, crossed his fingers that Vanessa would be there soon, and walked to the big glass doors.

After passing through a maze of security, someone eventually showed him into a conference room, where—thank God—Vanessa was waiting.

"Oh good, you're here," she said. "I have the PowerPoint all set up on the laptop here, if you want to flip through it before I turn the projector on."

Bless her, yes, he did.

They were the first presentation of the day, which the bigwigs at his company had lobbied for, because they all thought it was the best position. They were probably all kicking themselves now that they were stuck in L.A.

He skimmed the presentation and took the opportunity to make a few of the edits he'd been outvoted on. If he was going to do this, he was going to do it his way. Someone brought him and Vanessa coffee, but unfortunately, no one brought them snacks. Tech companies had such good snacks, but they were always stingy about sharing them, damn it. And he hadn't had breakfast. Oh well, this much coffee on an empty stomach would either make him keel over or give him all the energy he needed. He was excited to see which one it was.

Finally, a group of four people walked into the room without ceremony.

"Is this everyone from Legendary?" the guy in front asked.

Ben walked across the room to greet him.

"Just the two of us for now—I'm Ben Stephens, and this is Vanessa Hernandez. The rest of the team got stuck at LAX and they're on their way, but we know your time is valuable, so we don't need to wait for them."

Everyone sat down, and Vanessa cued up the presentation. And then the door opened again, and a woman stepped inside.

"Hi, all—sorry I'm late. It took longer to get through security than I accounted for. I guess the front desk didn't get the message that I'd be here today."

Everyone at the table stood up automatically. It was impossible not to, when you looked at her. She was astonishing.

Ben thought he knew what beautiful women were like, but he'd never seen anything like her before. He couldn't stop looking at her. She was luminous, like there was a spotlight on her somehow. She had golden brown skin, big brown eyes, and lips that . . . okay, he had to stop staring.

"Hi," she said. "I'm Anna Gardiner."

Everyone in the room had known that before she'd said it, of course. Anna Gardiner. The famous actress. Here for his pitch. His last-minute pitch. Thank God he hadn't known she would be here on his drive down; he would have needed a much longer pep talk.

"Ms. Gardiner!" Okay, from the tone of his voice, the guy representing the client hadn't known she was coming, either. "I'm sorry, I didn't realize . . . Of course, you had a standing offer to come today, but we . . ."

Ben walked around the table. Someone had to save this guy from himself.

"Ms. Gardiner, I'm Ben Stephens, from Legendary advertising agency. Thanks so much for coming today."

"Nice to meet you, Ben," she said. "Please call me Anna." Her voice was low, but warm. He wanted to listen to her talk for hours.

She smiled at him. Oh my God. He'd thought she was beautiful before, but with that smile aimed straight at him, "beautiful" seemed far too pedestrian a word for her.

He smiled back at her. Then he forced himself to remember why he was there today. Work, the pitch, he was their only hope, right. He couldn't let this surprise appearance of the most beautiful woman he'd ever seen blow him off course.

"Anna, then. I'm so glad you're here."

He went back to his spot at the head of the table and watched the client representatives surround Anna. He nudged Vanessa—she looked at him with eyes full of terror, but he shook his head.

"Go meet her!" he said under his breath. She still looked terrified, but she walked around the table and greeted Anna.

Once the introductions were over, Anna sat down at the foot of the table and looked at him expectantly. He nodded at Vanessa, who now had a huge smile on her face.

"If everyone is ready, we'll get started," he said.

Now that Anna Gardiner was here, he wasn't sure whom he was supposed to impress. The talent rarely attended meetings like this; he assumed they often had veto power over ad campaigns, but they were never in on the ground floor, making decisions; that was always the client.

But honestly, who the fuck cared about any of that right now? Because he sure as hell knew that the only person who mattered in this room right now was Anna.

He smiled at everyone in the room.

"Good morning, everyone. We at Legendary were thrilled to be invited to present our vision for this major ad campaign for your new phone. As you'll see, it's ambitious, but we're known for our ambition." Clients always lapped up that line; he could already see the dudes in the room puffing up their chests. "But it's also tailored just for you and your needs. Let's begin."

Anna sat back to watch. She'd come today for two reasons—to make it clear to this enormous corporation that she took the line in her contract about having veto power over the ad campaign seriously, and because this ad campaign was going to be very high-profile, she sure as hell wanted to make sure she trusted the people in charge. While her manager might claim she needed complete control over everything, that wasn't true. She just wanted to make sure that the people who were in control were worthy of it.

And she especially needed that right now. It wasn't, exactly, that this was a comeback—despite everything that had gone on last year, she'd still been working steadily for the past six months. But there was a lot riding on this, and she needed to know it would be damn good.

Her entrance also hadn't been as last-minute as she'd implied—yes, her manager had only called this morning to say she was coming, but that was intentional. She wanted to know what all of these agencies would put together if they didn't know she'd be there. It had killed her to be late—unlike most people in L.A., who notoriously ran behind schedule, she usually had to force herself to be two minutes early instead of ten minutes early—but in this situation, it gave her an advantage.

Her presence hadn't seemed to faze this charmer from the ad agency, though. Sure, he'd given her a very flattering look when she'd walked into the room, but he'd collected himself pretty quickly after that, and she liked everything he was saying during this presentation. A series of commercials and photo shoots for a new phone wasn't rocket science; she didn't think most of these campaigns would be all that different from one another, but the people running the shoots always made the difference—she'd seen that over and over.

It surprised her that it was just him and the young assistant with him. Not to stereotype ad agencies—especially the kind she assumed these big Silicon Valley companies used, but she hadn't expected a Black man to be the lead on one of these presentations. She'd actually expected to be the only Black person in the room for all of this. And she hadn't missed how he'd sent the assistant over to meet her, or how proud of her he'd looked when she'd walked back over to him. Treating assistants well was always a good sign.

"We wanted to make this phone seem like something that fits into the customer's lifestyle, not that they'll have to change their lifestyle around to fit it. And we want to show all of the great new bells and whistles of this phone, but in a relatable way. For instance, we want to show Ms. Gardiner—Anna," he corrected himself, with a nod and smile at her, "doing things like running around town, someone knocking the phone out of her hand on the sidewalk, or at the beach—and the phone will still work fine afterward. But also . . ."

She appreciated that he wanted someone to knock it out of her hand, and not for her to keep dropping it everywhere.

"And we want to exploit Anna's natural comedic talent—we've all seen how funny she can be, and this is a way to get people to not just remember the commercial, but remember the phone, too."

That might just be flattery, but it worked—she did have natural comedic talent, damn it! And she hadn't gotten to show it in a while. She started to ask a follow-up question, but the conference room door swung open.

"Our apologies, everyone." Two white men and one white woman all walked in and joined the Black guy—Ben, that was his name—at the head of the table. "You all know how it is, trying to fly into SFO first thing in the morning, so much fog. We can do quick introductions and then—" The one white guy who was clearly in charge had been looking around the room as he talked, and he'd looked past her at least three times, until he'd finally realized who she was.

She always loved that moment.

"Hi, I'm Anna Gardiner," she said. "Are you the rest of Ben's team?"

The guy in charge obviously did not enjoy being characterized as on Ben's team. She wondered if Ben would have done the presentation if they hadn't been delayed. If this was his understudy in the spotlight moment, he was taking full advantage of it.

"We're the rest of the team from Legendary. Wonderful to meet you, Ms. Gardiner. I didn't . . . We didn't . . ."

"I decided to come along today at the last minute. Nice to meet you, too."

There was a flurry of introductions, and then the rest of the Legendary team sat down on the other side of the table. The guy in charge started to stand up, but the woman whispered to him, then nodded at Ben. Ben smiled at everyone in the room again and kept going.

"One thing we really noticed as we watched the ads of your competitors was how often women are an afterthought—they're around in the ads, but so many of their concerns aren't."

Mr. Guy in Charge couldn't keep quiet for even a full minute.

"What Ben means to say is that we've seen a real gap that we can fill here, and we think Ms. Gardiner—as relatable and . . . confident as she is—is the person to fill it."

That long pause, that look he'd given the tech dudes—by "confident" he'd clearly meant "fat." Did he realize she was still in the room?

"Ben, what do you mean by 'so many of their concerns aren't' around in the ads?" she asked. She preferred to just pretend she hadn't heard that dude talk.

Ben looked right at her.

"I'm so glad you asked that, Anna." He smiled at her, a little crinkle in his eyes. She could tell he knew she'd cut his boss off on purpose. "I did a lot of research about how and why women feel like they're being ignored by phone companies, and there was a lot they had to say."

He'd been so careful to say "we" the whole time, but she noticed that "I" slip out just then. It made her like him even more. She smiled back at him. She had to flirt with this guy a little. She needed to have some fun with this, after all.

"Thanks so much, Ben," she said when he'd finished answering her question. "That was very thorough. I can tell you've done your research on the concerns of women."

He shot her a grin before he turned back to his PowerPoint.

For the rest of the time they had, the company people peppered Ben with questions, and he answered them all well, though his annoying boss felt the need to jump in repeatedly, too.

When they were done, they all passed around their business cards.

"Thank you all," Chad—or whatever his name was—from the tech company, said. "We'll be in touch."

"Thank you, it was great to meet all of you," Anna said. Ben and Vanessa both smiled at her—the one friendly, the other shy—on their way out the door. She didn't pay attention to what anyone else on Ben's team did.

She sat through the rest of the presentations, and they were all fine, but none impressed her as much as the first one. However.

She looked around at the group from the tech company.

"I liked the plan from Legendary the best. But if they get it, I want that first guy . . ." She flipped through the stack of business cards in front of her. "Ben Stephens, I want him to take the lead."

They all nodded at her, but she couldn't tell if they were nods just to pacify her or if they actually agreed with her.

"I liked him the best, too," the guy who hadn't said a word so far piped up.

"We have to take this upstairs for them to make the call,"

Chad said, "but we want to make this decision quickly, because we know you have a relatively short window for filming."

She nodded and stood up.

"Excellent. Please let my reps know as soon as possible. It was lovely to meet you all today."

She stood up to go, leaving the stack of business cards on the table.

On second thought . . .

She slipped the top card into her purse.

Two

ANNA TEXTED HER PARENTS FROM THE BACK SEAT ON THE way from Silicon Valley to Oakland.

I'll be there in time for a late lunch!

Her parents' house was out of her way, but she tried to never go to the Bay Area without seeing them. Her mom—a school principal—was off for spring break this week, and her minister dad had said he would come home for lunch to see her. It was still a slight sore spot for him that she wasn't coming home for Easter this year, but she hoped he didn't harp on that today. She'd used work as an excuse, but the real reason was that visiting her dad's church was too hard these days. Everyone made a big deal out of her—she had to say hi and take selfies and sign autographs for the whole congregation. And she was used to all of that, it was her job, but when she was with her family, she wanted to just be with her family. She wanted to be Anna Rose, not Anna Gardiner.

The car pulled up to her parents' home an hour later. The front door was open before she'd even made it to the porch.

"Anna!" Her dad had a huge grin on his face. "It's always such a treat to get to see you, even for only an hour."

Anna couldn't keep the tears from welling in her eyes as her dad pulled her in for one of his big bear hugs.

"Great to see you, too, Dad. Where's Mom?"

She walked with her dad into the kitchen, where her mom was exactly where she'd expected her to be—standing behind the stove.

"There's my girl," her mom said, and came around the counter to give her a hug. "Are you hungry? I made soup! Black bean and kale."

Anna pretended not to see her dad's grimace. Ever since his heart attack a few years ago, her mom had forced him onto a mostly vegetarian diet and a new exercise regimen. Ten years ago, that black bean soup would have had a big ham hock in it, and definitely no kale. But kale or no, Anna knew it would be delicious.

"Sounds great, Mom."

Anna walked around the counter to take down the soup bowls from the cabinet. She kept trying to buy her parents a new house, but at times like this, she was kind of glad they kept refusing to let her. This was still the same old kitchen where she knew where everything was. It was nice to come home to that.

They ate outside in the backyard. Her parents *had* let her pay for their backyard to be redone, at least. Her brother, Chris, had helped her spin that to them: she was doing her part for her dad's recovery, giving him a place to be outside, and not wanting him to dig around the garden by himself anymore, and her mom had said yes without consulting her dad. He'd been annoyed, but he'd gotten over it.

"It's so good to see you, honey," her dad said. She noticed that he was almost done with his soup, despite his pretense. "You look good. But how are you doing, really? And then, how is 'Anna Gardiner'?"

She laughed. Her parents always said that name in quotes, like "Anna Gardiner" was some completely different person than their daughter, Anna Rose. And while there was some truth in that—Anna Gardiner never would have put sour cream in her black bean soup, for example—increasingly it was hard to know where Anna Rose ended and Anna Gardiner began.

"Both of us are good, Daddy," she said, holding tight to his hand. "Working hard these days. Just trying to make you proud."

He scoffed.

"Like I could ever be anything other than proud of you, sweetheart. But really. These past few years have been hard." He didn't phrase it as a question. He didn't have to. "Are you happy in this Hollywood life?"

Anna leaned back in the deck chair and looked out at her parents' small, but cozy backyard. When she and Chris had been younger, there had been a kiddie pool out here—now there was a big grill and her mom's ever-growing garden.

"Getting there," she finally said, in response to his question. "I'm not unhappy, at least, not anymore. I'm taking care of myself, I promise I am." She looked pointedly at him. "Are you?"

He laughed.

"I'm fine! Stop worrying about me! Your mother takes care of me, and I'm happy to stay busy with the church." He put his spoon down in his empty bowl. "Speaking of that—no, don't sigh like that, young lady, I'm not going to tell you to go to church; you're an adult, that's your own decision. But I am going to ask you what else you're doing, to help people who aren't as fortunate as you."

Anna folded her napkin and avoided his eyes.

"Daddy, I'm doing a lot—I give money to charities up here whenever you guys or Chris ask me to, and there are a bunch of charities in L.A. that I give to as well."

He brushed that aside, like she knew he would.

"Money is wonderful, honey, and I'm glad you're in a position to give, but you know that's not what I asked. We raised you to be hands-on about this kind of work, you know that."

She sighed again. She should have been prepared for this.

"I know. But I'm still getting back on my feet; trying not to overdo it. Like *you* should be, by the way."

He patted her on the hand.

"Sometimes looking outside of ourselves can help, you know." He stood up. "I'm getting more of this soup; tell our daughter to stop worrying about me," he said to her mom.

As soon as he walked back into the house, Anna turned to her mom. She had that familiar kind-but-no-nonsense look on her face.

"He's okay," her mom said without her having to ask. "He has a doctor's appointment in a few weeks, and I'll let you know how that goes. He's still doing his exercising, and we eat well at home, but I can't watch him all the time, Anna, and I don't want to. He does lots of visits, and you know, people like to give him food; sometimes he drives around all day, and I have to pretend I don't see the fast-food wrappers in his car. But I said I want him to still be around for our retirement, and he'd better be taking that seriously."

Anna was glad her mom had given her this opening.

"Okay, so maybe that could be—"

Her mom laughed.

"Oh, Anna, no, I never should have said that. Please don't

start on me again about wanting us to retire early. We are taking more time, though—I've convinced your father to take some time off for my birthday. We're going to go to some national parks in Southern California—we can relax and do some hiking but still stay somewhere nice. I'm even taking a few days off work, during the semester, can you believe it?"

She couldn't believe it, actually. Maybe her parents were closer to retirement than she'd thought.

"Oh, that's great to hear. Just . . . keep me posted. You know I worry."

Her mom just looked at her, and then the two of them burst out laughing.

"Yes, Anna," her mom finally said. "I know you worry."

On the way back to the airport, she called her manager.

"Anna!" Simon picked up the phone right away. "How did your power move today go?"

She laughed. Simon had been very amused when she'd told him she wanted to make a surprise drop-in to the advertising pitches. He'd been her manager since she'd first started in Hollywood: they'd both been young and hungry when they started off and had grown and blossomed—and made a lot of money—together. And hopefully would make a great deal more.

"Very well, actually. They shouldn't have invited me if they didn't want me to come. Oh, and about that—can you pass along a message that I want it to be Legendary, but they have to put Ben Stephens in charge? I told them that today, but you're good at re-inforcing my messages."

That put it mildly. Simon was very well dressed and seemed relaxed on the surface, but he was a tiger on her behalf. She trusted him completely.

He was also one of the few people outside of her family and

her closest friends to know about Anna's paralyzing struggle with anxiety the year before. She was a lot better now; she hadn't lied to her parents about that. She almost felt like the old Anna was back. Almost.

"Will do. Who's this Ben Stephens and why him? Someone you know?"

It was very Hollywood of Simon to assume she wanted Ben in charge because she knew him.

"No, but I could tell he's excellent at his job, and he understands what I'm looking for, which is huge. Plus, he was the only Black person who presented all day. The other two firms both had someone sitting there, but it seemed like they weren't allowed to speak. I know it's all smoke and mirrors, but I trusted him as much as you can trust someone from an ad agency. But the ad campaign isn't the main reason why I'm calling."

Simon laughed.

"I'm all ears, but just a warning: I'm going to have to get off soon; I'm driving to a lunch right now."

Of course he was.

"Two things," Anna said. "First: What the hell is going on with *Vigilantes*? Have you heard anything? Is it even going to be ready for the premiere? Am I even going to be in the final cut? I barely showed up in the trailer, and there hasn't been a peep from them about wanting me to do press. I'm getting stressed about this, Simon. I don't even know if I lived or died! This uncertainty is killing me, no pun intended!"

Vigilantes was the comic book movie she'd filmed a handful of scenes in the year before. They'd hyped up her role when she'd signed on to the movie, but the premiere was coming up soon, and she still didn't know if the hype was real or imaginary. She'd had a director make her big promises before, only to cut her completely in postproduction. She really didn't want that to happen this time.

"I know," he said. "I made some calls about this a few days ago. They never should have scheduled the premiere for June; the studio didn't check with the directors on that. Their time line was . . . well, ambitious is the kind way to put it, and I'm rarely kind. They're scrambling to get it done. I think at this point the trailer means nothing—they just had to have something to put out there. Everything is still up in the air, but the directors love you, so that's promising. Don't count yourself out of this one."

Well, everything about that filming had been chaotic, so it made perfect sense that it was even more so in postproduction.

"Okay," she said. "I just . . . really want this one to be a win for me."

She blamed that filming—not totally rationally—for her crisis the year before. That's when the anxiety had gotten overwhelming. It had better have been worth it.

"No matter what, this will be a win for you," he said. "Like I always say, even if we can't control what other people do, we can—"

"Control the narrative." Anna finished his sentence. "I know, I know. I mean, yes, help me control this narrative, but also, please keep me posted if you find out anything more? And okay, the other reason I called: I read that script last night. For that film Liz Varon is directing. Simon—this is it. This is the one. I want this role. I have to have it."

He chuckled.

"I knew you would feel this way. I'll huddle with Maggie"— her agent—"and see what the story is there. Varon's in the midst of filming another movie, I do know that, so they're in no rush to do the casting. But she's got deep pockets with this one, which is sometimes good news and sometimes bad news—as we both know, often that means someone else is making the decisions. But I want to make this happen."

Usually, when Simon wanted to make something happen, it happened. Anna felt her shoulders relax.

"I do, too," she said. "This role . . . this is the one to get me back to the Oscars. I can feel it. I was right last time, remember? I have the same feeling now, but with a difference: I'll win this time. I know it. I want this role. Tell me what I have to do to get it."

"How could I possibly forget that you were right last time?" he asked. "Especially since you remind me of it constantly. Don't worry, I'll work on this ASAP. I have to run, but I'll keep you posted on all of this. And I'll make that call about the ad campaign right now. Ben Stephens, right?"

"Right. Thanks, Simon."

Anna ran her fingers over the edge of Ben's business card and smiled.

The woman Ben met for drinks that night—Lauren? Heather?—was very nice, perfectly attractive, and seemed interesting, but he couldn't concentrate on her. He kept thinking about Anna at the meeting that day—the interested look on her face while he was talking, that quick bark of laughter she let out at his best joke, and the sly grin she shot him after she cut off the head of his company and turned back to him. That interested look on her face . . . was it about him? Or about the idea for the ad campaign? Or did she just have resting interested face, and she hadn't been thinking about him at all?

It was probably that last one; she was Anna Gardiner, after all.

"What? Oh yeah, another beer sounds great, thanks," he said to the bartender. "Do you want another drink?" he asked the woman sitting next to him. Rachel. That was her name.

She shook her head and stood up.

"No offense, but you don't seem that interested in me. Have a good night, Ben."

Oh God, he was an asshole.

"Wait, Rachel."

She pulled her purse onto her shoulder and looked at him.

"What?"

"I want to apologize for being bad company tonight. It's not you—a really . . . weird thing happened at work today, and I can't stop thinking about it. I'm sorry for being a jerk."

She looked at him for a while and finally gave him a slight smile.

"Okay. Thanks for apologizing. Good night."

She patted him on the shoulder and left, just as the bartender put his beer in front of him. He didn't even really want it, but he took a sip as he thought about the day.

Everything about that day had been strange. The pitch had gone well, he thought, at least it had before the rest of the team had walked in. He grinned again at the expression on Roger's face when Anna had referred to them as "Ben's team." But after that, he'd just tried to keep going and forget about the rest of the team, which had been almost impossible with all of Roger's interjections, so he had no real handle on how everyone else in the room had reacted. Other than Anna.

He paid for the drinks and left the rest of his beer as he got up to walk home. It was a chilly April night in San Francisco, but he'd raced out of his house so quickly that morning that he'd forgotten his jacket. Why did he always do that? He'd lived here long enough to know what would happen.

He wondered where Anna was now. Had she flown back to L.A. right away after all of the pitches were done? Probably. She was probably out on some elaborate date with her famous boyfriend. Granted, his Google searches had said she currently didn't have a boyfriend, but someone like her must, right?

His phone rang, right when he walked into his apartment. His boss again. Why was she calling him this late at night?

"Hi, Lisa," he said cautiously when he answered the phone.

"Ben!" She sounded excited. That was a good sign. "I was going to wait to tell you this tomorrow at work, but Roger wants to meet first thing in the morning, so I thought you should be prepared for that."

It was nice of her to make sure he'd be there in time for Roger's meeting the next day, but she could have just texted him.

"Okay, what time? I'll be there," he said.

Had he really been late *that* often? Okay, yes, but like, ten minutes late, not "Lisa needs to call him the night before so he'll get to work on time" late.

"At nine, but I wasn't just calling for the meeting! Ben, we got it. Or rather, I should say, YOU got it."

Was she talking about the pitch?

"We did? What do you mean, I did?"

"They loved you today. So much so that they said we get the ad campaign, but only if you're the lead on it. From what they said to Roger, apparently Anna Gardiner was a big fan."

Anna Gardiner was a big fan of . . . him? A wide smile spread across his face. He'd better be able to tell *this* part to his brother.

"Wow. That's . . . wow. How did Roger take it?"

Lisa chuckled.

"Good question. He definitely seemed . . . bemused. He's very happy we got it, though, that's for sure. Tomorrow's meeting is to announce it to the team, and to plan for everything—I'm sure he's going to want you on set every day—just prepare for that."

Hmmm, that would not be a problem.

"Thanks for calling to let me know, Lisa. I'm thrilled. And don't worry, I'll be appropriately surprised in the meeting. See you bright and early tomorrow morning."

He got off the phone and turned on the TV but didn't pay any attention to what was on-screen. He would get to be the lead on this ad campaign? He'd only gotten to lead small, relatively low-budget ones so far. Holy fucking shit.

He picked up his phone again and checked his work email, and Roger, in true Roger style, had had his assistant send out a calendar invite for the meeting in the morning, without saying what it was for. If he'd seen that without talking to Lisa first, he would have freaked out. Thank God she'd called.

He glanced at his email to see if there was anything else he needed to know before he went to bed, and stopped cold.

To: Ben Stephens
From: Anna Gardiner
Re: Congratulations!

Hi Ben: I hope you've heard the news by now—I loved your presentation today, very glad you'll be in charge. (If you haven't heard, pretend to be shocked when what's his name who got there late tells you, I have a feeling you can handle that). One quick request: can you make sure whoever is doing the lighting for the shoot has worked with brown skin before? I've had some poorly lit disasters in the past few years.

Thanks!
Anna

Was that really her? No, it couldn't be. Anna Gardiner had *not* just sent him an email. Impossible.

But no one else would have these details, other than the partners who were at the meeting, and they wouldn't try to prank him like this. Holy shit. It must actually be her.

He hit reply so fast he almost sprained his finger.

To: Anna Gardiner
From: Ben Stephens
Re: Congratulations!

Thanks so much, Anna. Very much looking forward to working with you. Don't worry, I know just the right people to do the lighting. You can count on me. Email or text if there's anything else you need.

Ben

He hit send. He could not believe he'd just emailed Anna Gardiner. And given her his phone number, because why the hell not? Holy shit.

He skimmed the rest of his inbox. Oh, here was some random person emailing him; they must be trying to get his help getting a job or something, from the *Looking to connect* subject line. He got those frequently at this job, because of the big clients this agency represented, and he tried to help people out if he could. Well, he wasn't doing anything right now; he'd click on this email and see what he could do.

He skimmed it. And then read it again. He put his phone down, but after a few minutes of staring at the wall, he picked it back up and read the email again.

From: Dawn Stephens
To: Ben Stephens
Re: Looking to connect

Hi Ben,

My name is Dawn Stephens. And I'm sorry if this is out of the blue, but I think I might be your sister. Sorry for not leading up to that, it felt easier to just get it over with as soon as possible. Anyway, Melvin Stephens is also my father. I did one of those DNA testing things a few years ago, and I was just poking around on it and it told me there was someone else out there with my same father, and after some research I think it might be you. You look like him, anyway.

Here's a little about me—I'm twenty five, I live in Sacramento, I work with kids, and I just got into grad school to get my master's in education. I'm sorry if it's weird to email you at work—there were a lot of Ben Stephens on Facebook, so I didn't know if I'd find the right one. Anyway, I'd love to hear back from you and find out about you—I'm an only child, or, I guess, I thought I was, so it's both weird and exciting to find a brother. Or maybe other siblings too—are you also an only child?

You can email me back or text me if you want.

I hope you're doing well,
Dawn

He'd wondered at points over the years if his father had had another family out there. If that's why he'd left Ben and Theo and their mom, to start something new, because they hadn't been enough for him. He'd left so suddenly, all Ben could do when he was a kid was try to figure out why. Ben had moved past all of that, even gone to therapy about it. He hadn't thought about that for a long time.

Dawn. She worked with kids. That was nice. He wondered how—as a preschool teacher, or nanny or something? If she wanted to get her master's in education, maybe the former?

No. No, he wasn't curious about this woman; he didn't want to be. He had a brother, a perfectly fine brother, a great brother, actually, who was on the point of bringing his girlfriend Maddie into the fold to be his sister. He didn't need this Dawn.

He had to tell Theo.

Wait. No. She clearly didn't even know Theo existed. Theo didn't need to know about any of this. Theo had yelled at him for doing that DNA test in the first place—gave him a big lecture about private companies having your personal data and you don't know what they do with it and blah blah blah. He hated when his brother was right. Theo would just give him another lecture about that, and then . . . and then what?

Maybe this was just some kind of a scam. Someone trying to get money from him. Someone who knew his dad—that sounded like the kind of thing some friend of his dad would do. This woman probably wasn't even related to him at all. If she even existed.

When he glanced at his phone again, he had a new email.

From: Anna Gardiner
To: Ben Stephens
Re: Congratulations

Knew I could rely on you, Ben. Nice to meet you today, and glad that this all looks like it's moving quickly.

Looking forward to working with you too,
Anna

Ben pushed away all thoughts of the email from Dawn. Anna Gardiner was looking forward to working with him.

He turned the channel to the basketball game. The cheers from the crowd felt like they were for him. He sat back on the couch and grinned.

Three

ANNA WAS FIVE MINUTES LATE ON THE FIRST DAY OF THE shoot for the ad campaign. That was *not* a power move—she liked to be right on time to things like this, especially at the beginning, to make it clear that she respected everyone else's time and wasn't a diva. Well. Not much of one.

She walked from the hair-and-makeup tent over to where the crew was, and the first person she saw was Ben. She gave him a wide smile, and he smiled back at her. They'd emailed on and off since those first few emails—when he'd booked the crew, he'd sent her examples of their previous work, and she'd thanked him for it, and then congratulated him for his quick work when they'd set an official start date for the filming, only about a month after that first meeting.

"How did you manage to have perfect, fog-free weather on a beach in San Francisco?" she asked him.

His eyes crinkled at her.

"Oh, I didn't mention this at the pitch meeting?" He leaned in closer to her. "I'm magic."

She raised an eyebrow.

"You're magic?"

He nodded.

"I don't like to tell a lot of people about it—sometimes they get spooked, sometimes they treat me differently, I'm sure you get that kind of thing, too—but I can control the weather. I try not to use my powers *too* much, offends the gods and all, but for you? I managed it."

She laughed out loud.

"I can't tell you how much I appreciate that." She flashed the full force of her smile—a smile that *People* magazine had called "dazzling"—at him. He dropped the clipboard he was holding into the sand. She smirked. *Still got it.*

"Well, you're very welcome." Ben picked up his clipboard. "Can I introduce you to everyone? Unless you'd rather wait over in the tent for us to be ready?"

Anna nodded. She was glad he'd offered.

"Yes, thank you, I'd love to meet everyone."

He looked slightly surprised by her quick reply.

"Excellent," he said. "I always find with these things that we're all more comfortable if we at least can put a name to a face."

Ben took her around and introduced her to the camera crew. They were all still in the middle of setting up their equipment, so at least she didn't feel as bad about being late. Then he brought her over to his assistant.

"Glad to see you again, Vanessa," Anna said. She didn't miss Ben's quick grin at his clearly nervous assistant. That was sweet.

Everyone was very nice and low-key and only a little star-struck, which was exactly how she liked it—people who were too obsequious really stressed her out and made her feel embarrassed, but people who basically ignored her seemed like assholes. So far, no assholes here.

Ben had a low-voiced consultation with the camera guy while she was chatting with Vanessa, and then turned back to her.

"It's time to get you mic'ed up, but our sound guy is stuck in traffic, so I'm going to fill in for him for right now, if that's okay with you?"

Anna nodded.

"As long as it's okay with them, it's okay with me," she said.

Ben picked up the tiny microphone and its attached battery pack from the table. He stood in front of her and looked her up and down in a very clinical way.

"You don't have any pockets in this dress, do you?" he asked her.

She shook her head.

"Unfortunately not."

He made a face.

"I was afraid of that. Okay, do you mind if I attach the battery pack to your bra, or do you want to do it?"

Anna shrugged. She was used to this.

"I don't mind."

Ben came closer to her and held up the mic.

"Okay, I'm going to clip the mic to your neckline, if that's okay."

Anna took a step forward.

"Of course."

Ben gently lifted the neckline of her dress and clipped the mic on her. He didn't even touch her, but as she watched his nimble fingers on her dress, a shiver went down her back. He moved slowly and narrated everything he was doing as he did it.

"Great, it's clipped on there, all set. Now I'll just tuck the pack down back here," he said as he walked around her.

She lifted her hair and moved it out of his way. She could feel his warm breath on the back of her neck. She wanted to move closer but stayed right where she was.

"Now I'll slip this down your dress and clip it to your bra here."

She appreciated the way he told her everything he was about to do and warned her every time he was going to touch her. She'd been mic'ed up thousands of times by now, and this kind of care and attention to her comfort was rare. Most of the time it was a quick and silent procedure, though she'd had her fair share of guys, early in her career, who took the opportunity to grope her. No one had tried that in a long time, but she also couldn't remember the last time someone had made her comfort such a priority.

One of the things that had surprised her, a few years back, after she'd gotten that Oscar nomination and had hit so many magazine covers and so many more people knew who she was, was how many people felt entitled to her. To information about what she was doing and where she was going and who she was with, to her attention whenever they wanted it, and especially to her body. People would interrupt her when she was with her family, they would reach for her as she walked through a crowd, fans jumped to take selfies with her without asking and would throw their arms around her. And of course, men at parties and on set would casually brush her ass or the sides of her breasts like it was nothing, like her body was theirs for the taking.

But Ben touched her in such a businesslike, matter-of-fact way, and made it clear she was in control the whole time. He could have easily taken this opportunity to flirt with her some more, or touch her neck or waist or back. But he didn't do any of that. She was certain, more than ever, she'd made the right decision about this shoot.

"Okay, we're all set," he said, and took a step back. He looked over at the cameras. "And not a moment too soon. I think it's time for you."

She smiled at him and met his warm brown eyes.

"Great. Thanks."

They turned and walked across the sand to the cameras, where Anna did a series of sound checks to see how her voice and the mic held up against the waves and the wind.

She was absolutely not going to start something with Ben Stephens. Yes, she hadn't slept with anyone since last year, since the anxiety attacks had started, and okay, yes, she was ready for that drought to end. Yes, she'd been flirting with Ben since the moment she'd met him, but that was just the fun kind of flirting, where everyone knew it didn't mean anything. She'd had a firm policy since the very beginning of her career to never get involved with men she was working with—the Hollywood rumor mill was too vicious for her to get tangled up in it, at least, not on purpose. And sure, Ben wasn't a costar or anything, but they were still working together. No, she was absolutely not going to start something with Ben Stephens.

But it was really fun to think about.

Ben watched Anna as she chatted with the director. Damn, she was even more incredible than he'd thought initially. And he'd initially thought she was hot as hell. But he'd sort of assumed she'd be difficult, just because of the nature of her job and her status, but she didn't seem to be like that at all. She definitely carried herself like she was the star, which she was, but she was friendly to everyone there, and she seemed to be able to roll with the punches in a way he hadn't expected.

Okay, he had to focus and stop looking at her. This job was the biggest one he'd ever worked on at this level, and he wanted to kill it. Because if he did good work on this campaign, that was the entry point to do more work like this, and that was his goal. Which was why he had been up since well before sunrise and had been here on set since before the crew arrived, which was not the norm for him.

Plus, this was the thing he wanted to focus on, not the second email he'd gotten from Dawn the day before. He'd ignored the first one, in the hopes he wouldn't have to deal with it, but she'd sent another one—just as friendly and cheerful as the first time, with a note that maybe her first email had gotten stuck in his spam folder.

Wait. Were these emails some sort of precursor to hearing from his dad? He definitely didn't want that to happen. Shit. He'd have to email her back to make this stop, wouldn't he?

Okay, he'd figure out how to do that tonight.

It was a very long day, with many takes and long waits and repositioning and breaks to eat or fix Anna's hair or change the camera because of a cloud or change it back because the sun was out or lose perfect takes because of an airplane going overhead, but finally, after many hours, Ben and the director agreed they had what they needed, at least for the day.

He glanced around at the crew as they all packed up to leave. "Drinks?"

Everyone nodded forcefully. Yes, that was exactly how he felt, too.

Ben grabbed his bag and went over to check in with Vanessa. It had gotten chillier on the beach as the day had gone on, and everyone on set had bundled up in their hoodies and vests. Well, everyone except Anna, who kept having to run in and out of the icy water with just a cotton dress on. She hadn't even complained. He looked over at her now, a cardigan wrapped tightly around herself as she said good-bye to the director.

She looked up and saw him looking at her. Oh, awesome, perfect. She walked over to him.

"What's this I hear about everyone going to get drinks? Am I invited?"

Was she invited? Um, she would have been if he'd thought she'd wanted to come.

He fought back a laugh.

"Yes, *Anna Gardiner*, I have a feeling you're invited anywhere you damn well want to be, and yes, of course you're invited to come out with us for drinks. Apologies for not making that clear; I assumed you'd be busy."

She grinned at him and shrugged.

"My busy plans tonight involved the couch in my hotel suite and room service, and as much as I love room service, I'll be in that hotel for what, two weeks? I have a feeling I'll get to know that menu very well."

Was Anna Gardiner really going to go out for drinks with them tonight? He had to tell Theo this part. He needed to read that fucking NDA again.

"Where are we going?" she asked.

"Oh, a place not too far away, it's . . . Do you need a ride?"

She slid her phone out of her bag and glanced at it.

"I think my driver is here, but if he drops me off at a bar, it might be kind of . . . conspicuous. So sure, I'll take a ride, if that's okay."

Which is how he ended up giving Anna Gardiner a ride to a dive bar.

When they got in the car, she pulled her hair into a knot on top of her head and wrapped a big scarf around her neck.

"Is that your disguise?" he asked.

If it was, it wasn't going to work—she looked exactly like Anna Gardiner, just with her hair up and a scarf around her neck. Honestly, the scarf made her look even more glamorous than she had before.

"Not exactly," she said. "If people recognize me, they're going to recognize me, but also I don't think anyone knows yet that I'm in San Francisco right now, which is why it's probably one of the safest times for me to come out with you guys. This is more just to give me a little warning—people will have to stop and think and make sure it's me, and then I know it's coming. Though . . . if you can help me get a seat in a dark corner, that'll help even more."

He grinned at her.

"Didn't I tell you that you could count on me?"

When they got to the bar, some of the crew was already there and had commandeered a big table in the back. The director was already in the poorly lit seat against the wall, but Ben gestured to him, with a nod at Anna. He was prepared to say more but luckily, he didn't have to—Gene got up and moved over to the corresponding position at the other end of the table.

Anna slid into the seat and blinked at Ben.

"How did that happen? What other magic do you have?"

He winked at her and dropped his bag into the seat next to hers.

"What did I tell you? Also, I'm headed to the bar—what can I get you?"

She shook her head and pulled out her wallet. Oh God, was she going to be mad that he'd tried to buy her a drink? That's just what they did at these kinds of happy hours . . . but in retrospect, he should probably stop to think before he did something like that with someone like Anna.

She handed him a stack of twenties.

"I'll take a rain check on that, but can you get a few pitchers for the table from me, please? I'd do it myself, but . . ."

He shook his head.

"No, of course you can't. No problem."

Had she meant that about the rain check, or . . .

Probably *or*. Ben had no small ego about his way with women, but Anna Gardiner must have a boyfriend and also several more waiting in the wings. Oh, that reminded him.

"Are you hungry? They have wings here . . . and not much else that's good. The wings are spicy—just a warning—but if you like spicy, they're good."

She widened her eyes at him.

"I'm starving. Wings sound incredible right now, though I'm a little insulted that you felt like you had to warn me that they're spicy."

He came back to the table a few minutes later with Vanessa behind him, both of them carrying pitchers of beer, and the waitress following behind with pint glasses.

"Ooh, Ben, look at Mr. Big Shot over here buying drinks," the lighting guy yelled out. That motherfucker, after Ben had handpicked him for this job after days of research. They'd worked together before, but still.

"Don't get me wrong," Ben said. "I *am* Mr. Big Shot, but I am not your benefactor this evening." He nodded in Anna's direction.

Everyone jumped to thank Anna, but she waved that away.

"It was the least I could do after how great everyone was today. Cheers, all."

Ben slid into his seat next to Anna and poured her, and then himself, a pint of beer.

He lifted his glass to hers before he took a sip.

"Forgive me if I'm wrong here, but I wouldn't have pegged you as a big beer drinker," he said as she picked up her beer.

He was pretty sure he could see her smile behind the glass.

"I'm not, really. But this didn't seem like a sauvignon blanc or gin-and-tonic kind of situation. Or even a Manhattan one."

If they ever had that rain check, he'd remember all of that. He didn't really think that would happen, though, no matter how much she flirted with him. That was probably her default way of dealing with the world.

It was definitely *his* default way of dealing with the world. He'd tried to force himself to dial it back when talking to Anna, but he hadn't been . . . completely successful at that.

"So tell me: How does an ad exec like you know how to be a fill-in sound guy?" Anna asked him.

Astute of her to realize that most people in his job didn't know anything about the other side of the camera.

"I have all sorts of talents," he said. There he was, flirting again. Damn it. *Pull yourself together, Stephens.* "I actually used to do this kind of work awhile ago, before I made the jump to advertising. It's one of the things that got me interested in working at an agency—I worked on a few ad campaigns, and I could always tell when it was working and when it wasn't. And I wondered how it was all put together." He gestured down to Gene, who was now at the far end of the table. "He and I have worked together a bunch, starting when I was much more junior than I am now, and I told him I used to do this kind of work, so he's always been good about teaching me about the new stuff they use. Probably just so he can do things like today, and use me to pitch in and help out when there's a crisis."

There, that sounded nice and professional, and not like he deeply wished the two of them were alone, at some cozy little bar, in a booth in the back, sipping bourbon, instead of at a great big table surrounded by a whole lot of people.

"When did you do that kind of work?" she asked him. "The crew work, I mean."

Yes, okay, they could talk about his professional life; this was good. Anna seemed to like him, and he wanted that to continue—not just because she was the most attractive woman he'd ever interacted with, but because her respect and approval could do a hell of a lot for his career.

"Worked my way through college that way. I was sort of a late start to college anyway—I was doing other stuff, and then I sort of fell into the crew work accidentally. I got my first job as a favor from a friend of a friend, but I liked it and was good at it, so I kept going for a while, and then kept working on and off through college and after."

She raised an eyebrow at him.

"What 'other stuff' were you doing?"

Well, he'd walked right into that one, hadn't he?

"Oh. Well." He glanced around at the rest of the table, but no one seemed to be paying attention to him and Anna. "I was a backup dancer for a few years in my late teens, early twenties. I sort of ran away to L.A. to try to break in, and it worked for a while. But I had to find a way to pay the bills, which is eventually how"—he gestured to the table—"all of this happened."

She stared at him and set her beer down.

"Wait, no, you can't just slip that into a conversation and then try to turn it back to advertising. I need more information here—you ran away to become a backup dancer? Is this a secret? Does anyone else know?"

He hadn't expected her to be that interested in this—former wannabe stars must be a dime a dozen in her world.

"It's not exactly a secret—there are definitely videos online of me dancing, but I don't talk about it much." He nodded down the table. "Gene knew at one point, but I think he's forgotten. He's cool, though, so it's no big deal. Sometimes people can get weird about it. Wanting me to, like . . . dance for them like their own little minstrel show or something, and I'm not exactly into that. But it was a pretty fun time."

He did not think when he woke up this morning that by eight p.m. he'd be drinking beer and sharing confidences with Anna Gardiner, but hey, life had a habit of surprising him.

Anna didn't quite know what she'd expected when she'd invited herself along for this happy hour, but it definitely wasn't finding out that the delightfully charming man she'd been flirting with all day used to be a backup dancer. Shit. He must look very good underneath that hoodie.

No, she couldn't think like that. He was very fun to talk to, especially when he looked at her with that sexy grin, and stopped himself and looked away, clearly reminding himself that they were both at work. His self-restraint was even more sexy than the grin. But they *were* both at work. Plus, no matter how much she might be ready to break this terrible accidental celibacy streak, this was the wrong way to do it.

"How long did you do it? Dance, I mean," she asked him.

"For about three years, on and off," he said. "I loved it, but even though I was young and very, very stupid, I knew deep down that it wasn't going to last forever—I think that's also why I was attracted to the crew work; to build some sort of skills I knew I could keep doing."

He took a sip of his beer and then ran his fingertip down the condensation on the side of the glass. Anna let herself imagine what it would be like if he ran that finger down her skin. She took a gulp of her beer.

"It's probably why you're so good at what you do now," she said. "You had some time and space to figure out what you really wanted to do."

He raised his glass to her.

"Thanks for the compliment, Ms. Gardiner. Is that also why you're so good at what you do?"

Oh, he was very smooth. Usually, men like that felt fake, but Ben had this crinkle in his eyes that said he didn't take himself too seriously. She grinned at him.

"Funny, I never thought of that, but I think that's part of it. I wanted to be an actress when I was a kid, of course—in that way all theater kids do when they get onstage and get a taste of an audience—but I forgot about that dream after a while. Probably because I saw how hard it was for people who looked like me to get anywhere."

Ben sat back and smiled at the waitress as she put their wings in front of them. Everyone else at the table had clearly had the same idea, except for a few people who had gotten nachos.

"Why didn't you tell me there were nachos?" she asked as she picked up a wing.

He shook his head.

"They're terrible, that's why. I was doing you a favor."

She took a very tentative bite.

"Oh, this is actually good!"

He narrowed his eyes at her.

"You didn't trust me, I see. I promise you this: Ben Stephens never lies about chicken."

She laughed out loud, more at the serious look on his face than his words.

"I'll remember that."

His smile peeked out from behind his unnatural frown.

"What happened to change things?" he asked. "I mean, about what you were saying—to change your mind about acting?"

Huh, he'd actually been listening to her. How refreshing.

"I suppose I saw how hard it was for people who looked like me—women who looked like me—anywhere, not just in Hollywood. I'd been working as an agent, so I saw how shitty Hollywood was, but my friends were all over corporate America, and it wasn't any better there. So after a while, when I saw a role I wanted, I just said fuck it and decided to go for it."

Why was she telling him all of this? Granted, it wasn't much

more than what she'd said when she told her origin story to reporters, but it was a much more honest version of it.

Maybe it was the beer on an empty stomach. No, that wasn't
it; she was too savvy these days for a little alcohol to give her loose
lips. Was she just that starved for male attention that she'd open
up to any handsome face with good listening eyes?

No, she got plenty of male attention. She just felt like she
could relax around Ben. That in itself was strange; she hadn't felt
like relaxing around someone new in a long time.

Ben interrupted her thoughts.

"So was that all it took? You said fuck it and suddenly the roles
came flying to you?"

Anna laughed. Wouldn't that have been nice.

"My God, if only. No, it took years for me to break through,
which was enough time for me to get demoralized and discouraged and give up about fifty times, but somehow I always went
back out there. And then, somehow, things started going my way."

She let herself have a rare moment of pride. At how hard she'd
worked, how determined she'd been, at everything she'd fought
through.

"Well," he said, "I'm glad you kept trying; you do incredible
work. You should have won that Oscar."

She picked up another wing and grinned at him.

"Thanks, I think so, too." Shit. She never said that out loud.
She shook the wing at him. "If you ever quote me on that, you're
dead to me."

He put his hand to his heart.

"I, Ben Stephens, swear on this chicken I will never tell."

They both cracked up.

Four

BEN LECTURED HIMSELF ALL THE WAY TO THE SET THE NEXT day about how he would act toward Anna. They'd had a vibe going the night before, absolutely. *And* he'd driven her back to her hotel after everyone dispersed from the bar. If that had happened with any other woman, he would have ended up going back to her room.

But Anna wasn't any other woman. For one, she was Anna Gardiner. And two, they were working together. He could be casual and jokey with her last night at the bar, but today at work he had to be uptight and professional. Theo. He should try to act like Theo.

Speaking of Theo, he was having drinks with him tonight. Should he tell him about Dawn? Or about that email he'd sent her late last night, where he'd said if this was a ploy to get him back in touch with his dad, he had no interest in that? He and Theo rarely talked about their dad, but maybe he should warn Theo that she was out there, just in case she tried to get in touch with him, too.

He'd think about that. But first, he had to channel Theo today.

He lasted approximately thirty seconds. Anna was already there when he arrived, getting her hair and makeup done in her tiny dressing room in the house where they were filming the party scene, in that day. When he'd walked by and saw her there, it would have been rude of him to not stop and at least say hi, right? Right.

"Hey, Anna, did anyone take your picture on the way into your hotel last night?"

She laughed and beckoned him in, even though her hair was in big rollers.

"Yes, I told you they would." When he'd dropped her off at her hotel, she'd put lipstick on before walking inside; when he'd made gentle fun of her for it, she'd said it was because there were always people taking pictures of her in hotel lobbies, something that hadn't occurred to him. "I looked good in the photos, though, so I can't complain too much. Thanks for the ride. You know my hair and makeup team, right? Manuel and Jo?"

He waved at the people currently working on Anna.

"We met yesterday. Thanks for being here. FYI, most of this week is going to be jam-packed, but hopefully Friday should be more low-key. Just in case you wanted to make your room-service versus non-room-service plans in advance."

She laughed again, and he grinned as he left the room. He wasn't very good at channeling Theo, was he?

He spent most of the day standing with Gene, the director, watching the footage and strategizing on what more they needed to get since they had all of the extras around. He knew that the most important thing for him on this shoot was to make the client happy, and the best way to keep any client happy was to stay within, or even under, budget. The budget for this campaign was huge, yes, but between Anna and an almost two-week filming schedule—and all of the people who would need to be on set every day of those two weeks—that would account for a whole lot of it.

He ducked into a corner during a break to send Lisa an update and then checked his email. Shit. Another one from Dawn.

To: Ben Stephens
From: Dawn Stephens.
Re: Just checking in

Lol no, absolutely not, this has nothing to do with our dad. To be honest, I'm not really that in touch with him either—I hear from him every so often, but he wasn't that great of a dad to me. Just like to you, I assume from your email.

I guess I partly got in touch because of that—I wanted to see if I had more family around somewhere, since he wasn't so good at that part. It's mostly just been me and my mom, and I've always sort of wondered what it would be like to have siblings, so when I saw that there was one out there, I just wanted . . . I don't know, to get to know you. But if that's not what you want, it's totally cool.

Dawn

Shit. He reread his email to her from the night before, and it hadn't been particularly friendly. He didn't have to be a dick to this woman, no matter how he felt about his dad.

He hit reply and typed in a flurry with his thumbs.

To: Dawn Stephens
From: Ben Stephens
Re: Just checking in

Hey—Sorry about my email, I didn't mean to sound like I was accusing you of something. It's just that I haven't talked to my dad in a long time, and it was a lot to get your email. If we do have the same dad, I'm sure you can understand that.

Anyway, sorry if I sounded like a jerk. Tell me more about yourself. What kind of work do you do with kids?

Ben

There. That was better. He didn't know if she was actually related to him, but at least now he didn't feel like a dick.

Oh God, he had therapy tomorrow. He really didn't want to tell his therapist about this—she would want to know if it brought up stuff about his dad, blah blah, and they'd had enough of those conversations. At least, he knew he had.

He'd worry about that later.

As he sat in the bar that night waiting for his brother, Ben swiped through pictures on a dating app. Not her, not her, or her . . . yeah, nope to her, too.

"Finding any new victims?" Theo asked as he slid onto the stool next to Ben.

Ben dropped his phone into his pocket and turned to his brother.

"I prefer to think of them as the lucky ones, not victims, thank you very much."

Theo rolled his eyes and waved to the bartender.

"Why aren't you out with one of the 'lucky ones' tonight? To what do I owe this pleasure?"

Ben ignored that question.

"Why did I have a missed call from Mom today?" he asked. "It's Tuesday; she never calls on Tuesdays."

Theo sighed.

"She can't just call her son on a Tuesday?" he said, in a perfect imitation of their mom. Ben laughed and pushed Theo's drink in front of him.

"Ahh, so you talked to her."

Theo nodded.

"Carrie's having a baby. It's still supposed to be a secret, which is why Carrie hasn't told the family group text yet, but of course, Aunt Cynthia told Mom, who called to tell us."

Ben took a sip of his drink.

"This is going to be another one of those secrets that the whole family knows but we have to pretend we don't, right? At least Carrie will probably tell us for real via text, so it'll be easier to pretend we haven't known this for months."

"Exactly. Hey, how is that work thing going you can't tell me about? You said that thing that you had to do went well—any updates?"

He'd reread the NDA, and it was all about the phone itself. He didn't give a fuck about the phone; he just wanted to tell his brother about Anna, and he was in the clear.

"Okay, I'm going to tell you part of it, but you can't tell anyone. Obviously, you're going to tell Maddie, but she *really* can't tell anyone."

Theo looked suspicious.

"I promise. This had better be good."

Ben couldn't keep himself from rubbing his hands together.

"Oh, it is. Okay, so . . . that day I called you, it was to pitch an ad campaign starring Anna Gardiner. I can't tell you what *that* is about, but we got it. And I'm the lead exec on it. We started shooting yesterday."

Theo's mouth dropped open.

"Are you serious? Holy shit, Ben. That's incredible, congratulations! And you're the lead on it?"

He still couldn't really believe it, either.

"Yeah—I killed it at the pitch, and so the client wanted me to be in charge."

Theo clapped him on the back.

"See? I knew it. I told you you'd kick ass." He stood up and inspected the bottles behind the bar before he waved at the bartender. "Can we get some of that Booker's, please? One for each of us, neat. Thanks so much."

Good alcohol was one of the ways his brother showed love. Also bossy advice, detailed spreadsheets, and alphabetizing things. Very occasionally, blowing off work, but that was only for a true crisis.

"Thanks, man," Ben said, when the bartender set the bourbon in front of them.

"So does this mean that you've met her? Anna Gardiner, I mean? What's she like?"

Ben grinned as he took his first sip. Holy shit. He wasn't going to ask how much this cost.

"She's great. Really great. Good at her job, not a diva—except when she needs to be—really good to work with." He put his drink down. "And, can I just say—incredibly fucking hot."

Theo laughed.

"That sounds right—she's pretty gorgeous on-screen; I bet she's amazing in person." He narrowed his eyes. "You're flirting with her. Aren't you?"

Here came the bossy advice, right on schedule.

"I am NOT flirting with her. Okay, fine, I am, but, like—I'm not *hitting* on her."

Ben could tell Theo was fighting back a smile.

"You're so predictable."

His brother had a point.

"I know, but don't worry—first of all, you know I don't try shit with women I work with. But secondly, this is"—he lowered his voice—"Anna Fucking Gardiner. I'm not going to be that asshole who flies too close to the sun. Even though we did have a vibe going last night."

Theo's eyes opened wide.

"Last night? Did you go *out* with Anna Fucking Gardiner last night?"

Ben picked up his drink.

"I love that you actually think that, but no. I mean, yes, but not just me—everybody on set yesterday went out last night for a whole first-day-of-shooting happy-hour thing. I just happened to be sitting next to Anna. And"—he took another sip of bourbon—"yes, there was some *mild* flirting going on, on both sides, okay? But don't worry, I'm not such a fool as to think it's going to come to anything."

He let himself grin at his brother.

"But it's going to be damn fun while it lasts."

Theo clinked Ben's glass with his.

"I'll toast to that."

It was only after Ben was on his way home that he realized he hadn't told Theo about Dawn's email. Eh, it would have ruined the night. Next time.

Anna curled up at the edge of the couch in her hotel suite and poured herself a glass of sparkling water before she picked up the phone.

"Anna! Where have you been?"

Anna smiled and leaned back against the couch when she heard her best friend's voice. Penny had been her rock the year before; their phone calls and video chats and text messages had kept her going when she'd wondered if she would ever feel okay again, if her career was over, if she should just give up.

"Penny, I'm in San Francisco, you know that."

She could see the eye roll on her friend's face like they were in the same room.

"I know you're in San Francisco, I mean, like, metaphorically where have you been. I texted and called last night, and nothing."

Anna laughed at the outrage in Penny's voice.

"I was doing that terrible thing—I was working." She stopped and smiled to herself. "Well, fine, last night I wasn't working, I was drinking beer with a very attractive man, but mostly I've just been working."

"Ooooooooooh," Penny said, and the excited tone in her voice made Anna grin. "You were 'drinking beer,' hmm? Is that what we're calling it now? Tell me everything."

If only. She'd made a pledge to herself early in her career to never sleep with anyone she was working with. She'd seen how so many women got screwed over when they did that. But she *had* had a number of very intentional wrap-party flings.

"No, that's not what we're calling it now. The whole crew went out for drinks after the first day of shooting. He's very charming, but that's the end of it—he's working for the ad agency running this campaign, so I'm not going there."

Even though Ben seemed like he'd be a delightful person to break her long dry streak with . . . but no, she couldn't.

"Mmm, but you brought him up right away, though; it seems like you maybe *want* to go there."

Anna stopped to think about that.

"Part of me does, but, P—I don't know if I'm ready. I haven't, since before everything last year. And I just don't know if I can relax with another person like that yet. Or, I guess, trust another person." She sighed. "I never used to worry about that."

"I know," Penny said. "But also maybe you're building it up in your mind as something that you have to stress about, since it's been so long, and finding excuses not to do it?"

Penny knew her too well.

"Me? Build something up in my mind? Never. Fine, yes, but also that doesn't make it feel any less true right now. I'll get there eventually, don't worry." Anna took a sip of water and thought about Ben from the night before. "Okay, get this—he used to be a backup dancer. Years ago, I mean, but he still has that . . ." She paused, trying to think of the right words to describe it. "That way of moving, like he's light and nimble and on high alert, all at once."

Penny was silent for a while, for so long that Anna looked at the phone to make sure they hadn't been disconnected.

"Are you fucking kidding me?" Penny finally said. "You've got a backup dancer on the string and you haven't closed the deal yet? This is not the Anna Gardiner I know. Hell, it's not even the Anna Rose I know."

Penny had a very good point there.

"Oh, and—" She was just torturing herself now, but if she couldn't tell Penny, who could she tell? "He does that thing where he listens to me really intently, and then asks me questions about what I've told him, and let me tell you, after dealing with men in Hollywood who only want to talk about themselves, that had me ready to throw my panties at him."

"I would love to see you throwing your panties across a San Francisco bar, what a sight to see," Penny said. "You'd better throw them at this man at some point."

Anna sighed and pushed that fantasy away.

"I wouldn't count on it. Anyway, enough about me—how are you? How's business?"

Penny worked at a winery in Paso Robles. She and Anna had worked together at their first jobs after college and bonded over their terrible boss. That bond had lasted for more than ten years now, through many job and life changes.

"Business is good right now, thank God. We're still not out of the woods yet, but if we have a few more months like last month, I'll be able to sleep through the night for the first time in well over a year."

Anna let out a deep breath. What a relief.

"I thought you didn't worry about all of that accounting stuff and just stuck to the wine," she said, just to make her friend laugh. It worked.

"Yeah, that's me, just wandering around in a vineyard, tasting grapes, drinking wine in a backyard, and raking in the dough. Easy life, you know."

Now they both laughed. Anna knew how hard it had been for Penny. She'd fallen in love with the wine business a few years after they'd become friends, just when Anna was starting to find her way into acting. After about a year of thinking about it, she'd quit her job and gone to grad school at UC Davis to learn everything she could about wine, and then had become an assistant winemaker. Now she was one of a handful of female winemakers in California. And, as far as Anna knew, one of only a few Black women winemakers in the country. Penny loved her job, but small family-owned wineries like hers had a lot of ups and downs.

Well. Family- and Anna-owned, now.

"Don't worry, I'm protecting your investment," Penny said. Anna had bought into the winery the year before so they didn't have to go out of business; partly to save her best friend's job, but also to save a place that she loved. But Anna also loved having this secret from most of the world, and she especially loved that she got to share it with Penny.

"I'm a silent partner, remember? I'm just there for the wine, and the advice on how to stock my wine cellar."

Penny laughed at her.

"Oh please. You're also here for being able to say 'You know, when I was last at *my winery*,' as you lean back in your expensive chair with a glass of port in your hand."

Anna liked the sound of that.

"In that vision, I seem like some sort of James Bond villain—is that what I'm playing? I've always thought it would be way more fun to be the villain than to be one of his women."

Also, she wished she had a glass of port in her hand right now, instead of this sparkling water.

"I was actually picturing you in a Nancy Meyers movie, hanging out in a gorgeous kitchen as you pull a bottle out of the rack by the back door and pour wine into two enormous goblets that a very handsome older man hands you, but a James Bond villain sounds great, too." Anna could hear Penny take a sip of her wine. "You should wrangle yourself into a role like that after that Rebels thing comes out."

"*Vigilantes*, not Rebels," Anna said.

"Same difference," Penny said.

"But, ugh, speaking of *Vigilantes*—I still have no idea what my role is actually going to look like in the final cut of the movie. After all the fanfare about getting cast in it, how humiliating will it be if I get cut to a bit part? Oh God, I can only imagine what a nightmare the premiere will be if that happens."

She shuddered to think about it.

"Well, this is an easy one," Penny said. "You just won't go to the premiere if that happens. You'll have a prior engagement, preferably on a beach somewhere with me, drinking cocktails."

God, did that sound amazing.

"That's a perfect backup plan—you're brilliant. The only problem is that sometimes—most of the time—no one bothers to tell you about these things in advance. They haven't reached out to me about doing press for the movie, which makes me anxious. However, Simon texted me this morning that he had a 'very good meeting' with one of the directors. I don't know what that means yet; it could mean nothing, we'll see."

"Nah," Penny said. "Simon never bullshits you. Oh, also, what's going on with that other role you told me about?"

Anna got up and pulled a bottle of wine out of the mini bar. This wasn't a conversation for sparkling water.

"No news on that yet. From what Simon told me, the director really likes me, but the studio is leaning toward someone with a 'bigger box-office draw.' That's probably code for a white actress, but I'm not giving up yet. I want to fight like hell to get this role, but I just don't quite know how to do it. It's frustrating, because I have a whole plan for what I want the rest of the year to be: this ad campaign will go great, *Vigilantes* will come out and I'll be a hit in it, I'll film the Varon movie, it'll come out next year, and boom, back to the Oscars I'll go." And then she would finally be able to take a deep breath. "I don't want the studio to fuck up my whole plan, Penny! I need to talk to Simon about this; maybe he'll have a strategy to get me that role that I can't think of."

Simon usually had a strategy she hadn't thought of, actually.

"I bet he will," Penny said. "I have faith that between the two of you, you'll manage to get you this role. And I have faith that between the two of us, we'll manage to get you this man."

Anna rolled her eyes.

"Number one, I thought we were done with that part of the conversation. Number two, let's be clear, the issue isn't whether I *can* get this man, but whether I *should* get this man, and the answer to that question is no."

Penny cackled, and Anna laughed, too.

"See, this is what I like to hear! I rely on my famous big-city friend who snags men by the collar with a mere crook of a finger for all of my wish fulfillment. I'm just a small-town girl who sees the same boring men and annoying tourist types over and over again—even if I did find them attractive, they wouldn't say the same about me, since I'm in wine-stained overalls most of the time."

Anna rolled her eyes. When she and Penny had first become friends, Anna had been a shy twenty-three-year-old who was scared of dating and convinced men had never found and would never find her attractive. Penny picked up both men and women with ease, and Anna had watched from the background with awe. Then she'd started taking notes.

She'd been a quick study. The first time she'd left the bar with a guy, Penny had cheered. The rest was history.

"Sure, Wonder Girl," Anna said. "Wasn't that what that one guy called you?"

"It was *Super* Girl, I'll have you know, and also fuck you."

They both laughed.

"I'm just saying," Penny continued. "I know it's been awhile. And I understand why—last year was awful, you didn't want more complications, I get it. But you're back on your feet now. Right? So maybe you should do a little panty throwing. You know. To celebrate."

Anna laughed again, but she knew Penny was saying this as much for reassurance as she was for encouragement.

"I *am* back on my feet, Penny. And yes, I plan to do some panty throwing as soon as I can, don't worry. But I don't want to fuck up my career just when I'm feeling together. I promise, though: as soon as I throw my panties at someone, I'll let you know."

Anna went across the room to grab another bottle of sparkling water. She opened her underwear drawer as she walked by. Just a big pile of practical black panties. Some of them were thongs, but still. She might need to do something about that.

"You'd better," Penny said.

Five

A FEW DAYS LATER, ANNA SIGHED WITH RELIEF WHEN SOME-
one handed her a can of sparkling water during a break. It had
been a long day of filming all over San Francisco. This crew had
made it a lot of fun—she'd laughed a lot all day, especially at
Ben's ridiculous jokes—but she was worn-out.

"Thanks," she said, without looking at who had given it to her.

"No problem," Ben said. Her head snapped toward him. She
saw him grinning at her, and she grinned back.

"Tired?" he asked her.

She nodded.

"A little," she said. "Today has been an adventure. It's been
fun, though."

They'd spent the day racing around; she'd run up and down a
series of stairs all over the city, talking on the phone and getting
it knocked out of her hand repeatedly. She was hot and tired, but
in a good mood, despite all of that.

There had been a time when she'd have been self-conscious
for this whole crew to see her in the yoga pants that she'd had to
wear all day. She used to be ashamed of her body—of her butt

that made finding jeans that fit almost impossible, of her not-at-all-sample-size figure that made awards season a struggle, of her curves that had made her anxious in a bathing suit for most of her life.

At first, working in L.A. had made her feel so much worse. Everyone was smaller than she was, sometimes it felt like they were literally half her size, and she'd seen the way casting directors looked her up and down.

But at some point early on, she'd had to make a decision. She knew she was never going to be a size two, she knew she was never going to have that kind of ideal Hollywood body; no amount of starving herself or constant exercise would achieve it. So she'd had to decide whether to keep going in the business, just as she was, or give up and do something else.

She kept going. And then, amazingly, after her first few roles, so many women wrote to her to say how happy they were to see someone who looked like them on the big screen, how her beauty made them realize their own. Sure, it helped that she also saw the way men looked at her—both in public and in private—and how easy it suddenly was for her to get dates and anything else she wanted now, but that was just a side benefit. The men probably came easy to her because of her newfound happiness with herself, not the other way around. She realized, as she used her whole body to act, to exercise, to express herself, how much she loved her body, and how glad she was for every inch of it.

Last year, when she'd been so anxious and scared, she'd lost weight. And she'd gotten praise from all sorts of arenas for that, which felt so weird and disconcerting—did all of the people praising her really find her that unattractive before? But the worst part was she hadn't felt like herself. She'd gained some of the weight back now and felt like herself again. And she liked herself, in and out of the yoga pants.

"It's been a great day," she said to Ben, "even though I'm worn-out."

He smiled at her, and she suddenly wished they were alone.

"It really has been, hasn't it?" he said. She liked the way he smiled at her. Like they were sharing a joke, one only the two of them were in on.

"Maybe . . ." she said, and then stopped herself. What had she been about to say? Maybe he could come back to her room tonight? She couldn't say that. To cover for herself, she reached into her bag for her phone.

"I should check to see . . ." If what? If her agent called? Sure, yeah, that made sense. She was always checking for that anyway.

No emails or calls from her agent or from Simon, but she had two missed calls from her brother, and a text, too.

That was weird. Her brother was much more of a texter than a caller.

Call me when you get a chance

Oh no. That was an ominous text.

She held up a finger to Ben, still standing at her side.

"Hold on, I need to make a call."

She scrolled to her brother's name as Ben backed away.

"Hi, what's up?" she said when Chris answered the phone.

"Okay, so Mom told me not to tell you this, but I know you'd kill me if I didn't. But don't freak out."

She was already freaking out.

"What is it?"

He sighed.

"You know how they're in Joshua Tree this week, right? They drove down yesterday, and today they were in the park. Well, Dad tried to help someone whose car had broken down."

"Oh no," Anna said.

"Oh yes," Chris said. "Anyway, he landed in the hospital. They don't think it's his heart but they're not sure; the only reason I know all of this, FYI, is that Dad was apparently bragging about me to the guy whose car he was helping with, and handed him one of my business cards. Thank God the guy called me and then I called Mom."

Her dad was in the hospital. Oh no oh no oh no.

"Where are they?" Anna asked.

"A little hospital in Palm Springs, I'll text you the name, I know you're going to want to look it up. Mom sounded fine and forbade me to call you because she says you're working, but you're always working so I don't know why she thinks that's a reason not to tell you. She said Dad was asleep, but I don't know if that was true or just some bullshit she told me. You know her."

Anna sighed. Yes, unfortunately in this instance, she did.

"Okay. Thanks for calling. Where are you?" she asked her brother.

"I'm in Seattle at a conference. I'm supposed to be here through Monday, but depending on what I hear from Mom, I can fly down there tomorrow if I need to. I'll call you if I hear more. Don't freak out, okay?"

Don't freak out, indeed. Her brother had always been the level-headed one—calm, orderly, detailed, on the right path since birth. She was sure he wouldn't freak out about this.

"I'll try," she said. "Thanks for telling me. Keep me posted, okay?"

"Okay." He paused. "You're not going to do anything wild like shipping in an L.A. doctor to the hospital or airlifting Dad out of Palm Springs, are you?"

"No." She hadn't even thought about any of that. "I promise, I won't do any of those things." Though . . . that whole airlifting-him-out thing sounded like a great idea. She should make a few calls on that one. Just to see how possible it was.

"Annie. This is me you're talking to. I know that tone in your voice. Dad is going to be okay."

She turned around so no one in the room could see her.

"You don't know that," she said in a low voice.

Chris sighed.

"No. You're right. I don't know that for sure. But I talked to Mom, and I know she would have been more worried if there had been something to worry about. You know how she does that fake chipper sound to her voice thing when she's really scared? She didn't do it this time, I promise. And I swear, if I hear from her again, I'll let you know."

His voice had that soothing Mr. Rogers tone he probably used to reassure his students. It usually worked on her, too.

"Okay. Talk to you tomorrow," she said.

She hung up the phone and stood there facing the wall for a few minutes before she turned around. When she finally did, Ben was a few feet away.

"Feel free to tell me to go away," he said quietly. "But . . . is everything okay?" He looked so concerned, and had such a warm expression on his face, it made her want to burst into tears. She couldn't do that, though. Her mom was right, this was work, she had to keep going.

She nodded.

"It's fine, I'm fine." She tried to smile but failed.

Ben went back to the craft services table and brought her another can of sparkling water.

"You need to get out of here, don't you?" he asked.

She stared back at him. She wrestled with how to answer. She should stay; she should get her work done. But no, wait, she needed to take care of herself, remember? She was supposed to stop forcing herself to stay and get work done when she knew she needed breaks.

Ben looked at her as she silently battled with herself, then turned away.

"Gene?" he called out.

About a minute later, Gene clapped his hands.

"Folks, we're done for the day. See you tomorrow at . . ." He glanced at Ben. "Let's say nine a.m., for a treat. Good work, everyone."

Ben walked back over to Anna.

"Okay, let's get you out of here," he said.

She picked up her huge tote bag and looked around for her phone before she realized she was still clutching it in her hand.

"My car . . . I have to call for the driver. I don't think he's here yet."

Ben shook his head.

"Don't worry about your driver. I'll get you back to your hotel."

She followed him, with no energy to argue or tell him it wasn't his job to shuttle her around, that they already paid a service very good money to do that. As they walked to his car, she barely noticed the beautiful view of the San Francisco skyline from here or felt the chill in the air. All she could think about was her dad, in a hospital bed somewhere five hundred miles south of her.

She suddenly came to herself as they dodged traffic on the city streets on the way back to the hotel.

"Actually, Ben," she said, "can you take me to SFO instead of my hotel?"

He glanced over at her and barely blinked.

"Sure." He looked around at where they were and took a right at the next corner. "Hold on."

Anna looked down at her phone and scrolled to her assistant's name.

"Florence, hey," she said when her assistant picked up. "Can you get me on the next flight from SFO to Palm Springs? Text me when you have a boarding pass." She usually wasn't this short with her assistant, but she couldn't handle going into details right now.

She looked outside at the fog in the sky as they crept along 101 South to the airport. Why were airports always in such high-traffic areas, anyway? Wouldn't it make more sense to put an airport in an easy place to get to, so people didn't have to sit in traffic to and from it every time?

She looked over at Ben, who was staring at the road. He hadn't asked her a single question about what was wrong, what that phone call about plane tickets had been about, or why she suddenly needed to go to SFO. God, that made her like him so much.

"It's my dad," she said into the silence. "He and my mom are in Palm Springs—well, actually they were in Joshua Tree, and now he's at the hospital. My brother says he's fine, that it'll be fine, but . . . he had a heart attack a few years ago, and I'm always afraid . . ."

Ben turned to smile at her, and the look on his face felt like he'd given her a hug, even though he hadn't touched her.

"We'll get you there," he said.

He hadn't said it would be okay, or that her brother was right, or that her dad would be fine, or anything like that. She was so glad.

"I just . . ." Her phone rang before she could finish that thought.

"Okay, so how close to the airport are you?" Florence asked.

Anna looked around for landmarks.

"With the way traffic is . . . I'd guess around thirty minutes away, minimum."

Florence let out a sigh that Anna rarely heard. It was her bad-news sigh, and Florence almost never had to give her bad news; she was just that efficient.

"The last flight for the day is supposed to be at 8, but that flight has already been canceled. I have you ticketed on the flight at 6:10, but I don't know if you're going to make it."

Anna looked at the clock in the car. It was 5:30. Florence had worded her bad news very delicately.

"Shit. Okay. Okay, maybe you should . . ." Her mind went blank. What should she do?

"What about—" Florence started.

"Let me call you back." Anna ignored Florence's attempt to cut in. She needed to think.

"No flights?" Ben asked.

Anna bit her lip.

"The last one of the day is in forty minutes, and while it's much faster to get through airports when you're me, I still don't think I can make it." This was probably a sign that she should just go back to her hotel and wait for her brother to call her. "Thank you so much for trying, but I'll just go back to my hotel. My brother can get there tomorrow; he can call and let me know if . . . if everything is okay."

Ben turned to her, and that grin of his spread across his face.

"I have a better idea. I'm already heading south. What's a few more hours of driving?"

Anna stared back at him like she hadn't heard or didn't understand what he'd said.

"What?" she finally said.

He gestured at the road in front of him.

"What will it take, like, six or so hours to get there? Okay, maybe seven, because of traffic now, but I bet we can make up some time later. That puts you at the hospital at around one a.m.

It's not like you won't be awake then anyway; you'll be stressing about your dad all night; might as well do something productive."

He was looking at the road now, but he could tell Anna was still staring at him.

"You don't have to do this for me," she said.

He shrugged.

"What else am I going to do, go drop you off at your hotel and wave good-bye with you feeling like this? Please. I have a full tank of gas, I won't have a shoot tomorrow anyway because the talent has a family emergency—remind me to text Gene that, by the way, so the crew all knows they have a day off—and I've always liked Palm Springs. Hadn't planned to go there today, but"—he shrugged again—"why not?"

She leaned back in her seat, still looking at him.

"Why not indeed," she said.

She was silent for a while, and Ben couldn't tell what she was thinking. Did she want him to do this? Or was this another one of his wildly stupid ideas? Had he just kidnapped an A-list star? Shit, his boss was going to kill him.

He threw on his blinker to get off the freeway.

"Sorry—I'll turn around now and take you back to your hotel. You probably don't want—"

She cut in.

"No. I mean, yes, I do want." She gestured toward the road. "Drive on."

He grinned at her.

"Really?"

She grinned back. It was good to see her smile, for the first time since she'd gotten that call from her brother.

"Really."

He pointed at the phone that she still gripped in her hand.

"Great. Then use that, please, to navigate us over to 5."

She swiped open her phone and jumped to the directions. He felt a surge of adrenaline. They were really going to do this.

"Okay, we're going to stay on the 101 South for about an hour, then jump over to the 5."

He pressed his lips together and shook his head.

"Um, Ms. Gardiner? Did I read correctly that you grew up in the Bay Area?"

She looked sideways at him.

"Yes, why?"

"Okay—I was wondering if my memory was mistaken, since no native Northern Californian says 'the 101' or 'the 5,' for the love of God."

She laughed out loud, which had been his goal.

"Oh God, you're right. What a nightmare—L.A. has gotten to me! I'm so sorry, I can't believe I did that. Usually, I switch back when I'm up here without even thinking about it, but somehow I didn't this time. How can I repay you for this grievous error?"

"Hmmm." He pretended to think about this. "I guess that means our In-N-Out dinner will be on you."

"In-N-Out, what a great idea." She put her hand on his arm, and he was suddenly thrilled he'd tossed his hoodie in the back seat when they'd gotten into the car. Her warm hand rested on his biceps just for a second. Not long enough for him to flex, but long enough for him to feel the imprint of it after she moved her hand away. "I always used to stop there on the way when I drove home from L.A. I haven't been there in a long time, actually. Anytime I want fast food I get someone else to get it for me. In a few desperate cases, I've ordered delivery and tipped, like, four times as much as the food cost."

Ben shook his head.

"Stars, they're just like us," he said. "Wildly expensive delivery for In-N-Out. Not going to say I haven't wanted to do that, too, however."

She sighed.

"I know it sounds ridiculous, but I swear, it's not about me being too fancy to get in my own car and get myself food. I just didn't want to deal with people seeing me at a fast-food place and the pictures the tabloids would run and the terrible headlines. Inevitably it would be something about how fat I'm getting, or how I'm in the depths of despair because of a breakup with someone I was never even dating, and about how I lost this or that role because of my body, et cetera. And I didn't want to invite that on myself."

The matter-of-fact way Anna said all of that made him just as mad as what she'd said.

"That's such fucking bullshit," Ben said. "I can't believe you have to deal with that. You're one of the most beautiful women in America, and you have to sneak around to get a cheeseburger? That's ridiculous."

Just the idea of it made him fume.

She patted him on the arm again, but lingered this time.

"Thank you for your outrage. I'm so used to it I barely even think about it anymore." She shook her head. "No, that's not true—I think about it all the time, but it's so normal to me now I don't get mad about it anymore. It's just . . . the way it is."

Ben glared at the road in front of him.

"Well, I fucking hate the way it is, then." He sounded like a petulant child, but he couldn't help it. He knew, intellectually, that women got shit on for their bodies all the time, even though he didn't get it. He fucking loved women's bodies. The places they were strong, the places they were soft, the way they curved and rippled and moved and sighed when he touched them—he loved them all. How boring was it to want them to all be shaped the same? Where was the fun in that? And especially someone like Anna—why anyone would want her to change anything about herself, he had no idea.

"I fucking hate the way it is, too," Anna said. And then she laughed, and then he laughed, and they both laughed for the next few miles down the widening freeway, until they each stopped laughing and smiled at each other.

"Okay, so, important question," Ben said.

The smile faded from Anna's face.

"Okay," she said. "What is it?"

Ben swallowed hard.

"Can I trust you with the music? We need good music for a road trip, but I don't know what kind of nonsense actors listen to, and I can't have any of that highbrow intellectual crap. And"—he held up a hand to stop her from interrupting—"do not—do *not*—even say the word 'podcast' to me right now, do you hear me? This car is a podcast-free zone!"

She was laughing again, so hard she could barely talk. Good. He hadn't been able to get the stricken look on her face when she'd gotten off the phone out of his head. His mission since that moment had been to do whatever he had to do to make that look go away. And all he wanted was for her to forget for a few minutes about why they were in this car together, speeding south, and just enjoy the ride.

"First of all," she said when she recovered, "I'm insulted you even felt like you had to ask that question. Of course you can trust me with the music. Just because I'm an actor doesn't mean I have no taste." She stopped and pressed her lips together. "Okay, well . . . I mean, I may not have what many people would consider good musical taste, but that's not because of my job; it's more because I'm a teenage girl at heart when it comes to music. Especially music for a road trip."

He gestured to her phone.

"Come on. Show me what you've got."

She held up a finger.

"Second, you take that podcast thing back right now. The audacity to think that I would suggest a podcast for a late-night road trip, of all things! It's like you don't know me at all!"

Ben hid his grin. He didn't know her at all, but he liked everything he was getting to know.

"I deeply, sincerely apologize. I don't know what I was thinking." He shook his head. "No, I know exactly what I was thinking—that the last time I drove to Tahoe with my brother, he insisted on listening to some podcast about the Civil War! Which, yes, fine, it was interesting, but not road-trip material."

Anna was still smiling. Good.

"Okay, you're forgiven. I understand the effect a brother can have." She connected her phone with his car stereo. "Now. Is this your opinion of proper road-trip music?"

A few seconds later, the dulcet tones of Cardi B came rolling out of his speakers. He grinned.

"This is exactly what I was talking about."

They moved from Cardi B to Rihanna to Missy Elliot to Tupac to Beyoncé to Lizzo. Okay, yes, she knew what she was doing with this road-trip-music business.

Suddenly, after they'd been listening to music and not talking for a while, she turned to him.

"Your brother—is he your older brother?"

Ben nodded.

"He is. Only by three years, but sometimes he acts like it's by a dozen." He laughed to himself, picturing Theo, tipsy, with his glasses crooked, dancing his heart out at the last family wedding. "And sometimes he doesn't."

Anna smiled at him.

"You two are close?"

He could barely see the smile on her face now in the dim light from other headlights, but he could tell she was asking because she really wanted to know, not just to make conversation.

"Yeah," he said. "We are. We're very different, so sometimes that causes friction, and sometimes we irritate the hell out of each other, but in the end, none of that matters."

He wondered what Theo would think right now if he knew his brother was speeding toward Southern California with a famous actress in the passenger seat of his car. Actually, he could picture exactly the look on Theo's face. He almost laughed out loud.

You're on your way where? With who??

He'd have to text him when they stopped for food, just to experience this moment for real.

He still hadn't told Theo about Dawn. Or Dawn about Theo, for that matter. She'd emailed him back in response to his apology email—she was a first-grade teacher, and also a dance instructor. She'd included a picture of herself as a little kid, with her mom . . . and their dad.

It was definitely their dad in the picture—Ben rarely looked at old pictures of his dad, but he knew it was him because it looked just like Ben. It was uncanny.

The picture could still be fake, though. It could be just some random picture of his dad with some woman and her kid. He kept trying to tell himself that, but in his heart, he knew it wasn't true.

"What about you and your brother?" he asked Anna, to shake off thoughts of Dawn.

He could hear the smile in her voice.

"We're also very different, but he's great. He's a very buttoned-up professor at Cal, deeply academic, but also very funny. Every so often, some of his students realize who his sister is—Gardiner isn't my real last name, you know—and they freak out, which cracks me up."

"Is he also older?" Ben asked.

Her hair tossed back and forth as she shook her head, and she pulled a ponytail holder off her wrist and pulled it back.

"No—I'm two years older, but he's always seemed like the older one. Except when I'm embarrassing him, which I've always loved to do. I still do." She laughed. "I made him come with me to an awards show a few years ago, and afterward there was a whole series of articles about 'Anna Gardiner's hot brother.' He was mortified. I loved it."

Oh God, Ben would *love* to be able to embarrass Theo like that.

"That is absolutely something I'd do to my brother. For years, girls had crushes on him that he was totally oblivious to. Granted, it also took him a long time to realize he'd fallen in love with his girlfriend once it happened. My therapist says we all have blind spots; I guess that's Theo's. He's the smartest person I know, but sometimes I can't believe how very not smart he can be."

Anna laughed, but her laugh trailed away at the end. He saw that she was gripping her phone again.

"Hey," he said softly. "Your brother will call you if he hears anything."

She took a long breath. And then another one.

"I know," she said. "He will. I just . . . I don't want anything to happen to my dad."

He started to reach for her hand but then stopped himself. Just because she'd wanted him to take her on this impromptu road trip didn't mean she wanted him to touch her. But before he could move his hand back, she grabbed his and held on tight.

"We'll get to him," he said.

She leaned her head back against the seat and closed her eyes.

"Why were you and your brother going to Tahoe that time? Were you going skiing?"

Ben laughed.

"We're both too warm-blooded for that. No, it was in the summer, for a family wedding. One of my cousins. We almost got stuck driving with my mom and aunt, which would have been a nightmare. Don't get me wrong, I love them both very much, but they talk, incessantly, during every car trip longer than fifteen minutes. Neither Theo nor I would have made it. But we couldn't leave work as early as they wanted to go, so we got a trip to ourselves. We even . . ."

Ben looked over at Anna after he'd finished his story and saw that she'd fallen asleep.

Anna slowly opened her eyes. It took her a minute to realize where she was. In the car with Ben, on the way to Palm Springs, to see her dad. The motion of the car, the darkness, the cozy warmth, the sense of companionship she felt, all put a lazy smile on her face, despite the reason for the drive. She turned her head just in time to see Ben dancing along to "Oops! . . . I Did It Again"—hand motions and all—and she laughed.

"You're awake," he said, showing no embarrassment about his car dancing.

"How long was I asleep?" she asked.

He glanced at the clock.

"About an hour and a half. Good timing—there's an In-N-Out coming up in about thirty minutes."

She sat upright and stretched. She hadn't meant to fall asleep. Sometimes she did that as a stress reaction—when the world got too much for her, she would hide away and take a nap and let everything disappear. She'd managed to hold her panic about her dad at bay for the first few hours of their drive, but it had finally gotten to her. She rarely felt comfortable enough with other people these days to let herself fall asleep in front of them, though. She was glad she had this time—the nap had helped, at least somewhat.

"I certainly hope you would have known to wake me up for In-N-Out," she said.

He smiled at her for a second before he turned back to the road.

"I had a feeling that's what I should do, so I'm glad my instinct was correct."

She reached into her tote bag for her water bottle and drained it, and then grabbed the second one she had in there and offered it to Ben.

"Water? Driving is hard work."

He reached for it, and she uncapped the top before she handed it to him. He took a big gulp and gave it back to her.

"Thanks, you're right, I was thirsty. I usually plan better with snacks for things like this, but at least something did tell me to fill up my gas tank this morning." He grimaced. "Well, the 'something' was probably my gas light coming on yesterday on the way home from work, now that I think about it, but hey, I've driven for at least two days with that thing on before, so I'm still going to take credit for a smart decision."

Anna thought for a minute about what would have happened if they'd had to stop for gas before continuing down south. She would have had more time to rethink this ridiculous plan, she would have thought of multiple other ways to get to Palm Springs, and she wouldn't be in this car with Ben right now. She smiled to herself. She was glad he'd stopped for gas this morning, too.

Soon they saw the brightly lit In-N-Out sign from the freeway, and Ben zipped off the exit and drove them straight to the drive-through.

"I assume you don't want to go inside," he said. "I mean, I doubt there will be paparazzi here, but . . ."

She laughed and shook her head.

"Yeah, no, drive-through is great. We should eat in the parking lot, though—I want you to get a break from driving. Plus, I'm sure we'll both want a bathroom break." She lifted the water bottle. "And to fill these up for the rest of the trip."

"What's your order?" Ben asked as the In-N-Out guy with the walkie-talkie came toward them.

"Cheeseburger, Protein Style, with chiles. Fries and a Diet Coke, please."

After he ordered, Anna reached into her wallet and grabbed a twenty.

"Here," she said.

He took it without arguing with her, thank goodness. Men either seemed to want to sponge off of her, or got insulted when she paid for things, no matter how small. Ben definitely wasn't the latter, at least.

When they pulled into a parking spot with their food, Ben turned off the car and sighed.

"Tired?" she asked. She was glad he'd parked near a light, so she could see his face clearly.

"Just need to stretch a little." He unsnapped his seat belt and threw open the door. "I'm going to stand up for a second, but I'm going to attack that burger very shortly, don't worry."

Ben got out of the car and stretched his arms up high, and then bent down to touch his toes. He faced the front of the car, so Anna had a perfect view of his profile. Or, rather, the profile of his ass. She bit her lip. What a view it was. The man wasn't a backup dancer anymore, but wow, did he still have an excellent body. When he straightened up, she tore her eyes away from him and reached into the bag for her burger.

"Oh God, I didn't realize how hungry I was," she said after the first bite.

Ben sat down and picked up his own burger.

"I'm starving," he said. "Neither of us has eaten since, what, those brownies on set this afternoon?"

She took a sip of her Diet Coke.

"Sorry I fell asleep," she said. "We should have stopped earlier to eat—that was my fault."

Ben waved that off.

"Don't worry about it. If I'd known I would be this hungry, I would have sped through a drive-through while you slept."

He picked up his phone and checked the directions.

"We've made excellent time, by the way. Only about three more hours to go."

He reached for his drink and then dropped his hand and stared at her.

"I just realized something. You could have flown to L.A. To-night, I mean—there are a zillion flights from SFO to all of the L.A. airports; you could have gotten one. And then you could have rented a car or gotten a driver or something to get you to Palm Springs."

She nodded.

"I know," she said before she thought about it.

"You knew?" He stared at her. Now she wished there wasn't quite so much light in this car.

She reached for a fry so she wouldn't have to meet his eyes.

"I realized that at some point after we'd gotten on 5. But by that time, it was too late."

That wasn't precisely, exactly true. She'd realized it when they were only about thirty minutes into the drive, when there was still time to tell him to turn around and take her back to SFO. Her assistant absolutely could have gotten her on an L.A. flight at that point, and she definitely could have gotten a driver to pick her up and take her to Palm Springs.

But she'd realized it right when he'd made her laugh about the podcast thing, and right after he'd casually referred to her as one of the most beautiful women in America. The amazing thing was, she knew he hadn't said that to flatter her; he'd said it so matter-of-factly, it blew her mind. Sure, people had been calling her beautiful for years; it wasn't like she didn't know she was attractive. But somehow, the way he'd said that, and the way he'd talked to her, the way he'd made her laugh, had all calmed her down, had just made her feel so warm inside. She'd known she wanted to stay in this cozy little car, with Ben cheering her up and helping her relax and making her feel comfortable. And when she realized that instead she could get on a plane, the thought of making him turn around, of going through the airport alone, and trying to avoid people and not letting them see her or take pictures of her while she was so anxious and scared, and dealing with the long, cold drive to Palm Springs from LAX alone and friendless in the back seat of some town car or SUV felt so sad and scary and lonely.

She'd almost told him to turn around anyway, but then she pictured herself having an anxiety attack during the flight, surrounded by strangers and people looking at her, and she knew she didn't want to get out of this car. Here, in the car with Ben, was a happy place, full of dancing and conversations about snacks and pop music and someone she felt safe and comfortable with. No matter what was at the end of the drive, she had this. She needed it.

But now she felt guilty for forcing him on this road trip when she'd had another option. She was Anna Gardiner, after all; she had more money than she knew what to do with—she probably could have chartered a plane if she'd needed to. But no, instead, she'd made this unsuspecting guy—whose job probably depended on making her happy—drive her five hundred miles?

"I'm sorry," she said. "I should have—"

He held up a hand to stop her.

"And take a road trip away from me, are you kidding? I'm glad you realized it too late. Plus, we'll probably get there around the same time you would have, given L.A. traffic and how long it takes to get out of LAX."

She'd thought of that already, too, but more to justify for herself why her decision was the right one. It still didn't excuse making Ben drive, but she appreciated him saying so.

"Good point." She smiled at him.

He crumpled up his cheeseburger wrapper.

"It's a good weeknight adventure. I've been boring for a while. It's good to break out and do something a little wild again." He picked up his phone. "Speaking of, I've got to text my brother."

She opened the car door.

"I'll throw all of this away and fill up my water bottle. And go to the bathroom." She suddenly had no idea how she'd managed to hold it for this long, and raced inside.

Of course there was a line for the bathroom, but it was miraculously short. When Anna walked out, she turned in the direction of the water dispenser, until the teenagers who came out after her stopped her.

"Um, we were just talking about this and you look just like Anna Gardiner! But then we were like, what would Anna Gardiner be doing here, but maybe you're filming? Somewhere nearby?"

Oh shit. She'd been so in her own world, she hadn't remembered to pull her hoodie up over her head to walk into the bathroom. She didn't want to blow off these girls, but she also did not want to have to be Anna Gardiner right now, and take selfies with them that would absolutely turn up on Instagram or TikTok or somewhere else, and then have to answer questions about why the hell she was at an In-N-Out somewhere in central California late at night on a Thursday. She opened her mouth to say something, she had no idea what.

"Lulu! There you are!" Ben grabbed her hand. "Honey, we have to get back on the road, I've been waiting for you!"

She gripped his hand and smiled at the girls.

"I get that all the time, such a compliment! Have a great night. Get home safe."

They strolled back to the car, hand in hand, as Ben monologued, she assumed for the benefit of whoever might be watching them.

"So I said, are you kidding me? I've got to have those hogs by morning! And then he said, hogs! I thought we were talking about cows! Are you sure it's hogs? And so I said, of course we're talking about hogs! Why do you think I named my company Pigs R Us?"

By that time, they were back at the car, so Anna could get inside and let her laughter burst out of her.

"Pigs . . . R . . . Us?" she finally said, bent over so far her head was almost on her lap.

"Look, I had to say something!" Ben started the car. "Someone walked by with a Peppa Pig shirt on, and it made me think of pigs, so I just . . . went with it."

She rolled the window down, now that they were safely out of the parking lot and on their way back to the freeway.

"Also—do I look like a Lulu? Where did that come from?"

"Look, Little Miss Questioning Everything, which one of us got us out of there and into the parking lot without you having to pose for pictures or whatever, and which one of us stood there with a blank smile on her face with no idea what to say? Because

I know which one is which!" She could tell he was smiling, even in the dark. "Also. Your pants. Um, that's why the Lulu."

She looked down at the yoga pants she'd been in all day. At least if she had to do this road trip in the same outfit she'd been in since seven a.m., thank goodness it was this one and not the form-fitting dress she'd been wearing the day before.

"My pants? What do you . . ." She laughed. "Oh. My pants, I get it. How did you even know my brand of yoga pants?"

He flashed a grin at her.

"I'm in advertising, remember? I know a lot that no one would expect me to know."

She settled back into her seat, a smile still on her face. And then remembered something.

"Thanks. For the rescue back there, I mean. I wasn't thinking. I have no idea why I went into the bathroom without my hoodie up or sunglasses on or something."

That had been a very close one.

"It's been a long day," he said. "Even stars struggle with a day like you've had. Plus, you're a delicate flower now, you haven't been inside a fast-food restaurant in years. You forgot how to do it!"

She laughed and rolled her window back up as they got on the freeway.

"Yeah, I guess I did. And, yeah, it has been a long day."

Speaking of. She pulled her phone out of her pocket to check, but there was nothing from either her parents or her brother. If she texted Chris and told him she was on her way to Palm Springs, he would . . . actually, she had no idea what he would do. Part of her wanted to do it, just for the amusement factor, but no, it was late and he was probably worried enough as it was—she shouldn't freak him out.

What would be at the other end of this freeway? She'd been holding that fear at bay ever since she'd gotten into the car with

Ben, but she knew it was just hanging out there, somewhere behind her jokes and her attraction to him and the smile that hovered around her face.

Her dad's heart attack and subsequent surgery a few years ago had been hard enough. But at least then, they'd had a plan for the surgery, she trusted his doctors, and she'd been there the whole time during the surgery, in the waiting room with her mom. But even then, she'd been terrified. Terrified of losing him.

And now . . . he was in an unfamiliar city, with doctors who didn't know him and who might ignore him or mistreat him because of the color of his skin, in a hospital she didn't know, and it was an emergency, and she knew if she let the fear show its face, it would choke her. She tried to push it back inside, but she could feel it gaining force.

"Do you want me to drive?" she asked. "I feel bad you've been driving this whole time. We should have switched in the parking lot. I'm sorry I didn't think of it then."

Ben shrugged.

"Don't worry about it. You seem exhausted, no offense." He shook his head. "I shouldn't have said that—there's no such thing as 'no offense' when you're telling a woman she looks tired. I just meant you already fell asleep once and when you did, you were out like a light, and that's not the energy I like to bring to a drive down 5 at ten at night. Plus, I just drank a very large Coke—not diet, real, actual, Coca-Cola—which I got for both the caffeine and the sugar to hype me up to drive, so I can't waste all of that."

Just listening to Ben prattle on made her breathe slower. She took another breath in and let it out. Thank goodness she was with him.

For a moment, she let herself think again about what it would have been like to be in the back seat of some town car right now, with a silent driver, hurtling from LAX to Palm Springs, lonely and scared and with nothing to distract her except her phone, where she would probably be scrolling through social media and WebMD and all of the other places that would stress her out even more. And then she turned to look at Ben in the driver's seat, a smile dancing around his lips as he bopped along to Kesha, and she let out a breath. Thank God she was here.

"How on earth did you make the switch from being a backup dancer to being in advertising?" she asked him. Yeah, she was curious about this, but she mostly just wanted to get him talking again.

He laughed.

"Is it that weird of a trajectory? I think it was just that after having been on the other side of the camera for a while, both dancing and also with the crew work, I was so fascinated by how the whole package was made. I knew being in the actual production side or in front of the camera wasn't for me, so I tried to figure out what was for me."

His voice sounded so warm and comfortable next to her. She relaxed into it.

"Why didn't you think being in front of the camera was for you? I could see you there."

He laughed at that.

"I'm going to take that as a compliment," he said. She'd meant it as one, but he didn't give her a chance to say so. "But while I loved the dancing, it very much felt like a career for three years, five, max. Like a football player, except with less money and fewer concussions. And I didn't love it enough to be an instructor and give it my whole life. A lot of the guys went on to try acting, but I wasn't interested—what, I'd wait tables for years and maybe get one or two lines on some show eventually? I knew it wasn't my calling, and neither was doing camerawork, as fun as it is."

"How did you figure out that advertising was for you?"

He groaned.

"I'm so sorry I have to admit this, but it was my brother. I came home for Christmas, that last year in L.A., when I'd quit dancing and was still doing crew stuff but was sort of . . . aimless. And he tricked me into going out for drinks with him and said he'd pay, and I was too young and broke to realize there must be an ulterior motive. And then he asked me all of those fucking questions about where I saw myself in the future and what I love and what I wanted to be doing with my life and blah blah. I was so mad at him." He shook his head. "I kept thinking about what he'd asked me, even though I didn't want to. And I realized the thing that fascinates me the most is drawing people in, figuring out how they tick, turning something into nothing. So eventually I asked Theo if he knew anyone who did that kind of work. I didn't even realize what it was, at that point. He said it sounded a lot like what people do in advertising and marketing to him. And some friend of a friend of his who worked at an ad agency talked to me on the phone for like an hour, and everything they said sounded right up my alley. So I moved home—and back in with my mom, who was not thrilled about that—and went to school up here. I sort of assumed I'd move back to L.A. at some point, but I've liked my jobs in San Francisco, so I never left."

She liked the fond, exasperated way he talked about his brother.

"Plus, your family is all in the Bay Area, right?" she said.

He nodded.

"Not all, but mostly. I have some family and lots of good friends down South, of course. But . . ." He shrugged. "The Bay Area is still home. Despite . . . all of the changes over the past decade or so, it still feels that way."

That sounded familiar.

"Yes, definitely," she said. "I do love L.A. now, even though it can be . . ." She bit her lip and tried to think of the right word. "Overwhelming sometimes. But when I come up here—or, I guess, up there, since we're pretty far south now—it feels right." She laughed. "Sometimes I make excuses to go up there. Like this ad campaign."

He flashed her a smile.

"Well, I, for one, am glad you made excuses this time."

She felt an enormous desire to give him a hug. The only thing that stopped her was the impossibility of hugging someone who was currently driving a car down Interstate 5.

"Me, too," she said instead.

Six

A FEW HOURS LATER, THEY PULLED INTO THE HOSPITAL parking lot. It was a ghost town at this hour, with only a handful of other cars. They'd spent the end of the drive playing all the road games they could figure out how to play at night—license plate bingo didn't work so well, but then it was rare to see anything but California or Nevada plates in this area anyway. They'd also played progressively louder music, and told fake stories about the people in the cars around them. Anna told herself she was doing all of this to keep Ben awake and entertained in the wee hours of the morning, but really, it was to keep herself busy, so she wouldn't anticipate what was at the end of the drive.

Now they were finally here, and Anna was terrified about what she'd find inside that hospital.

Ben looked at her after he turned off the car.

"You okay?" he asked.

She nodded at him, and then shook her head.

"I'm not okay." She'd tried to practice saying that over the last year, but it was still hard. She made herself smile. "But we came all this way, can't miss the main event!" She tried to make a joke out of it, and very much appreciated that Ben gave her a pity smile.

"If you need a minute, it's fine," he said. "It's been a long day."

She unbuckled her seat belt. She'd dreaded arriving, but now that they were here, she had to get inside.

"No, I need to see them," she said. "Let's go."

Ben reached for his seat belt but didn't release it.

"I don't have to come in," he said. "It's totally okay, my feelings won't be hurt, I can just sit here and catch up on my—"

She shook her head progressively harder as he talked.

"No, please come with me." Wait, did that sound too needy? "You don't have to if you don't want to, but I'd hate to have you come all this way and then just wait in the car."

He unsnapped his seat belt and opened his car door.

"Okay, then. Let's go."

As they walked out of the tiny parking lot and toward the hospital doors, Anna fought back the impulse to reach for Ben's hand. That was ridiculous, she barely even knew him, why was she relying on him so much? No, she was a grown-up; she could handle this. She could handle it even if . . . No, no, she wasn't going to think about that right now.

She especially wasn't going to think about those hours that she'd sat in the hospital waiting room while her father had been in surgery, waiting and waiting to hear if he'd survived it. And she definitely wasn't going to think about that day last year when her dad had appeared at her front door, let himself in with the key she'd given her parents when she'd bought her house, pulled her into his arms, and let her cry for an hour. And then managed to get her on the road to pulling her life back together. No, she couldn't think about that, either, or she'd cry. And she couldn't cry now, she had to hold it together, for everyone in the hospital, for Ben, for her mom.

She let out a deep breath, and Ben looked over at her. Oh God, please let him not ask her if she was okay, because she wasn't sure she could pretend to be okay, but if she told him she wasn't okay, she knew she would fall apart, and she couldn't, couldn't fall apart.

"Glad we made it here," he said. "If I say so myself, driving was a brilliant idea."

She appreciated his effort to make her laugh, even if she couldn't quite do it.

"It absolutely was," she said.

Their knuckles brushed together as they walked through the automatic doors of the hospital.

"Hi, I'm looking for my dad," Anna said to the bored-looking woman at the information desk. "Phillip Rose?" The woman barely looked at her and turned to a computer.

"Rose, like the flower rose?" she asked in a monotone.

"Um, yes," Anna said. "Like the flower." How hard was it to spell "Rose," anyway? Were there that many variations?

She waited as the woman typed into the computer. And waited some more. How many Roses could there be in this small hospital? How many people could there even be? Why was this taking so long? Anna kept a pleasant look on her face, even though she could feel her heart beating, faster and faster. She felt her breathing getting shallow, so she tried to do the deep-breathing technique she'd learned, but it felt like there was something sitting on her chest.

Ben put a light hand on her back. She leaned into the gentle pressure, and he kept his hand there. She could breathe a little better.

Suddenly, the woman shook her head.

"No Rose here."

No. That couldn't be possible. She knew this was the right hospital. Maybe they'd had to move him to a different hospital?

"He came in through the emergency room. Earlier today. Or I guess it was yesterday now, but he—"

A deep laugh stopped her. She looked up, and there, coming down the hallway toward her, were her parents. Laughing and chatting with each other like they were strolling down the street on the way to a restaurant on a Saturday night, not like they were walking through a hospital on the way out of the emergency room.

"Dad? Mom?"

They both looked at her, and her father's face broke out into a grin.

"Anna, baby, what are you doing here?"

Before he'd finished talking, she'd made it to him and pulled him into a hug.

"Dad! You're okay! I was so worried." *Don't cry don't cry* she couldn't let herself cry.

"I told Christopher not to tell you we were here. I knew you would do something like fly down here," her mother said.

She hugged her mom, too.

"Shouldn't you know by now that Chris and I tell each other all of the important things? Wouldn't it be easier for you to just tell us all of the important things, too? Tell me now, what happened?" She turned to her dad. "Are you okay? Really?"

He patted her on the shoulder.

"Really, Anna. I'm okay, I promise. Just a little spot of heat exhaustion—I foolishly hadn't been drinking enough water out in the desert, and then I stopped to help someone change a tire, and well, the next thing I knew I was here. But don't worry. They checked me all out and gave me an IV full of liquids and I'm as good as new."

Anna looked at her mom.

"Is that true?"

Her mom pursed her lips, but nodded.

"Yes, Anna, it's true, we swear. You're such a suspicious child, you always have been. This is like when you found out about Santa Claus and grilled us about everything else. But we told the truth then, didn't we?"

Anna smiled at the memory. She'd been seven. Her mom had sworn her to secrecy, she'd said her brother still believed, and she didn't want Anna to ruin it for him, or for any of the other kids in her school. That had been one of the only secrets Anna had ever kept from her brother.

But her parents did have a habit of keeping important things from her. To "protect" her, or so she "wouldn't worry," et cetera, et cetera. She might be a thirty-two-year-old woman with a success-ful career who owned a house and had been on the cover of many magazines, but her parents still thought she was a child. Her mom looked like she was telling the truth right now, though.

"I remember," she said to her mom. "You'll call the doctor at home, right? And make sure he gets checked out then?"

Her dad rolled his eyes, but her mom nodded.

"I promise." She gave Anna another quick hug. "Now. As won-derful a surprise as it was to see you, it's been a long day, and I've got to get to bed." She narrowed her eyes. "You do, too, young lady. What did you do, charter a plane to get here?"

Anna shook her head, then realized she didn't know how to answer this question. Her mom would kill her if she knew she'd jumped in a car with a virtual stranger and had him drive her here. Especially without telling anyone.

Okay, well, her mom might have a point with that one.

"Um, I flew into L.A., then drove from there," she said. Yes, that thing she should have done.

Her mom looked around the lobby, and her eyes landed on

Ben, a respectful distance away, scrolling through his phone like he hadn't been paying attention. Though Anna was pretty sure he had been.

"Is that man with you?" her mom said in a low voice.

Something close to the truth was probably the best move here.

"He drove me here. From the airport." She just didn't say *which* airport.

Her mom nodded.

"Of course. Your driver." Anna opened her mouth to correct her mom, then closed it again. "Do you have a place to stay, or do you want to come back with us?"

Anna knew that if she went back to her parents' hotel with them, she would break down in tears, and no one needed that tonight. That could wait until she was safely alone.

Plus, her mom would wonder why, exactly, she didn't have any luggage or even any clothes that weren't the ones she was wearing. And she'd never been great at lying to them anyway, so the truth about the panicked drive to Palm Springs would come out, and then her mom and dad would both worry about her, and that was the last thing she wanted.

She waved a hand.

"No, no, Florence got me a room at the Ace, I'm fine."

Ben raised his hand from across the room.

"Miss, I'll bring the car around."

Anna hid a smile. She nodded at him, and he disappeared out the automatic doors.

"Okay, baby," her dad said. "I promise I'll take care of myself." He looked at her for a long moment.

"I promise I'll take care of myself," she repeated.

He nodded.

"Good. I would ask to see you for breakfast tomorrow, but I'm sure you have to head back to your shoot first thing, so we'll see you when we get back home, okay? You'll still be in San Fran-cisco?"

She would be, thank goodness.

"I'll still be there. Love you."

"Love you, too," her parents said in unison, and walked out the front doors of the hospital.

She stood there alone, only the bored woman at the informa-tion desk for company. He was fine. He would be fine. She took a halting breath and closed her eyes. Now she felt immensely fool-ish for that mad rush to Palm Springs. She could have just waited in her hotel room in San Francisco, they would have called in the morning, it would have been fine. She had overreacted on a grand scale, hadn't she?

A few seconds later, Ben pulled up right outside the hospital doors.

Anna smiled shakily as she walked to the car.

"I almost died when you broke out the 'miss' in there, you know," she said.

Ben grinned at her from the driver's seat. God, she felt so bad for bringing him along on this anxiety-driven mission.

"I almost said 'Miss Gardiner' but then I realized you probably didn't want No-Affect Lady at the info desk to realize who you were and decide to wake up, so then I was going to go with 'Miss Rose,' but I thought your driver wouldn't know your real name, so I decided to just stick with 'miss' alone, and I don't know why I'm still talking about this when the big news is that your dad is okay!"

He turned to her, a huge, warm smile on his face.

"The best possible news! I would say we have to celebrate, but it's almost two a.m. and we're in Palm Springs, so I don't think that's exactly possible, but still. I'm so happy for you."

She smiled back at him, then bit her lip.

"Thanks, Ben. But . . . I'm so sorry I dragged you all this way.

I shouldn't have freaked out after I talked to Chris. I should have just gone back to my hotel and eaten french fries or something and waited for news, and I definitely shouldn't have made you drive me five hundred miles south for no reason."

He dropped his hands from the steering wheel.

"Anna, what the hell are you apologizing for? Are you really telling me that you just found out that your dad is okay, and now you feel bad because you inconvenienced me? And here I thought you were a Hollywood diva who did whatever she needed and screw everyone else, but you're just a softie. Relax, I'm fine! I got an adventure and free In-N-Out out of this and a little birdie told me we're heading to the Ace tonight, and I love that hotel."

Now she had to laugh.

"Ben, I made that up, you know. I don't have a room at the Ace."

He started the car.

"Oh, I know. I did notice everything you told your mom about the trip down here was *almost* the truth, so we might as well make this one as close to the truth as we can."

She relaxed into the passenger seat and relinquished control.

"I knew my mom would lose it if she knew we drove down here—she already almost lost it because I showed up in the first place, even though she tried to pretend otherwise. So I wanted the trip to seem, you know . . . chill."

He shot her a look as he turned to get back on the freeway.

"Chill? Anna Rose Gardiner, or whatever your name is, I only know you a little bit, but 'chill' is the last word I'd use to describe you. And if I think that, I'm sure your mom knows it to her core."

The man had a good point.

"Okay, true, but, like . . . slightly more chill than it was." She turned to him and sighed. "What can I do to make this up to you? Basketball tickets or frequent flier miles or . . ."

Ben held up a hand to stop her.

"Anna. I promise. You don't have to do anything to make this up to me. This was fun—I mean, at least, for me, I had fun on the drive down here, you probably did not, now that I think about it, since you were on your way to your dad in the hospital, so now it feels insensitive that I just said it was fun, but anyway, really, you have nothing to make up for."

"I had fun, too," she said in a quiet voice. It was true. She'd been relaxed and happy and had enjoyed herself for most of the ride.

Ben turned and looked at her.

"You don't have to say that, you know," he said.

She put her hand on his.

"I did. Really. Thank you for making what would have been a really stressful trip mostly a fun one."

He beamed at her and looked away.

"You're welcome. It was truly my pleasure."

She didn't move her hand away until they pulled into the parking lot at the Ace.

Ben looked at Anna when he turned off the car. He had one important question for her.

"Okay. Am I going in there with Anna Gardiner, or Anna Rose?"

She dropped her head to her hands. Apparently, she hadn't thought of that. One more thing that let him know how stressed she'd been today, since he had the impression from their conversations that she always thought of things like that.

"Oh God, make it Anna Rose. I mean, or just your friend Anna, or some lady named Anna, or anything else, I don't know. But not Anna Gardiner. I don't want it to be a whole thing that I checked into a hotel in Palm Springs at"—she checked her phone—"1:42 in the morning. You know?"

He did know; that's why he'd asked.

"Okay, then. Put your hoodie up and let me handle this." He stopped to look at her. She'd had an incredibly long day, and that moment at the hospital with her parents must have been exhausting. "Actually, why don't you stay in the car and wait for me? I'll come back and get you when I get us rooms."

She shook her head.

"Absolutely not, I'm not that delicate. Plus, the rooms are on me."

He'd known she would insist on that.

"Yes, yes, fine, but, like, don't you think handing over your credit card will make it more likely someone will recognize you? I'll pay up front; you can pay me back."

He'd thought she would argue with him about that, but instead she just opened the car door.

"Okay, that makes sense, but I still want to come in."

There was no accounting for celebrity. Ben followed her out of the car and into the hotel lobby.

He walked up to the front desk and smiled at the woman staffing it.

"Hi, Niamh!" he said after a quick glance at her name tag.

She looked surprised.

"You know how to say my name! Everyone gets that wrong."

He smiled at her.

"My cousin's daughter is another Niamh, so I know the name well."

She smiled back.

"Well, please tell your Niamh I said hi. Do you have a reservation?"

He shook his head.

"Unfortunately, we don't, but is there any way my sister and I would be able to get two rooms for the night? I'm sorry we got here so late; it's been a very long day."

He gave her his best smile, but she shook her head at him.

"Welcome to Palm Springs, but we're fully booked tonight! There's a ton going on in town for the weekend. But you might have better luck at . . ." She turned to a computer and clicked around.

This was what he'd been afraid of. After Anna had told her mom she was staying at the Ace, he'd tried to book them rooms online but hadn't been able to. He hadn't known if that was because it was so late at night, or because they were booked, but he'd feared the latter. He'd almost told Anna that on the drive over here, but she'd seemed so stressed about everything he hadn't wanted to make it harder on her. Now he needed to do something about this.

He leaned on the counter and dropped his smile into a steady gaze.

"Look," he said, "if there's any way you can help me out with rooms tonight, I'd really appreciate it. I'm going to level with you—we're here because my sister and I were at the hospital; Dad collapsed in Joshua Tree today and we had to rush out here. We just left the hospital a few minutes ago. I know we should have called ahead, but . . ."

The clerk shook her head.

"Oh, that's terrible! I understand why you didn't call."

Ben felt guilty that he was sort of lying to her, but most of what he'd said was the truth. It just wasn't *his* dad.

"Thanks—it was pretty scary, but he's going to be okay, we think, thank goodness." He closed his eyes for a second and hoped Anna was taking note of his acting skills. "But I don't have to tell you that we're both exhausted after a long drive, and then the hospital, and driving around Palm Springs at night from hotel to hotel to see if anyone has room for us sounds like a nightmare that might last until dawn, and you could not possibly see two people more ready to fall into bed than the two of us."

Niamh patted him on the hand.

"Let me see what I can do."

At least this woman was the polar opposite of the hospital info-desk woman, who barely seemed sentient. After she clicked around for a few more minutes, she looked up at him with a big smile on her face.

"I thought so! Okay, we can take you!"

Ben cheered, and he heard a small "yay" from Anna behind him.

"Unfortunately, we only have one room—we were holding on to it for a VIP, but they canceled, so I can release it to you. You don't mind that it's only one room, since you're family?"

Well, shit.

"Actually, Niamh—"

"Anything is great, thank you so much," Anna said from behind him.

He turned around to argue with her, but she waved him off.

One room? He was going to have to spend the night in a hotel room with Anna and not touch her? This felt colossally unfair.

But what could he do? He handed over his credit card to Niamh, and she gave them two room keys and directions to their room.

"And I hope your dad feels a lot better!" she said as they walked out of the lobby.

"Thank you, so, so much," Anna said over her shoulder.

They were silent for the first part of their walk through the sprawling property to their room.

"I see you're also a fan of the 'tell as much of the truth as you can' form of lying," Anna said, when they turned the corner toward the empty pool. She pushed back her hoodie and grinned at him.

It was good to see her smile, after how stressed she'd looked for the past few hours.

"Oh, I think I invented that form of lying," Ben said. "It let me get away with a whole lot as a teenager. I rarely have reason to do it anymore, but it was good to keep those skills from rusting."

Anna laughed.

"Well, you were excellent in there. Thanks."

He handed her the key cards for the room.

"Hey—I can go somewhere else for the night; I'm sure there are other hotels where I can find a room. I was just saying all of that about not wanting to drive around so you could crash."

She brushed that off.

"You're the one who spent the past seven hours driving; you're probably just as exhausted as I am. And you were right, the thought of driving around town to find another hotel made me want to burst into tears. I'm thrilled we got a room here, and all because of your knowledge of Irish names."

Well, he'd tried. He gestured for her to precede him up the staircase that led to their room.

"Thank my cousin, who married an Irish guy."

Oh God, he didn't ask if it was one bed or two. If it was one bed, he'd have to sleep on the floor. Either way it would suck. This felt like some sort of curse.

Anna let them into the room with the key card.

"Oh, thank God we're here," Anna said. "I've had to pee for the past two hours, but then I got distracted at the hospital and didn't go when we were there. I'm dying here."

She dropped her tote bag on the desk and raced into the bathroom.

Ben put his messenger bag down and sat on one of the beds. There were two, which should have made him feel relieved. Instead, he felt like he'd lost his last chance. Like he'd even had a chance.

He had to stop thinking about this. No matter how beautiful Anna was, or how fun she was to talk to, or how much he enjoyed her company, or how much he was attracted to her, he needed to forget she would be in this room with him tonight. One, they were working together—he never got mixed up with people he worked with; two, she was a fucking famous actress and the whole world probably hit on her and he didn't want to be the whole world plus one; three, he didn't want her to think he'd driven her down here expecting some sort of payment. And those were only the first three of the probably twenty-five or so reasons he needed to not even look at Anna again until they were back in the car together tomorrow.

Anna came bursting out of the bathroom.

"Ben!" She had a huge smile on her face. He stood up and smiled back at her.

"Anna!" he said in the same tone of voice, and she laughed.

"My dad is okay! It finally just hit me." She closed her eyes for a second and let out a long sigh, and the smile on her face widened. "He's really okay."

Somehow, it felt natural for Ben to open his arms, and Anna walked right into them.

"He's really okay," Ben said. She hugged him fiercely, and then laughed out loud.

"I was so worried. My God, I was so worried on the drive down here. And you know I'm going to worry about him forever, but he walked out of the hospital on his own, and I could tell from the look on my mom's face that he really is fine." She leaned her head against Ben's chest. "I'm so thrilled and relieved and . . . just everything.

"My God, what a drug relief is," she said. She smiled up at him, that heightened, glassy look in her eyes that told him if he hadn't already known that she was so tired she was almost drunk. Then her smile changed. Softened. And she looked at him like . . .

No. Oh no. He knew that look. He knew it well.

That was a *kiss me* look if he'd ever seen one. And he'd seen them a whole hell of a lot.

But he couldn't kiss her. Hadn't he just detailed the many reasons why?

He realized his arms were still around her. He tried to take a step back, but just ended up backing them both up against the wall. He tried to let her go, he really did, but somehow, he couldn't.

Then she let go of him. He pushed away the jolt of disappointment he felt and tried to be relieved. Good, okay, good, that's what he needed, for her to stop this. She would let go and get under the covers and he would get under the covers of his own bed and attempt to fall asleep with her just a few feet away and then they would drive home tomorrow and never speak of this.

Then she took hold of his face with both of her hands, pulled it down to hers, and kissed him.

Seven

HE COULDN'T THINK, COULDN'T MOVE; ALL HE COULD DO
was kiss her. He hadn't let himself imagine this moment, but it
was somehow even better than he could have dreamed of. Her
lips were so warm, so soft; her body felt so good against his. My
God, how did she smell this incredible after seven hours in a car?
He couldn't get enough. He pulled her hard against him as they
kissed, and he could feel her smile as he ran his hands up and
down from her waist to her hips. He threw everything into that
kiss; all the times he'd wanted to kiss her, to touch her, and had
stopped himself, he poured all of those feelings into this moment.

They dove into each other, not talking, barely moving, except
when she pressed him harder against the wall, when he gripped
her ass, and then when he moved a hand up under her hoodie,
under her shirt, to feel the soft, smooth skin there. Suddenly, Ben
realized what he was doing and pulled away with a groan.

"Anna. Anna, we can't."

She hadn't stepped away; she was still right up against him,
looking at him with those soft eyes and plump lips.

"Why can't we?"

He looked at her blankly, all of his reasoning from when she was in the bathroom gone.

"You're . . . you." She laughed at him, and he realized how ridiculous that sounded. "I mean . . . You know what I mean. Plus, we work together."

Anna reached for his belt.

"Only for a little while longer. That doesn't count, really."

He was already so hard, after just a few moments of kissing her, it was embarrassing. And now she was unbuckling his belt? No, he couldn't think straight like this.

He stepped to the side, and her hands dropped.

"Anna, my God, I want this, I'm sure you can tell exactly how much I want this. I've wanted this since the first moment I saw you, but you've had such a long, emotional day, and I don't want you to do something you'll regret."

She pulled him back to her.

"I won't regret this." And then they were kissing again, and it was, oh God, even better than before. He bit her lip, and she laughed and then sucked his bottom lip in between hers, and her warm, luscious body pressed against his, and it felt like all he'd ever wanted in life.

Oh shit. Wait. He remembered that other reason.

It took everything he had, but he pulled away.

"Anna. Wait, hold on." She stopped and looked at him.

"I don't want you to think that you have to do this, that you owe me this for driving you here today. I know you felt guilty about that, but I swear, you don't owe me anything, you don't have—"

Anna put her hand over his mouth.

"First of all, you seem too smart about women to think I'm, what, acting here, and that I don't really want this." He raised his eyebrows at her, and she tilted her head. "Okay, good point, I *am* an actor, and a very good one, but I promise, this is not the kind of acting I would ever do, not one-on-one. Two, when I was trying to pay you back for this in the car, I was offering basketball tickets, not me! Three: Will you please just shut the fuck up and take your clothes off?"

Ben knew when he'd lost. Or, as the case may be, won.

He dropped his jeans to the floor and threw his T-shirt across the room.

"Happy now?" he asked.

She looked him up and down and smiled.

"Oh yes."

Ben's body was just as good as Anna had been imagining. Granted, he didn't look like one of the guys from *Magic Mike XXL*, and she didn't expect him to—he hadn't actually been a backup dancer for years. But he was still lean and athletic-looking and his chest was a gorgeous caramel brown. The man worked full-time, more than full-time, she'd seen it; how did he have this good a body? She had no idea, but she sure as hell enjoyed it.

He let her stare at him for a while, a little smile on his face, before he reached for her. He slowly unzipped the black hoodie she'd been wrapped in all night and tossed it to the floor. Then he stopped and bit his lip, an indecisive look on his face.

"Is something wrong?" she asked. Something had better not be wrong. She needed this.

"Not a single thing," he said. "I just can't decide if I'd rather take your top off first, or your pants. On the one hand, I'm generally more of a boob man than an ass man, but on the other, your ass has been driving me wild in those pants all fucking day."

It took everything in her not to strike a pose at that.

"All day?" she asked. "But I've been sitting on my ass for the past seven hours. How is it even possible that it's been driving you wild?"

He shook his head.

"Did you forget that before we got in the car, we had been on set together for a full day, a day where you repeatedly ran up and down stairs and I had to keep looking away so I wouldn't ogle you?"

Oh yeah. She had forgotten that.

"Then I would say you should save the best for last, but then, it's all pretty great," she said.

He pulled her hard against him and kissed her again, his hands first gripping her ass, then moving up and down her body until she was breathless. He put his hands in her hair and tugged out her ponytail holder. Her hair cascaded down onto her shoulders.

"My God, you're incredible," he said. Then he grabbed the hem of her T-shirt and pulled it up over her head.

Thank God she'd worn her best bra today, instead of the industrial sports bra the well-meaning but clueless shoot stylist had sent over. She'd regretted the good—but not particularly comfortable—bra a few times during the seven-hour drive, but the look on Ben's face made her mentally high-five herself.

He traced the edges of her bra with his fingers. Up and around, swooped down into the valley between her breasts, brushed over her nipples with his thumbs, the whole time staring at her in awe. She wished she could hold on to the look on his face forever.

Then he looked her in the eye and bit his bottom lip in the fucking sexiest way she'd ever seen.

"I think . . . I think I'm ready." And with that, he hooked his thumbs through her waistband and pulled her yoga pants all the way down. She kicked them across the room. And then she remembered something. She slid her thong off and tossed it to him. He caught it in one hand and smiled at her. Oh yes, this guy was good.

She grinned. Then she turned slowly around for him.

"Was it worth the wait?" she asked.

There was a time when she never would have done this. When her body hadn't been something to be proud of, but something she desperately wanted to change. When she'd covered herself up in both public and private, and known to her core that her life would improve dramatically as soon as she became a size six.

It turned out that her life improved dramatically as soon as she learned to stop thinking like that.

Ben pulled her back to him, ran a hand over her full, round ass, and shook his head.

"I definitely was not ready," he said, and she laughed out loud. He dangled her thong from one finger. "I mean, if I'd thought hard about this—which, by the way, I spent all day trying my best *not* to do—I would have realized you must be wearing a thong, because there wasn't a single panty line to be seen, but again, I was trying, so very hard, not to daydream about your fucking perfect ass that it never occurred to me, and now I'm just . . . overcome."

She ran a finger gently up and down the outline of his hard cock, still encased in his black boxer briefs, and smiled.

"Mmm, you don't seem overcome here," she said.

"Keep touching me like that, and I will be," he said.

He reached around and unhooked her bra, and she let it fall to the floor.

"Anna?" he said, after a few seconds of staring at her boobs. This was the first time in quite a while that she wasn't even tempted to tell a man who talked to her boobs instead of her face where her eyes were.

"Ben?" she responded.

He put his hands on her waist.

"Why, exactly, have we spent all this time ignoring that big, beautiful bed right behind you? Because I'm going to tell you right now, to do what I want to do with you for the next few hours, I'm going to need a bed underneath us."

While he'd been talking, he'd slowly backed her against the bed, and then pushed her over, so she fell onto it. He stood there and looked at her. She moved all the way up onto the bed and smiled up at him.

"Excellent call," she said.

Before she could blink, he crawled on top of her.

"Yes, I thought so, too," he said. And then he sucked one of her nipples into his mouth.

Holy shit, if this was what he meant by being a boob man, she never again wanted to have sex with someone who was *not* a boob man. The way he licked and sucked and squeezed felt like everything she'd ever wanted. She wanted him to touch her everywhere, she wanted him to keep doing this forever, no, now she wanted him to touch her in one specific place and he wasn't touching her there and she felt like she was going to scream in glorious frustration.

And then he slowly slid down her body and pushed her legs open.

"Now," he said, as his fingers tiptoed their way up her thighs. "I said I was a boob man, and that's true, I am. But I am also very fond of another body part."

She propped herself up on her elbows to watch him.

"Which body part is that?" she asked, pretty sure she knew the answer.

"This one," he said. He—finally—slid one finger inside her, and she let out a deep sigh. She could feel his breath on her, which meant he was almost there, and then . . .

"You know," he said, "if you—"

"You are the worst fucking tease in all of California!" she said.

He grinned up at her.

"Oh, you want this?"

And then his tongue was on her. It was hard and it was fast and it was exactly what she wanted; his fingers inside her, one hand gripping her breast, and his incredible mouth and tongue making her feel things she hadn't felt in a long time. She collapsed onto the pillows and writhed under his tongue. He kept a firm grip on her body, and she could feel the strength and power behind his touch.

She whimpered, which made him go even faster. He pushed his fingers deeper inside her, and she couldn't move, couldn't think, couldn't talk, and then he squeezed her nipple and she threw a pillow over her mouth so she could scream.

A few seconds later he sat up, a huge, smug grin on his face.

"So, it turns out you like that particular body part a lot, too?"

He still had his boxer briefs on—why hadn't she taken those off of him? She needed to remedy that but was too overcome to move. Instead, she gestured at them.

"Those. Off. Now."

She was delighted by how quickly he obeyed her. And then even more delighted once he did. His cock was oh so ready for her. She reached for him, but he held up a finger.

"Wait one sec."

He jumped off the bed and dove for his messenger bag.

"Here we go!" he said after he rummaged for a minute.

A string of condoms. She knew she'd chosen the right man to both drive her across California and also service her sexually upon arrival.

"Do you always bring condoms with you to work?" she asked, and he crawled back onto the bed.

He shrugged.

"Sometimes I go out after work. A man's got to be prepared."

Indeed.

She reached for him and kissed him again. This time the kiss was slower, more relaxed, more comfortable. She was in his smooth, strong arms, and right now, at this moment, she couldn't believe the luck and chance that had landed her here.

She snuggled closer to him. He ran his fingers through her hair and kissed her cheek. That felt great, but . . .

She wiggled out of his grasp and ripped open one of the condoms.

"This"—she wrapped her hand around his cock, and he breathed in fast—"has been hard for a damn long time now. I think it's time it got some action, don't you?"

She could feel his eyes on her as she slowly rolled the condom onto him and then moved her hand up and down his cock.

"Now that you mention it," he said, "I do think that."

He flipped her back underneath him, so quickly that she laughed out loud. He smiled down at her and then pushed her legs open to him. God, she loved sex. How had she gone so long without it?

"When you look at me like that—" He lowered down and kissed the hollow between her breasts. And then he slid up her body and inside her in one smooth motion.

Holy shit. First they moved slowly together, as they got the right rhythm. But even then, when it was slow and a little awkward, it felt so good to have him inside her that she wanted to scream again, just from joy. And then, suddenly, they figured it out, and they were moving together, faster and faster. He reared up, and his fingers pinched her nipple. Her vision got blurry, and everything in her body was focused on just moving faster and harder and then he shifted slightly, and that made light explode behind her eyes and she bit his shoulder so she wouldn't scream, and then he thrust hard into her and collapsed on top of her.

A few seconds later, he rolled off of her, got up, and threw away the condom. He got back in bed and pulled her against him. She liked how he did that—firmly, like there was no question that that's where she belonged.

God, that had been so good. This felt so good. What a relief, to be this satisfied again, to have this much fun again, to feel this much joy again. To feel happy, for the first time in so long. Especially since there was a time when she'd thought she'd never feel like this again. Anna let out a long, deep sigh, and let herself relax in Ben's arms.

Ben was almost asleep when Anna started crying. She didn't make a sound, but he could tell from the way her body was shaking, and from the tears that fell on his skin.

He brushed her hair back and kissed her on the side of her head.

"Is everything okay?" he asked. And then he wanted to slap himself. What a stupid fucking question. Everything was obviously not okay.

He tucked the covers tighter around them and pulled her close.

"I'm okay," she said. "I'm sorry. I should . . . explain."

He kissed her hair.

"Shhh," he said. "You don't have to explain anything." Wait. He released his hold on her. "But . . . if you want to be alone, I can go get a snack, or find another room, or something. Just say the word and I'm gone. I promise, it's fine."

She looked up at him.

"No, no, please don't go. It's not you. You're great. This"—she gestured to the two of them—"this is great. Stay here, just like this?"

He let out a sigh of relief and pulled her back against him. Oh, thank God, he'd been worried he was the problem, or that he'd done something to upset her without realizing it.

"Of course. I'll be right here as long as you need me to be," he said.

She looked up at him, tears still running down her face.

"Everything really is okay. That's why I'm crying. It's been so long since everything felt okay. Since I felt like I was okay. And it's been a long time for me. For this, I mean. Last year I—" She let out another sob. "I wasn't doing well. I wasn't okay at all. I was so . . . and now I'm not. I really am okay now. I'm sorry, you must think I'm—"

He stroked her hair. He had no idea what she was telling him, but he knew one thing.

"I think you're incredible, that's what I think."

She kissed him on the cheek and then settled her head back against his chest.

"Mmm, that feels nice," she said.

So he kept gently running his fingers through her hair, until he could tell from her regular breathing that she was asleep.

Eight

BEN JOLTED AWAKE, FAR TOO FEW HOURS LATER. WHAT WAS that noise? He had to make it stop. He pulled himself out of bed, and through barely open eyes traced the noise to his jeans, on the floor in the corner. He fished his phone out of them. Seven a.m. His alarm. Right. He hit off, but the noise didn't stop. He looked at his phone, then around the room. What was happening?

"My phone," Anna said from the bed. "My purse."

He grabbed her purse from the desk and brought it to her in bed. She dug through it and turned the alarm off. They looked at each other in relief.

"That was a very bad noise," he said as he got back in bed. Then he sat upright. "Wait. Work. Work is seven hours away." He reached for his phone again in a panic. No. Right. He'd sent out an email last night while they were at In-N-Out canceling today's shoot because of Anna's family emergency. He shot his boss a quick email to tell her what was going on—well, a tiny part of what was going on—and that he would work from home that day, and fell back on the bed. Only to find Anna staring at him with a small smile on her face.

"Apparently," he said, "the talent had a family emergency, so the shoot is canceled today. I'm working from home."

Anna draped an arm around him.

"Weird how that worked out."

He pulled her close. Her body was so soft and smooth and supple. He felt like he could touch her like this forever.

He also knew he might never get to touch her like this again, which made him appreciate it all the more.

"I'm . . . exhausted," she said.

He let out a bark of laughter.

"You and me both. Luckily, neither of us has to go to work today, so we can go back to sleep."

She burrowed her head into his chest. He rested his palm on her hip. God, did he love the way her skin felt against his. He moved his hand over just a few inches and cupped her ass. Well. That felt even better.

She lifted her head and pulled him down to kiss her. They kissed lazily, like they had all the time in the world. Like this was a slow, rainy Sunday morning, and all they had in front of them was a long brunch and an afternoon nap. She slid her leg up his body and wrapped it around him.

"Not so tired anymore, hmmm?" he asked. He moved his hand in between them so he could flick her nipple with his thumb.

"Mmmm, no, I'm still sleepy." She reached down and put her hand around his cock. "So can you do me a favor and fuck me right quick so I can go back to sleep?"

He laughed out loud, and she grinned.

"Happy to oblige."

They both fell back asleep soon afterward, and he didn't wake up again until his phone buzzed from the floor. Damn it, he'd meant to turn it on silent.

He leaned down to grab it—his brother, his fourth text since last night. Ben grinned and dropped his phone back on the floor, then turned to Anna's side of the bed. She was wide awake, wrapped in a towel, her phone in her hand.

"Oh, you're up. You've been up. You should have woken me."

She waved that away.

"You needed the rest—you're the one who did all of the driving yesterday, remember? And our postdrive activities were"—her eyes danced at him—"athletic."

Oh, thank goodness this morning wasn't going to be weird and awkward. He'd worried about that when he'd seen her already showered—that she didn't even want to talk to him enough to wake him up. That would have made the drive home supremely bad.

"They were indeed," he said. He got up and made his way to the bathroom. "Are you hungry? Because I just realized I'm starving. It's been a long time since that In-N-Out."

Anna picked up the room service menu and waved it at him.

"I'll call. What's your room service breakfast of choice?"

"Pancakes, bacon, coffee," he said. "I'm a simple man with simple breakfast tastes, Anna."

She picked up the phone.

"I respect that."

As he got out of the shower, he heard her open the door to room service. When he came out of the bathroom, he kept the towel around his waist, in case the room service guy was still there, but it was just Anna and the food in the room.

"You take long showers," she said.

He picked up a piece of bacon. Excellent; it wasn't that flabby, badly cooked room service bacon, but the good, crispy kind.

"I do. My brother used to get so mad at me for it when we were kids. I started taking longer showers first just to be a dick to him, because I was a little asshole, and then I guess I got used to them. I do all my best thinking in there."

She cut her sausage link in half and popped it into her mouth.

"What good thinking did you do this morning?"

He sat down on the bed next to her and poured syrup on his pancakes.

"I think we need to get you some clothes."

She shot him a perplexed look.

"That's not at all what I was expecting you to say."

He took a bite of his pancakes, then gestured to the clothes littering the floor of the room.

"You wore that outfit for, what, twenty hours yesterday? Do you really want to put it on today, for another seven-hour drive back north?"

"Well, not really, but . . ."

He kept talking.

"And God forbid anyone recognizes you today. Do you want to be in day-old clothes if that happens? I'm sure you have some makeup in that enormous bag of yours, and you can figure out your hair, but after that deer-in-the-headlights look you gave me at In-N-Out yesterday, I don't think you want to deal with people recognizing you today looking like this."

She raised an eyebrow at him.

"Are you saying there's something wrong with my hair?"

He leaned forward and kissed her lips. She had a smile on her face as she kissed him back.

"Your hair is incredibly hot this morning, but you probably don't want a stranger taking pictures of you looking quite so sexy at a rest stop along Highway 5."

She bit his lip softly, then pulled back.

"You have a point. For both the hair and the clothes. But how are we going to accomplish the latter? I can't try on anything, and I don't even know what stores they have here."

He ate some more pancakes before answering.

"Leave it to me. You don't have to look like a movie star, just not . . ." He couldn't figure out a way to end that sentence in a polite way.

"Like a scrub? I get it." She looked at him for a long moment. She was measuring him up, he could tell. "Okay, fine. Sure, why not? This will be an adventure, at least."

He put the last piece of bacon into his mouth and stood up.

"Excellent." He pulled his jeans on, and then his T-shirt and winced. "Don't worry, I'll find something for myself, too. I'll be back soon."

When he was safely in the car, he scrolled through his phone. He'd talked a good game in there, but he needed some help with this. Luckily, he knew exactly the right person.

"Hello?"

"Maddie! Oh, thank God. I need you."

There was a pause.

"What do you need, Ben?" his brother's girlfriend said in that long-suffering way older sisters always did. Granted, he didn't have an older sister, or any sister at all, but he could imagine.

Well. He might be wrong about that last part. He'd worry about that later.

"Okay, first," he said to Maddie, "I need you to swear you'll keep this a secret."

There was a much longer pause. Too late, Ben figured out why.

"Not from my brother! You can tell him all of this. Just from everyone else in the world."

"Oh!" Maddie's voice was relieved. "Yeah, I can do that. What's up?"

He took a deep breath.

"Okay, the background to this is very long and I'm sure my brother has told or will tell you some of it anyway, but I'm in a rush here so I'm going to cut to the chase—I am currently on my way to buy an outfit for Anna Gardiner to wear as we drive seven hours from Palm Springs back to the Bay Area. The goal is for her to not be recognized, but if she is, she needs to look good in pictures. You're a stylist, this is your job; please tell me what to buy for her, because I acted like I knew exactly what I was doing and I do not at all know what I'm doing."

Maddie burst out laughing.

"Only you, Ben, would call me with this dilemma and have it be real and not a hoax. Is there time for me to ask questions like why you're in Palm Springs and why you're driving from there home instead of flying, or why she needs you—of all people—to buy her a new outfit or at least ten other questions I have in my head?"

He was going to get the loudest voice mail message from his brother in about ten minutes.

"Not really, no, but I promise, I'll answer all of those questions and more when I get home if you help me out here."

Maddie laughed again.

"I figured. Okay, give me two minutes to look up pictures of her style, and three more to figure out stores. I'll text you. You owe me all of the details for this one."

He sighed.

"Trust me, I know."

As soon as Ben left the room, Anna had doubts. Many of them. He'd been so convincing when he proposed this shopping idea that she'd agreed. And yes, he'd been right that she didn't want to wear her same yoga pants and T-shirt and hoodie from yesterday again.

But what did he know about shopping for her—or any woman?

Did he have any idea what would look good on her? She had a bad feeling about this.

As she sat there and waited for Ben to come back, she got more and more stressed, but not just about the clothes thing. About the night before.

Not the sex—that part had been great. Really great. But why did she have to start crying afterward? And if she had to cry, why couldn't she have waited until she was sure he was asleep? And also, why did she spill her guts to Ben about *why* she'd started crying? Granted, she couldn't remember exactly what she'd said to him, and she was pretty sure she hadn't told him the whole story, but she'd still told him more than she'd told almost anyone. Ben had mentioned therapy in passing on the drive down here yesterday, so she knew at least he wouldn't be a jerk about that part, but still. Was he going to bring up what she'd said last night and ask questions she didn't necessarily want to answer?

And even if he didn't, was he going to want too much from her, after they'd had sex? Did she have to make it clear that that's all last night was? Ugh. Today had the potential to be very stressful.

What the hell was she even doing? With one phone call, she could be on a plane from Palm Springs back to San Francisco, with no need to wait for a weird and probably ugly and ill-fitting new outfit from a man who was excellent in bed but who she didn't know much else about. And did she really want to do another day-long drive today?

But . . . she couldn't abandon Ben like that. And if she was honest with herself, she didn't *want* to abandon Ben like that. She had no idea if their drive back up north would be as comfortable as their drive down south—sometimes sex could make things awkward, and it might be even more so after her middle-of-the-night, ill-advised, tearful revelations—but they still had another week of working together, so she might as well see what it would be like.

She pulled out her phone while she waited. There was a text from her brother.

> I should have known you would do that. How did mom and dad look?

Oops. She should have texted Chris last night to confess all after leaving the hospital. But, well . . . she'd been a little distracted.

> Don't let mom make you feel bad about telling me (I'm sure she's already tried). I didn't mean to come down to Palm Springs! But well, one thing led to another. And dad's ok, so all's well that ends well. (I know. I owe you one). Mom looked tired, Dad looked fine, after all that

By the time she poured herself some more coffee, Chris had already replied.

> She did already try, but it didn't work. And yes, you owe me one. But I know you're good for it. He really seemed ok?

She'd always known Chris wasn't as chill as he seemed.

> He really seemed ok. I swear.

She should also check in on her parents.

> How are you feeling today? Please take it easy, both of you!

Her mom was the one to text back.

Your dad is feeling fine today, but we're both a little tired.
Don't worry, all we're going to do today is drive around and
look at some trees—with plenty of water!

Hmm. That had better be true.

Ben wasn't back yet. Did he even know her sizes? She searched
through her email for his number.

Everything okay? Do you need any help with the shopping?

She realized a few seconds later that he didn't have this
number.

This is Anna, by the way.

He texted back right away.

Heading back now! How's your dad, have you heard from
them? (I knew this was Anna)

She laughed at that.

Just now, mom says dad's doing ok!

A few minutes later, Ben threw open the hotel room door.

"Okay, Cinderella, time for the ball!" He had a big grin on his
face, and two very full bags in his hands. Anna had to laugh, no matter how doubtful she was about this whole shopping excursion.

"What . . . what all did you get?" she asked.

He came over to where she was sitting on the bed.

"Well, I wanted you to have options! Plus, I had no idea how anything would fit, so I just grabbed what seemed like it would work. Oh, and I also stopped at Target"—he held up one bag—"to get something for me to wear. And some snacks, you know, for the road."

"Okay," she said. Was he stalling? It seemed like he was stalling. She wiggled her fingers at him.

"Show me," she said.

He smiled at her, but . . . shyly? She'd only known Ben for a little while, but that wasn't a descriptor she'd ever expected to use about him. She held back a grin. Despite her misgivings, this was pretty adorable.

"Okay!" he said. He dropped the bags on the bed and pulled something out of one of them. He held it up for her to see.

"Do you like it? I thought you might like it, but I wasn't sure. You seem like you like colorful things—I don't know why I think that, you were wearing all black yesterday, maybe it's too bright?"

He was babbling. It was so cute.

As was the dress. It was a T-shirt dress, pink, with a blue and orange embroidered design on it. Very Palm Springs.

"I love it. Let me try it on."

She grabbed the dress out of his hands and stood up, letting her robe drop to the floor. It was fun to see his eyes widen at her in a bra and nothing else.

She pulled the dress over her head, and he whistled.

"Well, I think that looks fucking incredible on you, but it might turn a few heads if you have to go to the bathroom somewhere."

She looked at herself in the mirror, and she could see what he meant. This dress hugged her curves perfectly, which meant it was a little snug—and a little short—for an incognito day.

He tossed another dress at her.

"This is the same dress, just in a different size and another color, in case you didn't want to be quite so visible."

This one was in black, but with orange and pink embroidery. She put it on and then reached into her bag and grabbed her enormous sunglasses.

"How's this?" she asked him.

He narrowed his eyes at her and shook his head. That wasn't what she was expecting.

"The dress is perfect, even though it obscures some of your glory."

She grinned.

"Nice way to put that, but?"

He took a few steps over to her and gently slid the sunglasses off of her face.

"But these sunglasses are too movie star." He reached into the Target bag. "Luckily, I got you these." He tossed her a pair of plain black plastic sunglasses. "And . . ." He looked down, not meeting her eyes. "I thought you might want these, too. I wasn't, um, sure on style, so I got a few options." He handed her the bag, and then turned to pull a T-shirt for himself out of a different bag. She glanced down and was charmed to see an assortment of underwear—some cotton, some silky, a few bikinis, one thong. All, if she wasn't mistaken, the right size. She plucked the red cotton bikinis out of the pile and pulled them on.

"It's like you're Santa Claus over there," she said. "What else do you have in those bags?"

He was pulling his jeans back up over his hips. He must have put on his own new underwear already. She'd unfortunately been so distracted by the underwear he'd bought her that she'd missed that.

"Just a plain black dress for you in case I'd gotten the other stuff wrong. Don't worry, the snacks are all in the car waiting for us." He took off his shirt, and she let herself stare openly. Mmm, yes, she was glad she'd given in to temptation. She hadn't even noticed that tattoo on his biceps last night; she'd been too busy. She wanted to trace it with her fingertips. And then trail her hands over to his chest and move her hands down, and down. The way his jeans clung to his hips . . . No, no, they didn't have time; they needed to get on the road soon if they were going to get back to San Francisco before too late.

He was suddenly much closer to her. His shirt was still off.

"We have thirty minutes before we have to be out of the room," he said in a low voice.

She reached for his chest. She couldn't help herself.

"Do we really?" she asked.

They made it, with three minutes to spare.

Once they were back on the freeway, with the date shakes he'd insisted on stopping for on the way out of town, she looked over at him. She suddenly started laughing and couldn't stop.

"What's so funny?" he asked.

She gestured at the car.

"Everything! All of this! You, me, the piles of Doritos in this car, my new clothes, your new clothes, that we're leaving Palm Springs right now when we should be halfway through our work-day in San Francisco, that you drove me down here in the middle of the night last night because you could tell I was freaking out, that my dad is okay, everything!"

"Don't forget that I had to wheedle our way into a hotel room," he said.

"Oh, right! How could I forget Niamh?" She went off into an-other peal of laughter, and he joined her.

They were quiet for the first few hours of the drive. Not in an awkward way, thank God, just relaxed, easy, comfortable. She put music on again, but it was less aggressively cheerful music than the day before, more Andra Day and Corinne Bailey Rae than Britney and Lizzo. They didn't talk much, and they didn't touch at all, but she somehow felt as close to him as she had in bed the night before. When she'd cried, and he'd pulled her close. And— in one of the sweetest things a man had ever said to her—had offered to leave the room if she'd wanted him to. That had only made her want to burrow herself even tighter into his chest.

And that, of course, was the thing that had made her spill her guts to him. She remembered now.

"Um, about last night," she said.

He shot her a grin, but his smile turned to something else when he saw the look on her face. Something softer. More kind.

"Anna. We don't have to talk about that if you don't want to."

She put her hand on his.

"No, I know. I want to. And telling you why . . . why I had a little breakdown last night, or rather, this morning, might help explain why I needed to come to Palm Springs so urgently in the first place."

He turned his hand over and held on to hers.

"Okay. I'm listening."

She took a deep breath. Why was she even doing this? She didn't have to tell him all of this. But she'd already told him part of it, and she couldn't take it back. She'd feel better if he knew the whole story.

"Last year . . . last year was really hard on me. The past few years were, really, but I guess I didn't pay attention—didn't have to pay attention—until last year. My career . . . my fame, I guess, came on so quickly. I'd been working quietly in Hollywood for years, and then I exploded, with that Oscar nomination and all that press a few years back. And it was incredible and gratifying and brought me more than I ever could have dreamed of." She let out a long breath. "And my whole life changed. Sort of before I even realized it was happening."

She stopped and closed her eyes for a moment. Ben didn't say anything, or ask any questions, or try to hurry her along. He just kept hold of her hand. Finally, she started again.

"Last year . . . I'd been working a ton—I did three movies back to back, I wanted to take advantage of the moment while I could, because I knew this stuff can be fleeting, especially for someone like me. And while I was working on *Vigilantes*, it's—"

"You're in that movie? That's so cool!" Ben said.

She laughed and then sighed. She hoped to hell she would actually be in it.

"Yeah, though I can't tell you much about it; I only have a handful of scenes." She took a deep breath. "Anyway, while we were in the middle of filming, I started having anxiety attacks. I couldn't breathe, the world would go fuzzy, my heart would beat so fast. Oh God, Ben, the first time it happened, I was so scared. I was in my trailer—I'd just gotten to the set. There were a bunch of photographers outside on my way in. They yelled something rude at me, about my body, how I looked that day—they do that, to try to get a bad picture," she said in response to Ben's outraged glare. "And I didn't react, I'm good at that, I just smiled. I look pleasant and blank-faced in the pictures, I saw them all later, even though they hurt to look at. But when I got to my trailer, I couldn't breathe. I felt like the walls were closing in on me, like I'd never be able to escape, like I'd have to have that blank smile on my face for the rest of my life, no matter what garbage the world threw at me."

She swallowed.

"I made it through that day, but it kept happening. And I felt so lonely, like there was no one I could talk to about any of this. I'd achieved so much, my life was a dream, shouldn't I be happy?

Shouldn't I be thankful? I still sort of feel like that, to be honest. I felt like an asshole complaining, or having a hard time with any of this. It's just part of the job—shouldn't I be able to deal with it?"

Why was she tearing up again about this? It was ridiculous. She took a few deep breaths, and Ben held tighter to her hand.

"So I didn't think . . . once the anxiety attacks started, I didn't want to tell anyone. I didn't even . . ." She wiped her eyes with the back of her hand. "I didn't even tell my family, or my best friend. I felt like I had to be strong, and if I told them, if I acknowledged that it was happening, it would mean I was weak."

Ben lifted her hand and kissed it softly.

"Oh, sweetheart. That's not how it works," he said.

She laughed, and a few more tears came out.

"Well, I know that *now*," she said, and they both laughed. "But then . . . no one expected me to get that Oscar nomination, you know—well, no one except for me—and after the nomination, I was so caught up in making sure I didn't go on to fail, to be a disappointment, that I had to work as hard as hell, and prove that I was worth the nomination and the accolades and the magazine covers and dresses, that I felt like I couldn't give in. I thought if I just pushed through, I could handle it. That it would all stop."

She'd felt so lonely then. With no one to talk to, no one to burden with this weight she'd thought she had to carry on her own.

"I bet that strategy worked out great, right?" Ben slid his hand onto her knee.

She laughed.

"You may be surprised to learn this, but no, it did not work out well at all."

It felt sort of . . . freeing, to talk to Ben about this. When she'd told her family and Penny, it had been in the moment, and they'd been so concerned about her that their worries had affected her. And when she'd told Simon, she'd just been terrified for her career, and she could tell he'd been worried about that, too. But Ben had no emotions—or any other needs—tied up in her, and seemed to take this in stride. It felt almost easy to talk to him about this. Maybe it was just easier to fall apart with someone who wasn't a part of her life.

"As a matter of fact, no, I'm not surprised that didn't work out well," Ben said. "I've tried to ignore my problems like that before; it's never really worked." He laughed. "But I still keep trying."

She liked the warm, solid feeling of his hand on her knee. Even though this thing with him couldn't go anywhere—she didn't even want it to go anywhere—that didn't matter right now. She'd just let herself enjoy it for the rest of the drive.

"Yeah. Well. I managed to keep it all—my anxiety, my fears, how I had trouble getting out of bed every day, all of that—a secret from everyone on set, thank God. But we were almost done filming, and I had a few weeks off afterward. I'd planned to head up to the Bay Area to see my family, but I knew they would see right through me, and I didn't want them to worry about me. So instead I canceled. I just locked myself in my house so I could hide away from the world."

His thumb moved back and forth on her knee. It made her slow herself down, deepen her shallow breaths.

"Did that help?" he asked.

She shook her head.

"I thought I would be relaxed, you know? Not have to worry about seeing anyone, any press, any photographers—not have to think about what they were thinking about me, if they'd noticed how I was acting, what they would say about me, how bad the pictures of me would be. But instead, it just got worse. I felt . . ." She took a breath that quivered, as much as she tried to stop it. "Like I was all alone in the world with this problem—me, I was the problem, and there was nothing I could do about it." She'd already said more than she meant to, but she couldn't stop now. "It was . . . it was a really dark time."

He glanced over at her, a soft, caring expression on his face. She hoped he didn't look at her too long like that—she'd cry again. Luckily, he looked back at the road.

"How did . . ." He stopped himself. "Sorry, I hate that I can't really look at you while you're telling me all of this. I don't want you to think I'm not paying attention."

She put her hand on top of his, and he immediately turned his hand over to hold on to hers.

"No, It's okay. I think . . . I think maybe it's easier this way for me. I haven't . . . this isn't something I really talk about a lot."

He nodded.

"That makes sense. And I hope you know, but in case you don't—I would never tell anybody about this."

She'd thought about that, of course she had. But he was the first person she'd even been slightly inclined to trust in a year and a half. Her therapist had kept telling her to trust her instincts about people. So here she was. Trying to trust them. She hoped to hell it didn't blow up in her face.

But she didn't think it would.

"Thank you for saying that. I think I already knew. But yeah, I haven't been public about any of this for a reason. I've seen the way the press—and the studios—treat women like me who are public about this stuff, and it sucks. How they get called crazy, how everything they do or say or wear or eat turns into evidence that they're unstable or losing it or something else like that. I don't want any of that to happen to me."

He held tight to her hand. She was really glad to be with him right now.

"I don't want any of that to happen to you, either," he said. "You don't have to answer this, but—you said you're doing okay now. How did you get out of that dark place?"

Tears came to her eyes again.

"My dad. He and I . . . we had a different relationship when I was a kid. I was a hothead, and so was he, and because of his job he had all of these rules I was supposed to obey, and I never wanted to, and he always discouraged me from acting—unlike my mom, who told me to do whatever I wanted as long as I could support myself. But we got along better as we both got older. He somehow figured out that something was wrong with me. He told me he had a meeting in L.A. and so he was coming over to my place. I tried to pull myself together when he came over. But as soon as he walked in, he took one look at me and asked, so gently, what was wrong. And everything came spilling out."

Even just thinking about that day was still so hard.

"So, when you knew something was wrong with him, you had to rush to him," Ben said. "I understand."

She brushed her tears away with the back of her hand.

"It was silly. I should have just . . ."

Ben touched his finger to her lips.

"No more of that, remember?"

She nodded.

"Okay, you're right. But yes, what you said. He helped me find a therapist and a psychiatrist. I got on meds and started seeing someone twice a week at first. Those first few months were really hard." She let out a breath. "Really, really hard. But now I'm doing so much better." She wiped her eyes again.

She glanced over at him. She liked the way his eyes crinkled up when he was listening.

"Anyway. Sorry for all of this. I'm a little embarrassed now.

Once I started talking, it was hard to stop. That's probably way too much information."

"No," he said.

She looked over at him, but his eyes were on the road.

"No, what?"

"No, it's not too much information. No, you have nothing to be embarrassed about."

"Oh." She took a deep breath. Tears came to her eyes again, but they were good ones this time. "Okay."

"I just wanted you to know that," he said.

She wiped her tears away.

"Okay, well, I guess I'll say this, too—I think I told you part of this last night, but before last night I hadn't slept with anyone since before all of that happened. I tried, early on, when I'd just started having anxiety attacks, but just being that close to someone made me anxious, and I was so paranoid, that this was all a trick, or that he'd put cameras somewhere, and so much other stuff. But last night . . . I didn't worry about any of that. It was just so great, and fun, and it felt like . . . I don't know, such a celebration. So I was crying just from relief, that I could have that joy again, that I feel so much better now, especially since there was a time when I thought I'd never be able to relax around another person again. Especially the kind of relaxation with no clothes on." She grinned at him, and he grinned back. "So. That's a very long way to explain . . . everything."

Ben was quiet for a while. He didn't know if Anna was okay with him asking her questions about everything she'd told him or not, but one question was at the forefront of his mind, and he figured there was no way he'd last the three-plus hours left in the drive without asking it.

"Thank you for telling me," he said. "But can I ask—why did you tell me? Don't get me wrong, I'm really glad you did. But . . ."

"But I don't know you that well, so why did I trust you?" Anna finished. He nodded, and she thought for a while. "It's because of how you responded. Last night, I mean. You could have pretended not to hear anything and just gone back to sleep, you could have just hugged me and not said anything. But not only did you soothe me and listen to me, but you said you'd leave if I wanted you to. I don't even know why you asked that, but it made me feel so comfortable with you—like you'd do whatever it took to put me at ease." She turned and looked straight at him. "Why did you ask me that?"

"Oh." Now he felt embarrassed by the conclusions he'd jumped to. He was very glad he had to keep his eyes on the road.

"I thought . . . I wondered if you'd had a bad experience sometime. With um, sexual assault, something like that. I thought maybe I did something that made you remember something you didn't want to, so I just wanted you to . . . I don't know, feel safe." He cleared his throat. "I'm glad you were crying for a happy reason and not that one."

She turned her whole body toward him.

"That's—" She stopped and swallowed. "That's so kind of you, Ben. And I'm glad I was crying for a happy reason, too."

He wished he could lean over and kiss her, but Highway 5 wasn't the best place to do things like that.

Was he ever going to be able to kiss her again? Or—the dream—see her naked again? They hadn't talked about it, but he'd assumed their fling was a purely Palm Springs kind of deal. Now that they were out of that hotel room, notwithstanding his hand on her knee and her hand on his arm, he was pretty sure that the whole relaxation with no clothes on between the two of them was a no-go.

Well, he supposed he'd have to be happy with the very excellent sex they'd had last night and this morning—the very excellent sex he'd had with Anna Gardiner!—and leave it there. Plus, they'd see each other on set on Monday; there couldn't be any secret winks or lingering glances then—that was for damn sure.

"I'm glad you told me about all of that. Thank you."

Why did he say thank you? Now he felt stupid for thanking her for that. But it had felt like a compliment, that she'd chosen to share all of that with him.

She put her hand on his. Her hands were so smooth, but firm.

"Thanks for not being weird about all of it. On one of the few dates I've been on since all of this happened, I mentioned my therapist in passing and the guy got so strange about it. I was like, my God, we're in L.A., doesn't everyone here have a therapist? Apparently not."

Ben laughed.

"Yeah, some dudes get so scared of therapy. Like, do you think they're witches who are going to steal your power, or something? It's just talking to people. One time I mentioned offhand to a friend I'd just come from therapy and he reacted like I said I'd just come from robbing a bank or something."

It had taken him a long time after that to mention it to anyone else. Not because he thought it was something to be ashamed of, but because he didn't want to deal with people who did. Especially after the time he'd mentioned therapy to a woman he was dating, who seemed to think it made him damaged in some alluring way, which had creeped him out.

"Yeah, it took me awhile to get over feeling like I should feel bad about all of this, or that something was wrong with me." Anna shook her head. "Well, to start getting over feeling like that, at least." She moved her hand off his. He wished she hadn't.

"Also, um. Can I ask you a favor?" she asked.

"Anything," he said.

"Can we talk about something else? I haven't . . ." Her voice wavered. "That was a lot, is all."

Ben didn't let his expression change, and he didn't reach for her hand, even though he wished he could give her a hug. She clearly didn't want to get emotional now. Lucky for her, he had a lot of practice at avoiding emotions.

"Absolutely." He thought fast. "Okay. What's your default breakfast order? You know mine. And please, do not give me any yogurt-and-acai-berries nonsense; it's just you and me in this car, no one is listening."

She laughed out loud, which had been his goal.

"You read that interview, did you? Yeah, that was bullshit, but I have to say these things sometimes, as much as I hate it. My manager made me do that one. I also went to a spin class with that interviewer, if you can believe that. Okay, okay, my real breakfast order is a modified version of what I got this morning."

He thought about her that morning, in a robe that showed an incredible amount of cleavage, a breakfast sausage in her hand. Good God. He'd had to bring this up?

"Scrambled eggs and breakfast sausages?" he asked.

She nodded.

"Yes, but ideally I'd also have very crispy hash browns, and if I'm being indulgent, sourdough toast. But they only had home fries on the room service menu, and those are usually too soggy for me, especially via room service. They had no sourdough, so I got the English muffin."

He thought about that for a moment.

"So you get no potatoes at all if you can't have crispy hash browns?"

She nodded very seriously. This seemed to be distracting her well.

"Yes. Or, rather, I'll get no potatoes at all if I can't have good, crispy ones. I try not to let the Hollywood weight thing get to me too much, but if I'm going to eat carbs, they'd better be my favorite kinds of carbs. So crispy potatoes or no potatoes at all."

"That's fair," he said. "I, on the other hand, will eat potatoes of any size, shape, and manner. Mashed, fried, scalloped, baked, hashed, totted, whatever you can do to a potato, I'll eat it."

They went on like that for the next hundred miles or so, talking hard about mostly nothing. Anna seemed to be smiling the whole time, and her body didn't have that stiff, anxious air that it had when she'd told him about her crisis and the aftermath.

"Heard from your parents lately?" he asked her, right as they drove past the off-ramp to SFO. He was so glad he'd made that ridiculous, nonsensical suggestion to drive her to Palm Springs the day before. He couldn't believe it had only been a day.

She held up her phone.

"They texted again a few hours ago, or my mom did, at least. 'Dad is feeling much better, we're taking it easy today. He wanted a date shake, but I told him no, it wasn't good for his heart, and he grumbled, but not too much. I promise I'll keep you posted on what his doctor says. Love you.'" She sighed. "I hope that's a real promise. Maybe it is, now that she's spooked I'll just show up, no matter what."

They both laughed. Ben was weirdly grateful for the traffic on 101; it meant this trip would last at least thirty more minutes. He was hungry and had almost suggested they stop for dinner, but that seemed too dangerous for Anna, especially since they'd gotten lucky when they'd stopped for food around midafternoon. No one had even glanced in her direction.

But he knew as soon as they drove up to her hotel, this was all over.

He held back a sigh and kept driving.

They were both quiet as they drove through San Francisco on the way to her hotel. It had been almost exactly twenty-four hours since they'd left the city, but it seemed like so much had happened in that time.

All too soon, Ben drove up the circular driveway to Anna's hotel.

"Well, we made it back," he said, and shook his head at himself. What did that even mean? Why was he even talking?

"We did," Anna said. A bellman opened her car door, and she nodded her thanks to him, then turned back to Ben.

"Thank you. For . . . well. For everything." She smiled at him, a small, quiet, private smile. He smiled back at her.

"You're welcome. It was my pleasure." He wanted to reach for her, but he didn't. "Now, get yourself some sleep; you must be exhausted."

She picked up her tote bag and laughed.

"I was just about to say the same to you." She got out of the car and waved at him. He wanted to get out, too, to say good-bye, to give her a hug, something, but he knew he couldn't hug her, and it felt like getting out of the car would just draw more attention to them, so instead he just waved.

"See you soon," he said.

She nodded quickly.

"Yeah. See you soon." She took her big movie-star sunglasses out of her bag and slid them on. She turned toward the hotel and walked up the stairs and through the revolving door. She didn't look back.

Ben thought about calling his brother on his way home, but as much as he couldn't wait to tell this story, he somehow didn't feel ready to start. He suddenly felt bone tired, the kind of tired that comes from two seven-plus-hour drives in two days and a very interrupted night of sleep in between.

He glanced at his phone when he walked into his apartment and was surprised by the rush of disappointment he felt when he didn't have a message from Anna. Why would she have texted him, anyway? He'd just seen her; they'd been together, almost nonstop, for more than twenty-four hours. He rolled his eyes at himself and scrolled through his texts from his brother, from Maddie, from a date from a few weeks back, from a high school friend, then dropped his phone on his nightstand and got in the shower.

After his shower, he collapsed on his bed and flipped through the delivery apps on his phone to try to decide what to have for dinner.

He woke up hours later, phone still in his hand, and squinted at the text on the screen.

> Someone took a picture of me in the hotel lobby here and put it on their Instagram. The dress looked great—nice job.

He grinned. He owed Maddie big.

> Oh ye of little faith. Didn't I say you could count on me?

Still smiling, he turned over and went back to sleep.

Nine

ON SATURDAY MORNING, ANNA ENDED THE CALL WITH SI-
mon with a big smile on her face. She immediately called Penny.

"Do I have a story for you," she said as Penny answered the
phone.

Penny almost purred.

"Oh, thank God. Yesterday was a deeply irritating day, and I
woke up grumpy about the entitled tourists who bugged the hell
out of me. I would much rather hear your story than give those
assholes any more real estate in my brain. Talk to Penny."

Anna poured herself some room service coffee as she thought
about where to start.

"Well . . . okay, so I did something kind of ridiculous and un-
necessary Thursday. I should probably start there."

"Whaaaat did you do?"

Anna could picture the gleeful smile on Penny's face.

"First off—everything is okay. I want you to know that so you
don't worry. But Chris called because Dad was in the hospital in
Palm Springs—my all-too-stressful parents were in Joshua Tree

and my dad collapsed. Don't worry, he's fine, it was just heat exhaustion, but I didn't know that then."

Penny sighed.

"Thank you for starting off this story by saying everything's okay. Let me guess, you chartered a plane and flew to Palm Springs, and your mom lost it, right?"

Anna laughed.

"You know me—and my mom—very well, but weirdly, you're wrong this time. So you remember how I told you about that guy Ben? The ad guy?"

"You mean the backup dancer? Of course I remember, but . . ."

"He drove me," Anna said. "To Palm Springs."

"He what???" Anna almost laughed out loud at the sound in Penny's voice. "From San Francisco? Did you forget about the existence of airplanes? Why, exactly—"

"And then I slept with him," Anna continued.

"Yessssssss." Penny let out a cackle, and Anna laughed along with her. "Okay, I'm angry at you that you didn't lead with that, but wait, now I've gotten over being angry and am only thrilled. Tell me all the good stuff, but first tell me that your dad is really okay?"

This was why she loved Penny. Anger and joy and concern about her family, all at once.

"He's fine—well, maybe not fine, but okay. We got to the hospital just as my parents were leaving; they said he was just dehydrated. And the reason I didn't fly is the boring part of this story. But I was already in the car with Ben, and he offered to drive, and I was . . . just so worried and anxious about my dad and I couldn't really think straight, so I said okay."

Penny knew how her mind worked. Anna knew she didn't have to say more.

"Anyway, after Ben and I left the hospital, we got to a hotel, and . . ." She grinned. "I basically jumped him. I was so relieved and happy and my God, so wildly horny, and he was so hot, and I have to say, I'd forgotten this, but . . . sex is pretty fantastic, Penny."

Penny chuckled again.

"It certainly is. There's the Anna I know and love. And I'm so glad you broke your dry spell with someone worthy of you. Are you going to keep sleeping with him?"

Anna sighed. That would be nice, but . . .

"Oh no, I can't. It was great, he was great, don't get me wrong." She thought back to that last time, right before they left Palm Springs. "Really great. But, that was just a fun, dry-spell-breaking little interlude—like you said, I'm ready for the old Anna to be back. And now she is, and I can move on." She laughed. "And listen to this! It must have been my good-luck charm, because Simon just called: it turns out they do want me to do a bunch of press for *Vigilantes*, so I'll be doing a ton of that as soon as I get back to L.A. No guarantees, but I hope like hell this means something good for what my role turns out to be in the movie."

"Seriously?" Penny said. "That's fantastic! I know how worried you've been about this. Your good-luck charm, indeed."

Anna grinned and leaned back in bed.

"I know, right? I can't believe it. Everything's turning up Anna: I have a whole plan now for what this summer is going to be like. I'm going to do the press junket for *Vigilantes*, strategize with Simon so I get that role I'm dying for, get some magazine covers, have fun with men again, all of that."

"Hmmm." Why didn't Penny sound excited for her plan? "That all sounds excellent, and I'm thrilled about *Renegades*, obviously, but—"

"*Vigilantes*," Anna said.

"That's what I meant," Penny said. "Anyway—you're still in San Francisco, right?"

Anna could already tell where she was going with this.

"Yes, for another week or so, but—"

"And you're currently in bed alone? I mean, I imagine you're alone; I don't think you'd be telling me all of this with him there next to you in your bed."

Anna sighed.

"Yes, I'm in bed alone, but I couldn't bring him back to my room! And I know what you're going to say, but no, I can't keep this going—we're working together! That would be far too complicated and dangerous. And plus—okay, so I told him about everything that happened last year." Penny tried to jump in, but Anna kept talking. "It's a long story, I told him sort of accidentally. And he was lovely about it, he said all the right stuff. But I don't want to see him make that face. You know that face. The patient, gentle, condescending face people make when they think they have to tiptoe around you. I want to remember everything with him as this good, happy thing and not have it be ruined."

There was more to it than that, but she didn't know how to explain it to Penny. She already sort of regretted telling Ben everything, letting him know too much about her, letting him see past the Anna Gardiner public persona. She worried that if she kept this going, even for the next week, she'd reveal far too much of herself to this man who had looked at her in bed like she was the sun and the moon and the stars all together. She didn't want to have to see that look change.

"Anyway," she said to Penny, "as great as it was, it can't happen again." *Oh shit.* "I meant to tell him that we couldn't do this again. On the drive back north yesterday. But I got distracted; I forgot. Damn it."

"Look," Penny said. "All I'm saying is that I haven't heard that lusty sound in your voice in over a year, and none of what you just told me is enough of a reason to not just keep this going until you have to go back to L.A. Wait. Unless he was an asshole. Was he an asshole?"

Penny immediately sounded mad at just the prospect of Ben being an asshole. This was another reason why Anna loved her.

"He was very much *not* an asshole. The opposite of an asshole, really. But that doesn't mean—"

"Blah blah blah," Penny said. "I know I know, you have a plan, you always have a plan. And yes, fine, *often* your plans make a great deal of sense."

"You mean *always* my plans make a great deal of sense, and that *often* they are successful. Remember my Oscar-nomination plan?"

Anna could almost see Penny purse her lips.

"You're going to bring that up for the rest of our lives to win every argument, aren't you? Okay, fine. I'm not getting off the phone because I can't come up with a reason I'm right. I'm just getting off the phone because I should have left for the winery ten minutes ago, but we'll talk later!"

Anna laughed as she hung up the phone. It had been great—even more great than she'd thought it would be—to tell Penny about her night with Ben and hear her squeal in joy. She'd forgotten how fun that was.

When had she made the decision to have sex with him? she wondered. Had she known by the time they'd walked into the hotel room? Mmm, probably; she'd seen both beds when they'd walked in and had been pretty certain one of them would be empty that night. Did she decide when Niamh had asked them if one room was okay? Maybe. When he'd saved her from the photo at In-N-Out? No, probably not by then, but that had definitely played a role.

Whenever it was, she was glad it had happened. But she still had to send this text.

> Hey—I meant to say this on the drive home yesterday, but I got distracted by everything else. Thanks, so much, for everything—I can't tell you how much I appreciated it. But what happened in Palm Springs can't happen again, for so many reasons. I hope you got some sleep last night, and I'll see you on set Monday.

There. That was done. That didn't sound too cold, did it? She hoped not.

Ben woke up to the sound of his phone ringing. He ignored it until it stopped, but then it started again. Finally, he rolled over and picked it up. Theo. Of course.

"Hello?"

"Oh, he finally answers the phone!"

Ben got up. He needed coffee for this conversation.

He squinted at the clock on his coffeemaker: 9:30 a.m. He'd slept for more than twelve hours, and he felt like he could still sleep a little more.

"It's not that late, you know," he said to his brother. "You should be flattered I even answered the phone."

He could hear Theo take a long gulp of his own coffee. Probably his third cup of the day. The asshole had a girlfriend; he probably didn't even have to make his own coffee like Ben was doing right now.

Ben stopped himself. No. Theo would never let someone else make his coffee.

"You knew I would keep calling forever until you answered," Theo said. "And with good reason, because you sent me some unhinged text I didn't quite believe about going on a road trip with a celebrity and then you called Maddie for advice on buying clothes for said celebrity, and you sure as hell had better tell me everything that happened in between those two things. Where are you? I assume you're alone, since you answered the phone and didn't just turn it off."

Ben sniffed the milk he'd pulled out of the fridge while Theo talked. Damn it. How had it gone bad in just two days?

"Home, and yes, unfortunately alone," he told his brother. He opened his freezer and pulled out a carton of chocolate ice cream. "We got back last night. Wait, let me pour some coffee, I'm still out of it."

He plopped a spoonful of ice cream in his mug and filled it up with coffee.

"Okay." He took a sip. "Where were we?"

"You are such an asshole," Theo said.

Ben laughed.

"I know, I know. Okay, the short version of the story is— Wait, first, you have to swear not to tell anyone any of this."

Not that he thought his brother would anyway, but he had to make it clear, for Anna's sake.

"Maddie already told me that part—yes, yes, we both promise."

Ben sat down on his couch and took another gulp of coffee. He should put chocolate ice cream in it all the time.

"Okay. So. I drove Anna to Palm Springs because her dad was in the hospital there—he's fine, but she was really worried about him, and there were no more flights for the day. That was Thursday evening. Yesterday we drove back, but since we left in a hurry on Thursday, she didn't have a change of clothes. That's why I needed Maddie. She came through, by the way."

"Of course she did," Theo said impatiently. "And?"

Ben grinned. He loved messing with his brother like this.

"Annnd, in between leaving and coming back, I managed to get myself trapped in a hotel room for a night with her, and holy shit, Theo. A gentleman never tells, but I've got to say, she's fucking fantastic. No pun intended."

"You owe me dinner!" Theo shouted in a muffled voice. When he came back to the phone, he sounded triumphant. "I *told* Maddie, but she didn't believe me! She may know celebrities, but I know my brother."

Ben felt weirdly touched that Theo had that much faith in him. But also . . .

"But really don't tell anyone any of this, okay? I'm only telling you, that's all. I didn't even . . . She and I had flirted from the beginning, but she's working with me, and you know how I feel about that, so I was sure it wouldn't go anywhere. Plus, she's . . . who she is."

That sounded silly as soon as he'd said it, but Theo got it.

"Yeah. Do you think you're going to see her again? I mean, other than on set."

He had no fucking idea.

"I sure as hell hope so, but who knows. But no matter what, I got a great story out of this that I'll never be able to tell anyone but you and my therapist."

He poured himself another cup of coffee when he got off the phone with Theo, and then checked his phone to see what had come in during his drive on Friday that he'd ignored.

He had many texts, but only one that mattered. Anna's.

Well, fuck. He'd expected this, of course he had, but when she hadn't said anything in the car yesterday, and when she'd sent that text about the dress the night before, he'd . . . hoped. Oh well.

It was my pleasure — all of it. No worries, see you Monday

What other disappointing messages did he have that he'd have to send cheerful, breezy responses to?

Thankfully, no one at work had seemed to realize that his version of "working from home" the day before had been checking email once every two hours or so at gas stations along Interstate 5.

He didn't have another email from Dawn, which he realized was the thing he'd been dreading. He still hadn't told Theo about her. Shit, he had to do that. He clicked back to the last email Dawn had sent and looked at the picture again.

It creeped Ben out, how much he looked like his dad. Mostly because he'd always worried that he'd be like him, too. That fear had been what had driven him into therapy, that his love for women meant he was destined to also abandon his wife and kids, just like his dad had done. Lately, his therapist kept telling him that he didn't need to go so far in the other direction and never get close enough to someone to make marriage and kids an issue, but that's not what he was doing. He just hadn't found the right person, that's all.

He suddenly felt bad that he hadn't even replied to this email. He didn't have to be that asshole.

To: Dawn Stephens
From: Ben Stephens
Re: Just checking in

Hey—I don't have any pictures of him and me as a kid handy, but yeah, that's my dad. This is weird, but I look a lot like him, if you had any doubt, here's a picture of me now. Anyway, I guess that DNA test must have been accurate. Sorry we both lost the dad lottery, but despite him, you seem to be doing pretty great. Congratulations on grad school, that's awesome.

Hope you're having a good weekend,
Ben

Ten

WEDNESDAY AFTERNOON, EVERYONE WAS IN A BAD MOOD on set. It was like the set had been cursed—everything that could go wrong that day had, between Gene getting in a fender bender on the way and getting there late, to craft services messing up breakfast, to it being so windy all day that they had to do a million retakes because the whistles of the wind outside were so loud in the background.

Anna sat wrapped in a sweater as she waited for yet another lighting change. Why did she have to be in this stupid sundress when they all knew it would be cold outside today? This was usually just part of the job for her, but today she was freezing and deeply irritated about it.

She glanced over at Ben, the one person on set who didn't seem affected by the gloomy day. He was over in the corner, chatting with the sound guy—and, from what she could overhear, trying to cheer him up. He glanced her way and caught her looking at him and winked at her. She blushed and looked away.

She'd meant to be chilly to him on set, to make it clear that the night—and morning—in Palm Springs had been a onetime thing, that even though she'd trusted him for some incredible reason with her biggest secret, she wasn't going to fall back in bed with him, no matter how much she liked him.

But Ben was so relaxed, so easy, so cheerful, that when he'd grinned at her on Monday morning over the craft services coffee and asked how she was doing that day, she found it impossible to not grin back and say she was well rested.

After that moment, she'd given up on her plan to chill Ben out. They'd been mostly normal with each other all day Monday and Tuesday, though she still had trouble looking him in the eye—every time she did, she remembered that look on his face right before that last time they'd had sex in the hotel room. Which was also why she'd avoided him at the end of the day, out of fear she'd accidentally invite him back to her hotel. He hadn't sought her out, either, which she insisted to herself was a relief.

And now it was this overcast, windy, dreary day, and Anna just wanted to get out of here and let herself stress in her hotel room about *Vigilantes*—even though things looked promising, she still didn't actually know anything—and the Varon film, which she wanted more every time she read the script, which she did far too often. Simon was going to be in town the next day; they were supposed to have breakfast to strategize. She had to make a list of things to talk to him about.

Why was Ben standing over there cheering up the sound guy and not her? Ugh, the weather was getting to her. She turned away from Ben.

And then the power went out.

There were a bunch of high-pitched screams—why, Anna didn't know; it was two in the afternoon, not the middle of the night. Someone ran outside to check the lights and discovered the whole block was out. Everyone freaked out, except for Ben, who picked up his phone. Anna walked over to him to see who he was calling.

"Power company," he said as she approached. "Want to see if they have any idea how long it'll be out."

She stood close to him as he was on hold, not saying anything. They watched the chaos around them together—everyone stressing about phone batteries and lighting and laptops; someone flicked the light switches over and over, like that would do anything; someone else took pictures at the windows, as if a middle-of-the-day power outage was an Instagram-worthy event.

Finally, Ben came to attention in a way she could tell meant he was listening to something on the other end of the phone, then sighed and hung up.

"They say this will last until eight tonight, at least. I bet a tree's down. I'd better tell Gene so we can call it a day here."

Ben strode over to Gene and whispered to him. Gene yelled, "Fuck!" just once, which made everyone turn and look at him.

"Power'll be out for the rest of the day," Gene announced to the room. "Go home, everybody, and drink some excellent alcohol. See you tomorrow."

Everyone groaned, then jumped up and bustled around to leave before Gene could change his mind or the power came back on. For some reason, though, Anna didn't move.

Ben came back to her side a few minutes later.

"You heard the man," she said. "It's time to drink some excellent alcohol. Want to join me?"

"Sure," he said.

Where do you want to go?" Ben asked when they got into his car. He tried to be cool, to ignore that Anna was in his car again, to act like it was just a normal "getting drinks after work with some-one he worked with" kind of thing.

Things had been weird between them for the past few days—she'd seemed to want to steer clear of him, and he never wanted to push himself where he wasn't wanted, so he'd avoided her, too. But today, she'd kept looking over at him—which he obviously only noticed because he kept looking over at her—and had actu-ally walked over to talk to him during the power outage. And now she was in his car.

"Oh," Anna said. "I didn't think of that. There's a bar on the top floor of my hotel, but I'm not sure if it's open at this hour. And I know the news is out that I'm here in San Francisco, and I'm not sure if I want to deal with being recognized today."

Why was she here in his car, then?

"Normally, I'd say we could go sit on my deck, but you probably—"

"Oh, that's perfect," she said.

He hadn't expected that.

"I'm going to warn you now, my place is kind of a mess," he said, "but I promise, I can make an excellent cocktail."

One of those things was a lie. His apartment wasn't a mess at all—he'd cleaned it all day Saturday, with nothing else to do after he'd woken up and talked to Theo and emailed Dawn. But women were always very impressed when you called an almost-immaculate apartment "a mess." For the most part, he tried not to play games like that—he'd tried some of those tricks to get dates when he was in his early twenties, and it just made him feel like an asshole. And then he'd realized all he really needed to do was listen to them and ask them questions and give them compliments that weren't about their boobs (okay, not *just* about their boobs). He didn't know why more people didn't try that.

But small white lies to make himself look slightly better to someone like Anna felt like an exception.

"Oh, that's okay," Anna said. "After living in a hotel, being in an actual home will be nice. And the cocktail will be even better."

"It's still windy outside, but we can sit out on my little deck and pretend we're at a beer garden," he said. He turned down his block. No parking. Of course. Didn't the universe know that he had Anna Gardiner in his car and should get a parking spot right in front of his building?

She scanned the street along with him.

"Is that . . . Oh no, it's a hydrant, damn. Sitting outside sounds nice, and I have many scarves with me. I come prepared for San Francisco weather. Oh, look!"

Ben swiveled his head to where she pointed and saw the car pulling out on a side street. He quickly turned left and made it to the spot before anyone else could approach it.

"Nice job," he said. "You haven't lost it."

"Haven't lost what?" she said, in what he hoped was a mock-offended voice.

"The ability to sense an open parking spot. Come on, you're not going to try to pretend you have to still look for parking now, are you? Doesn't everywhere in L.A. have valet?"

She laughed, and he felt triumphant.

"Not everywhere, but okay, fine, this isn't a skill I have to exercise that much anymore, that's true."

She wrapped her gray scarf around her neck and the bottom half of her face before they got out of the car, and she put the plain black sunglasses he'd gotten her at Target on, instead of her big flashy ones.

"You were right," she said as they walked toward his building. "These are much better for purposes like this. No one looks at me twice."

He wasn't sure if that was a compliment on his strategy or a knock on his fashion sense.

"Next time you need to dress like a normal person, you know who to call," he said, and she laughed.

"I'm this way," he said when they got to his building. He gestured for her to go ahead of him and unlocked the front door. "Up here."

He let her precede him up the stairs to his apartment.

Good God, why had he let this happen? She'd made it clear that she didn't want a repeat of Palm Springs, and he understood that. But this was going to kill him.

"Make yourself at home," he said as he opened the door of his apartment. That must have sounded ridiculous to someone who lived in what was probably an enormous gated house somewhere in L.A., and who was now walking into his spacious one-bedroom apartment. Everything about this was weird.

"What do you want to drink?" he asked.

"It's cold outside." She sat down on the couch. "Something that'll warm me up."

Well, that was vague and only slightly helpful. Thank God he did actually have excellent liquor on hand—all thanks to his brother, who'd told him he was ashamed to share bloodlines with Ben that time Ben had pulled a plastic jug of vodka out when Ben was twenty and Theo was a very-full-of-himself twenty-three. He'd given Ben expensive liquor for every birthday since. Now Ben could and did buy his own, but somehow the stuff Theo bought him was always far better.

He threw together Manhattans—one of the few cocktails he knew how to make—and poured the drinks into two glasses.

"Want to sit here or outside on the deck?"

Anna jumped up from the couch.

"The deck, definitely. At least, until I'm freezing and need to come back inside."

She slid open the door to the deck, since both of his hands were full, and they both walked outside.

"The sun!" She looked up and then smiled at him. "Maybe it won't be so cold out here after all."

He set their drinks down on the small IKEA table he'd labored to put together.

"It's the reason I live in the Mission—it's too cold everywhere else in San Francisco. If the sun is going to come out, it comes out here first."

She sat down and lifted her glass to him.

"To half days. I know I should be annoyed about this because it pushes the schedule back, but I feel like a kid who got let out of school early."

He clinked her glass with his.

"Oh, this is good," she said.

"One of my specialties," he said. Then he laughed. "Another way to put that is that it's one of the, like, three cocktails I know how to make."

She laughed out loud, and something in the tone of her laughter dispelled the awkward feeling he'd had around her since Monday. He smiled.

He leaned back in his chair, and she did, too. They were side by side, looking out over the tiny garden next door, with the sun trying to break all the way through the clouds.

They didn't talk much at first. They enjoyed the sun on their faces and the drinks in their hands and being there together.

Or, at least, Ben did, and he hoped Anna did, too. He was usually good at telling when women enjoyed being with him, but suddenly with Anna he had doubts. Was it because she was such a great actor that he wouldn't know if she was pretending? Or because he wanted her to like being with him so much he didn't know if he was just wanting it or it was actually true?

She could be anywhere right now, though, and she chose to be here. With him. He'd take it.

Anna smiled as she took another sip of her drink. Sitting outside on Ben's deck drinking a cocktail with him was definitely better than sitting alone in her hotel room stressing about her future.

"So what's up for you, after this shoot is over?" Ben asked.

Speaking of her future.

"I'm still kind of figuring that out now," she said. "I have a lot of promo for *Vigilantes* coming up as soon as I get back to L.A., so I have to gear up for that. But also, there's this film role I'm dying to get; I love the script, the director is incredible, and I've been wanting to work with her for years."

He raised his eyebrows at her.

"So what's the holdup, then?"

She sighed.

"The studio isn't convinced I have enough box office-draw, or at least, that's what they say."

He put his drink down and looked at her.

"What do you think the real story is?"

She leaned back in her chair.

"'Not enough box office-draw' in Hollywood usually means 'not white.' It's so frustrating that no matter how hard I work or how on top of things I am or how good I am, I'll always be second best. They'll always want a white actress first; they'll always pay her more money than they would have paid me. Because, you see, they're 'universal' and I'm not. And yes, sure, their movies do make more money at the box office than mine do, but is that because people like them more? Is it because they're white and I'm Black and people automatically like me less because of that? Is it because the studios believe in them more and promote them more and it's a self-fulfilling prophecy? Who knows. Likely a combination of everything." She sighed again. "Sorry for the rant; this has obviously been building up."

Ben shook his head.

"No apology necessary. Rant as much as you want. That fucking sucks."

She laughed and took another sip of her cocktail.

"It fucking sucks indeed. I really want it, though, so I'll do whatever it takes to get it. I'm hoping that I make a splash in *Vigilantes*, which would help a ton, but it's kind of a faint hope—I only filmed a handful of scenes for that, and for all I know, it could end up being a bit part. I guess we'll see. I'm having breakfast with my manager tomorrow; hopefully he'll have some ideas."

"I'll keep my fingers crossed for you," Ben said.

She grinned at him.

"Please do."

She was glad she'd come here today. Just talking about the stuff she was most stressed about with Ben made her feel calmer.

Why was that? She still barely knew him, even though it no longer felt like that after that trip to Palm Springs. She realized that she'd talked to Ben a lot about herself and her family during the drive to and from Palm Springs, but he hadn't told her much about his. She knew he had a brother he was close to—that was all.

"Do you see your family often?" she asked him. "Your brother is in the Bay Area, you said—are your parents here, too?"

Ben nodded.

"Yeah, my mom lives in the East Bay. I see her every few weeks or so. At least once a month she demands that my brother and I come over for Sunday dinner." He shook his head, but with a wry smile on his face. "She drives me up a wall, but she's hilarious. I never miss her summons for dinner, unless I'm out of town."

"What does she do?" Anna asked. She was suddenly very curious about Ben—who his family was, how he came to be the person he was. He'd mentioned his mom, but not his dad, but in that way where she didn't think she could ask why.

He drained his drink and set it on the table.

"She's a nurse. She has been my whole life. Or, at least, as long as I can remember. After . . . when I was little, she doubled up on her shifts for a while—Theo and I spent a lot of time with our cousins then. Once we got old enough to stay home alone, she would take the night shifts, which meant she was always there in the morning to get us ready for school and then again when we got home to supervise our homework. I was always sort of a class clown, but I never wanted to get in so much trouble that the principal would call my mom, because I knew if anything woke her up during the day, she'd be on the warpath."

He smiled reminiscently. Anna pictured Ben, twenty years younger. She could see him as a teen, with dancing eyes and a mischievous smile. His mom probably had her hands full.

"Has she thought about retiring? I only ask because I keep trying to convince my parents to retire, and it's not going well."

Ben laughed.

"From the glimpse I got of your parents, I can imagine that. And she talks about retirement sometimes, but sort of in that pipe-dream way. Like 'when I retire, your aunt Leslie and I are going to spend a month in the Virgin Islands' kind of way. Nothing serious, at least not yet." He paused. "Though maybe she's said more to Theo. He's always been the responsible one. I should ask him."

He didn't seem to have any bitterness in his voice when he made reference to his brother as the "responsible one." That was nice—she knew too many people who had been scarred by how their parents tagged them and their siblings as kids.

He picked up her empty glass and raised an eyebrow at her, and she nodded. He stood, taking both of their glasses with him, and walked back inside. She followed him.

"What does your brother do?" she asked.

He opened the freezer and pulled out ice cubes.

"He's the spokesman for the mayor of Berkeley," he said. "Great for me—with his help, I got the permits for all of the filming for this shoot much faster than anyone predicted."

She watched him pour liquor into the shaker.

"Big brother pulled some strings for you?"

He shook a finger at her.

"Never. My brother is far too by the book for that. But he knows everyone, so he told me who to contact, and as soon as I mentioned that he was my brother, everyone was all 'Ohhh, I love Theo! Anything to help out his brother!'" He stopped for a minute, the bourbon bottle in his hand. "I guess I should probably tell him that."

He gently shook the concoction and poured it into their glasses. He came around the counter to hand the drink to her. He stepped close to her, closer than he'd been to her since they left the hotel room in Palm Springs.

She'd forgotten how much taller he was than her, how he'd towered over her, even though she'd fit so well in his arms and against his body. She stared at his chest. She remembered how it felt against her cheek, how his arms felt around her.

"Anna." She looked up to his face. His eyes were serious, but that smile still hovered around them. "What are you doing here?"

She held her drink with both hands. The chill of it made her shiver. Or maybe it was the intense look in Ben's eyes. But she couldn't look away.

"What do you mean?" she asked, even though she knew exactly what he meant.

He moved even closer to her.

"Saturday morning, you texted me that what happened in Palm Springs between us could never happen again. Okay, I get that. Then on set for the past few days you haven't looked me in the eye. All right, I'm not going to push myself on you if you're not interested. But then today you asked me to get a drink, and I don't know why. Or why you're here, in my apartment, looking at me like that, and standing there being who you are and looking like you do, if you don't want me to touch you. Because I haven't touched you, but holy God, it is taking everything in my power not to. So I need to know. What are you doing here?"

He hadn't touched her at all, she realized. Not a hand on her back as they walked up the stairs to his apartment, not when he'd showed her the deck, not even when he'd given her the drink.

"What if I've changed my mind?" she asked him before she stopped to think about it.

His eyes bored into hers. She had no idea how, just minutes ago, she'd been chilly from the icy drink and the weather outside. Her whole body felt flushed, on alert.

"If you've changed your mind," he said, not moving closer to her, "you should probably put that drink down right now, so it doesn't fall to the floor and shatter when I rip your clothes off."

She looked down at the drink in her hand, and then carefully, deliberately, set it on the counter. She looked up and met his eyes.

Before she could say anything, his hands were on her. He pushed the V of her sundress down and to the side, and with his thumbs, pulled her bra down until her swollen breast and hard nipple popped out of it. He smiled, his thumb and fingertip caressing her nipple until she moaned.

"I've been wanting to do this for days," he said. "It's all I've been able to think about. I just wanted to touch you, here, and here." He moved his other hand up the inside of her thighs and slid a finger inside her underwear. "I've been wanting to do this with my fingers, and with my mouth." He pushed her backward onto the counter and sucked her nipple into his mouth. She whimpered.

"That noise. I've wanted to make you make that noise since Friday morning. My God." He went back to her breast and licked and sucked until she thought she was going to go wild. He pulled her underwear to the floor and kicked it to the side. She grabbed his head with her hands, pulled him to her, and kissed him hard. Why had she said they couldn't do this again? She couldn't remember now.

He put his hands under her hips, and before she even knew what he was doing, he lifted her onto the counter.

He smiled at her, that devilish smile she'd only seen from him in the hotel room in Palm Springs, and pushed her knees apart.

"If I remember correctly," he said, "I heard you make that noise a lot when I did this the last time. Let's see if I can manage it again."

She braced her hands behind herself and watched him push her dress up and bend down. But then, before he even touched her, he stood back up again.

"Wait, just to be clear," he said. "Is this one of those things we couldn't do again? I just wanted to double-check."

She glared at him.

"Fuck you."

He grinned.

"Was that a no? Because . . ."

Before he could say anything else, she grabbed his head and shoved it between her legs. She could feel him vibrating with laughter. Once he was safely where she wanted him, she let herself grin. From the very beginning, this guy had made her laugh. Of course he would make her laugh while they were having sex, why would she expect anything else?

As soon as his lips and tongue touched her, though, she stopped laughing. He clearly had paid attention to what she'd liked when they'd been in that hotel room. Then he'd tried different things, touched her in different places, sometimes soft, sometimes hard, sometimes fast, sometimes slow. She'd enjoyed it all, but now he was doing all of the things that made her slide her fingers into his hair and writhe and moan and finally throw her head back and shout.

He stood up, grabbed her by the waist and lifted her down, and then smiled at her. He looked very proud of himself.

"You never showed me your bedroom," she said. "You didn't give me a tour at all; we just walked in and went straight to the deck."

He pushed her hair back from her face.

"Do you have literally any idea how much I wanted to get you in my bedroom?" he asked. "I was trying not to be an asshole and lead you there as soon as you walked in here!" He looked so outraged and rumpled and sexy.

She pulled him down to her and kissed him. He wrapped her in his arms, like his arms had been waiting for her to come back ever since she'd left them last. Or maybe it just felt like that, because she'd been wanting this, more of this, since then, even though she'd told herself it was impossible. She could feel the smile on his lips as he kissed her back, as he danced his tongue against hers. In Palm Springs, their kisses had felt rushed, like they knew they were living on borrowed time, like every kiss could be their last. But this, this was the kiss of two people who had kissed before and knew they would kiss again. Of two people who not only liked kissing each other, but *liked* each other. She hadn't had a kiss like that in a long time.

He slid his hand up to cup her cheek, and the tender touch of his hand on her face made her heart turn over. She ignored that and just kissed him, enjoyed the hardness of his body, the way her curves fit snuggly against his chest, that way he rested his hand on her hip, in the same way he'd done before. Like he liked that part of her body, appreciated it, couldn't keep himself from touching it. She'd noticed that touch before, and she loved that he was doing it again now. She ran her hands up his back, under his shirt, feeling the warm, smooth skin there. She remembered when she'd woken up in the middle of the night next to him and kissed him softly on his shoulder blade; he'd turned over and opened his arms to her without even waking up.

"Can we go to the bedroom now, please?" he whispered in her ear.

She kissed his cheek and took his hand.

"Lead the way."

Ben walked with Anna down the hall to his bedroom. At every moment, he was afraid she'd shake her head, change her mind, put her panties back on, and leave.

But instead, she reached for him again, as soon as they got into his bedroom. He slid his hands up her body, backed her up until she hit his bed, and gently pushed her onto it. She fell backward and laughed, and he climbed on top of her and trapped her hands beneath his.

"Here's what I'm wondering," he said.

She looked up at him, with that same look she'd had in Palm

Springs, that look full of heat. When she looked at him like that, he would do anything she wanted.

"What are you wondering?" she asked.

"I'm just wondering why you still have so many clothes on," he said.

She gave him a slow grin.

"I was waiting for you to take them off of me."

He smiled.

"Let me take care of this first."

He jumped to his feet, dropped his pants and underwear to the floor, threw his shirt across the room, and then rolled back on top of her. She was already laughing.

"Do you always take your clothes off that fast?" she asked him.

He moved down her body until he got to the hem of her dress.

"Only when I need to," he said.

"Oh, you needed to," she said.

He slowly pushed her dress up to her waist, as she gave him a look so hot he felt like he was going to catch on fire. Her fingers trailed over his shoulder and back, and he wished she could touch him forever. He dropped kisses on her knee, her thigh, her hip, her belly, as he moved up.

When he stopped, she let out a quick sigh.

"Something wrong?" he asked.

"I don't want you to stop," she said. Even though he knew she was enjoying this—knew from her moans and sighs and shakes when he'd gone down on her in the kitchen—he felt a burst of triumph at that. He wanted her to want this as much as he did. To want him as much as he wanted her.

"Oh, don't worry," he said. "I wasn't going to stop." He sat back on his heels and looked down at her. "But we need to get the rest of this dress off of you. It's hiding two of my favorite things."

She pulled the dress over her head, unsnapped her bra, and tossed it to the side.

"You mean these?" She cupped her breasts, a huge smile on her face.

He crawled up her body until his head was level with her chest.

"Mmm-hmmm." He sucked one nipple into his mouth, then rubbed it between his finger and thumb. He'd noticed that she liked it a little rough. He was happy to oblige.

"Has anyone told you"—he repeated that move with her other nipple—"that you have just fucking incredible breasts?"

She tossed her head back so her hair spread out on his pillow.

"Not in quite a while," she said.

"Well." He bent his head down and took tiny bites up one side of her breast, then let his tongue circle around and around her nipple until he sucked it in, hard. Her hand ran down his back and cupped his ass, and he grinned. "I'm happy to make sure you know it."

Her hand slid from his ass to his hips, and then she wrapped her fist around his hard cock.

"Please," she said. "I need you."

That was all he wanted to hear.

He lunged up to his nightstand and grabbed a condom out of it. As quickly as possible, he rolled it on as she watched him.

"Now," she said.

He thrust inside her. Good God, she felt amazing. This time there were no slow, gentle, getting-to-know-each-other movements at the beginning. She rose to meet him, and they moved together, hard and fast. They both moved like they'd been dying for this, like they hadn't been able to think about anything else for days, like they might never get it again. And when they came— first her, then him, as he felt her contract around him, they both shouted with joy.

They collapsed afterward, in a tangle of arms and legs, too out of breath to move. Finally, Ben kissed Anna on the cheek and lifted himself up a few inches.

"You wouldn't be hungry, by any chance, would you?"

She turned to him, a sleepy, sated smile on her face.

"I can't even tell you how much I appreciate that question. I absolutely could be. What do you have to eat?"

He smiled.

"Tell me what you want, and it'll appear. Didn't I tell you I'm magic?"

Eleven

THEY ATE DELIVERY SUSHI AND DRANK WINE NAKED IN BED, and then curled up together to watch a show on Netflix. Anna couldn't help herself from sharing all the gossip she'd heard about the actors with Ben, who at least pretended to be interested in all of her behind-the-scenes details.

She knew she should leave and go back to her hotel, she absolutely knew that. But she was so comfortable here, in Ben's big warm bed, with Ben's arm around her, and her head on his shoulder, that she just couldn't move.

Finally, after three episodes, she forced herself to sit up.

"I guess I should head back to my hotel," she said.

Ben sat up, too.

"You don't have to. You can stay." He looked at her, then fiddled with the sheets. "I mean. If you want."

She did want. But she shouldn't . . .

Oh, fuck it. Why shouldn't she? This was the first time she'd been relaxed and happy and actually having fun in two years, other than a few short moments with Penny. Plus, the shoot was only for a few more days, and she'd be back in L.A. and he'd still be here in San Francisco and they'd never see each other again. So she might as well enjoy this while it lasted.

"Sure, I'll stay," she said. "I have to be up pretty early tomorrow, though—I'm having a breakfast meeting with my manager. I get the impression from your yawns when you arrive on set that you're not much of a morning person—is that going to be a problem?"

He gave her an outraged look.

"You dare to accuse me of not being a morning person? Just because I may not be able to speak a word to anyone else before I drink an entire cup of coffee does *not* mean I'm not a morning person! I love mornings! I just love to observe them from my bed, that's all." He grinned at her. "But for you, I'll manage to pull myself together and drive you across town at the ass crack of dawn."

She handed him her wineglass.

"Then yes, I'll stay. And fuck it—I'll take more wine, too."

She admired his naked ass as he walked out of the room, and then his naked everything else as he walked back in.

Suddenly she realized something he'd said.

"You don't have to drive me to my hotel in the morning. That's what car services are for."

He shook his head.

"Oh no. I know you're famous and stuff and don't remember how this works, but car services are all fine when you're being picked up at your hotel, or your expensive gated home, but not if you're being picked up at six-something a.m. on a random street in the Mission. Someone will definitely take a picture of you in your clothes from the day before and your hair not done, and I know you don't want that."

Right, of course. And also, how was Ben more knowledgeable

and understanding of her need to have a glam squad before she went out in public than any man she'd ever been with—including the actors, all of whom were more vain than she was?

"Okay, fine, but I'll owe you one for that. Don't let me forget it."

A very wide, very dirty smile spread across his face.

"Oh, I won't. Don't you worry your pretty little head about that."

She smacked him on the shoulder, and he laughed.

As she was falling asleep, she thought about what she'd said. That she owed him one implied they'd do this again. She knew she should regret saying that, but instead, she felt gleeful.

She woke up the next morning, Ben's hand on her hip. His touch did so many things to her—last night it had thrilled her, intoxicated her, but today it soothed and comforted her. That night she'd slept with him in Palm Springs, she hadn't slept well, which was pretty common for her. But last night, she'd fallen asleep so fast, and slept so well. Maybe it was that she'd been yearning for human touch for so long, and Ben was so good at that. She'd noticed that about him early on—he was always touching shoulders, or clapping people on the back—but only people he had a relationship with, people who appreciated it. He hadn't touched her once, though, until she'd made it very clear she'd wanted him to. And that made that heavy, warm hand on her hip feel all the more earned.

She turned over and nestled her head into his chest. His arms came around her, even though she could tell from his breathing he was still asleep. She knew it must be time to get up soon, but instead she breathed along with him and let her whole body relax. She didn't think about the Varon film, she didn't think about *Vigilantes*, she didn't think about her dad's health. She just breathed in and out, in the circle of his arms.

Too soon, her alarm went off. Ben slowly opened his eyes and looked down at her.

"It feels very early," he said.

"It is very early," she said. "But I have to get back to my hotel to meet my manager before I have to be on set, remember?"

He brushed her hair back from her face and landed a kiss on the top of her head.

"I remember. Unfortunately." He yawned, then pulled her in for a tight hug before getting out of bed. "I'll be ready in a second, I promise." He gestured to the door. "You take the bathroom first."

She jumped out of bed and went to the bathroom. She peed, splashed cold water on her face, brushed her teeth with the travel toothbrush she always kept in her tote bag, and pinned her hair up into a bun.

When she got back into Ben's bedroom, he was fully dressed, and her clothes from the day before were piled neatly on his bed. He'd even found her underwear.

"You're fast," she said.

"Lots of practice," he said with an exaggerated wink. She had to laugh at how corny he was. Even in the five a.m. hour, this guy could make her laugh. Ridiculous.

He disappeared into the bathroom, and she threw on her clothes and looked at herself in the mirror.

Her hair was still messy, her eyebrows were barely visible without makeup on, her dress was wrinkled, and she had an enormous pimple on her chin. But she looked . . . happy. Actually happy, for the first time in a long time. She'd had a whole afternoon and night where she'd barely looked at her phone, where she hadn't worked or thought about work, where she'd just relaxed and talked to Ben and had sex and watched Netflix and eaten food and had more sex, and those sixteen hours had been the best vacation she'd had in a long time.

Ben smiled at her when he walked back into the room.

"Ready to go?" he asked.

She wasn't, at all.

"Yep, I'm ready," she said.

They walked out of Ben's apartment, walked down the stairs, and opened the outside door. And then she stood, frozen, on the doorstep, until she whirled around and went back inside.

She turned to Ben with a glare as soon as the door closed behind them.

"Did you know that they'd be filming out there this morning?"

He took a step back.

"What? No, of course not!" he said. "Do you think I would have had you stay over if I knew there was going to be a film crew on my street at five thirty a.m.?"

She looked at him for a long moment. Some people absolutely would have had her stay over if they'd known that the next morning there would be not just a camera crew filming on his block, but a gaggle of paparazzi on the sidelines. Was Ben one of them?

No. He wasn't. If he'd wanted to publicize that he'd slept with her, he'd had plenty of opportunities to do so since Palm Springs, and he hadn't.

"No. Sorry. I don't think that," she said. "It's just . . . some people would do that. It's hard to . . ."

He put his hand on her shoulder.

"I get it." He steered her back toward the stairs. "Let's go back to my apartment while we figure out how to get you out of here."

When they walked back into his apartment, she glanced toward his deck.

"There's not a back door that way I just didn't see last night, is there?"

Ben shook his head.

"Not unless you want to jump off the deck, and I kind of don't think you're the type who does her own stunts, no offense."

Yeah, that was accurate.

"None taken. Okay. Shit. I guess I could . . . put on a hat?" She pulled out her phone to try to figure out what was filming outside. Maybe it would be over soon?

Nope, no such luck. And shit—that's why she'd seen paparazzi: there were two big-name stars in that movie. One of whom had been in the tabloids a lot lately. Damn it.

How was she going to get out of there? The thought of walking outside into all of that made her anxious. People knew she was in San Francisco; the photographers might be watching out for her. And she was wearing the same thing she'd worn to the set yesterday. She'd avoided situations like this—where she wasn't in control of how and when people took photos of her—for exactly this reason. Shit. She dropped her head into her hands.

Ben pulled his phone out of his pocket.

"I have an idea. Hold on."

Theo answered the phone after only two rings.

"Why are you calling me this early? Is someone in the hospital? Are you in jail?"

His brother had so much faith in him.

"Neither of those, but I need your help. Wait, actually, Maddie's, too, if she's with you."

Theo snorted.

"Oh, are you going to be the one to wake her up before six a.m. and deal with the consequences? Because I sure as hell do not want to do that."

Ben heard mumbling in the background.

"She says fine, she's up, what is it?"

Wait. Damn it. He hadn't checked with Anna to see if he could let Theo and Maddie in on this. Which, obviously, they were already in on it, but Anna didn't know that.

"Hold on. Give me a second."

He ignored the squawking from Theo and hit the mute button.

"Anna." She looked up from her phone and at him. "Can I tell my brother that . . . you're here? And his girlfriend? They're both trustworthy, I swear, they won't tell anyone, and just as important, they'll know how to solve this. My brother might irritate the hell out of me sometimes, but he's great in a crisis."

She looked at him for a minute and shrugged.

"Sure."

"Okay. Great." He unmuted the phone. "Here's the situation. Anna is here, at my apartment." Theo whistled, but Ben kept talking. "There's a film crew outside, on my street, with a bunch of photographers, which we discovered when we tried to leave to go to my car so I could drive her back to her hotel. How do we get her out of here without being photographed?"

He heard a gasp from Maddie.

"I know! I know how to do this!" Maddie said. Theo had obviously put him on speaker. "This is the moment I've been dreaming of for years! Okay, wait—what time does she have to be back at her hotel? Like, by absolutely what time?"

He repeated that question to Anna, who looked down at her phone.

"Well, my manager just postponed our meeting from six to eight, thank God. Luckily, Gene told me yesterday I don't have to be on set until ten today, because you guys are doing all of that crowd stuff first."

"Eight," Ben said into the phone. "Why, what are you—"

"Okay!" Maddie said. "We'll be there as soon as we can. Stay where you are!"

"Where would we go? That's the whole . . ." She'd hung up the phone. Well, if he trusted anyone in this world, he trusted his brother and Maddie, so hopefully their solution was real.

And hopefully, they'd make it to San Francisco from the East Bay in time.

Ben turned to look at Anna.

"Maddie says stay here, they're on their way."

She looked back at him and narrowed her eyes.

"Who . . . is Maddie again?"

He shook his head. Right. Even though it felt like they knew each other well by this point, they barely knew anything about each other's lives.

"Maddie is my brother's girlfriend. Between the two of them, I knew they'd have some sort of idea for how to deal with this, but I didn't expect them to come flying across the bay before six a.m." Anna still looked doubtful. "Maddie's a stylist; she's used to this sort of thing. She worked for that princess, the American one."

"Oh!" Anna's brow cleared. "Duchess, but okay. So she does know what she's talking about." She looked past him into the kitchen. "Is there any coffee in there, by chance?"

They were deep into their third cup of coffee by the time Theo and Maddie buzzed from downstairs. Thank God, because Ben had spent the past thirty minutes freaking out that maybe there'd been an accident on the bridge and his promise to Anna that he'd find a way to get her out of there unscathed would be a lie and he'd have to dress her up in four layers of his clothes to walk to his car.

Ben opened his apartment door and let in Theo, Maddie, and the enormous suitcase Maddie was carrying. That must contain her disguise options for Anna. His brother looked sleepy; Maddie looked excited.

"Anna, meet my brother, Theo, and his girlfriend, Maddie. Theo, Maddie, this is Anna."

It was, yes, slightly awkward to be introducing his brother and Maddie to Anna at his apartment at 6:15 a.m., but everyone involved pretended it was totally normal.

"Nice to meet you, Anna." Theo nodded at her, as uptight and formal at this hour of the morning as he always was.

"Nice to meet you, too," Anna said. "Your brother has told me a lot about you."

Theo turned to Ben, and the formal mask slipped from his face a little. If Theo said *Likewise* Ben might have to murder him on the spot.

"Mmm. Well. Only believe the good stories he told you. The bad ones are all lies."

Ben relaxed. He should have trusted his brother. In his defense, it had been a . . . while since he'd introduced him to a woman he was dating.

Not that he was dating Anna.

But still.

Maddie broke into his musings.

"Hi, Anna. Do you want to hear my plan?"

She held up the suitcase, and Ben couldn't resist interrupting her.

"What is *in* that thing, anyway? That's the biggest suitcase I've ever seen."

Maddie grinned at him. She looked more excited than he'd ever seen her.

"It's huge. I usually use it for big-deal shoots, or when I'm trying to transport a ton of clothes for a client. And I brought an assortment of random clothes and a few wigs over this morning, in case Anna wants to wear them on the way to the hotel, but also . . ." She paused and looked right at Anna. "It's big enough for you to fit inside."

Maddie must have lost her mind. Ben looked at Anna, expecting her to say that, but instead, Anna let out a peal of laughter.

"Like when . . . Oh my God, this is ridiculous and hilarious and borderline certifiable." She grinned. "And also, I love it. Why the fuck not?"

Ben saw quite a few reasons why the fuck not, actually.

"Hold on, hold on. How do you know Anna will be able to fit inside? What if she suffocates? Who's going to carry her? What if she hurts herself? Maddie, *this* was your fantastic idea?"

The two women ignored him. Maddie already had the suitcase open on the floor, and Anna was inspecting it with that wild grin still on her face.

"These are the things I said all the way across the bridge," Theo said to him. "She didn't listen to me, either, but I thought Anna might have some of those same concerns. I guess not."

Anna was already sitting inside the suitcase, laughing again.

Maddie looked up at the two brothers.

"Stop worrying! Oh my God, Ben, I thought you of all people would be into this, but you're just as much of a stress case as your brother here! You two will carry the suitcase, you're both very strong!" Well. She had a point there. "How far away is your car?"

"A few blocks away," Ben said. "But—"

"Good," Maddie said. "That's not far at all. You and Theo will carry Anna in the suitcase to the car—put her in the back seat, obviously. I'll get in the back seat with her. Once we're well on our way, I'll unzip her. We'll drive her to her hotel, and she can either walk in of her own volition, or we can zip her up before we get to the hotel and you guys can carry her in. Simple, perfect, no one will know it's Anna inside."

Shit. She was going to talk him into this.

Ben looked at Anna, who had gotten out of the suitcase and come over to his side.

"This sounds ridiculous," he said. "But I'm happy to help with this weird stunt if you're okay with it." He lowered his voice. "But if you don't want to do this, Maddie has the disguises, we can just do that, you know."

Anna put her hand on his arm.

"The whole idea of this brings me so much joy that we have to do it," she said. "It's so silly and outlandish and I love it. But thanks for giving me an out. I appreciate it."

She picked up her tote bag from the couch and pulled her wallet out of it.

"Here." She handed him a plastic card. "This is my hotel room key; we'll also need it to get into the elevator. I'm suite 212."

She handed her tote bag to Maddie.

"Can you take this for me? It would be too bulky inside the suitcase."

Ben looked at Theo, and Theo looked back at him.

"I think we're going to be carrying a suitcase with an Oscar-nominated actress inside to my car," Ben said.

Theo nodded.

"I think so, too. How did these women convince us to do this?"

Ben looked over at Anna. She was already inside the suitcase and looked positively gleeful as she sat there, chatting away with Maddie.

"I don't think they even tried to convince us," he said. "I think they just knew that we'd do whatever they wanted us to do."

Theo shook his head.

"That's depressingly accurate."

Five minutes later, he and Theo were walking down the street, carrying Anna. In the suitcase. It was hard-sided, which, thank

God, made it feel less like there was a person inside and more like it was just a heavy suitcase.

Except there was a person inside. Anna. Anna was the person inside. What the fuck were they doing?

Maddie had left the zipper only partway zipped in the middle, and at least when they were still in the apartment, Anna had said she could breathe fine, but Ben was still worried about that.

They walked past the filming for a whole block—there were a ton of people around for whatever they were filming, and lots more outside the barriers watching. Ben had even seen the temporary no-parking signs along his street earlier in the week, but hadn't paid attention, or looked into why. He kicked himself for that now—if he'd done that, he would have taken Anna back to her hotel last night, and they wouldn't be dealing with this today.

But. Then he wouldn't have been able to hang out with her last night, in that easy, relaxed way. And he wouldn't have been able to have sex with her again one more time before they fell asleep. And he wouldn't have been able to sleep next to her all night, or introduce her to Theo and Maddie, or do this ridiculous—but, he had to admit, kind of hilarious—stunt to get her past all of these people without them seeing her. Maybe he was glad he hadn't checked after all.

"So, um. How long are you going to be out of town for?" Theo asked as they walked past a big group of people.

"What do you . . ." Ben stared at him, and Theo stared back without blinking. "Oh! Right, yes, of course. Um. I'll be out of town for . . . a month! For work. Which is why I needed so big of a suitcase. Lots of, um, outfit changes."

Theo nodded.

"Outfit changes, yes, of course. That makes sense. All of the many different pairs of jeans and sneakers and hoodies you own." He paused for a second. "Actually, I'm sure your sneakers *could* fill up this whole suitcase if you tried. How many pairs of them did you bring?"

Well, let's see, if he did go out of town for a month for work, how many pairs of sneakers *would* he bring?

"Only ten pairs." He shook his head. "I didn't want to get my good sneakers too dirty, so I couldn't bring most of the best ones—only a handful of my favorites and then a few of the daily workhorses." Now he started thinking about which of his sneakers he'd pack. "As a matter of fact, I was really sad to leave some of them behind. It's a real shame. But we'll be at the beach, and you know what sand does to good shoes."

"No, what does sand do to good shoes?" Theo asked with a very straight face.

Suddenly Ben thought about Anna inside the suitcase overhearing this conversation. Would she think he was comparing her to his sneakers? Well, if she did, she should be honored—he treated his sneakers *very* well.

She probably wouldn't like the way he phrased that.

A laugh exploded from him, with no warning. Theo turned and looked at him, and his face crumpled. They stood still, both laughing so hard they were shaking.

"Guys!" Maddie said. "Don't we need to get a move on?"

Ben took a deep breath and tried to stop laughing. Yes, right, Anna was still inside the suitcase. He pulled himself together and walked on.

"I'm ashamed of you," he said to his brother. "Me, you'd expect me to lose it, but I had more faith in you."

Theo glared at him.

"If you make me lose it again before we get to this car, I'm going to tell Mom about this."

Ben stopped again.

"You wouldn't!"

Maddie poked him with her shoulder and he kept walking.

"Of course I wouldn't," Theo said. "But still." He looked from Ben down to the suitcase and back again. Yes, yes, message received, they had to get Anna into the car and out of the suitcase.

It wasn't his fault that this situation was hilarious. It wasn't Theo's fault, either. Come to think of it, it was . . .

"Ben? Isn't this your car?" Maddie asked.

Oh right, that was his car.

Not without some difficulty, he pulled his car key out of his pocket while he kept a grip on the suitcase with Anna inside. Why didn't he have one of those cars where it automatically unlocked when the key was in your pocket? Maybe he'd have one next time he had to carry an Oscar-nominated actress to his car in a suitcase.

Maddie opened the back door, and he and Theo carefully slid the Anna suitcase into the back seat. She pulled the seat belt out as far as it could go and buckled it around the suitcase.

Ben pulled out of the parking spot while Theo was still putting his own seat belt on.

"Unzip her, Maddie!" Ben said as soon as they were at the corner.

"Already done," Maddie said.

The lid of the suitcase flipped up, and Anna's head popped out.

"Just how many pairs of sneakers do you have?" she asked Ben.

Theo started laughing. Then Maddie. Then Anna. Then Ben. They all laughed so hard and for so long that someone honked at him to keep driving.

"I can't believe . . ." Ben said as soon as he could talk again, "that I just walked down the street with my brother, carrying Anna Fucking Gardiner in a suitcase."

"You two did a very good job," Anna said. "Really. Professional suitcase actress carriers couldn't have done it better. I felt extremely secure."

Ben turned to Theo and gave him a nod. *That's right.*

"Except for when you were both giggling so hard you almost dropped me."

Ben and Theo both started talking at once.

"We wouldn't have!"

"We stopped walking! To make sure we didn't!"

"We weren't giggling, we were laughing!"

Ben saw Anna and Maddie exchange glances in the back seat, and glared at them.

"Mmm," Anna said. "One question, Ben—when you compared me to a sneaker . . . was that supposed to be a compliment?"

See, he knew she wouldn't get it.

"Okay, first of all, I didn't *compare* you to a sneaker, I was just trying to make some fake conversation about what would be in my suitcase. You know, to throw people off the scent! But also, I treat my sneakers very well!"

Theo turned around to face Anna.

"He really does. He always has, actually."

At least his brother came through for him when it counted.

"He actually does," Maddie chimed in from the back seat. "A whole little shelf set up in his closet for them. Weird, but true."

Wow, Maddie defended him, too.

Wait a minute.

"Why is that weird?"

Maddie and Theo both laughed.

"I mean, Ben," Theo finally said. "You're not exactly Mr. Responsible."

He couldn't believe Theo was saying this with Anna right there.

"I am so!" Why did he sound like he'd reverted to childhood? "I mean, I'm perfectly responsible."

"Do you remember that time when you took a stranger's suitcase when you left the airport, and you didn't realize it for hours, well after the poor woman was freaking out?"

"First of all, that was not my fault! All black suitcases look alike. Second, that was ten years ago!"

"What about the time you left the key in the driver's-side door of your car on the street overnight?"

Ben had to laugh. That had been something of a miracle.

"And it wasn't even touched! I think everyone who walked by it must have thought it was a setup or something."

Maddie piped up from the back seat.

"What about when you helped me transport those dresses for that benefit and managed to spill coffee all over the valet when we got to the hotel?"

He couldn't believe Maddie was joining in on this. Though, what she didn't say, thank goodness, was that he'd been so busy flirting with the makeup artist that he hadn't been looking where he was going.

"The dresses themselves were all pristine, weren't they? Plus, I tipped that guy very well!"

Theo laughed again. Ben didn't trust that glint in his eye.

"Oh, and there was the time . . ."

He should have pushed his brother into traffic when he'd had the chance.

Anna laughed as she listened to Theo and Maddie making fun of Ben in the way only family can. Ben and Theo were so different—you could see that even in their posture in the front seat, with Theo's back ramrod straight, and Ben relaxed—but anyone would still be able to tell they were brothers from a mile away.

Ben seemed so outraged by all of the stories that Theo and Maddie were telling about him, but they all made her like him even more. She liked how they all obviously jumped to help one another in an emergency, and how Maddie treated Ben like a little brother. And now that she knew Maddie was a stylist, another mystery was cleared up. She was pretty sure she had Maddie to thank for her new Palm Springs dresses.

Maddie turned to her as they got close to the hotel.

"How do you want to do this?" she asked. "Are we going in through the front and then up to your room from there, or through the back so you don't have to get in the suitcase again?"

Anna thought about that. It had been cramped and uncomfortable in the suitcase, obviously. And she was tempted to call the hotel manager and tell her she was on her way so she could go in through the kitchen. But . . . the idea of being carried in a suitcase through that staid, elegant hotel lobby cracked her up. Maybe it was the diva in her, maybe it was the devil on her shoulder, but she grinned at Maddie after she thought about it for a few seconds.

"We've come so far, why take the easy way out?"

But wait. She'd better double-check that she wasn't taking the diva act too far.

She leaned forward.

"Guys—are you sure you're up for carrying me to my room? If not, we can—"

"Theo, I think she's calling us weaklings," Ben broke in. "She's saying we aren't strong enough to carry her up to her room. Are you going to take this lying down?"

Theo shook his head.

"Oh, absolutely not. That's an insult I won't stand for." He turned to the back seat. "Maddie. Zip her in."

Maddie saluted him.

"Yes, sir."

Anna folded herself back up. She was grateful for all of the yoga she'd done over the past few years, which made it possible for her to fold her body like this. And that movie she'd done early in her career where she'd had to hide under a bed for hours, which had forced her to get rid of any latent claustrophobia. Maddie zipped the suitcase most of the way closed, and Anna smiled to herself.

Then she thought of one more thing.

"Hey, Maddie?"

She could feel Maddie's head come down to the suitcase.

"Yeah? Everything okay in there?"

"Oh yeah, everything's fine. But, um, if you can, without being obvious—can you take some pictures of this? In the lobby, I mean. I desperately want to see this from the outside."

Maddie chuckled.

"Oh, don't you worry. There's no way I'd let this go without being memorialized. I'll head into the lobby while they're getting you out of the car, so I can get the best vantage point."

No wonder Ben had called his brother and Maddie. He was right, she was a pro.

She normally wouldn't have asked for evidence like this—she normally would have specifically banned evidence like this, actually—but while they'd been waiting for Theo and Maddie at Ben's apartment, she'd googled Maddie based on what Ben had said about her and had been reassured. If she'd worked for a member of the royal family—especially *that* member of the royal family—the woman must know how to keep her mouth shut; she probably had way more top secret photos on her phone than of a suitcase. And it was clear Ben had already told Theo and Maddie about them—he'd just said "Anna" on the phone to Theo, who had known exactly who he was talking about.

Plus, she probably wasn't the only one who had noticed she and Maddie had gotten along well; she was pretty sure there was no way Maddie would jeopardize her career—or any potential professional relationship—by blowing this secret sky-high.

Anna could feel the car slowing down. They must be pulling up to the hotel now. She felt that same giddy anticipation she'd felt when they'd left Ben's apartment. This was just so profoundly ridiculous, and she loved everything about it.

Early in her acting career, when it was just starting to get off the ground, she'd felt this kind of thrill about all of the fun, actressy things she'd gotten to do. When she'd met Denzel Washington, when she'd gotten fitted for an awards show dress for the first time, when she'd first been in *People* and *Us Weekly* in the same week. But then, all too quickly, that glitter had faded, and all of those previously exciting things had become imbued with stress. Now when she got fitted for dresses, she worried about whether she would win or lose at the ceremony. Now when she met another actor she'd respected for years, there were often so many cameras pointed at them she couldn't relax. Now when she was in *People*, she worried about what the less-kind celebrity press was going to say about her later that day.

It had been a long time since she'd just let herself relax and do something ridiculous like this, one of those wacky celebrity stunts she'd never believed could be true until she'd become one herself.

She certainly never would have expected that she'd let a guy she'd slept with—was sleeping with? Was it present tense or past? She'd figure that out later—and his brother carry her around in a suitcase to dodge the press. Or that she'd enjoy it. Life was full of surprises. All she knew was that walk from Ben's apartment to his car had been hilarious, and she hoped the trip from the car to her hotel room would be just as fun. She couldn't wait to see Maddie's pictures.

"See you in there," Maddie whispered when the car stopped. The car doors opened and she felt Ben, Maddie, and Theo all jump out of the car.

"Oh, no, thanks, we've got it," Ben said. To the bellhops? "Precious cargo."

Anna couldn't help but smile. She could just picture the smirk on his face when he said it. So many men had hit on her in so many elaborate ways, but Ben's corny compliments got to her.

And then, slowly, she and the suitcase slid across the back seat.

"One, two, three!" Ben said, presumably to Theo. At three, they lifted her out of the car and up the steps of the hotel.

She could tell as soon as they got inside, just by the quality of the sound. The wind from outside was gone, replaced by the din of tourists and travelers and bustling staff. But she had no concept of what direction they were moving in.

Oh no. What if someone stopped them on the way up to her room? Hotels like this had tight security, which she usually appreciated, but now it might be her downfall. What if someone thought Ben and Theo looked suspicious with that enormous suitcase and asked them where they were going? What would they say? She should have called ahead and told the hotel that she would be getting a delivery, and to let them up, just in case. Because now . . . oh God, if they tried to say they were with her, there was no way for her to verify it. Her phone was in her bag, currently on Maddie's shoulder, so even if she could contort herself enough to send a text message inside this suitcase, she wouldn't be able to.

Anna made herself take one long deep breath, and then another. Okay. This would be . . . a little weird, but it would be fine. She'd have to pop out of the suitcase; that was what she'd have to do. Hopefully the manager would question them somewhere private, so she wouldn't have to do it in the middle of the lobby. Despite her fears, she fought back a giggle at the mental picture. That would definitely get her some tabloid headlines.

"Excuse me." Ben and Theo halted at the woman's voice. Oh no. This was it, that must be the manager. She was a woman; she'd introduced herself to Anna early on in her stay. Anna had liked her, very no-nonsense but with a sense of humor. She'd at least laugh when Anna popped out of the suitcase.

"Guys. The elevator to the room is that way."

Maddie. The voice was Maddie. Anna's shoulders slumped in relief.

"I told you it was that way!" Ben hissed.

"You did not! You didn't tell me anything!" Theo whispered back.

"I nodded my head in that direction but you kept walking this way so I followed you because I thought you knew where you were going!"

"Why would you think that?"

"Because you usually do!"

Now Anna had to fight back laughter again. Soon they stopped walking, and she heard a very quiet *ding*. Ah, they must be in the elevator.

"Everything okay in there?" Ben asked. "Knock twice for yes, once for no."

Anna laughed and knocked twice.

"What were you going to do if she knocked once?" Maddie asked. "Drop her to the floor and unzip the suitcase now? The guy watching the hotel elevator video cameras would have gotten a kick out of that."

Anna giggled at that, but Ben ignored it.

"Don't worry, we're in the home stretch now! Elevator's almost there!"

"Oh my God, why are you talking to the suitcase?" Theo said. "Isn't the whole point of this to be stealthy?"

Theo had a point there.

"The video cameras in elevators don't have sound—did we all learn nothing from that video with Solange and Jay Z?" Ben asked.

Ben also had a point.

The elevator slowed, and then stopped, and the procession moved on. Anna should have told them they could set her down in the elevator, but that would probably hurt their egos too much.

"Maddie—"

Maddie cut Theo off.

"Going ahead now to direct you guys. Follow me."

Maddie must have figured out the way to Anna's suite without incident, because the next time they stopped, the suitcase jostled around some.

"Sorry . . . um, no one, just had to get the room key out of my pocket," Ben muttered.

And then, seconds later, Anna heard the door open, and they moved again, super quickly.

As soon as the door closed, she was slowly lowered to the ground.

"We did it!" Ben said. The zippers slid apart, and the lid popped open. Anna sat up and saw Ben's gleeful face. "I was worried for a second there in the lobby; we got a few weird looks, and I was trying to plan for what to do if we got stopped, but we made it!"

Anna laughed out loud.

"I panicked for a moment there, too, but I'm glad I had nothing to worry about." She grinned at him. "That was so much fun."

And yes, despite her brief freak-out in the lobby, this had been as fun as she'd wanted it to be.

Ben took her hands and pulled her upright.

"That was a blast."

Anna looked at Ben for a second. Oh, the hell with it. Maddie and Theo knew the deal.

She grabbed Ben and kissed him hard. He kissed her back without hesitation. He wrapped his arms around her and lifted her out of the suitcase. She tilted her head back, laughed out loud, and kissed him again. She felt victorious about this small, fun, silly thing she'd done for herself, and had enlisted this fun, silly, excellent fling of a guy to do with her. The kiss was a celebration of herself, of the pieces of herself she'd thought she'd lost and wasn't sure if she'd ever find again, of everything in her life that had brought her to this moment, of Ben and the strange but delightful way they'd come together.

When they finally pulled apart, Ben had that delicious, lustful smile on his face again. And Maddie and Theo, still standing by the door, had shit-eating grins on their faces. Ben glanced over at them, then quickly bent down to zip up the suitcase. Anna had a feeling they'd tease Ben about this hard. Just thinking of that made her smile.

"Um . . . we should take off," Theo said. "I have to, um, get to work. We'll take a cab back to my car."

Ben, Anna noticed, did not argue.

"Thanks for everything, guys," Ben said. He picked up the suitcase and handed it to his brother.

Anna walked over to Theo and Maddie.

"Yes, thank you both so much. Maddie, for the brilliant idea and Theo, for carrying it out." She winked at them. "Literally."

Maddie laughed.

"It was my pleasure. This was definitely a morning I'll never forget."

Anna thought of something right before they opened the door.

"Oh, Maddie, can you send Ben those pictures? And also . . ."

Maddie held up a hand.

"The only people who will ever see those pictures are standing in this room right now. I swear."

Anna smiled at her.

"Thank you."

Maddie and Theo said good-bye again, and Anna didn't miss the smug look Theo gave Ben. Anna turned around to Ben, suddenly shy to have him here in her suite.

"Um, I can go, too, if you want," he said, as he fiddled with the room service menu. Maybe he was shy about being up here, too.

She took the menu from him.

"I don't. Want you to go, I mean. But you know what I do want?"

He grinned at her.

"Breakfast," he said.

"Breakfast." She grinned back. "I have an hour before my meeting; we have time." She picked up the phone.

Fifteen minutes later, room service arrived with their huge breakfast spread.

"Okay, first of all," Ben said as he unfolded his napkin, "do you always get food that fast from room service? I feel like it takes at least an hour whenever I order it."

Anna picked up a sausage link.

"I sure do," she said. "It's pretty fantastic, I've got to say. Maybe not worth having to dodge paparazzi at unexpected times, but if I have to do that, I might as well get the benefit of lightning-fast service."

He opened the basket of pastries on the table between them.

"Do you do a lot of stuff like what we did this morning? Suitcase capers, I mean. Because, I have to admit, that was a hell of a lot of fun, but I can see how it would get old after a while."

She laughed.

"It was a hell of a lot of fun, wasn't it? And, no, I've never really done stuff like that before—probably because I'm mostly either in L.A. or living out of hotels while on set and having very prescribed comings and goings, so I've never had to. I'd probably hate things like today if I did it a lot, but today I was basically giggling the whole time."

Ben's brow cleared.

"Oh good. I was worried about you in there—I remembered you'd said some of your worst anxiety was because of all of the photographers outside the set that other time, so I didn't know if all of this stuff was hard for you for that reason."

She liked the way he asked that—he brought up her anxiety like he was talking about a sprained ankle or something—no hushed voice or expression like he was discussing something bad or like she was some fragile being who might fall apart. But also, she was glad he'd thought about it and had checked in on her.

"Thanks, I appreciate that," she said. "I did start to panic for a second in the lobby, but it didn't last long. Mostly, it was just fun, which I was grateful for. I haven't relaxed like that and had fun with"—she gestured to the room—"all of this, the fun part of being 'Anna Gardiner,' for a while."

There was a knock at her door. Probably room service, bringing something they'd forgotten.

Anna got up and looked through the peephole. Shit, Simon was here already? Okay, okay, she'd just have to play this cool. She could do that. She put a surprised smile on her face and opened the door.

"Simon! What are you doing here? It's only seven fifteen!"

Her manager strutted into the suite, looking very proud of himself.

"I told you I'm in town for my husband's sister's wedding, right?

Well, I had been convinced to go over to his other sister's house and consult on the flower arrangements before breakfast—I do not know why they couldn't have me do that last night, but Aidan's family is like that, you know—but his nephews were awake and running around, so I made sure to snap out my orders—sorry, advice—on the flowers as fast as possible. Nothing against children in general, it's just that those children are invariably . . . sticky." He shuddered. "And they always want to touch me, and this shirt is not for three-year-olds to . . . Oh! Good morning."

He'd gotten all the way into the room, chatting merrily to Anna, before he looked up and saw Ben, placidly eating a piece of bacon.

"Good morning." Ben stood up. "Anna, looks like you have some business to talk about, and I should take off anyway. Thanks for breakfast."

Half of her was grateful to him for leaving right away and making this easy on her, but the other half of her wanted to stop him, tell him to stay. But she knew she couldn't, not with Simon there.

"Thanks to you, too," she said, her voice as bland and businesslike as she could make it. "Simon, this is Ben Stephens, he's the lead at the ad agency for the phone shoot. We were just talking about the plans for the rollout of the ad campaign. Ben, this is Simon Drake, my manager."

Ben shook Simon's hand and saluted to her.

"See you on set," he said before he disappeared out the door.

Simon took the top off of his travel coffee mug and picked up the pot of coffee on the room service tray.

"I knew you'd have plenty of coffee for me, bless you. How's this shoot going, anyway?"

Oh thank goodness, he'd bought it. Anna did not want to deal with Simon questioning her about Ben and her love life and everything else this morning. She must have pulled off the business-breakfast pretense.

She filled Simon in on the shoot and let him rant about Aidan's sister's atrocious wedding color scheme as they drained the pot of coffee.

"Now, before we discuss both *Vigilantes* and our strategy for getting you that Varon film, one quick question: How long have you been sleeping with . . . Ben, is it?"

Anna panicked for a split second but recovered quickly.

"Simon, are you at the point where you think I'm sleeping with every attractive man? We're working together, remember? I don't do that."

Simon just smiled.

"I know you don't do that, which is why I'm certain there's a very good story to explain why you did it this time. And while I'd love to know it, you don't need to tell me. I mean, if it's really good, please tell me so I can leak it, but otherwise, I'll make sure the press knows you fell for him after you wrapped the shoot. Oh, you're an angel, this is going to be so good."

Anna stood all the way up.

"After? The press? Simon, what the hell are you talking about?"

The man actually rubbed his hands together.

"Anna! Wasn't this your plan all along? Don't you see? This is just what we need for your *Vigilantes* promo! This is our answer to the Varon film problem! The studio doesn't think you have enough star power to be a box office draw—the news of your secret relationship hitting the tabloids will show what a star you actually are! Everyone will be talking about you. All you need to do is keep this guy on a string—which won't be hard, given the way he looked at you when he walked out of the room—and we've got a few good weeks of stories, maybe even more. Just in time for you to get the role."

This definitely hadn't been her plan all along. She didn't want to drag Ben into all of this.

"Why not set me up with some actor slash fake boyfriend? Won't that make my profile way higher?"

Simon held up a finger.

"I've obviously been putting out feelers about that, but—"

"What? You have?"

Simon looked exasperated.

"Of course I have. But the only people available are either not high-profile enough for you, or they're assholes. And while I know you think I'd do anything for business, I'd never set you up with one of those guys."

She was weirdly touched by that.

"Thanks, I appreciate it," she said. "But if I can't date someone who isn't high-profile enough for me, why would you want me to date Ben, who isn't famous at all?"

Simon grinned.

"Oh, but true love gets headlines no matter what. Forbidden love? A secret relationship with an unknown? Especially one *that* attractive?" He closed his eyes. "Ahhh, the ways I'll be able to spin this are just incredible."

She needed to slow Simon down.

"Wait, but what if he doesn't—"

Simon opened his eyes.

"Don't worry—he obviously won't know it's fake! That's far too dangerous, civilians don't understand this stuff. Plus, what if he decided to make a little extra money and sell this story? That would be a nightmare. Just make him think you're going to keep this on-set fling going after you go back to L.A., that you care so much about him, you want to make it work, blah blah blah. You're a great actor—that's the easy part."

How was Simon starting to convince her of this? No, she couldn't do this to Ben.

"Simon, this seems like a terrible idea, for so many reasons. And you know I don't love talking about my personal life in the press."

He patted her on the shoulder.

"I know, but isn't that how we got into this predicament in the first place, where we need to get you extra press to pump up your box office draw? Remember: control the narrative. Eyes on the prize, Anna, and the prize is that Varon film, and I know how much you want it."

He was right about that. But there must be another way.

"I can't—"

"Don't worry," he said. "If you get bored by this guy—or if you're already getting bored—you won't have to string him along for more than a month or so. Hey, when does the shoot end?"

She definitely wasn't getting bored by Ben.

"The shoot ends tomorrow, if all goes well," she said. "Despite some delays, we're right on schedule. I'm supposed to go back to L.A. on Saturday night. But, Simon—"

"Excellent. Tomorrow night: bring him to the swanky rooftop bar here. I'll make sure a photographer is there to get snaps of you two looking cozy. Then get him to come down to visit you in L.A.—you can give him the ultimate Hollywood star kind of visit. You'll bring him along to the *Vigilantes* premiere; that'll get you a ton of buzz. You can get rid of him after that."

This would never work. Anna opened her mouth to tell Simon that, when he checked his watch and jumped up.

"I have to run. Remember, tomorrow night at the bar. We'll text about the timing. I'll arrange everything." He gave her a hug. "What a productive meeting this was. I'm so glad I was early."

He left in a flurry, with Anna staring speechless at the door.

Twelve

BEN SLOWLY GOT DRESSED THE NEXT MORNING BEFORE work. Would today be the last time he'd ever see Anna in person? Probably. Almost definitely, he was pretty sure.

She'd been weird yesterday. Not in the morning, not during and after their great suitcase caper through the streets of San Francisco. But afterward, when they'd both been at the shoot. He knew that obviously they couldn't let anyone know they were sleeping together—or *had* slept together? He wished he knew.

Probably the latter, because she'd barely looked at him all day. Before—before Palm Springs—they'd been friendly on set, laughing and joking around sometimes, or even just smiling at each other when something funny happened. Even after Palm Springs, even though Anna had kind of avoided him on set when she was around him, she'd treated him like nothing had ever happened between them, like they hadn't taken two long drives where they talked about their families and relationships and struggles—well, mostly she had, but still—and had a night and morning of fucking fantastic sex. That she'd been able to go back to treating him exactly the same as before had stung, even though he'd understood why she'd done it, and he'd tried—and, he'd thought, mostly succeeded—to treat her the same as he had before, too.

But the day before, he'd arrived on set expecting her to have a shared twinkle in her eye with him when they saw each other for the first time after the great suitcase adventure; but she'd barely even glanced at him when he'd walked into the room, and had gone right back to responding to whatever her hairstylist was saying. He'd tried to catch her eye a few times throughout the day, even though he knew he shouldn't, but nothing worked. Did she not want him to assume they'd see each other again—alone—before she went back to L.A.? If that was the case, fine, he was clear on where she stood, but did she really have to ice him out like this? Despite . . . everything, he'd thought they were friends.

He'd almost texted her when he got home the night before. He'd gone so far as to pull up her name on his phone. Their last texts had been the suitcase pictures that Maddie had taken in the hotel lobby—he and Theo both looked like they were desperately trying to keep straight faces, which was accurate, and you could just barely see the flash of Anna's yellow dress from the side of the suitcase where they'd left the zipper open a bit so she could breathe.

But he hadn't done it. Anna had so far made it very clear when she wanted him—he wouldn't push her.

When he got to the set, he told himself he wasn't going to look around for her, but he did it anyway. She was over at the coffee table, filling up her cup and laughing and chatting with the caterers. Why did she have to be so fucking nice to everyone? This would be much easier if she was an unfriendly nightmare like the actor in the last big ad campaign he'd worked on.

And why was she being so nice to everyone but him?

But just as he thought that, she looked around and saw him.

She smiled at him, that same smile that had made him drop his clipboard on that first day, and he smiled back. Of course he did. He walked straight over to her.

"Morning. Ready for the last day?"

What a stupid, boring, unoriginal thing to say to her.

She smiled back at him anyway.

"A little ready to go back to the sunny skies of L.A.—and to be back at my house, instead of a hotel room—but I'm sad it's the last day. We've had fun together, haven't we?"

She gestured to the room like she was talking about the whole crew and had a completely straight face, so he had no idea if she meant that in a universal "this shoot was so fun" kind of way, or if she meant that about her and him, specifically.

"Um. Yeah, we have," he said.

That time she grinned at him, and raised her eyebrows just a touch, and he grinned back. She took a step closer to him.

"Well, why don't we . . ."

Gene interrupted.

"Oh, Anna, great, you're ready. Can we test the lighting on you for a second? We had to make some adjustments today. Hi, Ben."

Ben held back a sigh. He even managed to smile.

"Hey, Gene."

What had Anna been about to say? "Well, why don't we . . ." What? "Sneak off to the bathroom for sex?" "Go back to your place again tonight?" "Never see each other again after we leave the set today?" It could have been anything!

But instead of grilling her about that, he stepped to the side, while she walked off with Gene, and poured himself a cup of coffee. Not that he needed it now—that tiny interaction with Anna had him wide awake.

He stood out of everyone's way as they tested the lighting and got everything ready for the final day. His role for the day was mostly a silent one—he and Gene had worked together so closely throughout all of this he knew he didn't really have to be there, but there was no way he would have missed the last day.

He scrolled through his phone as he stood there and watched, not really paying attention. Until he saw the email from Dawn.

To: Ben Stephens
From: Dawn Stephens
Re: Just checking in

Hey Ben! I'm going to be in SF next weekend for a friend's baby shower, and I was wondering if you wanted to meet up? I'd love to finally get to meet you and chat in person instead of over email! Totally understand if you're busy; just let me know if it works with your schedule.

xo
Dawn

He and Dawn had emailed back and forth a few times since that email he'd sent her over the weekend. Nothing major, just stuff about their families and what their lives were like, though he still hadn't told her about Theo, nor had he told Theo about her. He was going to tell Theo. He just hadn't found the right time.

He'd gotten used to emailing with her. Then why was it such a jolt for her to suggest meeting up?

He slid his phone back into his pocket. He'd think about how to deal with Dawn later. Now he needed to concentrate on the end of the shoot.

Actually, he should set up a date for tonight. Anna was leaving, the shoot would be over, he needed to get his life back. He hadn't been on an actual date in weeks! Well, that would end today.

Just as he pulled his phone out of his pocket to start swiping, a text popped up. From Anna.

> How about we celebrate the end of a successful shoot tonight? Want to meet me at the rooftop bar at my hotel?

He looked across the room at her, waiting in between takes, and she met his eyes and smiled. How had she read his mind like that? A . . . celebration with Anna was exactly what he needed tonight.

> Sounds good. What time?

Her reply didn't come until after the next take.

> 8? Text me when you get to the hotel and I'll meet you up at the bar

Okay, that gave him time to go home and change after they were done here. Depending on when they got out, he could maybe even get a haircut—he was overdue.

> See you then

He let himself grin. No one had to know it was about Anna, after all. This was why he loved dating—the anticipation was fun as hell. Who cared what happened after tomorrow? He couldn't fucking wait for tonight.

———

Anna paced around her hotel suite. It was seven thirty and she was completely ready, thirty minutes before she had to meet Ben upstairs. She was usually ready early, but this was early even for her. She hadn't been able to help herself, though. She'd been on edge for hours.

Simon had only gotten more and more into this plan since he'd come up with it. Especially once he'd done some background searches on Ben. He'd texted her that morning.

> Former backup dancer? Volunteers with Big Brother?
> Oh Anna, you chose so well. I couldn't be more proud.
> Photographer is all set, he'll be there by 8:30.
>
> Oh, and I heard from Varon—she wants to meet with you in a few weeks, "just to chat" about the film. You're so close, I think our plan just might put you over the edge.

That last text had finally convinced her—even though, as far as Simon was concerned, the plan had been in place as soon as he'd left her hotel room the day before.

She wanted that Varon film. After the last few years, she needed this win. She still had no idea what her part would be like in *Vigilantes*—despite all of the last-minute press she was doing for it, that movie might do absolutely nothing to raise her profile, or bring her closer to this role. The role she knew—*she knew*—would shoot her up into the stratosphere. She was tired of sitting back and waiting for good things to come to her; she wanted to take charge of her career again. She wanted the Varon film more than she'd wanted anything in years, and if this stunt was how to get it, then fine. She'd do it.

She'd make sure the pictures from tonight were fantastic, the tabloids would love it, and that studio would see just how much publicity Anna Gardiner could get when she wanted to.

Plus, it meant she'd get to keep hanging out with Ben, and that would be lots of fun. And he'd love this—why was she worrying about it so much? Only good things were in this for him! They would have a ton of fun for a month or so, and he'd made it clear he was the kind of guy who dated around a lot, so he'd be fine when it was over. Win-win.

Finally, it was 7:50. Time to leave her suite and head up to the bar. She wanted to get there before Ben, anyway, to make sure they had the best seat for her purposes. Granted, knowing Simon, he'd already called ahead to the bar and reserved the perfect location for her—and another for the photographer—but she wanted to be early, just in case. And Ben was always five minutes late, so even if the hotel elevators were slow, she'd still get to the bar well before him.

But when she got off the elevator on the top floor, she saw a familiar back walking away from the elevator bank.

"Ben?"

He turned around and smiled at her. He had on jeans and a gray button-down shirt, and . . . had he gotten a haircut?

"Hi." He smiled at her and brushed his hand over his head. Yes, he'd gotten a haircut. "Um, you look great."

She flashed a smile at him as they walked together toward the bar.

"Thanks." She looked him up and down and winked at him. "So do you."

He laughed and his grin got bigger.

"Always."

She felt very smug as they walked down the hallway together. They would look great together in these photos—she'd flirt like hell with him and make him grin at her like that; she'd make sure her best smile was on high wattage the entire time; the photographer would have many great options to choose from.

The hallway was decorated with pictures of the California landscape, and he pointed out one ahead of them.

"Aren't those the windmills on the way out of Palm Springs? Oh hey, speaking of, how's your dad? Are you going to get to see your parents before you go back to L.A.?"

Those were the windmills on the way out of Palm Springs. The city Ben had driven her to, just because she was terrified, and he could tell. Where he'd soothed her and comforted her, even before anything had happened between the two of them.

Ben had been nothing but kind to her, and this was how she was going to repay him? With deceit, throwing his life into chaos for a month or so, and then just dropping him?

And, oh God, what would this do to his job? This could be a disaster for him. Why hadn't she thought about that until now?

Fuck.

She knew why she hadn't thought about that until now— because she'd carefully avoided letting herself think about it. And so many other things.

She stopped walking.

What the hell was she doing? She would be the world's biggest asshole if she tricked Ben into a very public and very fake relationship with her.

"My dad is doing well—Ben, wait." He turned to her, but she couldn't even look at him. "Hold on. I need to . . ."

She couldn't do this to him.

They were almost at the bar. She couldn't go in there with him. The photographer might already be there. She turned around.

"Come to my suite instead of the bar?" She gave Ben a big smile.

She couldn't let him know what she'd almost done. "I changed my mind, I'd rather hang out there. Are you hungry? We can get room service! Some champagne, to celebrate the end of the shoot?"

Ben looked confused, but he turned around immediately.

"Sure, that works for me."

They walked back toward the elevator. Anna walked faster and faster, convinced that, at any moment, the photographer might come walking down the hall and see them and pull out his camera.

But thank God, they got in the elevator without anyone recognizing her.

Anna didn't look at Ben on the ride back downstairs—she just wanted to not be in public and to be back in her room where she could forget she'd ever thought this idea was good and order some snacks and have sex with Ben one last time and then go back to L.A. and make up a story to tell Simon about why his plan hadn't worked out.

When the doors opened, she swept out of the elevator and walked as fast as she could to her suite at the end of the hall. She pulled her key card out of her bag and opened the door.

"Okay, great!" She picked up the phone as soon as they got inside. "What do you want to eat? Charcuterie plate? Cheese plate? They have great wings here, too!"

Ben hardly even looked at the room service menu she thrust in front of his face.

"All of that sounds good," he said.

She nodded.

"Great. Great." She pressed a button on the phone. "Hi! Can I get the cheese plate, the charcuterie plate, and an order of the wings? And champagne! Yes, yes, the Moët is fine, great. Two glasses, two plates. Thank you!"

Okay. They had champagne coming, now she could just relax

and have a nice night with Ben here in her suite and she would forget that she'd been about to trick him into a fake relationship with her.

She walked over to him and wrapped her arms around him.

"Hi. I'm glad I have you all to myself."

She pulled his head down to kiss him. He kissed her back but pulled away after a little while.

"Anna. What's wrong?"

She took a step back.

"Nothing's wrong. Why do you think something is wrong?"

He narrowed his eyes at her.

"You wanted to come back to the room pretty fast, you know. And you seemed weird in the elevator. What is it?"

She reached for his shirt.

"I realized I'd rather be alone with you. I'm heading back to L.A. tomorrow night and this is our last night together." She slipped first one button open, then another. "I just couldn't keep my hands off you anymore."

He leaned down to kiss her. *See, there we go.* That was always the way to distract a man—tell them you couldn't wait to get into their pants.

But then he pulled away again.

"So the thing is, I know when a woman invites me back to her hotel room because she can't stand another minute without pulling my clothes off, and whatever happened in that hallway up there was not that. I know we don't know each other all that well, but give me a little credit. You don't have to tell me what's wrong if you don't want to, but don't lie to me."

Anna dropped her hands to her sides.

Ben stood there and looked at her. He just waited.

Damn it. Ben was so easygoing, so charming, that she kept forgetting how well he understood her.

She cleared her throat and let out a breath.

"Okay. Okay, um . . . Can we sit down?"

Ben sat down on one of the couches, and Anna sat next to him. She tried to figure out how to say this.

After a minute of silence, Ben turned to her.

"I can just go. If that's what you want. It's okay. I get it."

She shook her head hard. She suddenly knew that was the last thing she wanted.

"No. No, please don't go. I just . . . I was trying to figure out how to say this but I think I just have to dive in. You know how my manager came in the other day? When we were having breakfast here?" Ben nodded. "Right, okay, so. Well, he knows me pretty well, and he figured out there was something going on between the two of us."

Ben raised his eyebrows.

"And . . . he was upset about it?"

This story wasn't going to make sense to Ben, was it?

"No, to the contrary. He thought it was great. He . . . actually he wanted me to let the world think you were my boyfriend. To get more publicity for me and my career and have people wanting to know what was next for me, and that it would get me the role I'm in the running for. The one I told you about, the one I really want. "

Ben turned his whole body to look at her, his eyes all scrunched up in that way they did when he was trying to understand.

"Wait, say that again? Explain how I come into this?"

Anna let out a breath. At least she'd started.

"You know how we talked the other day about that movie I want, the Liz Varon movie? And how the studio is the holdup?" Ben nodded. "Okay. Simon thinks if I get some good headlines it will help me get it, and that stories about me and my hot new boyfriend will be just what I need."

He grinned when she called him hot, thank goodness. Flattery was always a good idea.

"Please thank Simon for me," he said. "But . . . were you going to . . ."

The flattery wasn't enough for him to miss that key point, though. She might as well confess everything.

"No. I wasn't going to tell you," she said. "Simon arranged for a photographer to be up in the bar tonight to get some pictures of us together, and then the plan was to get you to come to L.A. to visit me next weekend and let you think it was just because I wanted you to be my boyfriend and we could be out in public together some, even come to the *Vigilantes* premiere with me, and we thought that might be enough to be the career boost I need."

Ben didn't say anything.

She almost told him why she hadn't planned to tell him the truth—that Simon thought he might sell the story, or blackmail her, or something. But if she said that, Ben would think she didn't trust him. And she suddenly realized what she should have realized before: she trusted him completely.

She kept talking.

"But when we were walking down the hall upstairs I realized I couldn't deceive you that way, especially after everything you've done for me, and because . . . I guess because I like you, and the idea of lying to you about this for weeks made me feel like an enormous asshole. So that's what was wrong up there, that's why I turned around and made you come back to the suite—"

"That's why you were almost running back to the elevator, because you didn't want the photographer to catch us?"

He'd noticed that part, too.

"Yeah."

Ben nodded slowly. He didn't say anything for a long moment.

Anna expected him to get up and walk out the door. Instead, a grin spread across his face.

"So your only problem with doing this was deceiving me? Okay. Now I'm in on it. Let's do it."

Anna sat back on the couch and stared at him.

"What? Are you . . . really?"

Ben's grin got wider.

"You want a pretend boyfriend for a month? I can be your pretend boyfriend for a month. I don't have anything to do next weekend; I'll come to L.A. This sounds like a blast." He stood up. "Let's go back upstairs and make sure that photographer sees us."

Anna didn't move.

"Wait. Ben. Don't you want to think about this? I didn't expect . . . I didn't expect you to want to do this. Won't this fuck stuff up for you at work?"

He thought about that for a second.

"Good point. I'll talk to my boss—as long as I tell her in advance, it'll be okay. Plus, the client is thrilled about how well this ad campaign went, which means everyone in the office is thrilled with *me*. I might have to fudge the time line a little, but it'll work out. See, there we go, problem solved."

The doorbell chimed.

"Room service!"

Damn it. She'd forgotten about room service. She went to the door to let them in.

"Shall I open the champagne, Ms. Gardiner?" the waiter asked as he set up the food on the coffee table.

Anna looked at Ben, who shook his head. Maybe he'd reconsidered already.

"No, thanks," she said. She scribbled her signature on the bill and added a hefty tip. By the time the door closed behind the

waiter, though, Ben had already picked up the bottle and was pulling off the foil top.

"Room service is great, but why let someone else have the fun
of opening a bottle of champagne?" he asked. He popped the bottle and then filled two glasses.

"How about it, Ms. Gardiner?" Ben handed her a glass. "Do
we have a deal?"

If he wanted to do this, who was she to argue?

"We have a deal, Mr. Stephens." They looked into each other's
eyes as they clinked glasses.

Ben took a long sip and then buttoned up his shirt.

"Can we still make it for that photographer? I don't want to
spoil Simon's plan."

Anna laughed and checked her watch. Incredibly, it was barely
eight thirty.

"We can still make it. But we can also wait to do that part
later, now that I'm not trapping you into this."

Ben shook his head.

"No time like the present, like my mom always says. How do
I look? Am I wrinkled?"

She grinned as she looked him over. She was in a much better
mood about doing this now.

"You look perfect."

He took her arm and stopped right before they opened the
door.

"Wait. One quick question. If the answer to this is no, I won't
change my mind, just so you know—I just want to temper my
expectations. But . . . do we still get to have sex?"

Anna laughed out loud.

"God yes. As long as that's okay with you?"

Ben backed her up against the door and kissed her hard.

"What do you think?"

Anna breathed him in, let her hands trace over his arms and chest. She kissed his collarbone, his cheek, his lips. Damn, being with him felt so good.

"I think I don't want to go back upstairs."

Ben kissed her again, then backed away.

"Oh no, Ms. Gardiner, you're not getting out of this that quickly. Let's go."

He opened the door with a flourish, and she grinned at him as she stepped into the hallway.

Thirteen

BY THE TIME THEY MADE IT TO THE BAR, IT WAS EIGHT FORTY-
five. Someone immediately set drinks in front of them as soon as
they slid into their booth.

"Did you call and order drinks ahead for us?" Ben asked as he
picked up the pint of beer the waiter had given him.

Anna rolled her eyes and took a sip of her pastel-colored
cocktail.

"No. This has Simon's fingerprints all over it. I'm sorry he decided what you should be drinking tonight. I promise, that's not
how the rest of the night is going to go." She stopped for a second
and then grinned at him. "Well. Not most of it, anyway."

Ben looked at her over his glass. He'd been pissed at first,
when she'd told him why he was really there that night. That
she'd only asked him out to trick him into getting photographed
with her, and then trick him into dating her, and it was all to benefit her career. He was still kind of pissed, actually, even though
he'd agreed to do this. He hadn't lied to her when he'd said that it
sounded like a blast—it did, especially since he'd get to keep
sleeping with Anna the whole time. Was he glad that he had a

built-in excuse to be away from the Bay Area next weekend? Yes, fine. Was he fucking thrilled to get to keep sleeping with Anna? Absolutely. So, sure, he'd do whatever playacting Anna wanted him to do. Why not?

He looked across the table at her. God, she was beautiful. She almost shone, sitting there across from him, taking tiny sips of her pale purple drink. She smiled that glittering smile at him, not the way she did when it was just the two of them, but the way she'd only smiled at him a few times—that first day on set, and then the day before, when she'd . . . Wait a minute.

"Is the photographer here?" he asked her as he lifted his beer in front of his mouth.

Her expression barely changed, but her eyes did. They looked—surprised? Impressed?

"How did you know?" she asked.

He reached across the table and took her hand. If they were going to do this, they might as well do it.

"That look you just gave me. I just realized you're acting when you do that."

She held on to his fingers and rubbed the back of his hand with her thumb. He wondered if she'd be anxious now, because of what she'd gone through before with the press and everything else, but she seemed as relaxed and confident as he'd ever seen her.

"When I do what?" She raised one eyebrow at him, and he raised one right back at her.

"When you do that Helen of Troy smiling thing."

She laughed out loud. She tossed her hair out of her face and smiled at him like she had in the hotel room, that morning in Palm Springs. Did she know how sexy she was?

"This is so much more fun with you in on it," she said.

Yeah. She knew. He played with her fingers and shook his head.

"You're a nightmare, you know that?" he said to her. "You and your movie star-smiles and sexy little hair tosses and that sway you put in your hips when you know I'm watching you."

She laughed at him again, their fingers still intertwined.

"Oh, I'm the nightmare? Excuse me—who, exactly, was the person who sweet-talked us into a room at a sold-out hotel just last week by flirting his head off with the clerk, and making sure she knew immediately the woman he was there with was his sister? Because that was one of us at this table, and I'm pretty sure it wasn't me."

Ben grinned at the memory. It had gotten them what they needed, hadn't it?

He raised her hand to his lips and kissed it as he looked her in the eye.

"We seem to be well matched, then."

He could tell by her wide eyes and closed lips she was doing everything possible not to laugh.

"Well played for the camera. You're such an asshole. Do you practice these things?" she asked.

He shook his head.

"I think I've just always known." He lowered his voice. It was time to get her back a little. "Just like I've always known that you like it when I pull your hair when I kiss you. Just a little. Just enough to make you tingle."

She swallowed. He let his grin widen.

"I do like that," she said. "In the same way you like it when I climb on top of you, and you're at my mercy."

Oh, she was going to try this, too, huh?

"Mmm, that's because it gives me better access to those incredible breasts of yours," he said. "I know you love it when I bite your nipples, especially afterward, when I lick them to make them better." God, he loved the look on her face right now. "And thank God you love it, because I really fucking love doing it." She was breathing heavily now, and he could see her chest rising and fall-ing. "Did you wear that dress tonight because you knew I wouldn't be able to help myself from staring at your cleavage?"

She nodded.

"I did. Did you wear those jeans tonight because you knew I would spend the whole time we were in here thinking about your ass?"

He had, as a matter of fact.

"Hey, I saw the way you looked at me the other day when we were in my apartment. A man's got to do what he can to get ahead. All's fair in love and war, isn't that the saying?"

He couldn't believe his luck. He'd just signed on for a month of sex with Anna, for the cost of, what, a few magazine pictures? And it got him out of town right when he wanted to be unavail-able. Perfect.

"I like it when you look at me like that," Anna said.

He let his eyebrows go up again.

"Like what?" he asked, even though he knew what she was talking about.

"Like you want to tear my clothes off with your teeth," she said.

Ben bit his bottom lip and let his fingers trace patterns over hers.

"More like I want to crawl under the table and slide my tongue into your pussy," he said. She shivered. He felt triumphant.

"Finish that beer, asshole, and as soon as we get back to my suite, I'm going to hold you to that."

They left the bar thirty minutes later, after Ben pulled all the cash he had out of his wallet and threw it on the table. Anna shook her head at him as they walked back to the elevator for the second time that night.

"You didn't have to do that—everything is charged to the room."

Ben shook his head.

"I did indeed have to do that—there was a photographer there! No one will ever be able to imply I was a bad tipper."

He took her hand on the way to the elevator. Holding hands with Anna felt exciting, illicit. He'd never before been able to touch Anna in public, and now he could, and it was all because of a big joke they were playing on the rest of the world. This was going to be so much fun.

They didn't talk on the elevator back to her room. They barely looked at each other. But he could feel the electricity running through and around and between them. It was so tangible, he could almost feel his hair crackle.

They got off the elevator and walked down the hall to her room, still hand in hand. She walked differently when she was public Anna—he noticed that after they got back from Palm Springs. She stood taller, her shoulders more proud, her head high. At other times, she was more relaxed, softer, warmer. He found both sides of her impossibly sexy.

She opened the door to her suite, and as soon as they got inside, she grabbed him by the shirt and pulled him toward her. He felt a button snap off of his shirt. He fucking loved it.

He backed her up against the wall and kissed her hard. She reached for his remaining buttons.

"You turned me on so fucking much up there," she said as soon as he moved his mouth from her lips to her neck.

"I know," he said. He pushed the V of her dress to the side and brushed the tip of her nipple with his thumb. He could feel her tremble.

"I liked it," she said.

He pulled her bra out of the way and touched his tongue to her nipple.

"I know," he said.

She grabbed his hand and guided it to the inside of her thigh.

"You made me so wet," she said.

He dropped to his knees and grabbed her underwear with both hands. With one twist, the thin lace fell off of her body. He didn't apologize.

"I couldn't wait," he said. And then he slid his tongue inside her. He licked and sucked and bit and hummed until she writhed above him. And then he slid a finger inside her and sucked harder until she gasped and collapsed to the floor, bringing him along with her.

They lay there panting together for a while, until she turned and grinned at him.

"Are you always this good at fulfilling your promises?" she asked.

He traced his finger from the hollow of her breasts to her collarbone to her cheek.

"Always," he said.

Eventually, they made it to the bed. Anna pulled off his clothes on the way, and then laughed when he picked her up and tossed her on the huge bed. He crawled on top of her and stared down at her body. She loved the way he looked at her, like he couldn't get enough, like he was planning how to touch her next, like he was thrilled to be around her.

Luckily, that was also how she felt when she looked at him.

She pulled him down and kissed him. They kissed slowly, their hands roaming, exploring, their bodies intertwined. They had plenty of space, plenty of time to do whatever they wanted. And all they wanted was each other.

Hours later, Ben got up and wheeled the room service cart into the bedroom, and they finally ate the food she'd ordered in a panic hours before. She ordered more wings, and another bottle of champagne and they feasted, naked in bed, laughing the whole time.

Finally, they fell asleep together, sated in all of the best ways.

When she woke up the next morning, Ben was already awake, already smiling at her.

"Good morning," he said.

She kissed him softly. Had last night really happened? It must have, because he was here. She'd worried last night that she'd regret telling him everything, but this morning, here in bed with Ben, she couldn't regret a thing.

She put a finger on his biceps and traced the outlines of his tattoo.

"Whose initials are these?" she asked.

He laughed.

"My mom's. I got it in my early twenties—she was so mad at me. It took her, like, a year to forgive me. But apparently now she brags about it to my aunts, which I only found out because my cousin told me. So you never know about parents, do you?"

She lay back on her pillows and smiled.

"You really never know. When I was a kid, I never felt like I could talk to my dad about anything—he was so strict, he only grudgingly allowed me to be in school plays and stuff because my mom didn't give him the opportunity to say no, and now he's my biggest fan." She opened her eyes all the way. "Speaking of, what time is it? I have to pack and get out of here and be at my parents' house for lunch—I'm flying back to L.A. tonight, but I'm going to have lunch with them and my brother first."

Ben looked over at the bedside clock.

"It's only eight, you have plenty of time." He turned back to her. "But before you start getting ready—what happens next? With the pictures from last night, and this whole thing?"

She was glad he'd asked that.

"The pictures will probably come out sometime over the next few days—maybe as early as tomorrow. Oh, that reminds me: today—right now, if you can—you need to lock down your social media as tightly as possible. They'll find you, trust me. Make everything private, make any profile pictures of like, a tree or something, not you."

Ben nodded.

"Okay, I'll do that right away. And as soon as I get home, I'll call my boss."

Thank goodness he'd be able to warn his boss.

"Right, perfect. My people will handle all of the press—I'll send you everyone's number so you have it, and they'll all have your contact info. If you get any calls, or anyone recognizes you and stops you to ask about me, be friendly, say something meaningless—we'll get you some easy talking points—and don't answer any questions."

He nodded.

"I can do that."

"You'll come down to L.A. next weekend," Anna continued. "I'll get my assistant to book your tickets." He opened his mouth, but she put a finger on his lips. "Please don't fight me on that—I really don't want you to put yourself out for this whole thing."

He bit his lip. Damn, it was sexy when he did that. Especially when he wasn't even trying to be sexy.

"Okay, but can this be an ongoing conversation? I didn't agree to do this for you to spend money on me."

She knew that. It was probably a lot of the reason they were even doing this in the first place.

"You can pick up the bill wherever we go out to dinner next weekend—does that work?" She didn't wait for his response. "I haven't figured out the details for next weekend yet—I'll keep you updated about that. And I'll tell you if you need to pack anything special."

He laughed.

"Please do. I'll have to get Maddie working on my wardrobe."

Good idea. Ben dressed fine, but he might need some help to be camera-ready.

"So, that brings up something else," he said, his smile fading. "Can I tell my brother—and Maddie—the truth about all of this? Or . . ."

She could tell he wasn't going to like this answer.

"I'd rather you didn't. It's not that I don't trust your brother and Maddie—I mean obviously I trusted them the other day—but if people are going to ask them questions about you, and about us, it's probably better that their answers are genuine."

He didn't look happy but didn't argue with her.

She slid her hand up his face and cupped his cheek.

"Thanks. For doing all of this for me. I know it probably seems ridiculous, but I really need a win here, and this might get me there."

He kissed her.

"My pleasure." He moved his hand from her hip to her waist and then up, until his thumb brushed back and forth over her nipple. "I mean that quite literally."

She reached for him.

"I know you do."

Fourteen

ANNA WOKE UP IN HER OWN BED THE NEXT MORNING, BLISS-
fully sore from her very athletic activities with Ben the day before. She had a million things to do now that she was back home
in L.A.—unpack, update Simon about the Ben thing, check in
with her stylist about what to wear to all of her upcoming events,
therapy, and, ugh, an appointment with her trainer later that day.
But even that last thing couldn't dampen her enthusiasm for all
of this, because the reason for everything on her to-do list, the
reason she'd made this whole plan in the first place, was the Varon film. It felt so close that she could taste it.

But first, she needed coffee.

She went downstairs to the kitchen, took the fresh container
of oat milk out of her fridge, and poured hot coffee into her mug.
God bless her assistant—she'd known without even having to
check that Florence would program her coffee maker to brew at
eight a.m.

She sank down on the couch to drink her coffee and scrolled
through her text messages. She grinned when she got to Ben's:

I'm sore today in more locations than I can count, thanks to you

She grinned and texted him back.

Thanks to me??? Who started it?

The answer to that was debatable, she realized. Not that she'd let Ben know that.

As she kept scrolling her phone rang.

"You call yourself a best friend?" Penny said when she picked up the phone. "I cannot believe that you told the press about your new boyfriend before you told me."

That meant that (1) the pictures must be out, and (2) she'd forgotten to let Penny in on all of this, what with . . . everything that happened after she and Ben got back from the bar.

"Right, sorry. About that."

"See? See! I knew there would be an 'about that.' There's always an 'about that' with you!"

Anna took a gulp of coffee to sustain herself through Penny's rants.

"I know, I know. But this time . . . So the Ben thing isn't . . . quite . . . what the tabloids are probably saying. See, what Simon and I decided . . ."

Penny groaned. She wasn't a huge fan of Simon, even though she acknowledged he was good for Anna's career.

"This had better be good."

Anna got up to get more coffee.

"It's not just good. It's great. See, I have a plan."

"You? A plan? No, seriously?" Penny said. "Well, I never."

Anna couldn't help but laugh.

"No, but really, listen."

When Anna finished explaining the whys and wherefores of the plan, there was a long silence.

"Why this role? Why are you doing all of this—a fake boyfriend, dancing around for the tabloids—who you hate—all of that—for this movie? You get movies and TV shows thrown at you all the time, you could shout from your house that you wanted a new starring role and scripts would come flying down your chimney. Why do you care so much about this one?"

Anna stopped to think about how to explain that.

"I don't want just any role anymore. I want . . . I want to show the world what I can do. And I guess I want to show myself that, too. I want roles that can make me better. And damn it, I want to get back to the Oscars, and I want to win this time. And this movie, this role, with this director . . . I think it can do everything I want."

Penny was silent for a while again.

"Then, if that's what you want, let's make sure you get it," she finally said. "Also, I forgive you for not calling me, but that is if and only if I get to meet this Ben."

Anna laughed.

"P, we aren't really dating, I just told you."

"Oh, I know," Penny said. "But I saw the way he looked at you in those pictures, and the way you looked back at him, and I need to see if this guy is as hot in person as he was in the photos."

Anna thought about what Ben had been saying to her in the bar when those pictures were taken and felt her cheeks get warm.

"Hotter," she said.

She and Penny giggled like teenagers.

Ben walked into his therapist's office on Wednesday evening and dropped down into a chair.

"Dr. Lindsey, hello!"

He'd been so busy at work today that he hadn't figured out what he was going to talk about in therapy. He hadn't told Dr. Lindsey anything about Anna, and he didn't intend to. Once he started, he'd have to explain the whole damn thing, and she would absolutely say something to him in her very dry way about it, something that sounded like a normal bland comment, and then he'd wake up in the middle of the night and realize what she actually meant.

And he hadn't told her about Dawn, either. He kept meaning to, every session. But it felt like it would be a long and difficult conversation, with lots of "What do you think you should do?" and "How did you feel about that?" and "Did this bring up any feelings about your father?" and he didn't want to think about any of that, much less talk about it.

No, he'd talk about work—how Roger had congratulated him for his work on the phone ad campaign, that he finally might get to work on a campaign for his favorite sneaker brand; maybe he could throw her a bone and mention that Theo and Maddie might get engaged soon, so she could do her whole "How does that make you feel?" thing about that, et cetera.

"Ben." She nodded at him, a faint smile on her face. He always tried to make her laugh, but it was almost impossible. He'd only accomplished it three times in the three and a half years he'd been seeing her, but those three times were like gold.

"How are you doing this week?" she asked him.

He nodded quickly.

"Oh, good, good. It's been a good week—really busy, but good." He'd said "good" three . . . no, four times. He should just keep talking so she didn't notice. "Work, especially—last week we wrapped up the shoot of that big ad campaign I led, and everyone was really pleased at how it turned out. The proof will be when the commercials and ads all come out, of course, but I'm keeping my fingers crossed for that."

She nodded in her slow way. He could never tell if it was a positive nod or a negative one.

"Tell me about it."

So he did. At length.

". . . and you should have seen him—this six-foot-three, 250-pound guy jump up on a table and scream because he saw a mouse; we were all dying laughing!" He hoped he'd get a laugh from that story, but it was just that faint smile again.

"Ben, quick question for you—you've spent twenty minutes telling me about the shoot and everyone involved. Is there a reason you haven't told me that you're in a relationship with Anna Gardiner? Who, as you told me awhile ago, was the talent for this campaign, though you haven't mentioned that today?"

Oh. Oh shit. How did Dr. Lindsey know about that?

"The pictures are everywhere, you know," she said in answer to his unspoken question. "I do have the internet."

Of course she did. But he'd never thought of Dr. Lindsey doing things like actually using it.

"Right. Um, it's just because . . . I guess I was working up to it."

She nodded. This nod seemed imbued with disappointment.

"I see. I wasn't rushing you. Feel free to tell me on your own time. I was just curious."

He rushed to fill the silence.

"The thing is . . . about Anna. I mean, about me and Anna. It's not exactly true."

Shit. Why had he told her that? He hadn't meant to tell her that. He hadn't meant to tell her about any of this!

She raised an eyebrow at him.

"What do you mean, 'not exactly true'?"

Shit. Now he had to tell her the rest of it. Well, some of it.

"It's just that we—I mean she—I mean it's sort of a publicity thing for her. She needed a date to a thing coming up, and I guess her manager thought she needed a boyfriend for some good press, and since we had already, I mean since we became friendly while she was working the ad campaign, we thought, he thought, and she agreed, and I thought it sounded like fun, so anyway . . ." He made himself stop talking. Maybe they could just gossip about what an adventure this would be for a little while and then his session would be over.

"You said 'since we already . . .'—since you already what?"

Why did she always manage to pick up on the smallest things?

He let out a sigh and gave up.

"Since we'd already slept together. A few times. It started almost two weeks ago, when I drove her to Palm Springs."

And then the whole story spilled out. He didn't tell her the part about Anna's anxiety attacks, but he told her everything else.

"You and your brother carried her in a suitcase?" She laughed out loud. Laugh number four! And he hadn't even tried this time! "I can't believe she agreed to that."

Ben grinned.

"She loved it. We all laughed so hard about it. And it was right after that when I accidentally met her manager."

Dr. Lindsey looked at him for a moment.

"So Anna met your brother. Did you tell him the truth about all of this?"

Of course she'd asked him that. The one thing about all of this that he felt bad about.

"No. Anna didn't want . . . she asked me not to. Just so if the press asked him anything, his responses would sound real."

Theo had called him when the photos had come out—Maddie

had seen them right away, of course. They'd both been so happy for him. He'd hated lying to them.

"Anyway, it's only for a month or so. No big deal. It just sounded like fun to me. And Anna's great. So. That's all."

She was still silent. He didn't know what she was thinking.

"When I saw those pictures, I'd hoped . . ." She stopped and started again. "Have you given any more thought to what I said a few weeks ago? About how you might need to work on your ability to have permanent relationships, just in general? Because this seems like a venture in the opposite direction."

Ben looked out the window. Just the stupid sky. Why wasn't there anything interesting to see out her window?

"I know you think there's something wrong with me, because I like dating around and don't want to settle down, and that's all about my dad or whatever. But I just haven't found anyone I care enough about, that's all. And how could I turn down this offer from Anna? Not everything is about my fear of being abandoned or abandoning other people or whatever you want to call it."

Dr. Lindsey shook her head and smiled at him.

"I've never called it that, Ben. And I don't think anything is wrong with you. You know that's not what this is about. But attaching yourself to someone you think of as unattainable seems like . . . a particular kind of choice, don't you think? At least I'm glad that Anna is in on it, and doesn't think the string of dates you take her on is a relationship."

"Hey!" he said. "I'm up front with people about just wanting something casual."

She sighed.

"I know you are, but—"

"Yes, fine, a handful of them have thought we *were* in a relationship, but I think that's all due to my natural magnetism," he said.

That didn't even make her smile, but then, this time he hadn't expected it to.

"But isn't this better?" he asked her. "No one is expecting anything different from me this time! Actually, Anna almost tried to trick me into being in those photos and coming down to visit her in L.A.—her manager didn't want me to know it was all fake, but Anna felt bad, so she let me in on it. I was kind of pissed about that at first, actually."

Dr. Lindsey raised an eyebrow.

"Did you tell Anna you were pissed?" she asked.

Oh God, he shouldn't have said that.

"It wasn't a big deal," he said. "Plus, it wouldn't have accomplished anything."

He'd gotten his tiny revenge on Anna at the bar, which had led to really hot sex later—it had been fine.

Dr. Lindsey massaged the side of her neck.

"The accomplishment there would have been yours. It can be valuable to share your emotions, good and bad, with people. Not to change their behavior, but for you to tell them how you feel. And to acknowledge your feelings to yourself."

What was even the point of that?

"It doesn't matter—Anna and I won't be doing this for that long; there was no need for all of that."

Dr. Lindsey opened her mouth and then closed it. She took a deep breath before she finally said something.

"Ben. What are you so afraid of happening? If you're honest with someone about your feelings? If you stay with a woman long enough to get attached to her?"

She always said stuff like this and he didn't understand why. Why was she making this small thing into such a big one?

"I'm not afraid of anything! It's just easier this way. More fun. I do get attached to people, you know that. But—"

Her buzzer rang.

"My next client must be downstairs. But, Ben, I want you to think about what I said. And what I asked you."

He picked up his messenger bag and stood up.

"Yeah, fine, I'll think about it."

He had no plans to actually think about anything from that session, though, other than how thrilled he was he hadn't accidentally let anything about Dawn slip out. He could only imagine what Dr. Lindsey would have to say about that.

Fifteen

ON FRIDAY NIGHT, SIMON WAS WITH ANNA IN THE BACK SEAT of the limo on the way to the airport to pick up Ben. Simon had reacted . . . strongly, when she'd told him there had been a slight change in their plan.

It had all started out well when Simon had first called.

"The pictures looked fantastic, Anna! And I congratulate myself on a great job with the statement."

Simon had put out a very coy statement about how Anna wouldn't comment about her personal life but she was very happy, et cetera, et cetera. It had done exactly what they'd wanted it to do.

"Congratulations on a great job with the statement, Simon," she said.

"I know, I know, thank you. He's coming this weekend, yes? Like we planned?"

"He's coming this weekend, yes. Florence is getting him a ticket to arrive on Friday night."

Simon hummed in approval.

"Great, perfect, wonderful. And he has no clue this is all for show?"

Anna couldn't help but laugh.

"Oh no. He has every clue. I told him."

There was a long, ominous silence on the other end of the line.

"What do you mean, 'he has every clue'? What do you mean, you told him? Have you lost your mind?"

She should have expected him to react this way.

"I haven't lost my mind, I swear. I promise, it's fine. He gets it. He's savvy, he's amused by the whole thing, he was playing for the cameras when we were at the bar as much as I was." That was technically true, but only because she had the feeling that neither of them was performing—they were as intent on each other at the bar as those pictures looked. "Plus, this makes it easier. This way, I can make sure he does everything I want him to do, instead of just hoping he does."

Simon's voice got louder.

"Sure, you can make sure he does everything you want him to, until he spills his guts to the world for a fat check, or until he sells pictures of you to a tabloid, or until he blackmails you that he'll do one of those things unless you keep giving him money."

She should have known Simon would assume Ben would be an asshole. That was his job, after all.

"Ben won't do that. I know, that's what everyone thinks when they get caught up with someone like that. But he's proven himself in a few ways already, otherwise I wouldn't have even considered this. I'm not a babe in the woods here."

Ben knew so much about her after Palm Springs, and he'd kept his mouth shut. She wasn't worried that he'd change that now. Simon might think she was a fool for this, but she trusted Ben.

"Well, you're acting like it," Simon said. He sighed. "I don't mean to sound like an ass, but it's my job to protect you, both as your manager and as your friend. You've had a tough time in the past year or so, and I don't want some hot grifter to come into your life and fuck up all of the hard work you've been doing lately, that's all."

Anna figured that the only way for him to relax about this was to meet Ben. Therefore, the trip to the airport.

"I still can't believe . . ." he said, as they waited in the car.

"Simon. Give it a rest. He knows. It's done, it's been done. It'll be fine."

He grunted. "I'll be the judge of that."

A few seconds later, her phone buzzed.

Just landed—I'll be outside in a few minutes

She texted him back.

The driver is waiting for you at baggage claim. See you in the car

In a little while, the driver opened the back door with a flourish, and Ben slid into the car.

"Good evening." He smiled that slow, sexy smile at her, and she was suddenly very resentful that Simon was here in the limo with them. Ben sat next to her and leaned in for a kiss.

"Good evening, Ben," Simon said.

Ben stopped and turned to the other side of the car.

"Simon." He didn't visibly react, but Anna felt like a jerk for not warning Ben that Simon would be with her. She should have told him.

"Nice to meet you again," Ben said to Simon. "What a welcome mat this is."

Simon nodded briskly.

"Yes, right. Welcome to Los Angeles, et cetera." He checked that the opaque glass barrier between them and the driver was up and the intercom was off. Then he turned back to Ben. "I'm here because I want to be crystal clear that you understand all of this. As Anna may—or may not—have informed you, my original plan was slightly different. This is very important for Anna's career, and I want to make sure you understand the landscape, and your role here."

Ben's eyes narrowed slightly, but the pleasant expression on his face didn't change.

"Yes, Anna let me know that you thought the better way to go about this would be to trick me into it. I'm glad she disagreed." He sat back against the plush limo seat, somehow getting farther away from Anna in the process. "To be . . . clear, Simon—just because I have a pretty face doesn't mean I'm stupid. I know the drill. Anna and I are friends. I'm not going to embarrass her. She's told me exactly what she needs from me."

Simon sat forward, but Ben relaxed against his seat. He didn't look at Anna. She wished he would. She wished Simon would, too. She'd thought he just wanted to meet Ben for real this time, to reassure himself about him. She didn't think he'd start grilling him as soon as he got in the car.

"Guys, we don't have to—"

Simon ignored her.

"You know that as soon as the premiere is over, she's done with you, right?" Simon looked right at Ben. "If you try to do anything in an attempt to capitalize on this, I'm telling you now, it will not go well for you. Anna's had enough to deal with in the past few years—I don't want this—you—to make things harder on her than they need to be."

"Simon. That's enough," Anna said. "Ben's not the enemy here. He and I talked about all of this at length. Everything will be fine."

Ben didn't look at her but kept that same light, friendly, angry smile on his face.

"You heard her, Simon. Everything will be fine. I appreciate that Anna is your client, but I sure as hell don't work for you, so do me a favor and don't talk to me like I'm the help."

Anna tried to diffuse this again.

"Ben, he just wanted to—"

"This is very high stakes." Simon looked straight at Ben. "If you fuck any of this up, it'll be Anna who will pay the price. And this—all of this—is highly confidential." He pulled a sheaf of papers out of his bag. "Speaking of, here's an NDA that we'd like you to sign."

Simon hadn't told her he'd not only put together an NDA, but brought it tonight.

"Simon! Enough." Anna put her hand on Ben's knee. "He knows how important this is. He doesn't have to do that. Relax."

Ben didn't look at her, but took the papers from Simon.

"I'm happy to sign an NDA, Simon."

Simon handed him a pen with a very smug expression on his face.

"Excellent, I've flagged the pages where . . ."

Ben was still talking.

"Obviously, I'll need a lawyer to look at it first, so I'll get back to you later this week."

Anna bit her lip so she didn't laugh out loud. He was good.

They traveled the rest of the way to Simon's house in silence. After they dropped him off, she turned to Ben.

"I am so, so sorry about that. I just thought he wanted to go over the game plan, not give you the third degree."

Ben shrugged and tossed his arm around her.

"No big deal, don't worry about it. Now can I do what I've been thinking about ever since I got in this limo?"

He pulled her face to his and kissed her, hard and long. She gave herself over to that kiss. There was more that she'd wanted to say about Simon, and to make sure Ben wasn't upset, but she forgot everything other than what it felt like to kiss him, to touch him. God, she'd missed his touch.

"You've only been thinking about that since you got in the limo?" she asked, as they finally pulled away. "Because I've been thinking about this all week."

His hand slid up her thigh.

"Mmmm. One question: How long will it take us to get to your place?"

She tried to think, but she couldn't quite concentrate, not with his fingers pulling at her nipple in that way he knew she loved.

"About half an hour," she said.

He bent down to kiss her neck.

"Good," he said. "Now, tell me what you've been thinking about all week, and I'll tell you what I've been thinking about."

The look in his eye was that hot, insatiable look from the bar that night. But this time, no one was watching them.

"Well," she said, as she reached for his belt, "before you got in the limo, I was thinking that it's been almost a whole week, and I didn't know how I could survive being in here with you for the whole hour it would take to get back to my place."

He looked down at her fingers, which had already unzipped his jeans, and smiled.

"And what did you think we might do about that?"

He tugged her dress down and popped her nipple out of her bra. He squeezed it between his thumb and forefinger until she arched her back.

"I thought . . ." She wrapped her hand around his cock. It was already hard. "I thought that if you came as prepared this time as you did the other times, that we could take care of that right here in the car."

He reached down, flipped his messenger bag open, and pulled out a condom.

"If?" he asked, his eyes locked on hers. "Are you saying you doubted me?"

She tore the packet open and unrolled the condom over his cock.

"Not for a second." She straddled him in one fast move. She loved the surprised, aroused look on his face. He reached up under her dress and hooked his fingers around her thong.

"Tear it off," she said.

He took it with both hands and ripped. He dropped the pieces to the floor.

"Oh, you liked that last time, did you?" he asked.

"I liked that a lot," she said. "That's another thing I've been thinking about all week."

She leaned forward and kissed him hard. He tangled his fingers in her hair and pulled her toward him. They kissed as they jolted on the road, and she wanted him so bad she almost came just there.

"But I've been thinking about this part even more," she said. She lifted her hips and slid herself down, down, until he was deep inside her.

He looked at her with that intent look in his eyes, and it made her feel like she was going to catch on fire. She wanted it hard, and fast, and now, and she could tell from the way he looked at her and touched her that he did, too. So she rode him just like she'd fantasized about, and it was even better than she'd imagined, because he had his hands around her waist, clutching her, moving her up and down, his breath on her neck, his lips on her collarbone, his tongue on her nipples. And when he brushed her nipples with his teeth, she went faster and faster until he clutched her even harder and gasped into her chest, and then she arched her back and collapsed into his lap.

"What were you thinking about this week?" she said in his ear, after she finally slid off his lap and back onto the seat next to him. She picked up her torn underwear and put it in her purse.

He leaned in close to her.

"I was hoping," he said in her ear, "that you had some bacon around for breakfast tomorrow. I can do a breakfast sausage but, you know, it's not ideal."

She smacked him on the shoulder and they laughed together until they pulled up to her house.

After they had dinner, and another round of sex—longer and slower this time—they went outside to Anna's backyard with a bottle of wine. The sun had gone down, but it was still warm outside, with a cool breeze. Ben took a sip from the glass she poured him and looked out over the pool.

"Was everything okay at work?" Anna asked him. "I mean, about all of this."

Ben had been more nervous to talk to his boss about their "relationship" than he'd let on to Anna. Thank goodness, that conversation had gone well.

"Mostly fine—my boss was great about it when I told her, and thanked me for warning her in advance. No one else has really said anything." Roger had dropped by his office that week, and Ben had sort of expected him to bring it up, but he'd just congratulated Ben for the shoot—the client was thrilled with the results, and that it had come in under budget, even with the delays. Apparently, when a billion-dollar tech company wanted to give them more business because of Ben, no one at work cared what else he did, at work or at home. "Though some people have given me some looks like they're dying to ask me about you." He laughed. "I haven't encouraged them."

"Good." Anna smiled at him. She was sitting cross-legged next to him in that way she always did. Her hair was pulled up on top of her head, and her lips were still pink from how much he'd kissed her. He smiled back at her.

"So. What's the plan for tomorrow?" he asked her.

"Something super wholesome, I thought. Well, Simon and I thought. The farmers market."

He ignored the "Simon" part of that sentence. That fucking guy. If it hadn't been for Anna, he would have refused to have anything more to do with this whole thing, once Simon talked to him like that. He'd also been annoyed at Anna for blindsiding him with Simon in the limo when he'd thought he'd have her to himself. But he pushed that away.

"The farmers market! The perfect place for me—I just love to cook so much! You know how I feel about fresh fruit and vegetables, can't get enough of them!"

She pointed at him.

"You kid, but I want you to keep that energy for tomorrow. I want oohing and aahing over avocados and the most beautiful stone fruits of the season, you hear me?"

He saluted her.

"Aye, aye, Captain. Just tell me what a stone fruit is, and we're good."

So the next day, they got out of Anna's car near the Silver Lake Farmers Market. Ben had to laugh—though only internally, since he didn't want Anna to think, like Simon did, that he was making light of all of this—at how far they'd driven to get there, and how very long it had taken to find parking. What if all of the stone fruit was gone by the time they got there?

They got out of the car, and Anna looked him up and down.

"Thank Maddie for me, will you?" she asked. He felt a ridiculous glow of pride.

"Will do," he said. He slid his hand into hers. "Shall we?"

They walked toward the farmers market, hand in hand. Ben turned to Anna to ask her something, but before he could say anything, she jumped in.

"Remember, you're supposed to look besotted with me," she said, gazing up at him adoringly. It was wild how much her bossy, commanding tone didn't match the glowing smile on her face.

Ben didn't know why she felt the need to say that to him—besotted was the only possible way to look at Anna right now. She had on this light, flowing sundress that clung to her breasts, her hair was in soft curls past her shoulders, and he didn't know if it was just because he was here in L.A. or if she'd gotten more sun in the past week or what, but there was this . . . glow about her. He couldn't believe everyone around them didn't stop to stare.

"What if I just think about the way you woke me up this morning when I look at you?" he asked.

She lowered her lashes and then fluttered them—actually fluttered them!—at him, and he had to laugh.

"Excellent idea," she said. "Aren't you glad you're staying until tomorrow, when there can be a repeat performance of that?"

He rubbed his thumb back and forth inside her palm.

"Mmm, tomorrow might be my turn to do that for you," he said. "It's only fair, you know."

By that time, they'd made their way into the market. Ben didn't know if any photographers had been around yet—he probably should have been looking out for them, but he'd been focused on Anna. He supposed it was probably better that he didn't know, if the goal was for him to seem like he had no idea anyone was taking his picture. He obediently squeezed avocados and exclaimed over nectarines and examined herbs, as Anna beamed at him. By that time, he'd seen a few photographers around, trying to hide. Just to put his own spin on this thing, he stopped at the flower vendor and presented Anna with a bouquet of peonies.

"Oh, you're very good," she said, looking up at him from under her lashes.

He thought so, too.

After about twenty minutes, Anna turned around.

"I think we're all set to cook dinner tonight—is there anything else we need?"

He knew that was the signal that they'd gotten what they'd come here for. He wondered what would happen if he said, "Oh no, I want to stay longer—maybe check out those stands way down at the other end to see if they have any french fries." He let himself grin at the thought, and then took her hand and walked back with her to the car.

They stopped at a cupcake store nearby and got a few for later—spicy chocolate, lemon meringue, and s'more. Once they were on their way back to Anna's house, Ben turned to her.

"So that went well, I imagine, from that smug look on your face?"

Anna grinned over at him.

"Very. Especially that moment with the flowers—that was perfect." It had been, hadn't it? "Granted, you never know what photos turn out like; some people definitely try for unflattering angles where I'm in the middle of saying something and my eyes are closed and my face looks all smushed up. But we did as well as—honestly, even better than—I'd hoped."

He asked the question he'd been wondering all day.

"How did you know that photographers would be there? Are they always at that farmers market, or . . . ?"

Anna laughed and shook her head.

"Oh, you sweet summer child, no. We made sure they'd be there."

Ben narrowed his eyes at her.

"Made sure— What do you mean?"

Anna's smile grew wider.

"Well, usually it means that someone on our side calls them, but we've already done that once, and we don't want to push our luck here—that can get messy. So this time Simon convinced one of his other clients—much more of a fame whore than me, no offense to him, we all have to do what we have to do in this business—to go there today, too. So *they* called them. We just reaped the benefit."

His mind was blown.

"You call them. Wow. I'd always just assumed . . ."

Anna patted his arm.

"That all of this was organic? Yeah, no."

He couldn't believe how naive he'd been.

"I had no idea. Is it always like that?"

He felt like he was in a play within a play. They were pretending to be dating in front of people who pretended they'd just happened to come upon them when every part of it was a lie. What a weird, fucked up, fascinating world this was.

"It's not always like that—sometimes it really is organic: they happen to be in just the right place, or the wrong place, from my point of view, in situations like that." Oh God, he felt like an ass now, given what she'd told him before. He opened his mouth to apologize, but she kept talking. "There are some places they just hang out, but after a while you grow to know where those places are, so you can avoid or flock to them, as your attention needs take you. And sometimes people get caught in the attention to someone else—if they're following someone super famous, or if someone else has called them and they see you, they'll get you, too. But a lot of the stuff you see in tabloids or whatever, they look like candids, but they're not, trust me."

Ben thought about that for a while. It all made perfect sense, now that she'd explained it. Except . . .

"Can I ask you something? Something personal?"

The smile faded from Anna's face, but she nodded.

"Sure."

He tried to think of the best way to ask this.

"It's just about . . . what you told me on the way back from Palm Springs. You said the photographers made you anxious and panicked, which I totally understand. But today, you seemed fine—unless maybe you weren't fine and you were just acting? In that case . . ."

She shook her head.

"No, I was fine. I actually thought that was kind of fun, didn't you?"

She glanced over at him with a grin on her face.

"I thought it was hilarious, actually. I was cracking up inside the whole time."

She laughed.

"I thought so—me, too. And you're wondering why I was okay now, and not before? I guess the difference is that for things like today, I'm in control. Obviously not over what they say about me, or what the final pictures look like, no. But the where, when, how, who—all of that I do intentionally. It's not something I have to do because I can't escape from them. I mean, yes, it's also because now I'm in therapy and on meds and doing so much better, but that's another big part of it." She made a face. "My therapist thinks I shouldn't feel the need to control everything quite so much. I'm . . . working on that."

Weren't they all working on something? Or supposed to be, anyway.

"Okay," he said. "Thanks. For answering me, I mean."

She dropped her hand on his knee. That was usually his move. Now he understood why it so often worked.

"You're welcome," she said. "And thanks for today. For doing all of this, I mean. Dealing with Simon—I'm really sorry about that, by the way, he insisted on meeting you, I should have warned you—and the flight down here and making adoring faces—"

"Besotted, I believe the word was," he said.

"Oh right, sorry, making besotted faces at me. Thank you for all of it."

He put his hand over hers.

"You're welcome. But really, don't thank me too much—this is fun for me. And now the whole world thinks I'm dating Anna Gardiner? Win-win."

She laughed, but tightened her hand on his knee.

"Okay, but just let me say this. I have no idea if any of this will work, but I guess . . . going back to what I just said, I guess I feel better about it all now, because I've tried to snatch some of the control back. I'm not just sitting around hoping for my career to happen to me; I'm taking charge of it. And I like taking charge."

Ben looked at her sideways.

"You do, do you?"

She smiled without looking at him.

"Well. Sometimes. Other times . . ."

He had an excellent idea for what they could do when they got back to her house.

Sixteen

"*PEOPLE*? WE MADE IT TO *PEOPLE*? THE MAGAZINE, NOT JUST the website?"

Anna had tried not to get her hopes up too high about what could happen from the farmers market photos—she'd thought the day had gone well, but you never knew how pictures could turn out, or what terrible angle some photographer who had a grudge against her could find to make her look sad or angry or sullen. But apparently, all of that worry had been for naught.

"We made it to *People*," Simon said. "The magazine, not just the website. Or, rather, you and your little friend made it to *People*. I have to give it to you, that buying-flowers bit was a fantastic idea, congratulations for thinking of it."

Anna scrolled through the photos Simon had sent over—one with them strolling, hand in hand, into the farmers market, and one with Ben presenting her with that bouquet of flowers. She could feel how smug her smile was.

"The flowers thing was all him. He didn't even tell me about it, he just stopped and bought them, so that look of surprise on my face is genuine."

She looked over at the flowers, in a vase on her bookshelf, and smiled wider.

"Hmm, interesting," Simon said. "Well, now I'm glad that I leaked all of that stuff about what a great dancer he was and how everyone on set loved him and how respectful he is to women."

Anna laughed. Simon didn't fool her.

"You did that for me—or rather, for your interests—not for him. Speaking of our interests—any updates from the studio? Or on when that meeting with Varon is going to happen?"

Because that's what this was really for. Not fun farmers market jaunts and beautiful bouquets from Ben, or weekends full of great sex and a lot of laughter. All of that was well and good, but they weren't going to get her what she wanted, which was the Varon movie.

"Varon still isn't back in L.A., but apparently she'll be back soon. Nothing from the studio yet, but the buzz around you is getting bigger, between all the press you're getting for *Vigilantes* and this Ben thing. He's coming back down this weekend, right?"

"Yeah," she said to Simon, even though he already knew this. He apparently thought Ben was going to bail on her at every moment. "He's back on Friday—we're still on for the Lakers playoff game Saturday night."

"Ah yes, the Lakers game you insisted on."

Simon's original plan for Saturday night had been for a super public double date for her and Ben with one of Anna's very A-list friends and her former football-player husband. But when Anna found out there was a Lakers playoff game that night, she had forced Simon to get them tickets instead. She didn't care about basketball, but she knew Ben did.

"Does he have any idea how high-profile this is? Have you talked to him about this? Please make sure he knows how to behave with the cameras on him constantly like they will be at the game. And also, you should . . ."

"Yes, he knows. Don't worry, Simon. He won't swear at a player with the cameras rolling, or yell at anyone around us, or any of the other nightmare scenarios you're making up in your head. But I'll remind him, just in case."

She wouldn't, but if it made Simon feel better that she said so, fine.

Anna hung up and kept working for the next few hours—a call with her stylist to discuss her outfits for the game that weekend and for the premiere in a few weeks, a call with her financial planner, prep for her *Vigilantes*-related interview the next day, emails to Florence about her schedule, reviewing charity requests.

Her phone rang just as she got off the phone with Florence. Her brother.

Oh no.

"Hi, what's wrong?" she said into the phone, her heart beating fast.

"Nothing's wrong, Anna!" Chris said. "I can't just call my big sister without a crisis?"

She flopped back against her cozy office chair.

"Okay, but you *don't* ever call your big sister without a crisis, so . . ."

Chris laughed out loud.

"That's not . . . completely true. But obviously now I have to call you more so you don't sound panicked every time I do. Anyway, it's not a crisis; everyone is fine. I just had a quick question, and I figured calling was faster than texting."

That sounded like bullshit, but okay.

"What is it?"

"Well, two questions, actually. The first I emailed you already, but I know things can get lost in that inbox of yours, so look out for it and let me know if you have any questions." This must be a request for money for one of his pet projects; she would give some, of course, they both knew that. Chris was involved in a bunch of charities, which she kept hoping would get her dad off her back, but it hadn't. "But as for the second . . . Okay, full disclosure, Mom asked me about this and wants me to get info from you, but I won't say anything if you don't want me to."

He was taking awhile to work up to this, which was rare for Chris.

"What is it?"

"Well. Mom saw those pictures from last week, and then again in *People* today, and she showed them to me, and . . . what's going on with you and this guy?"

Anna had to laugh.

"Chris, I told you guys what was going on when we had lunch at Mom and Dad's, you know this is all fake."

"Yes, you told us that, but . . ."

"But what? Didn't I tell all of you, a long time ago, that I'd tell you anything that mattered in my personal life before it hit the press?"

The few actual relationships she'd had in Hollywood, she'd told her family about well before they were public, for this exact reason—she didn't want them to read gossip about her and think they were finding out along with the rest of the world.

"I know, I know, but . . . what Mom said to me—and I agreed, after I looked at those pictures—was that you looked different in them. Happier, I guess. And she liked the way that guy looked at you. So she thought maybe there was something else happening."

Hoped, Anna was pretty sure he meant. She loved her mom very much, but she desperately wanted Anna to be partnered and settled down, a thing that was not in Anna's plans for at least a few more years.

"I am happier, happier than I have been in a while, but it's not because of Ben—it's because I'm feeling better and taking care of myself and working, but not too hard, all of those things Mom and Dad want me to do." She shook her head. "I can't believe she called you and made you look at pictures of me in *People* magazine."

Her mom didn't even used to read *People* magazine.

"It wasn't that bad—I stopped by the house to drop off some books for her school. And then she made me look at pictures of you in *People* magazine."

They both laughed.

After she got off the phone, Anna thought about what she'd said to Chris. It wasn't exactly true, that her happiness had nothing to do with Ben, but not in the way her family thought. It had nothing to do with Ben himself. Ben was great, absolutely, she always had fun with him; the sex was truly excellent. But this "relationship" with Ben was the first time since her crisis where she felt like she was taking control of her life, that she was in charge of her career, that she wasn't sitting back and letting things happen to her because she was too anxious or exhausted or overwhelmed to make decisions. It felt fantastic.

Thursday, Ben texted Anna on the way to work.

> I'm sitting on muni and this woman is looking from her phone to me and then back to her phone and then back to me—is this always what happens when someone with you ends up in People magazine?

Anna had texted the day before to tell him about the pictures in *People*, but not before one of his aunts had texted them to the family group text. The group text had been out of control ever since the first pictures had come out, with his older cousins all making fun of him, but also privately trying to get him to spill some dirt, his younger cousins all making memes out of the pictures of him and Anna, and his aunts and uncles all saying that they couldn't wait to meet her, and reprimanding their offspring for teasing him. Ben loved it. He only wished they'd all actually get to meet Anna.

Not because he wanted her to be his girlfriend for real, obviously not. That seemed like a lot of work—all that travel, all of the performing for the cameras, having to interact with everyone on "Team Anna" from her eager assistant to her ass of a manager and everyone in between. Nah, it was just because he knew his family would all get a kick out of her, that's all.

He still felt bad that he hadn't told Theo the truth. Theo would be so disappointed when it all ended. He'd tell him everything then, though he had a feeling Theo would just be even more disappointed.

When Ben got to work, he immediately got pulled into a meeting about the pitch for the sneaker company, which he had a million ideas for. When he finally got to his desk and scrolled through his email, one popped out at him. Another from Dawn.

From: Dawn Stephens
To: Ben Stephens
Re: So cool!

OMG, just saw you in People! No wonder you weren't in town last weekend when I was in the Bay! That's wild that you're dating Anna Gardiner—is she nice? That's a silly question, I'm sure she's nice if she's dating you, lol. Anyway, I hope she's treating my brother well and that you had fun with her in LA last weekend!

xo
Dawn

Hope she's treating my brother well.

He'd—sort of—gotten used to thinking of Dawn as his sister. Theoretically. But he had a visceral rejection to the idea that he was her brother. He was Theo's brother. That's all. Forever, it had been him and Theo, together against the world. He'd let Maddie into the fold, because he'd known from first glance that she was good for Theo and that she loved him—he'd known that well before she seemed to know it—but also it was different; she was his girlfriend. It felt like this woman, this Dawn, was trying to steal something from his relationship with Theo.

Fuck that.

He clicked away from the email without replying.

Seventeen

ANNA SAT NEXT TO BEN AT THE LAKERS GAME, HER HAND IN his. She continued to be impressed with how well he was managing all of this—they'd been holding hands or whispering to each other, or chatting with the other celebrities sitting around them throughout the game, but even though half the things he whispered in her ear during the game were wildly filthy, he was totally PG in all of his outward behavior. He didn't even put his hand on her knee, just on her shoulder as they sat there, or the small of her back on the way into the arena. And he'd once or twice brushed her hair away from her face when they'd been facing each other, in a way she knew the cameras would love.

"You're very good at this, you know," she said the next time he did that.

He gave her a sweet smile.

"Next time you say that to me, I want you to be naked," he said. She choked back her laughter as his eyes twinkled at her.

"I'm going to kill you for that one when we get home, you know," she said. "Well. First I'll suck your cock in the limo on the way home. And then I'll kill you."

He took her hand again.

"I know you're going to want some reciprocity first, sweetheart," he said. Suddenly she had a vision of him the night before, sliding his fingers under her skirt as soon as he leaned over to kiss her in the limo when she'd picked him up from the airport. She uncrossed and recrossed her legs. The asshole was right—he was good at so many things.

But it wasn't just the performance of their relationship that he was doing well with tonight. They were sitting next to a notoriously aloof actress, someone Anna had met a number of times and had thought disliked her because of how unfriendly she'd always been. But because of the cameras, Anna had been forced to introduce her and her preteen son to Ben at the beginning of the game. Ben had managed to draw her out so well that by the second quarter, she was chatting away to Anna about what she was wearing to her next premiere and how nervous she always was at awards shows.

She even hugged Anna when the game was over and her kid high-fived Ben, who had clearly been a big hit with him.

Ben pulled out his phone when they got into the limo to go home and chuckled.

"I texted my brother some of the pictures I took courtside and he's dying. He might actually kill me the next time I see him. He's going to get me back for this so bad."

The warm, excited smile on Ben's face made Anna smile, too. She was glad the game had made him happy. She'd been on edge all week, jumping every time her phone buzzed, for no real reason she could identify. Probably just everything—the upcoming premiere, the endless waiting for news about the film role, the frequent stories about her and Ben, her dad's routine doctor's appointment this week. Tonight had relaxed her, though. A little.

She leaned over to glance at Ben's pictures. He'd taken a ton from the halftime event with the little kids trying to land free throws—none of them had made it, but former players had come out and helped them dunk in the end, and then announced big charity donations to wild applause.

"That was pretty cute," she said.

He relaxed against her.

"It really was." He looked over at her. "Do you do stuff like that? Not on the court, I mean, but the charity stuff? I've always thought that must be a fun part of being someone like you."

She shrugged.

"Sort of. I mean, not like that, but I give money, whenever someone asks me to. My brother has lots of pet charities up in the Bay Area, so that makes it easy."

She could feel his eyes on her, even though she wasn't looking at him.

"But you don't? I thought you'd want to be more involved personally. Maybe with a mental health charity, something in the Black community; the way you talked about it, it seemed like—"

"I get enough harassment from my dad about this, I don't need it from you, too," she said.

He held up his hands.

"Sorry for asking. I didn't realize this was a sensitive subject."

She shook her head.

"It's not sensitive. I'm just not in the mood to talk about that, that's all." She changed the subject. "Did you watch a lot of basketball with your dad and brother growing up?" she asked.

His face closed up and he looked away from her.

"Theo and I did."

"Not with your dad?" she asked. Ben never talked about his dad. There was clearly some mystery there. She suddenly wanted to know.

"No. Just me and Theo." He dropped his phone into his pocket.

"I thought what's her name was nice. That woman sitting next to you. And you said when we sat down that she didn't like you."

Anna opened a bottle of water.

"I thought she didn't. Guess I was wrong about that. Do you not get along with your dad?" She knew she was pushing on this. She could tell Ben was trying to change the subject, but somehow, she really wanted to know.

"I wouldn't know. I haven't seen him since I was a kid." Ben turned away to look out the window at the freeway traffic.

"Oh. I'm sorry. I didn't . . ."

He turned back to her and shook his head.

"It's fine. Don't worry about it." He slid an arm around her. "Why are we wasting all of this time in this limo? Aren't there other things we should be doing?"

He pulled her to him and kissed her. She kissed him back, and it was as good as it always was, but something kept nagging at her. When he slid his hand up underneath her shirt, she suddenly realized what it was. She pulled away.

"Have you ever noticed that when you get upset about something or there's something you don't want to talk about, you try to distract me with sex? It works, don't get me wrong. But you could just tell me you're upset, or that I shouldn't have pushed at you, or whatever. You don't have to pretend everything is fine and just fuck me."

Well, that had come out harsher than she'd meant it to. Ben pulled away from her.

"I apologize if you didn't want me to kiss you," he said. "Just FYI, when I kiss you, when I touch you, when I fuck you, it's because I want to, and for no other reason. I was under the impression you wanted it, too."

She dropped her hands from his chest. Why did men always do this shit?

"That's not what I meant and you know it. You can just tell me to stop asking you about your dad, or tell me that you're annoyed I kept pressing you on that when it was clear you didn't want to talk about it—I'm sorry! I shouldn't have done it. It's just that I feel like you know a lot about me by this point—I've told you a lot of personal stuff and you've been great about all of it, don't get me wrong. But I feel like I don't know you all that well except that you're funny and kind and go out of your way for people and you're great in bed, and those are all good things. But—I don't know, maybe I wanted to know more. You've told me you're in therapy, great, why do you go? You don't have to tell me that, I guess, that's probably too personal to ask, but it feels ridiculous that there's a 'too personal' between us with all of this. I guess one thing I know about you is that you avoid conflict and pretend it away or fill it with sex, which . . ."

She stopped and thought about that. About other times he'd done that. He'd been looking down, not at her, but now he looked up.

"You were mad at me," she said. "Weren't you? That night I told you about my plan for all of this. You were mad that I was going to trick you into this."

He didn't say anything.

"Answer me!" she finally yelled.

"Yes! Fine!" he yelled back. "Yes, I was pissed about that, okay? It felt pretty shitty, that you had a whole plan to lie to me and manipulate me, like I was just some cog in the Anna Gardiner wheel. Are you happy now? I'm not mad anymore, I got over it. What was even the point of being mad at you about it? It wasn't going to get me anywhere or do anything good. If I remember correctly, and I think I do, you did your fair share of trying to distract me with sex that night."

That was why he'd started all of that wildly hot dirty talk in the bar that night. And maybe it was why they'd had sex all night after getting back from the bar and hadn't stopped to talk about anything else.

She put her hand on his and waited until he looked her in the eye.

"I'm sorry," she said. "You're right. You were right to be mad. That was fucked up. I'm sorry I wasn't honest with you. I'm sorry that I almost went through with a plan that treated you and your feelings like they didn't matter."

His eyes fell. He didn't turn away from her, but he looked down for a while. She let the silence between them grow.

"I'm not . . . great about conflict," he finally said. "It's something I'm . . . supposed to be working on. You know. In therapy. But it's hard. And I don't like it. And it always feels easier to smile or joke or fuck it away, I guess."

She put her hand on his face and then leaned forward and kissed his cheek. He put his arm around her and pulled her close to him.

"It's a lot easier," she said. "But sometimes it's also a lot more rewarding to share your feelings and your hurt with someone else. That's, um, something I've had to work on, too."

He brushed her hair back from her forehead and kissed her softly there, but he didn't say anything else. Okay, she would let this go. He was obviously done with this conversation now—not that he'd even wanted to have it in the first place.

She felt like a jerk for pushing him about his dad, and then pushing him on this, and making him have this conversation he clearly hadn't wanted to have. Why had she even done it? Because she'd been anxious and wanted to pick at a scab? Because they'd been pretending to be in a relationship to the outside world, so she felt like she had to start a fight to make it feel real? Because she really wanted to know more about him and was frustrated that he held her at arm's length—emotionally, at least—that he only shared so much, then no more, and she thought if she hammered away at him, he might crack?

Probably all of the above.

"Thanks for the apology," he said, as they pulled into her driveway. "For that night. For what you almost did." He smiled down at her, meeting her eyes for the first time in a while. "And you didn't do it."

The driver opened her door, and Anna nodded her thanks as she got out.

No, she hadn't done it. She was more and more grateful for that every day.

Ben followed Anna into her house. He'd been worried, when he first came here, that it would be some big, fancy, expensive glass house, where he'd be afraid of breaking things and wouldn't want to sit on the furniture. And it did look imposing from the outside, with big hedges and a gate and a long driveway to keep people out. But the inside just felt like Anna—expensive, yes, but also relaxed, fun, joyful. It was colorful and spacious and felt like a home, and he was already sad he'd only get to visit a few times more.

"Do you want a drink?" Anna asked him when he followed her to the kitchen. "I could use one."

He nodded and watched her drop ice cubes into two glasses and then pour bourbon on top. She handed him a glass, and their fingers touched. It still felt so electric between them. He wanted to ask her if it was this way for her with other people. It probably was—she was just like this.

It wasn't this way for him with other people. Yeah, sure, he'd had great sex before, lots of times. But he'd never felt this way, this hunger to be with someone, around them, in their bed and out of it, touching them and talking to them. And the more they were together, the better the sex was. The better everything was.

He wanted to kiss her, to touch her, but after what she'd said in the car—and what he'd said—he felt hesitant. He didn't want her to think he was just doing it to brush off their fight.

Despite the fight, though, he was glad he'd told her he'd been mad she was going to trick him into this. He hadn't realized how much he'd needed to get that off his chest.

She took a sip of her bourbon and licked the tiny drop off her bottom lip. He looked away. Damn it, this woman was fucking him up. He was glad when she walked toward the living room.

"Coming?" she said over her shoulder.

He followed her. Of course he did.

When they sat down on the couch, he sat a respectful distance from her, but somehow, once they'd turned the TV on and found their way to the sixth episode of the show they'd started watching together, first in San Francisco at his apartment, then here last week, he was right next to her. Or she was right next to him? He didn't know exactly how it happened.

After they'd watched one episode, he looked down at her.

"Do you want . . ."

"In the car . . ." she said at the same time, and then they both laughed.

"You first," he said.

She smiled.

"Thanks. I was just going to say . . . I'm sorry about starting all of that. In the car, I mean. I shouldn't have pushed you. I've just been on edge all week, about this role, and if I'm going to get it, and the damn movie premiere, and what my role in *Vigilantes* will end up being like, and . . . everything."

He looked down at her. He started to put his arm around her, but stopped himself.

"Are you afraid that the premiere and everything around it will bring up bad memories of last year?"

She nodded.

"A little, I guess. And with that coming and all of the uncertainty around the Varon film, it's just . . . a lot right now." She sighed and leaned her head back on the couch. "She called me this week. Varon did. We chatted about the part. We're going to have lunch next week."

He sat up straight and looked at her. Why didn't she sound more excited?

"But that's great news, isn't it?"

She shrugged.

"I don't know. She told me that the studio is still on the fence, and that she doesn't have free rein here, so I don't really know what it means. But we're having lunch on Thursday. Which of course means I'm going to be a stress case all week."

She leaned her head against his chest. He put his arm around her then—how could he not?

"Anyway. I'm sorry I took that out on you. And I really am sorry. About everything else."

"I know you are," he said. "Thank you for saying so. I'm sorry, too." He brushed her hair back from her face. "I'm glad we talked about all of this." And he was.

She pulled him down to her and kissed him. God, it felt so good to feel her lips on his, her body against him, her hands on his shoulders, his hands on her waist, her hips.

They pulled apart, and she reached for his shirt.

"I thought—" he started, and stopped.

She sat back but kept her hands on him.

"You thought what?" she asked.

Damn it. Now, after what she'd said in the car, he had to say it.

"I thought, after what you said, that you didn't . . . I didn't want to . . ."

She smiled slowly and cupped his cheek with her hand.

"Is that why you were being so standoffish when we got home? Ben, I wasn't saying that I want any of this part to change. I just want us—both of us—to be able to be honest with each other. Okay?"

"Okay," he said. "I promise."

He leaned down to kiss her, and she kissed him back, hard. He pressed her down onto the couch, and she slid her hands up his chest. He pulled her very snug T-shirt up and let his hands roam all over her body. He traced the lacy borders of her bra with his thumbs.

"My God, when you touch me like that . . ." she said.

"I know," he said. "Me, too."

Later, in bed, in the dark, she kissed him on the cheek before she snuggled into his chest.

"The game was fun," he said. "Courtside! I'm never going to get over that."

She tilted her head back and smiled up at him.

"I'm glad. You've done so much for me, I wanted you to be able to have a little fun with this."

He brushed her hair back from her face so he could see her eyes.

"Wait. Did you plan that for me?"

She tried to look away, but he wouldn't let her.

"I just thought . . . this whole thing has been about me. I thought . . . you'd like this better than you liked the farmers market."

Why was he so touched by that?

"Anyway." She slid her hand over his. "Thanks for making all of this—the celebrity stuff, I mean—fun for me again."

He pulled her close.

"It's fun for me, too."

"Good," she said. "I'm glad that you're okay about what I said earlier. I'm glad that . . . that we're okay."

He swallowed. He didn't know if it was because of the darkness, or the conversation from the car, or the sex, but he suddenly wanted to tell her the thing he'd told no one else.

So he did.

"I, um. I have a sister." It was the first time he'd said it out loud.

She pulled back, and he could feel her looking up at him, but he didn't look down. It was easier if he couldn't see her.

"I thought it was just you and Theo."

He nodded.

"That's what I thought, too. Until a couple months ago. She emailed me, out of the blue. She's my dad's . . . daughter. So she must be my sister. Half sister, I guess. Dawn. She lives in Sacramento. We've emailed. For a little while now."

He rolled onto his back, and Anna laid her head on his chest. Good. He needed that right now.

"Have you met her?"

He closed his eyes.

"No. She wants to meet me. A few weeks ago, she said she was coming to the Bay Area for the weekend. But it was the first weekend I was here. So I didn't see her then."

She put her hand on top of his, where it lay on her hip, and moved her fingers in slow circles on his skin.

"What does Theo think? Has he met her?"

He swallowed.

"Theo doesn't know. She didn't email him—I was the one who took one of those stupid DNA tests; that's how she found me. I haven't told him."

The slow movement of her fingers stopped when he said that. A few seconds later, she started again.

"Why haven't you told him?"

"Because I don't want to meet her!" He hadn't realized this

until that moment. "I don't want her! I don't want a sister! I have Theo, I have my mom, I have my cousins, I don't want anything having to do with my dad. I don't want his second family to try to intrude on mine. He left, he's done, I'm done with him! I went to fucking therapy, I talked about my fucking feelings, I moved past everything, I figured it all out, I was done! And now she's trying to waltz into my life, to be part of my family, to take my brother away from me, I don't want it! I don't want any of it!"

Anna put her arms around him and pulled him against her. He tucked his head into that space between her shoulder and her neck. She rubbed his back and didn't say anything. They breathed together for a while, until his burst of anger subsided.

He pulled away and put his head back on his pillow.

"I'm sorry. I didn't meant to . . ."

She put a finger on his lips.

"I'm glad you did. You don't need to be sorry."

He sighed.

"I haven't even told my therapist about this."

He could feel her looking up at him.

"Why not?" she asked.

He took a long breath.

"It feels like . . . after all the work we did, that she did with me, that she'll be disappointed in me. For not, like, thinking this was no big deal, for not being ready to embrace this woman with open arms, the way she seems ready to embrace me. For not being fixed."

Anna took his hand.

"Oh, Ben. She won't be disappointed in you. Life is a constant work in progress, you know that. There's no being 'done' with any of this stuff."

He looked at the ceiling.

"I guess I *wanted* to be done. For her to be proud of me. It feels like something is wrong with me that I'm not ready for this."

He hadn't planned to tell Anna this, not any of it, but now that he'd started, everything was pouring out.

"I think this would be hard for anybody, no matter how well adjusted they were, or how many years of therapy they'd done," Anna said. "It's a big deal!"

That made him feel better, that she thought it was a big deal, too.

"But . . ." Oh no. He didn't want her to say "but." "You said you think she's trying to take Theo away from you." Her voice was very gentle. "Why do you think that?"

He took a long breath.

"It's been just me and Theo. Forever, it's been just me and Theo. We watch over each other, we take care of each other— well, mostly he takes care of me, but I've had my moments—we take care of our mom. We always have. We irritate the hell out of each other constantly, but we're always there for each other. A girlfriend is one thing, especially Maddie, because she's great. A wife, fine, I can live with that, since I'm pretty sure that's where they're heading. That's not a sibling. There is one person who has Theo as a brother; I am the brother to one person. I don't want him . . . or us . . . to change."

Oh God. Now Anna was going to think he was an asshole.

But her hand was still in his.

"Oh, Ben. Love isn't a zero-sum game, you know. You don't have to meet this woman if you don't want to; you don't have to invite her into your life. But one thing that I've known about you from the very beginning is that"—she slid her hand up to his chest—"you have a very big heart. And I know your heart could expand to embrace Dawn, and you would lose none of your love for your brother. And I saw him with you, I could tell how much he loves you—there's no way that anything would make him love you any less. I'm certain of it."

He took her face in his hands and kissed her softly on the lips.

"Thank you. That's . . . I have a lot to think about, but thank you."

She curled her body back against his.

"You're welcome. And thank you for telling me."

After a little while, he could tell by her regular breathing that she'd fallen asleep. But he lay awake for a long time.

Eighteen

"THEY'RE ALL UP IN THE DRESSING ROOM," FLORENCE SAID to Ben when she let him into Anna's house the following Friday morning.

"The dressing room?" Was that some sort of code that he didn't know?

"I'll show you," she said.

They stopped at the door of what he'd just assumed was a guest room next to Anna's bedroom.

"Oh. The dressing room," he said.

Some people might call this room an enormous closet, but that would understate it. Clothes lined the room on all four sides, with breaks for floor-to-ceiling mirrors. One big corner had shelves just for shoes, and then another was full of purses. There were more racks and bins for things like sweaters and . . . ahh, that's why Anna seemed to have on a different bra every time; it was like a whole lingerie shop over there. Damn, he thought he treated his sneakers well.

"Hi, Ben!" Anna said from a platform in the middle of the floor. She was wearing a black, very slinky dress that emphasized her curves and barely covered her breasts. One woman was kneeling at her feet, and her stylist was a few feet away, looking at her with a frown on her face. And, oh, excellent, there was Simon, scowling away in the corner.

Anna had told him that she'd be in the midst of a fitting for her premiere dress when he arrived, but he hadn't realized just what a fitting like that would entail.

Ben cleared his throat.

"Hi. Is it my job to take off my jacket and sweep it over you if some of that fabric slips a little too far when we're on the red carpet?"

Everyone in the room laughed. Well, everyone except Simon.

"That's what the fitting is for," Anna's stylist said. "Don't worry, she'll be more covered up at the premiere."

He hadn't been . . . worried exactly, but he was relieved he wouldn't have to live in fear of a wardrobe malfunction. And very pleased he'd gotten to see Anna in this version of the dress.

"That is, if I even wear this one," Anna said.

"You should wear this one," Simon said.

Anna ignored him and pointed to the corner.

"There are a few other options I haven't gotten to try on yet; we're figuring this out now. They have your tux, by the way, if you want to try it on."

Ben dropped his bag by the door.

"Sure, why not?"

"Why not" was that he had a feeling that if he tried on his tux, the fitting would take even longer, and he was already frustrated that the first time he saw Anna after a week apart was in the presence of Florence, Anna's stylist, whoever that other person was, and of course, Simon.

He hadn't seen her since Sunday night, and while they'd texted all week, it wasn't the same. He wanted to be able to kiss her hello, tell her how incredible she looked in that dress, ask her how her meeting with Varon had gone, and so many other things. That was partly why he'd come this morning instead of tonight after work, so he could spend more time with her. But he'd forgotten—or maybe hadn't realized—how much went into being Anna Gardiner.

He should probably go over there and kiss her hello in front of all of those people so they could ooh and aah and then tell people about how cute Anna and her boyfriend Ben Something were, right? But it felt . . . wrong to do that. As much as he was fine with holding hands with Anna in public and acting just like she wanted him to, he appreciated that they still had their private whispers, so it felt like it was a big inside joke for the two of them. But he didn't want to kiss her for public consumption, even just "public" for the people on her team.

Ben picked up the hanger with the tux on it and went into the bathroom to change. He felt sort of silly doing that, he was sure Anna was changing in the middle of the room, and all of those people probably saw men in various stages of undress all day. When he'd been a dancer, he'd gotten used to changing in front of a million people. But that was a long time ago.

When he came back into the room, Anna was in a different dress. Everyone turned to whistle at him. Even—he was shocked to see—Simon.

"Anna, did you know he looked like this in a tux when you started dating him?" her stylist asked.

Anna shook her head, but with a wide smile on her face. That smile made him realize how stressed she'd looked the rest of the time. Was it the premiere? Was she anxious about what that would be like, with all of the photographers and the cameras?

"I didn't know he looked this good in a tux," she said. "But I highly suspected." Her eyes were locked on his. He blushed and went to stand where the stylist pointed, so they could pin the cuffs and hems and . . . the sleeves?

"You're taking in the sleeves?" he asked her.

She looked at him, then over at Simon.

"We thought we might as well take advantage of those biceps of yours," she said.

He knew who the "we" was there, but he'd let that go.

He left the room again to change back into his regular clothes, which took longer than usual because he had to do it without stabbing himself with a pin, but he managed. When he came back into the room, he stopped cold at the doorway.

"Wow," he said. "You look incredible in that dress."

Anna looked up and into his eyes. A slow smile spread across her face.

The dress was red, with a simple, snug, strapless top and a very full skirt. It wasn't as overtly sexy as the first dress, but that wasn't why he liked it. It just looked like Anna to him. Bright and powerful, but also fun and beautiful.

"I like this one, too." He liked that smile on her face. "Simon likes the first one better, but I've always wanted a tulle dress." She looked at herself in the mirror, and then at her stylist. "I've never worn one—people have always told me that with my shape, the big ball-gown skirt doesn't work on me, but . . ." She looked in the mirror again and swung her hips from side to side. "It's just so fun."

Something happened to him as she danced in the mirror. He couldn't keep his eyes off of her. Fuck it, he didn't care how many people were in the room, he had to kiss her. He moved toward her. She turned and smiled right at him.

"Okay, if you're sure." Her stylist stepped in front of Ben. He stopped.

"Remember the Golden Globes?" Simon said. "You loved that dress, too. That time, I also said—"

Anna turned away from Ben and looked at Simon.

"I remember the Golden Globes, how could I ever forget? Yes, yes, you were right that time." She looked at herself in the mirror again. "Get them both ready, Devora? I'll decide next week."

Simon looked irritated, but then, Ben figured he probably did, too. He sat on the couch amid the piles of clothes to wait.

He wished he could send Maddie pictures of all of this—she would love to see the clothes Anna was choosing from, and he'd be able to ask Maddie all of the questions he didn't want to ask out loud right now. Not with Simon around, anyway. What happened at the Golden Globes? Did Anna pay for all of these clothes? If not, did she get to keep them? And his tux—where had that come from? Anna had just told him she'd take care of it and he hadn't argued with her about it, but now he wanted to know if she'd paid for it or if some designer had given it to her for him.

Holy shit. He was really, actually going to be on a red carpet with her. He'd known that from the beginning of this whole charade, of course. But he hadn't really thought about what it would be like. Would he have to pose for pictures with her?

If so, he hoped someone would give him some tips.

"Okay, I think we're all set," Devora said, and unpinned the red dress from Anna. Anna stepped out of it and . . . holy fucking shit. He'd seen her body, nude and in lingerie, so many times now, but it blew his mind every time. He tried to disguise the naked hunger that he was sure was all over his face, but when she looked at him, it was almost impossible. She beamed at him.

Anna threw on a sundress, and Ben tore his eyes away from her. He saw Simon looking at him, but he couldn't care less. Everyone in the room other than Ben was getting ready to leave, and after too many side conversations and "just one more things" and "have you thought abouts" and "Oh wait, Anna, I forgot to tell yous," they all finally left Anna's house. Everyone but him and Anna.

"Hi." Ben met her by the stairs when she came back up after walking Florence out.

"Hi, yourself." She walked toward him. She had that look on her face again, the one he'd noticed earlier. The worried, anxious look. He pulled her into his arms, and she nestled her head in his chest.

"What's wrong?" he asked.

She laughed.

"How did you know something was wrong? It's nothing."

He tilted his head back and looked at her. She smiled when she saw the expression on his face.

"Okay, it's not nothing," she said. "It's nothing new, nothing major, that's what I meant. It's just everything—I've gotten my hopes so high over the past few weeks about everything, and this fitting just made me think about what if I'm wrong about all of it? What if I show up to this *Vigilantes* premiere and smile and pose on the red carpet and then I'm barely in the movie? I'll be so crushed, so humiliated that I did all of this for nothing. I want this role in the Varon film so bad I can taste it, and I'm just so worried that all of this won't work. I'll feel like such a failure, and everyone will see that I've failed, and laugh at me, and I won't know where to go or what to do."

Her arms were tight around him, and all he could do was brush back her hair in that way he knew soothed her.

"Do you want to sit down?" he asked.

She lifted her face up and kissed him softly on the lips.

"Yeah. Thanks."

They went to his favorite couch in her den, the cozy little room that just had a TV and couches and a coffee table and felt lived in.

"I'm sorry this is all so stressful," he said. "How did the meeting with Varon go?"

She let out a long sigh, and his stomach dropped until she started talking.

"It was great. She was great. But it just made me want it even more—I want it so bad, Ben. I see so much in this role. It could be . . ." She closed her eyes for a moment. "Everything I want. At first I just wanted it because it felt like it could be the thing that would get me back to the Oscars, to maybe even win this time. But now . . . now it's not about that. Well. Not just about that. She gets me, I get her, I feel like I could really . . . grow in this role, I could learn so much from it, from her. But that may have just made everything worse, because it's still the same situation as before—I have to get the buy-in from the studio, and I have no idea what they're thinking. I think Varon was trying to make them show their hand a little by having a public meeting with me—she knows how this game is played, too—but who knows, that might just piss them off."

He hated to ask this, but—

"What does Simon think?"

She looked up at him with a wry smile on her face.

"I know you and Simon didn't—exactly—click, but he's my fiercest advocate, you know."

Ben sighed.

"I know. That's why I asked. I figured if there was something to worry about, Simon would know."

She leaned back against him and pulled him down until they were both lying back on the couch.

"He says we're doing all the right things—he never bullshits me, so I know it's true. But I think he's also worried." She put her hand in his, and he squeezed. "He gave me a pep talk today, said I'm doing a great job, just keep doing what I'm doing, and we'll know more in a few weeks." She laughed softly. "That made me feel better, it always does when he gives me a pep talk, but this time I didn't even ask for one, so he could obviously also tell something was up."

He lifted their hands and kissed hers.

"Okay. Do we have plans tonight?"

Anna shook her head.

"No, everything is tomorrow and Sunday. Tomorrow night we're going to a play and then dinner. Sunday is just a paparazzi-bait trip to the grocery store."

He kissed the side of her head.

"Perfect. Then how about we stay right here, on this more-comfortable-than-it-has-a right-to-be couch, until your heart stops beating like you just ran a marathon? And then maybe we can go outside and get in that pool of yours I have yet to experience. Or we can do whatever the hell else will take your mind off of all that other stuff."

Anna propped herself up on her elbow and looked down at him.

"I have a better idea." She reached for his belt.

He smiled at her and pushed up her dress.

"Mmm, is this where I get to take off these perversely sexy underwear of yours?"

She laughed as he peeled them down.

"Perversely sexy? My Spanx? You must be kidding."

He shook his head.

"Absolutely not. Thongs are great, I love them, sexy as hell, don't get me wrong. But these things feel like the kind of thing you don't usually let men see you in."

He could see her think about that.

"No. You're right, I don't. Almost never, actually."

He smiled and slipped them all the way off.

"That's what I thought. That's what makes them sexy."

She pulled him up and kissed him.

"You are a constant surprise to me," she said. "I'm so glad you're here."

So was he.

Anna was awake, barely, but not ready to actually wake up. She was still in bed, curled up against a sound-asleep Ben. She liked this time of the morning, when she could just lie here with him and breathe in and out; feel him breathing in his sleep, feel his hand on her hip and his chest against her back. His breathing and his touch made it so she couldn't worry about anything.

Well. So she couldn't worry as much, anyway.

Her phone rang, and she reached for it to turn off the sound before it woke Ben up. She glanced at the screen: Penny. What was she calling for this early in the morning?

Anna slid out of bed carefully and grabbed her robe on the way out of the room.

"Hello? Is something wrong?"

"No, nothing's wrong, why are you whispering?" Penny asked. "Oooh, because the maaaan is there. Ooh, this makes this even better."

Anna padded into the kitchen to pour herself coffee.

"Makes what even better?"

"I'm going to be in L.A. today!" Penny said.

Anna pulled off the scarf from around her hair.

"What? Without telling me?"

"What do you think I'm calling for right now? It was a last-minute thing—can we meet up? Can I meet HIM? A restaurant is doing a whole big dinner tonight with our wines and at the last minute asked me to come so I can do the whole winemaker song and dance. I'll be heading that way in a few hours with a bunch of cases of wine in my trunk. I have to get there super early to set up—want to bring HIM to meet me there? I'd come over after the dinner but I have to drive back to Paso Robles tonight."

Penny was one of the few people she'd change any plans for.

"Why don't you spend the night here tonight? That way you don't have to drive back home in the dark and all full of wine."

Penny laughed.

"I won't be full of wine—I can't drink much at these things; I have to keep my wits about me. And I have to be at the winery bright and early tomorrow for a meeting with my interns."

Anna heard a step in the hallway and turned to see Ben amble into the kitchen. She grabbed a second mug out of the cabinet for him and poured coffee into it. He took the oat milk out of the fridge and handed it to her, and took the sugar out of the cabinet for himself.

"Okay, then. I can—" She looked over at Ben, sleepily blowing on his coffee like he did every time. "We can meet you at the restaurant. What time?" He looked up at her and raised his eyebrows. She grinned at him. He smiled slowly at her and opened the sliding glass doors to her backyard.

"I love the sound of that 'we,'" Penny said. "How about three? I'll be there by two thirty at the latest, but they'll be finishing up lunch then, so it's probably better if you get there after they're all closed. Just text me when you park and I'll let you in. Make sure HE knows how excited I am to meet him."

Anna looked in Ben's direction. His back was to her, and she was pretty sure he was out of earshot, but she lowered her voice, just in case.

"He has a name, you know. Ben. Please be nice. Simon wasn't . . . excellent, and I don't want him to think everyone in my life is going to hold his feet to the fire."

Not that it really mattered, she reminded herself. They only had this weekend and then the premiere left to go.

Penny chuckled.

"Oh God, why did you make the poor man meet Simon? I know he's exactly what you need as your manager, but . . . ouch. Don't worry, I'll be great! It's just me!"

"Mmm, yes, I know, that's why I said something," Anna said. Penny just laughed and hung up.

Anna followed Ben outside.

"Hey, so, change of plans," she said when she sat down on the couch next to him. "My best friend, Penny—I've told you about her . . ."

"The wine person?" Ben took a sip of his coffee.

She nodded.

"Yeah. Well, she's going to be in L.A. today. I know you have some work to do, but I haven't seen Penny in way too long, and . . ."

"And she wants to meet me?" he said with a raise of his eyebrows.

Anna tried to fight back her smile but didn't succeed.

"Yeah, she wants to meet you. Is that okay? You don't have to come if you don't want to. I can go meet her alone. We still have the play later tonight, so if that's all the activity you feel like doing today . . ."

He waved that off.

"You talk about Penny a lot; I'm glad I'll get to meet her. Just let me know when I should be ready."

Ben lifted his coffee cup to his lips, then stopped.

"Wait, just so I know—what does Penny know here?"

Anna laughed.

"Penny knows everything." She grinned at him. "Well. Almost everything. Don't worry."

So at a few minutes before three, they pulled into a parking spot on Figueroa. Ben had driven so she'd be able to text Penny right away to let them in.

The restaurant door opened as they walked toward it, and Anna swept inside, Ben behind her.

"Anna!" Penny pounced on her, and they fell into a hug, both laughing. And at least on Anna's side, crying a little. Even though they only lived about three hours away from each other, that three hours could be five or more if there was a lot of traffic, and between her career and how hard Penny had been working over the past year, they hadn't seen each other in months.

Finally, they broke apart, both grinning.

"I missed you," Anna said.

"I didn't miss you at all," Penny said. She also had tears in her eyes. Anna grinned at her and turned to Ben, who was still standing by the door.

"Penny, I'd like you to meet Ben Stephens. Ben, Penny Malone."

Ben reached for Penny's hand.

"Very nice to finally meet you, Penny," he said. "I've heard a lot about you."

Penny's eyes danced.

"Likewise." Oh no. Was Penny going to embarrass her? Yes, of course she was.

"Does a booth work, Ms. Malone?" Someone from the restaurant came up to Penny and studiously didn't look at Anna. "I'll keep setting up in the back room."

"A booth is perfect, thank you." They followed him to a booth in the corner, which was already set up with a cheese plate and wineglasses.

"I figured if I had you here, I might as well have you taste some of your investment," Penny said when the restaurant guy walked into the back room and left the three of them alone.

"Investment?" Ben asked as he slid into the booth next to Anna.

"Oh, Anna didn't tell you?" Penny pulled her corkscrew—the engraved one Anna had given her when she'd gotten the winemaker job—out of her pocket and started opening one of the bottles on the table.

Ben looked at Anna. Right. She hadn't told him this part.

"Penny likes to overstate my involvement, but yes, I am a minor—"

"Major," Penny said.

"*Silent* partner in her winery," Anna finished. "It's very easy work for me—I just had to write one check, and now I get all of the wine I can drink."

Penny poured wine for all three of them, then sat down on the other side of the booth. She lifted her glass.

"Cheers to new beginnings, and complicated partnerships."

Ben's eyes crinkled at that.

"Excellent way to put it." They all clinked glasses, and then he took a sip of the wine. "Since you're the expert, can you tell us about this wine, or is that a boring question for you to have to answer when that's your job?"

Anna slid her hand on Ben's knee under the table. That was the perfect question to ask Penny.

"I'd love to tell you about our wines. I brought some of my favorites for tonight—we do a lot of Italian-style wines, and this is a Barbera style that I bottled a few years back—shortly after I came to the winery, actually."

"That's good with food, right?" Ben asked.

Anna turned to him and narrowed her eyes. She'd never heard him talk like he knew about wine before. He saw her glance and laughed.

"I only know that because of my brother—as you might imagine, he's very into wine."

Yeah, Anna could see that.

They sat there for the next hour, drinking wine—mostly Anna, since Penny was working and Ben had said he'd drive home—and eating cheese and talking. Not about anything major, and Penny didn't even ask Ben that many questions about why he was doing this with Anna like Anna had thought she might. They talked about wine, and Penny's adventures with tourists, and the times Ben went wine tasting with his brother, and when Anna and Penny had gone to France together a few years back. Anna hadn't realized just how much she'd missed Penny until she was here together with her and Ben. She was glad Penny had insisted on meeting him. He'd been such a big—if temporary—part of her life these days; she was glad Penny finally knew him as a person, and not just a series of stories.

All too soon, Ben nudged her.

"I hate to do this, but you told me to tell you when it was four, since you want to make sure to get out of here to give Penny time to finish setting up."

She looked at her watch, and he was right. She reached across the table and grabbed Penny's hands.

"We can't go this long again before seeing each other, okay?"

Penny nodded. Were those more tears Anna saw in famously stoic Penny's eyes?

"Absolutely. I'm holding you to that. This week we'll pick a date for next time. Next month?"

Ben slid out of the booth and smiled at Penny.

"It was really great to meet you," he said. "And I'll make sure to tell my brother about your winery. He'll want to get some wine."

Penny reached into her pocket and handed him a business card.

"Have him contact me." She winked. "I'll give him the friends-and-family discount."

They were still all laughing together when Penny unlocked the restaurant door. Anna stepped outside, and a flash went off in her face.

She stopped, startled, and it happened again.

Oh God. The restaurant owner. He must have called them.

Ben put his arm around her.

"Let's get you to the car."

She couldn't move. The photographer was still in front of her.

"Ben. Ben, I . . ."

He started walking and gently pulled her forward.

"Remember what you told me. Put that smile on your face. You can do this. The car is right down the street."

Her heart was beating so fast. She felt woozy, like she was going to faint. She couldn't do this.

But she had no other option. She couldn't turn around, so she had to go forward. So she walked on, Ben's arm around her. She smiled; at least she tried to. She could feel her heartbeat in her hands, her head, her feet, she couldn't breathe, but she walked until they got to her car, holding on to Ben, the photographer ahead of her the whole way, with that smile on his face that showed he knew how much she hated this.

Ben opened the passenger door for her, and she collapsed inside. Thank God he had the keys; her hands were shaking too much to have even opened the door. He got in the car and pulled away seconds later.

"It's okay. You're okay. I'm with you," he said.

She barely heard him. What if someone was behind them? She had to keep smiling, keep looking calm, just in case, in case . . .

"No one is following us," Ben said. "I'm watching for that. Don't worry." He reached over and took her hand. "Breathe."

She gripped his hand, but she could only take shallow breaths.

"I can't . . . it isn't . . ."

Ben gripped her hand.

"Shit. Okay. I'll . . . shit. What can I do to help? Do you want me to pull over?"

She shook her head.

"Home. Just get me home," she managed to say.

"Okay," he said. "I can do that."

She tried to breathe slower, to count her breaths, but she still just felt like she was gasping for air.

She'd gotten through this before. She could do it again. She closed her eyes and concentrated on the pressure of his hand.

"Can you . . . can you talk to me? Just . . . anything."

He squeezed her hand.

"Talking, that's something I'm good at. Okay—do you want to hear the story of how Theo and Maddie got together?"

He didn't wait for her to say yes, thank goodness.

She held his hand tightly, tried to breathe, rolled down the window so she could feel the air against her face, tried to breathe, listened to the warm, easygoing sound of his voice say something about a hospital and forgotten sweatpants and pizza and a locked closet door, and she slowly stopped feeling like she was gasping for breath. By the time they pulled into her driveway, her pulse felt almost normal.

As soon as they were inside her house, she turned to Ben. His arms were already reaching for her.

He pulled her close, and she held on to him as hard as she could. His tight embrace was just what she needed, just what she'd craved during that whole terrible drive home. It was so good to have his arms around her, to feel his heart beating along with hers, to have his slow, even breath to follow. She felt limp, exhausted, like she could fall asleep in his arms standing right here. But being with him, like this, made her feel better, like she would be okay, like he'd said to her in the car, like she hadn't been until this moment.

And then the tears came. Slowly at first, just trickling out of her eyes, and then as his hands rubbed up and down her back, she let herself sob into his chest.

Ben kissed her wet cheeks and then led her to her favorite couch in the den.

"Hey," he said as he sat down and pulled her back into his arms. "Is now a good time for me to tell you all the ways I fantasized about punching that photographer in the face and running over his camera with the car? Or do you want to wait to hear that later?"

She laughed as he wiped her tears with the bottom of his shirt. Oh God, she must look like such a mess.

"Maybe later," she said. "We can trade fantasies."

And then she started crying again.

"I'm just so ashamed," she said. "I thought I was better. That I was okay now! That I wouldn't freak out like this again. But one flashbulb and it was all the same."

He rubbed her back in slow circles.

"You have nothing to be ashamed of."

She should have known he would say that. It was nice to hear, but it didn't change anything.

"Hey." He pulled back from her until she looked up at him. "Look, I know when I was growing up people talked like there was something wrong with you if you needed therapy. Some people still talk like that. But you and I both know that's not true. Don't we?"

She knew where he was going with this.

"Yes, fine, but that's not—"

"As a matter of fact," he said, "just recently, someone really smart told me that life is a constant work in progress. You're still working on all of this. That's okay."

She tried to glare at him but couldn't help but smile.

"There is nothing I hate more than people throwing my own words back in my face."

He brushed more tears away with his thumbs.

"I thought you might feel that way."

She sighed and sat back against the couch.

"It just feels like . . . like I should have gotten over this by now. It's part of my life—it's part of the job! I've known this for a long time; it shouldn't bother me anymore. It doesn't do this to other people. Why can't I be stronger?"

Ben pulled the blanket off the back of the couch and tucked it around her.

"This doesn't have anything to do with how strong you are. We all need help sometimes. Lots of times. And some things are hard for everyone. That other actress you sat next to at the Lakers game— wasn't she saying she gets really stressed at premieres?"

She hadn't realized he'd heard that part of their conversation. But still.

"Also, I just feel so stupid—I should have been on higher alert today; I should have guessed that restaurant guy would call them when I showed up to see Penny. What perfect free advertisement for him. But—"

"That's why the photographer was there?" Ben asked. He started to stand up, then shook his head and sat back down. "You know what? I'm sure Penny will deal with him."

Anna thought about that for a second and then laughed.

"I'm sure Penny will." She looked around for her phone. "Actually, I should let her know I'm okay. I don't know if she saw any of that, but if she did, she'll be freaking out."

Ben went and grabbed her purse from where she'd dropped it by the front door.

"You text Penny; I'll get you some water."

Anna reached into her purse for her phone. Yes, Penny was freaking out. And yes, she was going to deal with the restaurant guy.

Fuck. Anna, are you ok?

I'm going to destroy this motherfucker

No, first I'm going to make sure everyone at tonight's dinner loves the wine

Then I'm going to destroy this motherfucker. A food poisoning rumor should do it, I think

Or maybe rats, that one would be fun too

Tell me you're ok

No really, tell me you're ok

Anna, if you don't fucking text me back

She should have thought to text Penny as soon as they got home.

I'm ok! I swear. I wasn't. But Ben helped. And yes, we would both like you to destroy that motherfucker, please.

Ben came back from the kitchen with two glasses of water and two bottles of sparkling water.

"I thought you said you were never a waiter, but those are some waiter skills right there," she said.

He set everything down on the table.

"Oh, I didn't say I was never a waiter, just not here in L.A. I learned excellent skills that way. Did you check in with Penny?"

Anna drank half the glass of water in one gulp. She should go get her meds from her bedroom—why she'd stopped carrying them around with her in the first place, she had no idea—but she couldn't move right now. In a few minutes.

"Yeah. She's debating between a food-poisoning rumor or one about rats."

Oh thank god. Thank Ben for me, will you?

Anna glanced down at her phone, then back up at him.

"Also, she says thank you. And, um. So do I."

He took the glass of water from her and put it back on the coffee table.

"You're welcome. But I didn't do anything. You got yourself through that. I just drove us home."

They both knew that wasn't true, but Anna didn't bother arguing.

He picked up his own glass of water.

"I know you hate changing plans, but I'd like to suggest we blow off the play tonight."

Oh God, the play. She'd completely forgotten about that.

"Great idea. I can't imagine anything I'd less like to do right now. Let me have Florence deal with that."

She fired off a text.

"Okay. Great. We have all night. What do you want to do?"

He turned to her and shrugged.

"I'd be perfectly happy just sitting right here with you all night."

Anna laughed.

"Ben, you're a much better actor than I've given you credit for."

He looked confused, then annoyed.

"What, you mean obviously I just want to have sex? Christ,

Anna. That's not the only thing I think about, you know. I was actually thinking about you."

Oh. She'd hurt his feelings.

She reached for his hand.

"Ben."

He looked at her.

"I'm sorry," she said. "I was just trying to . . . lighten the mood a little. I know you were thinking about me. I appreciate that, more than I can say."

The tension around his jaw relaxed.

"Okay. Sorry."

She hooked her finger under his chin and kissed him. It was long, and slow, and gentle, and it almost made her cry all over again.

He smoothed down the back of her hair.

"I have an idea," he said. "Why don't we both change into those great robes you have upstairs, and then we can watch a terrible movie and you can tell me all the gossip you know about it. And after that, if you're hungry, I can make us pancakes for dinner."

She took a long, deep breath.

"That sounds wonderful," she said.

Nineteen

IN THE CAR ON THE WAY TO ANNA'S HOUSE ON WEDNESDAY morning, one sentence ran through Ben's head on a loop.

You know that as soon as the premiere is over, she's done with you.

He wanted to discount it, because Simon had said it to him, and Simon was the worst. Except it was true. In all of their conversations about their "relationship," the premiere had been the end point. Anna needed him to be her public boyfriend for some paparazzi shots, and to show up with her on the red carpet, and that was all. Afterward, Ben's services were no longer needed.

He'd thought that was fine, at the beginning. But now . . . now he didn't know how to deal with this. It had been a long time since he'd had a connection with someone like he had with Anna, and he would miss it. He would miss her. And he would worry about her, and how she was doing.

She'd seemed fine on Sunday, after everything that had happened on Saturday. They'd done the stupid grocery store visit Sunday morning—even though he'd tried to talk her out of it, she'd insisted. She'd looked up into his eyes and smiled when she knew the cameras were on them, like nothing had ever been wrong. She hadn't seemed to want to talk about everything on Sunday, and he hadn't pushed. He'd been impressed with how fearless she'd been as they walked out of the store on Sunday afternoon. He supposed this was her job, and it was important for her to just get back to it. But God, he hated that she had to pretend away so many things just to survive.

But that wasn't his business, he reminded himself. Because tonight was the premiere. And then afterward, this was done. They were done.

That would be fine. He'd been in a weird mood for the past few days, but that was probably because he'd been traveling so much, and his whole regular schedule was off. He would be happy to go back to his normal life—to get to have dinner with his mom and Theo on Sunday, to see Dr. Lindsey every Wednesday, even though he'd been avoiding her for the past two weeks—to throw himself back into things like work, and dating, like he had before. He'd slept with the same woman and only the same woman for almost two whole months now. He needed some variety. Yes. Variety would be good.

When he got to Anna's house, Florence let him in.

"Hi, Florence," he said. "Where's Anna?"

"She's swimming. You got the agenda, right?"

Florence had sent him an agenda for today. Yes, he'd gotten it. Had he read it? Well, that was a different story.

"I got it, yeah," he said. "Are we . . . supposed to be somewhere soon?"

Luckily Florence seemed like she frequently dealt with people who didn't read their agendas.

"Not for two hours." That was soon, from his perspective, but okay. "The limo will pick you up here and take you to the hotel—

your premiere clothes are already there, and the glam squad will meet you there. I'll be there, too, a little later, to take some candids for social, and then you'll go from the hotel to the theater."

What she didn't say, but that he already knew, was that his job was to show up, wear what they told him to wear, and not act like an asshole. He could manage that.

"Great. That sounds great. Thank you for making this so easy for us," he said.

Florence picked up her bag and opened the front door.

"That's my job," she said. "But working with people like Anna— and you—makes everything easier for me, too." She stepped outside. "Okay, I'm taking off. See you over there. Text me if anything comes up."

Ben set his bag down and walked into the backyard to find Anna. She sliced through the water quickly and cleanly, a black swim cap on her head. She didn't see him yet, so he sat down to watch her. She'd told him that she loved to swim, and that she got this house partly because the high walls around the pool made it so she could swim anytime, without worrying someone could see her. Last week, they'd gotten in together late at night and spent hours floating there. But he'd never seen her swimming in it like this before, like she could go back and forth forever.

After a while, she surfaced at the shallow end and saw him.

"Ben! When did you get here?"

The smile on her face was so warm, so genuine.

"Not too long ago. Florence let me in, but I didn't want to disturb you."

She pulled herself out of the pool, and his eyes widened.

"You . . . do you always . . ."

She pulled off her swim cap and shook her hair. The water streamed over her breasts and ran down her legs.

"No, I don't always swim topless." She grinned. He knew she

knew what this was doing to him. "But I do when I have some-thing big coming up and I'm swimming during the day—swimsuits give me such distinct tan lines, no matter how much sunscreen I put on. There's body makeup that can deal with all of that, but it's a pain in the ass. I'd rather just make sure I don't have tan lines in the first place."

She walked over to him, and he pulled her down onto his lap. She swung her legs sideways and kissed him.

"You like that, I see."

He ran his lips down over her warm brown skin.

"I like it a lot."

They made it to the hotel in the nick of time, though they kept the limo waiting for a while at Anna's house. As soon as they walked into the suite, it was like he didn't exist—one person im-mediately started blow-drying Anna's hair, another reached for her nails, and a third patted cream on her face.

She winked at him from across the room. At least there was plenty of space in this suite. He had an hour to sit on the couch and work—he was "working from home" today, but since all this was going to end soon, he'd better actually get work done. He had to prove he was more than just a famous person's boyfriend.

You know that as soon as the premiere is over, she's done with you.

He shook that off. At least Simon wasn't there today.

"Ben," Florence called from across the suite. "They're ready for you."

He closed his laptop and walked over, ready to put his tux on, until someone beckoned him into the corner.

"Makeup time."

Right. He'd forgotten that someone would probably want to put makeup on him.

Anna grinned at him from her own chair, where two people were twirling her hair around scary implements.

"It's just a little lip balm and moisturizer," she said. "Did Florence warn you about that?"

He shrugged.

"Probably? She's very detailed, but"—he lowered his voice—"I only skimmed her instructions."

Anna laughed. She looked happy and excited about tonight, which relieved him. She was a great actress, yes, but by this point, he could sense her emotions, even if she was trying to hide them. That she didn't seem anxious about tonight meant he could relax, too.

Though . . . if he saw that photographer from last weekend, it would be hard not to trip him.

Finally, their hours of grooming ended just as Devora walked into the room.

"Anna! Ben! Tonight is going to be amazing."

She unzipped one of the enormous garment bags on the clothing rack and handed Ben his tux.

"Here you go—let me know if you need anything."

He appreciated how everyone who worked for Anna was very helpful and polite to him while at the same time making it clear that Anna was their only priority. He was sure none of them would ever just hand Anna a dress and tell her to let them know if she needed anything.

He ducked into the bedroom and pulled on the perfectly fitted and pressed tux and shirt. At least there was air-conditioning in this room so he wouldn't swelter on this summer day in long sleeves, but he had a feeling he was going to be hot as hell on the red carpet. Maybe someone had a solution for that. He walked out of the bedroom barefoot, jacket over his arm.

"Devora, I just realized . . ." He stopped cold.

Anna turned at his voice. Despite everyone with them in the room, he knew her smile was just for him.

She was in the red dress. He'd been sure she would wear the dress Simon had liked. He hadn't even asked her about it; he didn't want to make her feel bad when she had to tell him. But she was wearing the dress he'd told her he loved.

"The dress," was all he could say. "It's . . . you look so beautiful."

Beautiful wasn't even the right word. He didn't think he could be surprised anymore by Anna, or his reaction to her, but in that dress, with that thrilled, happy, proud look on her face, she shone so brightly it was almost hard to look at her. She beamed as she looked back at him.

"Thank you," she said. "You look pretty great yourself."

Devora looked up from adjusting Anna's dress.

"Was there something you needed?"

Was there something he needed? He looked at her blankly before he realized.

"Shoes! I need shoes."

Devora looked at Anna, and they both smiled. Devora took a box off the top of the clothing rack and handed it to Anna, who walked over to Ben and gave it to him.

"I hope you like them," she said.

Why did they both look like that about some shoes to wear with his tux? Whatever they were, he'd act excited about them.

He opened the box, pushed the tissue aside, and froze.

"How did you do this? How did you know?"

He'd coveted these sneakers for months. They wouldn't even be out for weeks.

Anna had a huge grin on her face.

"I checked in with Maddie. And then Devora pulled a few strings."

He shook his head. He couldn't believe this.

"Wow. I'm . . . Wow."

She laughed and kissed him on the cheek before she went back to Devora.

He sat down to put the sneakers on. And he went back to watching Anna. They'd done something complicated to her hair that made it all flow in waves over one shoulder, and she had very long, very expensive-looking earrings on. Ben couldn't believe he was here, tonight, with her. He couldn't believe any of this had happened. He'd always been pretty sure of himself—with life, with work, with women, all of that. But Anna suddenly felt other-worldly.

Devora and the makeup artist and the hair person all finished their last circles around Anna. She slid her phone into her tiny purse.

"Are you ready for this?" she asked Ben.

"Ready as I'll ever be," he said.

They walked through the hotel, and he realized that Anna's shoes made her much taller than she usually was, even when she was wearing heels.

"I'm sure people always say this to you," he said as they followed Florence to the freight elevator, "but I'm impressed that you can walk so easily in those things."

She relaxed against him as they rode down the elevator.

"Many years of practice," she said. "I'm sure I'll pay dearly for it later in life, and I already have to do all sorts of exercises to strengthen my ankles, but these fabulous shoes are worth it. I'm glad I get to keep them."

He touched her earlobe, and the strings of diamonds swung back and forth.

"Do you get to keep these?" he asked.

Her eyes sparkled at him.

"Wouldn't that be incredible, but no."

They got in the limo in the garage; there were a bunch of other limos there, he assumed waiting for other people also going to the premiere. Anna waved at someone getting into the one next to theirs.

Once they were in the car alone, Ben turned to Anna.

"I can't believe we haven't gone over this, but is there anything I should know for tonight? Not, like, the logistics, but the people— is there anyone you can't stand who you want me to spill a drink on? Anyone who is actually your friend and I don't have to be suspicious of?"

Anna giggled. He'd said all of that partly to relax her, if she needed it. After all, this was the movie that she'd been filming when her anxiety had gotten so bad, so he'd worried that tonight would be hard for her. But she seemed fine.

"This is the rare movie where when I say all of that bullshit in interviews about how we all got along great, it's actually true. But maybe that's because we all filmed so separately that I really only worked closely with a handful of people. And plus, I only filmed, like, seven or so scenes, so I barely know anything that happens in this thing. I still don't even know if I live or die. The plot tonight will be as much of a surprise to me as it will be to you."

She touched his hand.

"Oh, speaking of logistics—on the red carpet tonight, you and I will take a few pictures together, and then someone with a headset on will pull you aside, and you'll step back and I'll do the whole song and dance for the photographers. Just wait for me, and then we can go inside."

He thought about that.

"What if I want to do my *own* song and dance for the photographers? I look pretty good in this tux, you know."

She adjusted his bow tie.

"You do indeed." She touched a finger to her lips, and then to his. "I can't kiss you and mess up my makeup, but don't worry. Later I'll show you exactly how great you look in that tux."

Ben let his eyes move slowly up and down her body.

"I can't even tell you how much I'm looking forward to that," he said.

A few moments later, the noise around the limo increased dramatically. They'd been barely moving once they left the hotel, but they slowed down even more.

"Holy shit." Ben looked out the window at the wall of people lining the streets. "Is it always like this?"

Anna shook her head.

"Just for the big ones. And awards shows, obviously." She grinned. "It's kind of fun to be in a movie that gets all of this. I've done some pretty big stuff, but usually not on this level. They stagger the red carpet arrivals, from least to greatest—I'm in the B+ zone, from what I can tell about the timing. I think that's a good sign? Anyway, none of these people are here for me—well, very few of them, anyway—but it's fun to be a part of it."

A few minutes later, the limo slowed even more, and then stopped. Anna squeezed Ben's hand.

"Glad you're here with me tonight," she said.

Before he could respond, her car door opened, and she stepped out of the car.

He got out on his side, and the cheers almost deafened him. He hoped people from that asshole studio who thought Anna wasn't marketable enough were paying attention.

He joined her at the edge of the walkway and took her hand. It felt natural to do that after the past few weeks.

"Very few people are here for you, huh?" he said to her under his breath as she smiled and waved and blew kisses at the crowd yelling her name.

"That's what I thought," she said when they finally started walking toward the theater. "I guess there are more here for me than I thought."

They walked and waved, walked and waved. A few people even shouted Ben's name, which amused both him and Anna.

Finally, they got to what Florence had informed him was called the "step and repeat," where there were the big movie posters for background, and rows of photographers there to take pictures of them. They held hands as they waited their turn, and Ben looked around at the wild scene that surrounded them.

"Nervous?" Anna asked him. "I was so nervous at my first one of these, my God."

He smiled at her slowly and shook his head.

"With you here next to me? Impossible."

Just then, someone with headphones on came up to Anna.

"Ms. Gardiner? They're ready for you."

"Thanks so much," Anna said. Ben offered her his arm, and they swept into the center of the lights.

Ben *had* been nervous about this part, even though he hadn't wanted to admit that to Anna. He'd been worried he'd embarrass her, that he wouldn't stand in the right way or look in the right place or would have a deer-in-the-headlights blankness on his face and everyone would criticize Anna for whatever he did wrong. But once they were standing there, the lights and cameras all on him, he realized that what he'd said had been right. He had nothing to worry about with Anna there with him. She coached him through the whole thing.

"Just look right to the center," she said as they took their mark. "Everyone is going to try to get you to look at them and their camera, but don't pay them any attention—we will just go center, then left, then right. So for now, just look straight ahead and smile."

The lights and cameras on them were almost blinding, but he

did what she said. He smiled straight ahead, but he had no idea what to do with his hands or feet—thank God Anna's arm was through one of his, but was his hand just supposed to . . . dangle there like that? What did it do normally? He couldn't even remember now.

He obeyed her pressure on his arm and turned with her, first to one side, then the other. And then, before he left to join the person beckoning to him to leave Anna's side, he looked down at her.

"Have I told you yet tonight you look beautiful in that dress? I'm so glad you wore it."

She turned her attention from the cameras to him, and her smile softened.

"I'm so glad I wore it, too."

They smiled at each other like that for just a second, and it felt like they were all alone, no cameras, no lights, no people, just the two of them.

"Um, Mr. Stephens? Can we get some with just Ms. Gardiner?"

He nodded, but he didn't look away from Anna.

"Knock 'em dead," he said to her.

He followed the harried-looking woman to the far side of the step and repeat. He stood there watching Anna as she posed and laughed and gave the world that dazzling smile that now made him think of that moment in the bar when he'd felt he'd truly understood her.

She gave a final wave to the photographers. Then, as he watched, she did a series of interviews with reporters, where she laughed and sparkled and said complimentary things about the movie that he knew were bullshit but sounded very convincing. Finally, she came and joined him.

"Okay." She squeezed his hand. "That part is over. Now it's just like a normal movie night, except in formal wear."

They walked slowly toward the theater—slowly, because every ten seconds Anna would stop and air-kiss someone and introduce him, and then they'd all keep walking and it would happen again.

Once they got inside, there was more circulating—he knew his role in all of these interactions was to smile when Anna introduced him, tell whoever it was that he "loved their work!" and see them light up and turn to Anna and say "You've got a good one here." It happened four times in a row. The fourth time, he and Anna barely moved away before they both burst out laughing.

"If you can say one thing about Hollywood people—and I include myself in this—we're nothing if not predictable about how much we love praise," Anna said.

Ben laughed and touched her arm.

"Yes, but when I say it to *you*, I mean it," he said. "I don't know who most of these people are."

Soon the lights flickered, and they all made their way into the theater. Their seats were in a section reserved for the cast. He'd always been very picky about where he sat in a movie theater, but not even he could complain about this.

When the lights dimmed, all of the chatter quieted. The director and producer—at least, that's who Ben assumed it was—went up onstage and introduced the movie, to much applause, and as soon as they took their seats, the movie started. He and Theo usually went to see movies like this together. He'd always been secretly relieved that Maddie had never wanted to come along. He loved Maddie, but this was their thing. He'd have to bring Theo the action figure that had been waiting on his seat.

He enjoyed the hell out of the movie from the start, though he wasn't a harsh critic of movies like this—all he wanted were some laughs and a few good explosions and he was perfectly happy. The first time Anna was on-screen, he looked over at her, and she had a wide grin on her face. She leaned over to whisper to him.

"I can't wait to see the special effects. Ooh!" Just then, on-screen Anna shot fire out of her fingertips and the whole crowd applauded, Anna included.

Midway through the movie, someone walked into a room carrying a huge suitcase. A very familiar-looking huge suitcase.

Anna grabbed Ben's arm. They looked at each other, their eyes wide, their lips pressed together, both shaking with painful, silent laughter. Finally, something funny happened on-screen, and everyone else in the theater laughed, so Anna and Ben could let out their shouts of laughter. They leaned against each other, laughing and shaking so much they were helpless. He put his arm around her and pulled her close, and she rested her head against his shoulder. It made him so happy that despite her dazzling smile and stunning looks, he still felt like he knew the real Anna, the person who was funny and loving and kind and anxious and courageous and a constant joy to be around, no matter her mood. He felt like he could be like this forever, close to her, laughing with her, with their public face and inside jokes.

And that's when he realized it.

He was in love with her.

That's why he'd felt so bad for the past few days. It was because he knew this was the end, and he didn't want it to be the end, because he was in love with her.

Oh God.

Anna tried to repress her triumphant grin as they walked into the party after the premiere, but it was a serious challenge. She'd been so worried that despite the recent push to have her do promo for the movie, her resulting role would be almost nonexistent. But somehow, in the editing and the CGI-ing of the movie, her role had magically become a pivotal one. She'd been so happy, so relieved, in the theater she'd almost cried. She did cry when her character got huge cheers from the crowd in the theater in the final scene. And she hadn't died! Which might mean another big paycheck in the future, if she was lucky.

But even better than that, if what her gut was telling her was right—and it often was, at least for things like this—this role was going to be great for her career in so many other ways. The box office for this movie would be over-the-top no matter what, but if her reviews were excellent, and if the press came calling, that would mean very good things for her ability to get everything else she wanted.

Like the role in the Varon film.

Damn, did she feel victorious. All of her stress, all of her hard work—it had all been worth it.

Her smile got wider.

"Anna!" One of the other women in the movie—whom she'd filmed no scenes with; it was that kind of movie—opened her arms. "You were incredible! Wasn't she incredible, Jeff?" she said to the man next to her, presumably her husband. "And I love your dress!" Anna had only met her twice before, but she gave her an enormous hug and vigorous air-kiss. Which, she was glad to see, a photographer was just in the right place to catch.

Since last year, she'd worried that her anxiety would bleed over and infect the things she loved about this job—the acting itself, most of all, but also parties like the one tonight. Where she and her colleagues could embrace and celebrate one another, make connections, even make friends. Some of her best Hollywood friendships had come from industry parties like this one, mostly starting from tipsy chats in the bathroom, like with all good parties. And tonight, she was so relieved that she could still find joy in nights like this that she almost laughed out loud.

And she loved her dress, too. She usually wore sleek, appropriate, boring looks to things like this—she didn't love any of them, but they were what designers would make for her size, and she looked good in them. She never got on any best-dressed lists for them, but she never got on any worst-dressed lists, either. Except for that time at the Golden Globes, when she'd gone rogue. But this dress was the opposite of her usual dresses, and she felt incredible in it. It was fun, and a little frothy, but still elegant. It felt like her. She was so glad Ben had encouraged her to wear it.

She introduced Ben to everyone, and they all exclaimed over him and air-kissed him, which she was pretty sure amused them both. He'd been on the quiet side since they'd left the theater, but no matter how much of an extrovert someone was, parties like this were overwhelming the first time. At one point he disappeared, then came back and handed her a plate of finger food— everything small enough that she could pop it in her mouth with one bite and not mess up her lipstick. Bless him.

She was happy that Ben got to see her in her element tonight, especially after last week. She hated that he'd seen her fall apart like that—it was one thing for him to know what she'd been through last year, but another for him to see it. She didn't want him to think she was the fragile, needy person she'd been last week; she didn't want anyone to think of her like that.

Tonight she was a star, and Ben had a front-row seat. Every so often she could feel his eyes on her, and she would look at him and smile. Maybe the next time he came down . . .

Oh. Right. There wasn't going to be a next time. She'd forgotten.

Well, but did it have to be that way? They could keep this going for a while, couldn't they? Why had they given the premiere as an arbitrary end date, after all? That had been all Simon, but she might need this to continue for a little while longer, just through the press for this movie, and whatever came afterward. She'd see what Ben thought.

"Are you bored? Do you want to go?" she asked him under her breath.

He shook his head.

"I'm happy to stay as long as you want to—this is a great night for you; you should enjoy it."

She kissed his cheek.

"Thank you. I hope you're having fun, too."

He touched her arm.

"Of course I am."

But she wasn't convinced by the look on his face. She knew him too well by now for that. She started to ask him if something was wrong, but then he smiled that wicked smile of his at her.

"I'll be having even more fun later."

She laughed and started to answer but heard her name again and turned away from him.

Thirty minutes later, though, she touched his hand.

"You ready? Let's head for the door."

She didn't stop to wait for his answer.

"Are you sure?" he asked her as they made their way out. "You seem like you're having fun."

She nodded.

"I am. But I learned awhile ago I have to leave these things when I'm still having fun—much better to do it then than five minutes after it all stops being fun."

They slipped out the back door, and Ben quickly found their waiting limo.

"You didn't say good-bye to anyone," Ben said once they got inside. "I wouldn't expect you to be the type to disappear like that."

She laughed.

"I didn't used to be, but you've got to do it at these things! Otherwise you're there twice as long."

She pulled her phone out of her purse. She had to text Simon about tonight.

He'd texted her already.

My phone has been ringing off the hook about you tonight.
Have a lot of champagne, we'll talk tomorrow.

She grinned.

On it. Not to jinx anything, but . . . I'm feeling good about
tonight. Really good.

Me too.

Ben was silent next to her, but she flicked the light on in the back of the limo, leaned in close, and took a selfie with him. He smiled obediently when she held up her phone.

"Had to memorialize tonight just for me," she said.

He gestured to her phone.

"Was that Simon?"

She put it back in her purse.

"Yeah—he's already been hearing a lot of buzzy things about tonight! Ahhh, I'm trying not to get my hopes up, but—"

Ben put his hand on her cheek.

"That never works. Get your hopes up all you want—life is more fun that way."

She put her hand on top of his.

"You're right. I will."

She'd expected, after what he'd said at the party, that Ben would be all over her in the limo. But he seemed content to sit there with his arm around her and his hand in hers as they drove home in the glowing nighttime sky. She almost turned to kiss him, but he'd seemed a little off for the past few hours, so she held back. She wanted to give him room to breathe, too, like he'd given her the week before.

When they got home, she took off her shoes by the front door.

"My feet are going to kill me tomorrow—ask me then if I thought these shoes were worth it," she said as they walked together into the kitchen.

She reached into the fridge and took out the pizza she'd had Florence pick up this morning.

"Now we can eat—I never actually get to really eat at those things—I'm always too busy talking to people. So I planned ahead for when we'd get home starving." She smiled up at him and noticed that he'd loosened his tie. "But thank you for getting me snacks tonight; that was the best."

He smiled down at her. Something was different in his smile.

"What is it?" she asked him. "Is something wrong?"

He hesitated, then shook his head.

"Nothing at all." He took the pizza box from her and set it down on the counter. "I just have to do this."

She expected him to kiss her, but he didn't. He took her hand and led her to the bedroom.

He turned on the light when they got into her room and just looked at her for a long moment. Finally, he reached for her hair, and slowly, delicately, took out all of the bobby pins holding it in place, one by one. When her hair was free, he kissed one shoulder, then the other. He walked around behind her and lifted her hair out of the way and kissed the nape of her neck. The ripples of his kiss shimmered over her whole body.

He slowly pulled down the zipper on her dress and followed the line of the zipper with his kisses. Soft. Gentle. But with so much promise of what was to come. When the zipper was finally all the way down, she let the dress fall to the floor and stepped out of it. She turned around to look at him and saw the hunger in his eyes. But there was joy, too, and kindness, and that laughter that was always just under the surface with Ben.

She reached for him, but he stepped back.

"Not yet," he said.

She dropped her hands. She would let him be in control to-night.

He unhooked her bra, and as he took it off her body, he cupped her breasts in his hands, just for a second.

Then he moved his hands over her whole body. He lingered on her hips, her waist, her thighs. He slowly pulled down the shape-wear he'd called sexy last week. She usually made sure to get rid of it before any man saw her in it—she'd abandoned pairs more than once in bathroom stall garbage cans before leaving parties—but tonight, she hadn't bothered.

He ran his hands all along the sides of her body. His touch was intoxicating her, almost drugging her. She wanted him to kiss her, she wanted to pull his clothes off, but she wanted to stay right here in this moment forever.

He took her face in his hands. He looked at her and she looked back, right into his eyes. She was glad there was enough light in the room for her to see the expression on his face. It made her shiver.

Then he kissed her. His lips were firm and tender, but de-manding. She gave him everything he wanted, and she wanted it, too, all of it. She pulled his tie off and dropped it to the floor, and reached for the buttons on his shirt. This time he let her. As they kissed, she slipped each button open slowly and carefully. She pushed his shirt off of his body and reached for his belt. Soon his pants dropped to the floor.

He stepped out of his clothes, took her hand, and led her to the bed.

As soon as they lay down, his hands and lips and tongue were all over her. Touching, probing, licking, sucking, like he couldn't get enough of her. Or maybe that was just how she felt, like his touch and his body on hers made her crave more and more.

She pulled him up so she could kiss him, and this time she traveled down his body, this time she made him shudder and sigh and whisper her name. Just as she put her lips around his cock, he stopped her.

"No, please. I want you. I need you." He leaned over and pulled on a condom while she lay back and watched him.

He knelt on top of her and slowly lowered himself inside her. She gasped as he entered her, at how good this felt, at how much she wanted him, at how right it felt to be there together with him. They knew each other so well by now, what they liked, how they liked to be touched, all those secret places and slight movements that made the other cry out. But it still felt different every time, it still felt new and exciting, it still felt like there was so much more to explore and discover.

He started moving faster, and she was close, so close, and she rose up to meet him. He reached down and touched her, just where she needed it, and she cried out, but she kept moving with him until she heard him gasp and moan, and they collapsed together.

When their breathing slowed, he turned to her, that grin of his back on his face.

"Okay. Now we can have pizza."

She laughed and started to get up, but he stopped her.

"No. I'll get it."

He came back upstairs a few minutes later carrying the pizza box, a big bottle of sparkling water, and a stack of napkins.

"I know, you're classy, I should have brought plates, but there's only so much a man can carry."

She just laughed and took the pizza from him. They sat in the middle of her bed and had a picnic.

"Day-old lukewarm pizza has never tasted so good," she said as she reached for a second slice.

Ben smiled at her. Then he froze. And slowly lowered his own half-eaten second slice to his side of the pizza box.

"Um. Anna."

She looked up from her pizza to him.

"Yeah?"

He swallowed.

"A few weeks ago." He stopped, and started again. "A few weeks ago you said there's a thing that I do, that when I'm upset or I don't want to deal with something, I turn to sex. And I told you I wouldn't . . . I wouldn't do that with you anymore."

She lowered her pizza to the box.

"Yeah?" Something must have happened tonight to upset him. Had she said something? She had to wait for him to tell her.

"The thing is, I realized tonight. I'm in love with you."

Twenty

ANNA JUST STARED AT HIM.

"What?"

"I love you. I've fallen in love with you." Now that he'd said it, he couldn't stop. "I realized it tonight. During the movie. And I wasn't going to . . . I didn't know how to deal with that. You were right, I do use sex as a distraction—to distract myself as much as other people. But I couldn't leave tomorrow without telling you."

She kept staring at him.

He hadn't known what he'd expected to happen when he said all of this to her. He hadn't really expected anything. He hadn't really planned to do this at all.

But he wished she would say something.

"Ben. I . . ." She stopped.

Okay, well. That's not what he wished she would say. Not "Ben" in that condescending, gentle way.

He picked up his pizza. There was nothing he wanted less than to eat it now.

"Never mind. I get it. It's okay."

She put her hand on his arm. He shook it off.

"Don't," he said. "Please."

She didn't say anything else.

Eventually, she got up and took the rest of the pizza down to the kitchen. He went to the bathroom, cursed at himself in the mirror, and was in bed by the time she came back into the room.

She turned off the light without saying anything and got in her side of the bed. Her bed was so big that they each had plenty of room. He'd never realized that before, since they'd always slept together in the middle. But now she was on her side, and he was on the other side, and no one reached across the center.

When he woke up the next morning, she was still asleep. He found his phone and turned off the alarm that was set to go off thirty minutes later, and got in the shower. If he was quiet enough, maybe he could shower and get dressed and leave before she even woke up. He felt like a coward even thinking that, but he just couldn't face the pity that he knew would be in her eyes today.

But his luck had abandoned him. When he came out of the bathroom, her bed was empty, and he heard the unmistakable signs of coffee making from the kitchen. Okay. He could do this. He'd faced worse. He pulled his clothes on, threw all of his stuff into his overnight bag, and walked into the kitchen.

"Hey," she said in a cheerful voice. "Florence got us pastries for this morning. I just heated them up in the toaster oven."

She was going to pretend last night away. Thank God. The last thing he wanted was to have some sort of heartfelt "You're really great, but" "I'm just not in a place for" "Don't worry about me" kind of conversation with her. He'd had those before, lots of them. But he'd always been on the other side. He'd thought his side sucked. He'd had no idea.

"Oh, awesome, I'm starving," he said. His voice even sounded normal to him. His car to the airport would be here in an hour; he could handle being like this for an hour. Once he left here, he was headed straight from the plane to his office, where he had so much work he had to do he wouldn't have to think about this.

He picked up his mug and added the sugar she'd taken out of the cabinet for him. The coffee was strong, like her coffee always was, and today he needed that. He had to talk, to fill the silence for the next hour.

"Any more word from Simon since last night?" he asked.

Her face lit up.

"He's sent me a ton of fantastic reviews of the movie, and specifically of me in the movie. And everyone loved my dress! Thank God, because I loved it, too, and I would have been insulted if anyone called it fugly this time."

The toaster oven timer went off, and he took the pastries out of it. He needed something to do, so he wouldn't think about that dress and her in it. And when he'd taken her out of it.

"Oh, that's great," he said. "I hope that means more good news is coming for you." He inspected the plate of pastries. "Florence is an angel—ham and cheese croissant, cinnamon roll, and a raspberry Danish? Bless her."

He picked up the raspberry Danish. He wanted the croissant, but he knew Anna would want that one.

They passed the next hour with conversation about the movie, that one actor who had gotten incredibly drunk the night before, and the ad campaign for sneakers he'd been working on. The pitch was coming up, and he was excited about it. Had been, anyway. He managed to act upbeat and relaxed the whole time—he was great at that.

Finally, there was a ring at the gate that meant Ben's ride to the airport was there. Anna buzzed the driver through, and Ben picked up his bag.

"Thanks so much, Ben. For everything," Anna said. "I couldn't have made it through these past few weeks without you—I appreciate everything you did for me so much. I have no idea how I'll ever be able to repay you."

He grinned at her and shrugged.

"No repayment necessary. I had a blast. Do you have any idea how much my friends are freaking out about all of this? I'll be able to start stories with "While I was dating Anna Gardiner . . ." for years to come. And my family is losing their shit. I had a great time. Good luck with the Varon film and everything else."

She grinned back at him.

"Thanks, I'm keeping my fingers crossed. And, you know, I'm up in the Bay Area at least a few times a year to see my family; maybe sometime when I'm around, we could get together again, catch up."

He started to say sure, that would be great, she should text him. But he couldn't do it. He shook his head.

"I don't think so, Anna. Take care of yourself."

He turned and went out the door.

Anna stood, motionless, in her kitchen after the front door closed softly behind Ben.

What had just happened? Had Ben really said that last night? And then said what he'd said, just now?

Her heart was beating fast. She didn't know how to react, how to think. She hadn't expected that. She hadn't expected anything like that.

No. She couldn't think about this. This was too much.

She had enough to deal with right now, from putting her world back together and taking care of her mental health to fighting tooth and nail for her career to trying to take care of her parents from afar. She didn't have space in her life or in her heart for one more thing. Ben knew that.

He hadn't meant it. He couldn't have. Ben wasn't the type to fall in love—she knew that, they were very similar in that way. That was part of the reason she'd trusted him to do all of this in the first place; she knew he wouldn't care when it was over!

She thought of that crushed, broken look on his face, right before he walked out the door.

No. No, she couldn't deal with this.

She pulled off her pajamas, put on a swimming suit, and got in her pool. She tried not to think about Ben's eyes when he'd seen her get out of the pool topless the day before.

She swam laps, back and forth and back and forth, to try to feel better, to forget what Ben had said, to get back into herself.

Her phone rang just as she finished getting dressed. At first, she ignored it. If it was Ben, she didn't want to deal with it; if it was Simon, she could call him back.

She looked at the screen just in case. Penny. Okay, fine.

"Hey," she said as she picked up the phone.

"You looked incredible last night!" Penny said. "That dress was different from what you usually wear, and I loved it. Not that I don't usually like your dresses, well, except for that time at the Golden Globes."

Everyone brought up that fucking dress she'd worn to the Golden Globes.

"Look, that one was an experiment, okay? It didn't go well, we don't need to ever speak of it again."

"I know, I know," Penny said. "I'm just mentioning it in the context of how last time you experimented was bad but this time was great."

Anna dropped down on the bed.

"This one was great, wasn't it? I loved it. Ben helped me pick it out." And then she burst into tears.

"What did he do? Anna, do you need me to come there? Do you need me to destroy him? What do you need?"

She wiped her face with her pillowcase.

"He told me he loved me."

Penny was silent for a few seconds.

"And what did you say?"

Anna knew she was going to ask that.

"Nothing! He caught me so off guard, Penny! I had no idea what to say. He just sprang this on me last night—I didn't expect it at all. I have so much going on right now, nothing like this occurred to me. I tried to say something, but it wasn't going to be . . . and I'm sure he could tell that because he stopped me. Anyway, this morning, things were weird, and now he's gone and I feel like the world's biggest asshole."

See, this was why she only ever got involved with other actors—there were no surprises with them.!

"You aren't the world's biggest asshole," Penny said. "There are many people vying for that title, and you're nowhere near them. What do you mean, things were weird this morning?"

Talking to Penny always made her feel better.

"I don't know, we talked and drank coffee and stuff while we waited for his car to come, but . . . it was . . . off. But he didn't say it again, and he didn't seem like he was, I don't know, thinking it. Maybe he didn't mean it?" Anna pictured Ben's face, right before he'd turned and left her house. She must have just imagined that look on his face. "He probably didn't mean it."

"Do you think he meant it?" Penny asked.

"He couldn't have. At first I thought he meant it. Last night, I mean. It just came out of nowhere; I was so shocked, I didn't know what to think, or how to react. But now I think he must have been just caught up in all the glamour of the premiere and the Hollywood thing and seeing me on-screen and being with me at the party and all of that. Or maybe this is all because of last week: he thinks I'm weak and fragile, he just wants to take care of me. I never should have told him about last year in the first place—men always like that kind of thing; it makes them feel strong."

Yes, that made more sense. He couldn't have meant it. She got up to go get some water.

"Okay, but are you sure he's like that? He didn't seem that type," Penny said. "You guys seemed to really get along well. Are you sure that you don't think you—"

"Penny, Ben's great, I liked him a lot, and yes, we got along great! He's the first guy I slept with in over a year, of course I feel happy, warm feelings for him, especially since he was so kind, so fun, so . . ." She stopped, and shook her head. "Also, the sex was fantastic! But that was just sex! This thing with Ben was just an interlude, a way to get me from point A to B, A being Anxious Anna still recovering from everything, who hadn't let a man see her naked in over a year, B being a Bad Bitch who stars in box office hits and gets magazine covers and beckons at whatever man she wants and he comes running, throwing his clothes off in the process."

By this time they were both laughing.

"A Bad Bitch?" Penny said.

"Look, it was alliterative, okay? You know what I mean! Him falling in love with me was not in the plan! We both knew what this was when we went into it! And yes, sure, Ben makes—*made*—me feel incredible! But those weren't real feelings, that was just good sex emotion! I trusted him to know the difference!"

Penny was still giggling.

"Okay," she said when she recovered. "You know, look. You *are* Anna Gardiner, international movie star, after all. Maybe the good sex emotion you give out is just that much more convincing than other people. Ben probably does know the difference for normal women, but for you, he was just so overcome in the moment. Maybe he didn't actually mean it; he just thought he did. But he'll get over it fast."

Yes! See? This made sense!

"Penelope Malone, you're a genius. Of course that's it. See, I should have called you right away."

Oh no, she shouldn't have said that. Now Penny would gloat . . .

"I *am* a genius, as a matter of fact, and you *should* have called me right away. Anything else you need me to solve for you?"

Anna just laughed.

Penny's voice softened.

"No, really, I mean it. Are you okay? You know I'm here for you, no matter what, right?"

She did know that.

"Yeah. I'm okay. But, I've been thinking about . . ." She shook her head. "No, it's nothing. Never mind, forget I said anything."

"Anna."

"Okay, fine, I'll tell you, but I'm not going to do this. It's just that I keep thinking about something Ben said a few weeks ago— not about all of this. But I was saying something about all of the charities who ask me for money, and he said maybe I should do more, instead of just sending a check. Like my dad has been wanting me to do for forever. And Ben suggested a mental health charity, help them raise money and reach out to people, raise awareness, that kind of thing. But. That seems . . ."

"Hard?" Penny finished for her. "And that you might have to talk about things you don't want to talk about? Yeah, probably. But if you keep thinking about it, maybe there's a reason?"

Anna closed her eyes.

"Maybe. But I'm still not going to do it."

Penny's voice sounded tentative.

"Will you be mad if I say I really liked Ben?"

Anna sighed.

"No. I really liked Ben, too."

Twenty-One

BEN WALKED INTO DR. LINDSEY'S OFFICE THE FOLLOWING Wednesday. Since he'd last seen Anna, he'd worked multiple twelve-hour days—including one on that Thursday when he'd gone straight to the office from the airport, and one on Saturday, prepping for the sneaker pitch. Sunday he'd only worked five hours, and with the rest of his time that day he'd cleaned his apartment from top to bottom. He'd planned to reinstall all of his dating apps, to go out on a bunch of dates, to sleep with someone else, to get Anna out of his mind and soul. But he hadn't done it.

He'd dreaded this appointment with Dr. Lindsey. He hadn't told anyone what had happened with Anna. What was even the point? He knew that after a while, she'd mention in some stupid article that she was single again—that had been in her and Simon's plan, after all—and then he'd say something to his family about it. Someday, he'd figure out what to do with those sneakers Anna gave him. For now, he just muted the family group text, avoided Theo's calls, and left the sneakers where they were, shoved in the back of a closet. But he worried that Dr. Lindsey would see right through him.

He sat down on her couch, determined to just get this appointment over with and go on with his day.

"How was your week, Ben?" she asked to start him off, the way she always did.

He shrugged.

"Not terrible—the premiere with Anna was last week." God, it hurt to even say her name. He was pathetic. "So that was fun. That whole thing is over now, though."

She looked over her folded hands at him.

"And how do you feel about that?" Of course she asked that.

He was going to lie, was going to say he felt fine, that he was ready to get back to his normal life.

But he just couldn't do it. Why the fuck was he in therapy in the first place if he wasn't going to talk about the hard stuff?

"I feel like shit about it," he said. "I told her I fell in love with her. After the premiere. I didn't realize it until then. So I told her." He could feel himself getting choked up. Fuck. He had to stop talking for a second, so his voice wouldn't betray him. "It didn't go well."

He looked down so he wouldn't have to see the look on Dr. Lindsey's face.

"Oh, Ben. Oh, Ben, I'm so sorry. From the way you talked about her, I wondered if maybe . . . but I didn't—forgive me for saying this, but I didn't think you'd tell her."

He looked up at her. She looked so kind he had to look away.

"No forgiveness necessary. I honestly hadn't planned to tell you, either, but"—he lifted his hands—"I had to tell someone, and that's kind of your job. Anyway. I feel like shit. I guess I already said that, but . . . I don't know, I don't know how to deal with this, and it sucks. Can you . . . What can you do to make me not feel like shit?"

She laughed, but kindly. Laugh number five!

"Oh, Ben. I'm so sorry. Unfortunately, there's no quick cure for feeling like shit after a breakup—if there was, I'd probably be out of a job. But—can I ask you—why did you tell her?"

He looked down at his hands.

"She said—a few weeks back, we were being kind of snippy with each other, and then I kissed her, just, I guess, to make it all stop, and she said something that I feel like you've been trying to tell me for . . . years now. That I use sex as a distraction when I'm upset or I don't want to deal with something. And so that night, after I realized that . . . I loved her, and after we had sex, I thought about that. And also about what you said not long ago."

She looked surprised.

"Which thing I said?"

"That thing about how sometimes it's important to tell people how you feel just to say it. I hadn't . . . I didn't really understand what you meant then. But I guess I figured it out."

"Are you glad you told her?" she asked. "Even though she didn't respond in the way you wished she would?"

He thought about that for a long time. About how broken he'd felt in Anna's bed that night, how he'd wished he could take it back, how ashamed he'd been, how stupid he'd felt.

And then he'd thought about what it would have felt like to keep pretending forever. To have her come to the Bay Area to see her parents and text him, and pretend all he wanted from her was a few hours of mutual pleasure. To pretend that to her, and to himself.

"Not at first. At first, I was so humiliated. I hated doing it. I hated myself for doing it. Everything about it felt awful. It was one of the hardest things I've ever done. I've hated every day since." He bit his lip. "But yeah. I'm glad I did it."

He took a deep breath.

"And while I'm talking about things. There's something else I haven't told you. I found out a few months ago that I have a sister. Dawn."

Dr. Lindsey nodded slowly. That made him realize just how much he'd shocked her when he told her what he'd said to Anna—she'd been so visibly surprised then that she was almost relaxed at this bombshell.

"Oh wow. Okay, that's a big deal," she said in her soothing voice. "From your father, I assume? How did you find out?"

And then he told her the whole story. About the emails, and what he'd said to her, and what he hadn't told her. And that she wanted to meet him.

"And I've been . . . avoiding her ever since then," he said. "She sent a few emails about the Anna stuff when she saw it in the news, but I kept taking longer and longer between replies to her, and I finally just . . . stopped." He swallowed. "Hearing from her . . . it brought up some stuff about my dad, that I thought I'd dealt with. And I guess I was worried that this would mess up what Theo and I have. But that seems stupid now. Maybe I was just afraid of more change. And of having to think about—and talk about—my dad again, when I thought I was all done with that."

Dr. Lindsey raised her eyebrows.

"You thought you were all done with that?"

He laughed out loud, and she joined in. Six!

"Anna . . ." He let out a breath. "Anna said something similar when I told her about it."

Dr. Lindsey smiled at him.

"You and Anna talked about a lot, it seems."

She had no idea.

"Yeah. We did."

He left Dr. Lindsey's office feeling exhausted and wrung out, but also relieved. It had hurt—a lot—to tell her about Anna, and about Dawn. But somehow he felt better. Like he didn't have to deal with all of this alone.

Speaking of.

I know you're busy, but when are you free for a drink? Yes I'll come to the east bay.

Theo texted back a few minutes later.

He's alive! This week is a nightmare, but next week?

Okay. He could wait until then.

Anna woke up to the sound of her phone ringing. It was late, she was usually up by then, but she hadn't been sleeping well. It had been taking a long time to fall asleep, and then she would wake up in the middle of the night and stare at her ceiling for hours, before she finally fell back asleep right around sunrise.

She sat up and tried to clear the sleep out of her voice.

"It's not official, but . . . you got it," Simon said when she answered.

She froze.

"I got it? IT? I got it?"

Simon laughed.

"The Varon film. Yes. Maggie should get the official call for you in the next few days." He laughed again. "But you know me, I wanted to be the one to share the news first."

Of course he did.

Anna dropped back down on her pillows.

"I can't believe it. After everything. I got it."

After Ben. After she'd broken Ben's heart, just for this. And she'd gotten it. Was it worth it?

Yes, of course it was. Plus, hadn't she realized she hadn't really broken Ben's heart, that he hadn't meant it?

"Also," Simon said, "we need to talk about the rollout. Once they announce this, everyone is going to want to talk to you, so I thought we should strategize about this first, so we can have a plan. Maybe come up with some reporters you've liked in the past, and do the interview with them. You can slide in there that you're single now, too, so we can close that whole chapter. Oh, speaking of, I forgot to ask—did everything go okay there? With the end of it, I mean."

Why had he asked her that?

"Oh yeah, everything went fine. No problems." That wasn't exactly a lie—Simon wouldn't consider Ben's heartbreak a problem he had to be concerned with.

"Good. That all went much better than I thought it would. Anyway, about the reporters—you liked that woman who interviewed you for *Vogue* awhile ago, right?"

Anna had liked her, as a matter of fact.

"Oh yeah, she was great. Let's get her, if we can." She and Simon came up with a list of a few more potential journalists for the interview.

She took a deep breath right before they got off the phone.

"Oh, and Simon. Can you get me some names of a handful of good charities that deal with mental health that might need some help?"

There was silence on the phone for a moment.

"Are you sure about this, Anna?"

She closed her eyes.

"No. But get me the names anyway, okay?"

A week later, a red sports car pulled up to Anna's house. A Black woman with her hair up in a topknot got out and waved to someone inside, who drove off.

"Nice ride," Anna said, when she opened the front door. "Hi, Nik, good to see you again."

Nik Paterson grinned.

"Hi, Anna. It's not my car—mine broke down this morning, so I had to hitch a ride."

"Coffee?" Anna asked Nik as they walked toward the kitchen. "I seem to remember that you drink as much as I do."

Nik laughed.

"You have a good memory. And yeah, I'd love some coffee."

They made small talk about the weather, her new kitchen— she'd moved into this house since the last time she'd talked to Nik—and car disasters they'd experienced.

Once they had coffee in hand, Anna walked her out to the backyard. It wasn't too hot yet today, so she figured it would be nicer to do this out there than inside. She already had—Florence already had—sparkling water out there waiting for them.

"So." Nik took out her phone, a notebook, and a tape recorder. "Do you mind if I record this?"

"Not at all," Anna said. She took a sip of coffee, hoping it would give her courage. Despite what she'd said to that charity yesterday, she still didn't have to do this. They would understand, Simon would make polite excuses, she'd write a big check.

"Let's talk about this movie you're doing with Liz Varon. This sounds like the perfect vehicle for you."

That could be empty flattery, but Anna didn't think so. She'd read some of Nik's other pieces.

"Thanks, that's just how I feel," she said. "As soon as I read the script, I called Liz. I felt like the role was mine from the first page, that I wouldn't be complete until I played her, and until I got to work with Liz. I really can't wait. It's going to be tough, but I'm ready for it."

They talked about the role more, and then Anna's role in *Vigilantes*. Anna was very diplomatic about her work there, and Nik gave her a knowing look about it but let it pass. Nik knew this business as well as she did; she understood.

"What was filming that role like?" Nik asked her. "There were so many demands on you then, especially following your Oscar nomination—you filmed three movies back to back to back, didn't you?"

Anna nodded.

"I did, in three different locations. It was . . ." She looked at Nik's friendly, open expression. "It was really hard on me, actually. I've had . . . I've experienced anxiety for a long time, though for a lot of my life I didn't realize what that was, I didn't have the language to explain why my stomach hurt like that, why I could barely function some days. When I was a kid, my parents didn't know how to deal with it. I think . . . you know, we don't talk about mental health enough. My dad is a minister; we didn't talk about therapy when I was a kid, just prayer. So I just thought that if I pushed on and worked harder and ignored my stress and anxiety, I'd get over it, and it would all be fine."

Nik gave her a small smile.

"And that didn't work out well?"

"Not at all!" Anna said, and they both laughed. "After . . . during, I should say, during that filming, I struggled a lot. I seemed fine on set, I don't think anyone noticed, but inside . . . it was rough. Finally, after filming was over, I . . ." She closed her eyes. "I'm sorry, I haven't really talked about this with a lot of people."

Nik's voice was gentle.

"It's okay. This stuff is hard, I know."

Anna nodded. She opened her eyes and continued.

"After the filming was over, I had a real crisis. I think having to go there every day and be around people kept me from thinking about everything. But then I was just alone with my thoughts and it was all . . . really hard."

She stopped talking and took a long breath. Nik didn't say anything, but the silence was an easy one.

"I'm glad I had my family—they really helped get me through the past year." She smiled. "My dad has evolved a lot—now he both prays for me *and* helped me find a great therapist. Therapy has helped a lot. And my friends were wonderful. Ben's been so supportive. Now I know that when my anxiety gets bad in the future, I won't feel so lost about what to do. Because this is a hard business, you know that, and I'm glad I know what I need to do to keep myself well." She wiped her eyes. "But it's not just people like me—there are a lot of people who need support to get through the hard times, and aren't as fortunate as I am. And as we both know, health care is inaccessible for so many people in America, and mental health care even more so. And that's why I'm going to be working with an organization here in L.A. that concentrates on getting free and low-cost mental health services to people— especially people in the Black community—who don't have the resources I did. I want everyone to be able to have the tools and support I had—that I have—and I want to help combat the stigma against getting help for mental health. This feels like a great way to start."

Nik smiled at her.

"A really great way to start," she said.

They talked for a while longer, about why she'd been so excited about the Varon role, about working with the guy who was going to be her costar, whom she'd met briefly a handful of times but had never worked with before, about her house, and how much she loved her swimming pool, but the hard part was over.

When they were winding down, Nik picked up her phone.

"I'm sorry, I have to send a quick text to get picked up."

Anna waved that away, and walked her through her garden as they waited.

"I should probably tell you I work really hard on this and I commune with nature as I weed and water and clip flowers, but really I have an excellent gardener who comes twice a week and does all of that and leaves me big vases full of flowers in my house."

Nik laughed.

"Hey, we can't all be good at everything."

The gate rang, and Anna buzzed Nik's ride in. She walked her outside to see the same red sports car driving up.

"Oh, is this a friend of yours? I assumed it was an Uber or something, but you usually don't get the same one."

Nik smiled.

"It's my fiancé." Anna looked down and saw what she hadn't noticed earlier: the simple gold solitaire on Nik's finger.

"Oh! Congratulations." Anna seemed to remember Nik had started dating one of her former costars. "It's not . . . that guy I worked with, right?"

Nik laughed. Hard.

"No, oh God, no. I met Carlos right after—just as, actually— Fisher and I broke up. Carlos is . . . really great."

Carlos got out of the car and bowed to both of them.

"Your chariot awaits, ma'am."

Anna laughed, and Nik rolled her eyes, but with a grin on her face.

"He's also a ham. And a big fan of yours."

Anna walked over to the car, her hand outstretched.

"Carlos? I'm Anna. Nice to meet you."

Carlos grinned as he shook her hand.

"A real pleasure to meet you, Anna."

Anna turned to Nik.

"When's the wedding?"

Nik and Carlos looked at each other and laughed.

"That's still . . . under discussion," Nik said. "We have slightly different visions for a wedding, but we'll get there soon."

Anna looked at Nik and Carlos as they smiled at each other. She could feel the love flowing back and forth between them. She wanted . . . no. Not now. She couldn't think about that now.

She gave Nik a hug good-bye and watched them drive away.

Twenty-Two

BEN WAITED AT THE BAR FOR THEO. HE LIKED THIS PLACE—
he'd been wanting to come here for a while, but between work
and . . . Anna, he hadn't been over to the East Bay in way too long.
And between his work on that sneaker pitch—which had finally happened the day before, and he'd been great; Roger had even congratulated him afterward—and Theo's planning for city council meetings,
it had taken awhile before they'd actually been able to meet up.

He kept thinking one day he'd wake up and not care about
Anna anymore. That he would be over her, like she never existed,
like he'd never met her and fallen in love with her, like she hadn't
become wedged into his life. It hadn't happened yet. He thought
about her every night as he fell asleep, her name was on his lips
every morning as he woke up. One night he dreamt she was there
with him; waking up that morning had been awful.

He hadn't even realized he'd been falling in love with her. If
he had known, could he have stopped himself? He knew that this
wasn't what she wanted; he shouldn't have let himself do it.

But he couldn't regret a single moment he'd spent with her.

Suddenly his brother dropped into the seat next to him.

"I can't believe you're here before me," Theo said.

"I'm always here before you," Ben said. "You're always running even later than I am; you just seem so responsible and put together that everyone forgets that about you."

Theo laughed as he nodded at the bartender and pointed at Ben's drink.

"I'm glad I seem that way, at least. So, how are lifestyles of the rich and famous over here?"

Oh. He'd been concentrating so much on telling Theo about Dawn he'd forgotten he had to tell him about Anna, too.

"That's . . . all over," he said.

Theo raised his eyebrows.

"Just like that? When you were at that premiere with her everything looked great between the two of you."

He should have told Theo the truth from the beginning.

About everything.

"Yeah, well. I thought it was great, too. But, the thing is, none of it was real." Theo started to say something, but Ben held up a hand. "Let me back up."

He told Theo about what Anna had asked him to do and why.

"I'm sorry I didn't tell you. She didn't want anyone to know, but I should have pushed harder on that. And please don't tell me I never should have done it—the universe told me that loud and clear." He stared down into his drink. "I fell in love with her."

Theo looked at him, then signaled to the bartender again.

"Can we get two of those grilled cheese sandwiches, please?" He turned back to Ben when the bartender was gone. "Okay. You've got to tell her. Remember when I—"

Ben interrupted.

"Let me stop you right there. I told her. It . . . didn't go well. So. It's all over."

Theo was silent for a moment.

"Fuck. Ben, I'm sorry. What did she say? Are you not rich enough for her, or famous enough, or—"

Ben shook his head.

"Don't. I know you're trying to help, but she's not like that. I'm not saying she's perfect, but that didn't matter; I loved everything about her. It was just . . . she didn't love me back, that's all."

Fuck if that didn't hurt to say.

Theo put his hand on his shoulder.

"Damn. I'm really sorry. That fucking sucks."

Ben let out a long breath. It felt good to hear someone else say that.

"Yeah. It really fucking sucks." He looked at his brother, then looked down. "I don't . . . I don't know how to get through this. I keep thinking I'm going to feel better, but I just feel worse. How do I do this?"

Theo's hand tightened on his shoulder.

"I know. I've been there. Have you tried getting drunk with your brother? That's helped me a lot, in the past."

Ben waved at the bartender.

"First of all, I should have called you a long time ago. Second, I can't think of anything I'd rather do right now than get drunk with my brother."

The bartender set two more drinks down in front of them. He started to pick one up, and then paused. Shit. He had to do this first. He took a deep breath.

"There's one other thing. Speaking of telling people things . . . there's something else I have to tell you. A few months ago, I got an email from someone named Dawn. Dawn Stephens. She's . . . it seems as if our dad had a daughter. After he left."

Theo set his glass down and turned to Ben.

"How did she find you?"

Ben shrugged.

"Well, this is when you can say I told you so—it was that stupid DNA thing I did. I guess she did it, too, and she found my name, and then she emailed me."

Theo nodded slowly.

"Did you email her back?"

He hadn't even said he told him so.

"Yeah. At first just to see if she was really who she said she was—I thought it might be some sort of scam or something. But she sent some pictures. Of herself as a kid with him. And of herself now."

Theo picked up his glass but didn't take a sip.

"Did you—have you met her?"

Ben couldn't believe Theo would ask him that.

"Of course I haven't; I wouldn't meet her without talking to you about it."

Theo put down his glass.

"Well, you emailed her without talking to me about it."

Ben turned to face him.

"I know. I'm sorry about that. I was just worried that—I wanted to make sure it was something, before I told you. And then when I knew it was, I guess . . . I guess I was scared to tell you about her. That it made the whole thing feel . . . real."

Theo didn't say anything, so Ben kept talking.

"I didn't even tell her you existed. She asked me early on if I had any brothers or sisters, and I just ignored the question. I was scared that—I didn't want anything to come between us. And I was worried that this could. That she could."

Theo shook his head.

"Between you and me? Nothing can ever come between us. Not this, not anything else."

Ben looked at his brother and smiled.

"Yeah. Yeah, I know that now."

Theo took off his glasses, cleaned them with a bar napkin, and put them back on.

"Well. A sister." He looked at Ben. "I think we should meet her. Don't you?"

Ben nodded.

"Yeah. I do."

On the way out of the bar, a lot of bourbon later, Theo clapped his hand on Ben's back.

"Look. I won't talk shit about her, because you don't want me to. But that Anna is missing out. No way she can find anyone else as great as you."

Ben didn't argue with his brother, even though he was pretty sure she could. He wished he could text Anna about the drunken email he and Theo had just sent to Dawn.

To: Dawn Stephens
From: Ben Stephens
Re: Hi

Hi Dawn

It's Ben—and his brother Theo. I'm sorry I've been out of touch and I'm really sorry I didn't tell you about Theo before but this whole thing has been a lot more to take in than I let on. but we were thinking

Theo here: what Ben is trying to say is, after consulting his older and wiser brother, he decided we should all meet up. Also, hi! You have two brothers! We both want to meet you!

Theo thinks he should be the one writing this email because he's a professional at this stuff or something but I stole my phone back from him. Anyway, I'm really sorry! And yes I have an older brother and seems like you do too unfortunately for both of us. We'd love to meet you. What are you up to next weekend? We can come up to Sacramento?

Ben
(and Theo)

He knew, for his own self-respect, he couldn't text Anna about tonight. But he really wished he could.

Anna had warned her parents in advance she'd decided to be public about everything. She'd been worried about that—they'd never suggested that she'd keep it a secret, but they'd also never suggested she tell anyone, and she knew the past year had been hard on them, too. But they'd taken the news quietly, and had just said they supported her in anything she chose to do. She wasn't quite sure if that meant they approved or disapproved. She knew she should be past needing the approval of her parents, but, well, she wasn't there yet.

Nik sent Anna an email as soon as the profile was up. Anna had been waiting for it; she knew it was supposed to come out that day. Had she said everything she'd wanted to say? Had she said it in the right way? She hoped so.

As soon as she got the link to the piece from Nik, she texted it to her parents and her brother. And then she read it. And let out a sigh of relief. She didn't love the photos they'd picked to go along with the piece, but other than that, she couldn't find anything to complain about. Nik hadn't misquoted her, the links to the charity she'd mentioned were all working, and she at least felt like she'd gotten all of the important things across, both about the Varon film and about mental health. She texted Florence that she could press publish on the social media posts, and told her to let the contact at the charity know they could announce her involvement.

Then her fingers hovered over one more name in her phone.

She never would have done this if it weren't for Ben. He'd brought it up, he'd given her the idea in the first place, he'd been the one to help her deal with her shame, and think about what she could do to help others. She wanted him to know about what she'd done, but even more, she wanted to thank him.

But she couldn't do that. Her plan was going just the way she'd wanted it to. Now that she didn't have to stress about the Varon film and everything else, she could relax and have some fun. One of the other actors—one of the hot ones—from *Vigilantes* had slipped her his number at the premiere when Ben wasn't around. The premiere had been more than three weeks ago, and she hadn't texted that guy yet, but she should. Tonight, even. Yes, tonight, she'd text him.

She didn't want some big love story in real life; that was just for movies. That seemed too stressful—all that relying on other people for your happiness. What if it went wrong? Then she'd just be back where she was now, but even sadder.

Not that she was sad. She wasn't; she was thrilled about everything. She just felt a little at loose ends, that's all.

She put her phone down, but it almost immediately buzzed. She picked it back up.

Proud of you, Anna baby.

She let the tears that had been in her eyes flow.

Thanks, Dad.

A few minutes later, her gate buzzer went off. She looked at the security camera, and it was Simon. Did they have a meeting scheduled today? Probably. She hadn't been paying much attention to her calendar over the past few days.

She buzzed him in and wiped her eyes.

When she opened the front door, she was composed.

"I'm sorry, Simon—I hadn't realized we were meeting today; Florence and I must have gotten our signals crossed."

Simon walked inside, as impeccably dressed as always.

"We weren't. Sorry for barging in. There's something I wanted to chat with you about."

This was weird. But it must not be bad news—Simon was always good about giving her bad news straight out, with no "we need to talk" preamble. It was one of the reasons she liked working with him so much.

She brought him into her office and sat down at her desk.

"What is it?"

He stood there looking at her for a moment before he sat down.

"The *L.A. Times* piece is out. Did you see it?"

She nodded.

"Yeah. I was happy with it. I mean, I'm always going to have things to criticize about what I said and didn't say, but I think I got all of the important things across."

Simon sighed. What was it? What had she forgotten? What had she said wrong?

"Simon?"

He pulled out his phone and read from it.

"'And my friends were wonderful. Ben's been so supportive,' Anna said, in an apparent reference to her new boyfriend, Ben Stephens.' That's the only thing you said about him in the interview. Unless she just didn't print the part where you said that you're single now?"

She hadn't even realized she'd said that.

"I totally forgot about that part. I didn't even mean to say that. About Ben, I mean. I was just concentrating on saying all of the right stuff about anxiety and my career and everything else. Okay, well, I guess we'll just have to figure out another way to do that."

He sat back and crossed his legs.

"You know, normally, I'd buy that. But not from you. You're good at this, you know how to do this stuff, but instead you said 'Ben's been so supportive.' What's going on between the two of you, Anna? Is there something you haven't told me? Not that you have to tell me the details of your personal life, I hope you know that, and if you want me to butt out, just say the word, but from what you said last week, I thought the Ben thing was all over. But I know you too well to think that you just forgot to tell the world you're single. In your mind, you're still with him. Aren't you? Are you two still—"

She shook her head.

"No, no, that's all done. I told you, I just forgot, that's all."

She stood up.

"Was that everything? Because my trainer is coming over soon, and I have to . . ."

Simon didn't move.

"You fell for him. Didn't you?"

She sat back down.

"No! What are you talking about? That isn't—that's not what I wanted. We had a perfectly nice little fling; it's over now, I've moved on."

Simon just looked at her.

"Fine! He told me he loved me! Are you happy now? After the premiere. But I'm sure he didn't actually mean it. People just say things, you know that. He was probably just caught up in the glamour of the night and everything. He left the next day, and I haven't heard from him since; see, that's proof, he didn't mean it, it didn't matter."

"I saw the way he looked at you," Simon said. "That wasn't the look of a man who didn't mean it."

Anna brushed that aside.

"I told him to look at me that way. That was for the cameras. You should know that better than anyone."

Simon shook his head.

"No. I'm talking about when there were no cameras around."

Anna knew what Simon was talking about. She pictured Ben's face, when he'd looked at her like that. She shook that off.

"Simon. It was business, you know that. He did help me through some stuff, and I was really grateful for it, I guess that's why I said that in the interview, but that doesn't mean anything like you seem to think it means!"

Simon leaned forward.

"What did he do—when you said he was so supportive? Were you talking about that day outside the restaurant when those photos got taken?"

She looked away.

"It wasn't just that, there was a lot more to it, but yeah. I was really . . . that was a hard day. And he was great. Really great. But that doesn't mean anything."

She wanted to take that back as soon as it came out of her mouth. Of course it meant something. It had meant everything to her. But she had to make Simon understand it was all over.

"And yes, okay, I keep thinking about him, of course I do. But like I said, I'm done with that!"

She had to be.

"Anna." He waited until she turned to look at him. "You don't seem done."

She felt tears well up in her eyes.

"He saw me at my worst, okay? And he was wonderful, yes. But I don't want someone who has seen me at my worst! I want someone who falls in love with me at my best!"

Simon touched her arm.

"I understand that, but—"

"I don't want love and all of that! I just want the old Anna back—the Anna from before everything happened! That Anna was great—she had so much fun, she went to lots of parties and dated lots of men and managed to ignore her constant anxiety!"

They both started laughing. Anna grabbed a tissue from her desk and wiped her eyes.

"Do you really want that, Anna?" She'd never heard Simon sound so gentle. "The old Anna was great, don't get me wrong, that's why I wanted to work with her in the first place. But what if the old Anna is gone? There's a whole new Anna in her place. I like her a lot. It seems like Ben did, too."

She dropped her head into her hands.

"I'm scared, Simon. What if it all falls apart? What if I fall apart?"

Simon put his hand on her shoulder.

"Then you'll put yourself back together again. You've done it before, you can do it again. If you don't want him—if you really don't want him—ignore me. But I don't want you to let this go because of fear."

She looked up at him.

"I know I can put myself back together. But I don't want to have to do that again! I'm fine now. I'll be fine without him." She felt tears come to her eyes again and willed them away. "Why are you saying all of this—you didn't even want me with Ben! You didn't even like him."

Simon stood up.

"I liked him fine. I didn't want you with him because I thought he was going to hurt you. I want you to be happy, Anna. Obviously, yes, I want you to make both you and me a lot of money, but—don't ever tell anyone I said this—your happiness matters even more. And the thing is . . . Ben made you happy."

He walked to the door.

"I don't want to push you on this; you need to do whatever you need to do here. Either way, I'm here for you. Just tell me if you need me to leak your breakup to whatever magazine and I'll do it. No judgments. Ever, you know that, right?"

She stood up and hugged him.

"I know. Thank you for that."

He turned around, his hand on the doorknob.

"I saw the way you looked at him, too."

She sat still in her office for a long time after Simon left. Then she took out her phone.

Do you think he meant it?

Penny didn't ask what this was about. She didn't have to.

Do you?

Anna didn't answer. Then, Penny texted her again.

Do you hope he meant it?

Anna put her head down on her desk and didn't respond for a long time. Then she texted back one word.

Yes.

Twenty-Three

IT WAS MONDAY MORNING, AND BEN WAS GETTING READY for work. Running late, getting ready for work. At first, he didn't even hear the knock at his door.

Had he ordered something? He'd ordered new sneakers the other day, but they weren't supposed to be here until tomorrow. Was one of his neighbors mad at him for playing music late at night? He couldn't help it, he was depressed, okay?

He tried to put a friendly expression on his face as he opened the door.

"Hi," Anna said. "Your neighbor let me in. Can I come in?"

He took a step backward, not really to answer her, but because he was so confused she was here. Was this another one of those dreams? What was going on?

She walked through the door and stopped in the middle of his kitchen.

"Hi," he finally said. "Um, are you . . . is something wrong with your dad?"

That was the only reason he could think of for why she'd be here.

She shook her head.

"No, he's fine. I just . . . I had to ask you something."

Oh God. Did she want him to keep doing it? To keep pretending to be her boyfriend, because she had some other event or the studio wanted more proof that she had fans or some other stupid reason? He couldn't do it.

"What do you need?"

He crossed the kitchen and picked up his coffee mug and poured more coffee into it, just to give himself something to do, so he wouldn't look at her. He didn't offer her any. He had a feeling she wouldn't be staying long.

"Why did you say that?" she asked. "What you said. That night. Did you mean it?"

He set his mug down, so hard that coffee sloshed over the sides of the rim. *This* was what she'd come for?

"What the fuck do you think, Anna? Why do you think I said it? Do you think I make a practice of saying things like that to women? Of telling women that I've fallen in love with them, just to give them the fun of being able to reject me afterward? Did I not flatter you enough when I said it, is that the problem? Did you want me to tell you how beautiful you are, how talented you are, how lucky I felt when I was with you? Well, fuck that, I'm not going to say any of it. Yes, I meant it. Yes, I fell in love with you, but it wasn't for any of those reasons, even though they're all true. It was because I understood you, and you understood me. It was because I was so happy, every moment that I was with you. It was because you're funny, and smart, and thoughtful. It was because you called me on my bullshit, but I didn't want to run away. It was because after you forced me to be honest with you, I realized that I couldn't lie to you about anything, ever again. So yes, I meant it. Is that enough for you now? Did that give you what you came here for? Did you ask because you want to know if I can keep up with this charade? If so, no, I'm not going to participate in whatever scheme you and Simon have come up with this time. I'm out. If that's all, I'm running late for work. If you'll excuse me."

He opened his apartment door.

She didn't move.

"I guess I deserved that," she said. She wiped her eyes. He tried not to feel bad about making her cry.

"I didn't want this, Ben," she said. "I wanted a fun little fling with you, one that would bring me back to how I used to be. I wanted you to help me get press and good publicity and convince that studio I should get that role. And that's all I wanted from you. But from the beginning, you wouldn't let that happen. Everything with you felt too close, too intimate. It scared me. I didn't want you to get that close to me, at least I thought I didn't."

He closed his apartment door. He stood there, his back to the door, waiting to see what she would say next.

"I wanted to be back to the old Anna. I wanted accolades about my performances and magazine covers and I wanted that Varon movie. I wanted my agent and my manager to get calls about me every day, and I wanted to get my pick of what to do next. And I've gotten all of that, Ben, I've gotten everything I've ever dreamed of. But none of it matters without you."

He was frozen to this spot, right by his door. Was she really saying this? Did she really mean this?

"I hope—my God, I hope—that you can forgive me for how long it took for me to realize this, but I've fallen in love with you. I love you. I'm in love with you. And"—she took a step toward him and smiled tentatively—"it's not because of how hot you are, or how good you are at your job, or how good you were at being my fake boyfriend. It's because of how kind you are, how big your heart is, how much love you give to the world, how happy I always was whenever I was around you. Even now, right this minute, when you are standing there staring at me, and I don't know what you're thinking, and I don't know what you're going to say, and I'm so scared it's not going to be what I want you to say, I'm just happy, being here, with you."

He took one step toward her. And then another. And then he opened his arms, and she flew into them.

"I love you so much," he said, she said, they said.

He brushed her hair back from her face and kissed her. She pulled him closer and kissed him back. The tears fell from her eyes onto his cheeks.

"Are you sure?" he asked. "If you're feeling guilty, or something, I don't—"

She put her finger against his lips and looked him in the eye.

"I've never been more sure of anything," she said.

Anna took his hand and led him into his bedroom. She plucked the bottom of his shirt out of his jeans and pulled it up over his head. He reached for her, but she stopped him, so he stood there and watched her. She unbuckled his belt, unzipped his jeans, and let them drop to the floor. She kissed his collarbone, his shoulders, his arms, his chest. She ran her hands over his body, memorizing what it felt like, even though she hadn't forgotten a single thing about him.

Finally, she dropped her hoodie to the floor. He reached for her again, and this time she gloried in it. In the way he undressed her, touched her, looked at her, kissed her, laughed with her, loved her.

Afterward, they lay together in bed. Kissing, touching, talking.

"That charity thing that you suggested—I'm doing it," she told him. "I did an interview talking about it. It was really . . . hard. But I think it's going to be good."

He kissed her softly on the lips.

"I read that interview. I tried not to, but I couldn't help myself. I was—I am—so proud of you."

She smiled.

"I was pretty proud of me, too."

He dropped his head back on the pillow.

"I told Theo about Dawn. We're going to meet her soon. It's all still so weird for me. But I'm glad I told him."

She smiled at him.

"I'm glad, too."

She intertwined her fingers with his and lifted their hands to kiss his.

She couldn't believe she was here, with him, for real this time. She was so happy.

She was about to say that out loud, when he bit his lip.

"Shit. I should be at work. Right now. Hold on."

He jumped out of bed, grabbed his phone, and typed busily with his thumbs.

"There."

He dropped his phone and got back into bed with her.

"Do I get you all to myself today?" She kissed him softly. "What should we do?"

That wicked grin she loved so much spread across his face.

"How about a road trip?"

Epilogue

ON SATURDAY MORNING, ANNA SAT IN THE BACK SEAT OF Theo's car, Ben's arm around her, her head tucked into his chest. It felt like they'd barely let go of each other in the past week. Now that they were together, for real, all they wanted was to *be* together.

Monday, they'd jumped into Ben's car and had driven down to Anna's house in L.A. The whole drive down there they'd talked and laughed and cried and talked more—about everything that had happened in their lives in the past few weeks they hadn't gotten to tell each other, about how hard those weeks had been on both of them, about what Simon had said, about what Theo had said, about how and when they'd each realized they'd fallen in love. Ben had flown back up to San Francisco Tuesday morning and Anna joined him there Wednesday night. They were going to fly back down to L.A. late Saturday night, so they could drive Ben's car back up the next day.

They hadn't—quite—figured out what the next few months would look like for the two of them. She was going to start filming soon, he had this new ad campaign he was working on, they both knew they wouldn't be able to be together this much. But some-how, they both knew they'd make it work.

Now they were on their way up to Sacramento, so Ben and Theo could meet Dawn. Anna and Maddie were coming along for moral support. From the tense look on Ben's face that morning, he needed it.

"What are you and Maddie going to do while you wait for us?" he asked her.

She laughed.

"We're going shopping. There are apparently a handful of bou-tiques nearby that Maddie's been dying to go to for a while. I'm excited to see what she finds."

He nodded. That tense look was still on his face.

"Nervous?" she said to him in a low voice.

He started to shake his head and then stopped himself.

"Yeah. I . . . I just want her to like me. I feel bad, about blow-ing her off before. And I've never had a sister; I don't know how to . . . I don't know, I'm probably making a bigger deal about this than I should be, but—"

"No," she said.

He smiled down at her.

"No?"

"No, you're not making a bigger deal about this than you should be." She reached for his hand. "Don't feel bad. Her email back to you was so nice. And of course she'll like you. Even Simon likes you."

He laughed.

"That might be overstating it a little."

She laughed, too.

"Only a little. But you won over both of my parents last night, which FYI is not easy."

He grinned at her.

"Well, that was different. All I had to do was sing their daughter's praises, which comes very naturally to me."

It had been so good to be with Ben at her parents' house, to see him talking and laughing with her parents and her brother. It had felt right.

He leaned down and kissed her on the cheek.

"Thank you. For coming with me today. It's really good to have you here."

She felt herself tear up again, just by that sound in his voice and the tender look on his face.

"It's really good to be here for you," she said.

He traced her lips with his finger.

"You make me very happy," he said. "Do you know that?"

She squeezed his hand.

"I know. I love you."

Theo cleared his throat.

"Ahem."

They looked up. They were stopped at a light, with Theo and Maddie grinning at them. Anna blushed, but Ben just grinned back.

"Yes?" he said to his brother.

"We're about a block away from the restaurant," Theo said. "Dawn texted—she's there at a table."

Ben took a deep breath.

"Oh. Okay, great."

They pulled into a parking spot, and Ben took off his seat belt. Anna grabbed his hand before he got out of the car.

"Do you have any idea how happy you make me?" she asked him.

His entire face bloomed into a huge smile.

"Yeah," he said. "I do."

Acknowledgments

I didn't think I could write this book. At first, it felt impossible to write a book during a global pandemic, especially a book about love. But then this book became my joy, during a very hard year. I am grateful beyond words for everyone in my life who helped me find love and joy and creativity in the hardest of all years to find all of those things, and who made it possible for me to tell Ben and Anna's story.

Holly Root and Cindy Hwang: I thought I was grateful for the two of you before this; I realize now I had no idea how incredibly lucky I am to have you as my agent and editor. Without your patience, support, and above all, your faith in me, this book would not exist. Thank you both, from the bottom of my heart, for everything.

Jessica Brock, how would I do anything without you? I hope I never find out. Fareeda Bullert, thank you for one million things, but especially the title. Angela Kim, Craig Burke, Erin Galloway, Megha Jain, Rita Frangie, Ayang Cempaka, Eileen Chetti, Lisa Davis, Yasmin Mathew, and everyone at Berkley and Penguin Random House who works on my books, you've all gone above and beyond in the past year. Your jobs got infinitely harder, and I'm still amazed at how wonderful you've been. Thank you for every email and brainstorming session and phone call and everything else. I appreciate all of you so very much and hope we never have to put another book out together during a pandemic. Thank you to Alyssa Moore, Melanie Castillo, and all of you at Root Literary for all of your hard work throughout an incredibly hard year. Thank you to Alice Lawson and everyone at Gersh for your unfailing support of me and my books. Huge thanks to Reese Witherspoon and the whole team at Hello Sunshine for being the best cheerleaders out there.

Amy Spalding and Akilah Brown, thank you for all of the emails and texts about names, geography, snacks, and so much more. Jessica Morgan, thank you for your wisdom, your friendship, and your encouragement about everything from writing to buying just one more pair of earrings. Kayla Cagan, thank you for your advice and jokes and thoughtfulness. Nicole Chung, I cannot wait to give you the biggest hug in the world. So many writers have been there for me since the beginning, and especially this year; thank you Jami Attenberg, Melissa Baumgart, Robin Benway, Austin Channing Brown, Nicole Cliffe, Heather Cocks, Alexis Coe, Ruby Lang, Danny Lavery, Lyz Lenz, Samin Nosrat, Rachel Fershleiser, Helen Rosner, and Sara Zarr for your advice, handholding, expertise, and support.

Jill Vizas, where does friendship stop and family begin? I'm not quite sure, but I know we crossed that line a long time ago. Simi Patnaik and Nicole Clouse, I wouldn't have made it through this year without you two. Janet Goode, I miss you and I love you so much. Lisa McIntire, thank you for everything, but especially that thing you said in a text message that I thought about for many months and then put in this book. Kimberly Chin, thank you for all of our backyard meals, hopefully we'll get to eat a meal together inside someday soon. Enormous thanks to Christina Tucker, Alyssa Furukawa, Samantha Powell, Dana White, Alicia Harris, Nanita Cranford, Melissa Sladden, Jina Kim, Joy Alferness and the entire Alferness family, Sarah Mackey, Margaret H. Willison, Kate Leos, Lyette Mercier, Micah Ludeke, Katie Faulkner, Maret Orliss, Catherine Gelera, Kate Flaim, Maggie Levine, Sara Simon, Julian Davis Mortenson, Nathan Cortez, Sarah Tiedeman, Kyle Wong, Ryan Gallagher, Toby Rugger, and Jessica Simmons for your friendship and love.

Special thanks to every member of every single one of my group texts. I've treasured all of the jokes, selfies, venting, love, tears, hugs, support, and so much more. Get ready for sustained, very tight hugs in the hopefully near future.

Thank you to my family, who have loved and supported me so much throughout my whole life. To my own enormous family group text: you all knew I would put you in a book someday, didn't you? My cousins, I love you so very much. A special shout-out to my cousin Leann, since I keep putting the names of the people who live in your house in my books, I can't help it. (I'll get to the rest, I promise). And of course, thank you to my mom and dad, who have taught me so much, and have always had faith in me, even when I had none. I love you.

Librarians and booksellers, you all had to change how you did your jobs on a dime, and I'm in awe of your resilience, your creativity, and your ability to keep telling the world about your favorite books, no matter what. Special thanks to my hometown bookstore, East Bay Booksellers, and all of the staff there, who helped me get hundreds of signed books out to readers during a pandemic—you all blew me away with your organization, enthusiasm, and good humor in the face of everything. Thank you so much.

And a huge thank-you to all of my readers. Thank you for buying my books, getting them from the library, recommending them to friends, posting on social media, and everything else you do. Your notes and messages about my books have been such a balm for me during hard times, and I think about them so often. I'm grateful for every single one of you. Thank you all, for everything.